By Stephen Hunt

The Court of the Air
The Kingdom Beyond the Waves
The Rise of the Iron Moon
Secrets of the Fire Sea
Jack Cloudie

JACK CLOUDIE

STEPHEN HUNT

JACK CLOUDIE

TOR®

A Tom Doherty Associates Book

JACK CLOUDIE

Copyright © 2011 by Stephen Hunt

A Tor Book
Published by Tom Doherty Associates, LLC
175 Fifth Avenue
New York, NY 10010

www.tor-forge.com

Tor® is a registered trademark of Tom Doherty Associates, LLC.

Library of Congress Cataloging-in-Publication Data

Hunt, Stephen, 1967–
Jack Cloudie / Stephen Hunt. — First U.S. edition.
    p. cm.
"A Tom Doherty Associates book."
ISBN 978-0-7653-3320-9 (hardcover)
ISBN 978-1-4668-0205-6 (e-book)
1. Steampunk fiction. I. Title.
PR9199.3.H8235J33 2013
813'.54—dc23

2013015153

Tor books may be purchased for educational, business, or promotional use. For information on bulk purchases, please contact Macmillan Corporate and Premium Sales Department at 1-800-221-7945 extension 5442 or write specialmarkets@macmillan.com.

Originally published in the United Kingdom by *HarperVoyager,* an imprint of HarperCollins*Publishers*

First U.S. Edition: August 2013

Printed in the United States of America

0   9   8   7   6   5   4   3   2   1

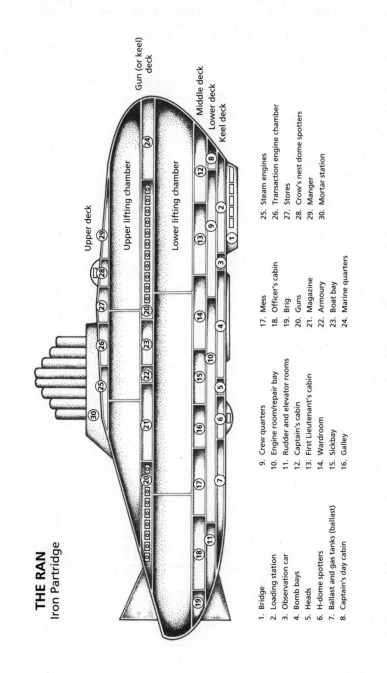

THE RAN
Iron Partridge

Gun (or keel) deck

Middle deck
Lower deck
Keel deck

Upper deck

Upper lifting chamber

Lower lifting chamber

1. Bridge
2. Loading station
3. Observation car
4. Bomb bays
5. Heads
6. H-dome spotters
7. Ballast and gas tanks (ballast)
8. Captain's day cabin

9. Crew quarters
10. Engine room/repair bay
11. Rudder and elevator rooms
12. Captain's cabin
13. First Lieutenant's cabin
14. Wardroom
15. Sickbay
16. Galley

17. Mess
18. Officer's cabin
19. Brig
20. Guns
21. Magazine
22. Armoury
23. Boat bay
24. Marine quarters

25. Steam engines
26. Transaction engine chamber
27. Stores
28. Crow's nest dome spotters
29. Manger
30. Mortar station

If you can smell the scent of death on the air and you do not know where the smell is coming from, then the smell is coming from you.

Ancient Cassarabian proverb

CHAPTER ONE

Middlesteel, the Kingdom of Jackals' capital city

Jack Keats was pushed aside by the others in the gang as the shout echoed out from the shaft in the wall. They were deep in the bowels of Lords Bank, having broken in through the sewers. But even so, if the boy kept yelling like that, one of the bank's night watchmen would hear the racket and then every member of the young gang would be done for.

'I told you it was a mistake bringing the boy,' said Jack. 'He's too young.'

'Shut your cake-hole,' snarled Boyd. It was hard to tell whether the gang's leader was snapping at Jack for questioning his authority, or venting his aggression towards the boy crawling deep into the shaft running alongside Lords Bank's main vault. Boyd leant into the dark shaft, looking in vain for any sign of the small boy's flickering gas lantern.

'He's scared down there,' said Jack. *And of course, my fingers aren't trembling from fear. That's just the cold.*

'He should be more scared of me,' spat Boyd, bunching his fist in anger before turning on Jack. 'Yeah, and you've got two brothers his age locked up in the sponging house. And that's where they'll stay unless we get inside this vault. So you think of your kin, not 'im down there.'

'The workhouse,' said Jack. *You ignorant fathead.* 'They're in the workhouse now, not the debtors' prison.'

The five others standing behind the gang chief sniggered at the distinction and Jack's superior tone of voice, all of them grimy and dust-covered from breaking through the brick foundations of the sewer to get this far. Maggie was with them and she gave him a despairing look – the kind that said this was not a good time to be wearing his education on his sleeve. She had shown him the ropes of street life in more ways than one. Eating stone-hard bread in a debtors' prison and broken by the family debts, or washing down the same rations with the gravy water that passed for soup in the workhouse. Any difference between the two was paper-thin, and Maggie knew it.

'Well, pardon me,' laughed Boyd. 'You're not the son of a gentleman farmer down 'ere. You're shit, just like us. On the job, on the make.' Boyd pointed down the shaft towards the young boy. 'He's small, useful shit. You're clever shit, and I need your fingers, so don't give me no excuse to break some of 'em for you.'

Jack guessed this wasn't the time to point out the meaning of a double negative to the hulking thug. 'And what about you, Boyd?'

'I'm the biggest shit of 'em all, Cracker Jack. I dream up the juicy jobs; I saw how your clever fingers might drag us all out of the gutter. After we pull off this job we'll dress like swells and eat like lords from the best the city's got to offer.'

Jack stared into the dark shaft where the boy was coughing. But only if their little shaft rat found the vault's timing mechanism and managed to jam it, only if he held his nerve and kept the special tool Jack had forged wedged into the machinery for long enough. And only if Jack was every bit as good as he believed himself to be.

'Talk to the runt,' Boyd ordered Maggie. 'Steady his nerves.'

Maggie moved to the hole and started whispering and cajoling. She was as much a mother as most of the young street children and pickpockets in the slums behind Sungate had known, although she was barely an adult herself. Her pleas and support must have had the desired effect, though, because Jack heard the cogs of the transaction-engine lock they had just exposed snap into place. It had shifted from its nighttime lockdown mode to its daytime setting, and that meant the vault could now be opened. Provided you bore the two golden punch cards of the chief cashier and chief clerk of Lords Bank, inserted in unison. Or, failing that, if you possessed a talent for opening such things.

The others in the group watched in quiet reverence as Jack dipped inside the toolbox he had lugged through the dark, stinking sewers, and began picking away at the exposed mechanism of the vault's steam-driven thinking machine, taking readings from the symbols along the bank of slowly rotating drums. It took twenty anxious minutes to re-jig the punch-card reader to accept his input, but the physical work was in many ways the simplest part of this crime – pure mechanics, that any engineman skilled enough could undertake. But the next part of the job was one only the most talented cardsharp would be able to carry off. Jack would have to match his brain against the thick layers of cipher and code that lay between him and a series of steel bolts as large as his legs, persuading them to withdraw and admit the gang into the vault . . . into a whole new existence. *Let me be good enough. Sweet Circle, let me get this one thing right. Just for today, let me be good enough.*

5

'That's it, boy,' muttered Boyd behind Jack, in what the ruffian probably mistook for encouragement rather than distraction. 'You do this and you'll be able to buy your two runts out of the poorhouse. You'll be able to complete your training with the Brotherhood of Enginemen – hell, you could buy a seat on the guild's council.'

Jack grimaced at the delinquent's meagre conception of his life before his father's debts had seen his family incarcerated. *What comfort, to be appreciated by you, you simple-minded thug, but nobody else. This is what I've sunk to.* Jack didn't need to finish his guild training; he had already moved far beyond that. What he needed now was to buy his way into sitting the examinations and pay for his apprenticeship papers. Without that, no mill owner or dusty office of clerks was going to allow him within a thousand yards of any engine-man's position. A closed shop, like so many of the skilled trades.

'Quiet,' hissed Jack.

'I've seen you do this a dozen times.'

'Not like this.' He brushed his dark hair out of his eyes. 'This isn't a lock on a jeweller's shop or some merchant's townhouse. This is a strong cipher, written by people who knew what they were doing. Proper cardsharps.'

Yes, the sort who were only too glad to turn him away from every job he had begged for, a ragamuffin without guild papers. Unwanted competition.

'Please, Jack.' Maggie's voice sounded from next to the shaft. 'Quickly. I can hear little Tozer down there. He's crying.'

'Button it up, runt,' Boyd hissed down the shaft. 'You keep your hand stuck in the timer as long as we need it there.'

Boyd could smell the money now, he could taste it. And the Circle knew, Jack had seen Boyd like this before. His shoulders started rolling from side to side, as if he was balancing the weight of all the mouths that needed feeding among his little mob. Boyd was always dangerous during such times. Pity the maid-of-all-works who stumbled across him rifling through her mistress's cabinet when he had a necklace in one hand and a blade in the other.

Jack turned his attention back to the transaction engine, his clever fingers going about their work. Whatever puppy fat there had been on those fingers had disappeared years ago. He was bony now. Thin and desperate. There wasn't a mirror in the derelict rookery apartment that Jack and the others called home, but he knew what he would see if he looked in one now. Street eyes. The trusting innocence of youth replaced by the narrow, darting glance of the slums. Old man's eyes in a face too young for them. They were the same eyes he looked into when he saw his two brothers during the weekly visiting hour at the workhouse. Poor little Alan and Saul. Half his age, but they already had those eyes. Unless Jack could steal a different life for them. Buy time enough to forget the images of their father coughing his last breath away inside the damp confines of the sponging house. *Am I any better than father was? I thought that after his death saw our family discharged from the debtors' prison, I would be able to get a job – begin a new life, a new start. How little did I know. It was my failure that saw my brothers end up in the workhouse, my mistakes, not father's. Trading the sponging house for the poorhouse, one low class of prison for another.*

Jack had the measure of the cipher now: he held it in his mind, still twisting and turning on the engine's drums, as he removed the little portable punch-card writer from his sack. He began to stitch a series of holes in the first of the blank punch cards that had been stolen to order for him. No one else could keep their decryption routines so short, not an ounce of wasted code. Jack's key was done within five cards.

Feeding them into the exposed injection reader, he heard ten seconds of clanking and clunking in answer from the depths of the engine, and then the massive vault door slowly began to inch upwards, revealing the first glimpse of what lay within. A chamber as big as a Circlist church hall, steel walls marked with thousands of deposit-box drawers and a metal floor crisscrossed by waist-high bins filled with notes and coin of the realm. Lords Bank was the richest counting house in the country, patronized by the wealthiest industrialists, merchants and landowners in the Kingdom, and here their wealth stood revealed, inch by slow inch; until the door stopped opening, squealing rollers matched by a scream from the shaft.

Jack's eyes darted to the drum's new configuration, the icons of symbolic logic lining up in a fierce new pattern. 'The vault's shifted back to nighttime mode.'

'You little runt!' Boyd yelled down the shaft.

'I dropped the tool out of the timer,' the boy's trembling voice came back, 'just for a second, that's all.'

There was the distant sound of alarms on the many floors above them, the guards and watchmen no doubt rousing as the late-night peace of their marble temple to money was rudely shattered.

Boyd smashed his fist in fury against the stalled vault door, a thin strip of the paradise snatched away from him still teasingly visible. 'My fortune. My bleeding fortune.'

One of the young thugs dragged the gang's leader back, pointing up at iron tubes pushing out of the ceiling. 'Dirt gas. Got to go!'

'Tozer,' Maggie yelled into the black square of the shaft entrance. 'We have to pull him out.'

Boyd shook his head, roughly shoving the rest of the gang back in the direction of the bank's breeched wall and the sewer tunnels.

'He'll suffocate down there before he climbs out,' said Jack.

Boyd seized Maggie's arm and pulled her away from the shaft. 'You stay then, Cracker Jack. See if you're clever enough to breathe dirt gas.'

Jack's head turned, hearing both the whimper of the six-year-old thief and the distant gurgle of liquid gas passing down the pipes above him, already reacting with the air and turning into sweet, deadly, choking smoke.

No time. He's as good as dead down there. I've failed him too, just like I always do my family.

'Never was any good lifting wallets either,' said Boyd, nodding in satisfaction as he saw that Jack had decided to cut and run like the rest of them. Clever hands like Jack's were hard to find in the slums.

Jack tried to ignore the echoing screams that followed him out into the sewers. *Coward, I'm a useless coward.*

The agonizing sound finally died as the gang turned into the light from the constabulary's bull's-eye lanterns. Then the shouts of uniformed brutes wielding police cutlasses and heavy pistols charging down the sewer tunnel were all that the hungry young thief could hear.

CHAPTER TWO

The Empire of Cassarabia – Haffa Township

There was only one upside to being a slave, Omar considered, from his vantage point on top of the desalination tank. Why, if he had been born a freeman like Alim, he too might be wearing a perpetual frown of worry across his face all the time. Freemen in Cassarabia always had something to worry about, it seemed. Politics. Religion. Trade. The weather. Alim was probably worrying why the salt-fish in the tank below Omar weren't being released into the next tank down the line, ready to go about their profitable business of separating the salt out of the sea water, leaving pure clean drinking water behind them, before disgorging pellets of table salt onto the beds of the third tank lined up under the shade of the water farm.

But nobody expected initiative from a slave. Indeed, it was very carefully beaten out of them. Omar had been ordered to scrape the salt residue out of one of the drained tanks, readying it for a new batch of salt-fish. Omar hadn't been instructed to then open the lock gates and set the desalination process in motion again. A freeman would care about having fresh drinking water to sell at market. A freeman could have their wages docked. But a slave? Slaves weren't encouraged to show their initiative, for such an attitude led to escape attempts across the desert.

'Omar Ibn Barir,' shouted Alim, spotting the young man lazing on top of the water tanks. 'Do you expect the water farm to run itself?'

Well, miracles do happen, master. But failing that, how about you just shout at me until I do it for you?

Omar pushed himself up and off the water tank. He could always tell when Alim was annoyed with him, because he used his full name. The *ibn* to indicate he was property, and the house-line of Barir to indicate where all his devotion should rightly be directed. 'I was resting, Master Alim. Saving my strength for my next duty.' He indicated the parallel run of desalination tanks in front of them. 'Have you ever seen the bottom of a filter tank scrubbed so clean of salt? There are chefs in the souks of Bladetenbul who will say twenty prayers of thanks to the one true god that there was a boy called Omar so diligent that the sacks of salt they buy from us are as plump as a caravan master's belly.'

'It is you who should say twenty prayers,' said Alim, 'for being so fortunate as to be born a slave into the house of Marid Barir, for no other master would spare you the floggings you so richly deserve.'

Omar did not risk the old man's ire by noting that few other civilized masters would have employed a grizzled freeman like Alim, either, his rough nomad manners barely softened by the decade he had spent inside the town of Haffa. Bred a slave, Omar counted the russet-faced Alim as much a father as he had known in his young life. The only male company he was familiar with, the only man he had worked alongside for years.

11

Such as it could be divined, the good opinion of Alim mattered to Omar. Often he was gruff, but when the old nomad could be roused to humour, his laugh would explode like a thunderstorm, his body shaking and jolting almost uncontrollably under the shade of the water farm. Omar had noticed the old tribesman seemed to find less to laugh about these days.

Alim looked up at the tank where Omar had been lounging. 'A fine view of the caravan road.'

'There is no sign of the water traders yet,' said Omar.

'It is not water traders, I think, that you were looking for.'

Omar tried not to blush, affecting an air of nonchalance, as if he had no idea what Alim was inferring.

'Shadisa will not come by today,' said the old nomad. 'She has gone down to the docks to inspect the fishermen's afternoon catch for the great master's table.'

Omar shrugged, as though the news made no difference to him.

'Ah, Omar,' sighed Alim. 'If you were a comely female and she the son of a freeman, rather than a daughter, you might have a chance. But what fortune or alliance does a male slave bring to an honourable family? The stench of salt-fish and the fifty altun it would cost to purchase your papers of ownership from Marid Barir?'

'My smell is not so bad.' *And I am born for more than this, you grumpy old goat. I can feel my greatness like the burning fingers of the sun, trembling and ablaze within me. A pity you do not see it.*

'You have worked here so long that you have lost your sense of it,' said Alim.

'Whatever my smell, Alim, you cannot fail to admit that I am handsome. When I catch my reflection sometimes, I believe that the one true god must have sent an angel from heaven to bless my cradle.'

'He sent something, boy. A lazy joker to swell my workload here.'

In one matter the old nomad was correct, Shadisa would not come by today. Omar knew. There had always been a connection between the two of them. He could sense when she was coming or when she was near. Sometimes when he was in the great house of their master, he would imagine she was in a certain part of the house and if he ventured close to there, he would find that his sixth sense was proved correct. Old Alim had laughed when Omar told him about this ability. There were men whose bodies had been twisted by womb mages who had such abilities, the nomad had explained, scouts in the elite regiments of the caliph's army – units such as the imperial guardsmen – the cutting edge of the caliph's scimitar. They hunted by smell, or perhaps the unseen magnetic patterns of the mind's thoughts. A mere slave boy had no such illustrious heritage, Alim had laughed. Just the unrequited longings of what he would never have.

But Omar knew better. He only had to meet someone once, take note of them, and then he could then feel their presence if they were near enough. It was as if an invisible thread connected him to them, a tingling warmth he could feel in the depth of his being. Alim was the only one he trusted enough to tell of his gift. It really was not a wise thing for slaves to reveal such abilities, less they be judged a threat and culled. Wild blood, the same as the nomads who haunted the dunes. Too many changes by womb mages and the witches of the desert, percolating through undocumented bloodlines. Who knew what changes had been wrought in the past, what gifts were hiding in his flesh? He hadn't even spoken to Shadisa about this matter.

Ah, Shadisa. Omar still recalled the first time he had noticed Shadisa. She had been a young helper in the kitchens of the great house, her bare elbow balanced on one of the tables as she challenged the other children on the staff to arm-wrestle her. Barely nine himself, he had taken up the challenge and asked Shadisa what she would give him if she lost. 'A kiss,' she had brazenly answered. One Omar had sadly never claimed, for her long perfect arms had proved disconcertingly muscular, and he had lost to her in seconds.

He was a lot stronger now, of course, a titan among men as he imagined it. It had been so much easier when they were younger. While it was true that the life of a freeman's daughter in the town was little better than that of a slave – always subject to the arbitrary whims of her father – when they had been children so much less had been expected from either of them. There had been time enough for Omar and Shadisa to sneak off to the beaches along the south. Empty golden sands, the two of them climbing palm trees and casting dates down into the sand drifting like mist along the surface where the ocean winds stirred it. Building fires from driftwood and making palaces and castles from sand mounds. Their favourite tree was an old betel palm that had embedded itself along the back of the shoreline, its feathered leaves perfect for hiding them as they waited to ambush other children. In its mottled shade they would sway and discuss who were the bigger tyrants among the great house's staff and the water farm's workers, quickest with the switch and harshest with the load of duties. Spending time larking about the sands with Shadisa seemed the most natural thing in the world – the one thing he had to look forward to, the one thing he could count on.

That time seemed so distant now, like remembering a lost age of magic. As they had grown older, he had vowed to let nothing separate them. Certainly not the growing differences in their bodies, swelling in increasingly interesting fashions. The way his heart would jump when she held his hand. The way he would find himself looking for excuses to seek her out, or invent chores to bring her out to the water farm. But as they grew older, so did Omar's awareness of the relative differences in their position. He was a slave; she was the daughter of a freeman. When they had both scurried around under the threat of the switch as children, that difference had seemed academic, simply a word. *Nothing in it.* But as adulthood beckoned, with each new season their relationship threatened to widen into an unbridgeable canyon. With the passing of every year, they got closer to the point where Shadisa would be expected to meet no man socially save with the company of a chaperone, and a mere slave, *never*! Omar knew of Shadisa's father, a very hard man who never smiled, with a reputation for greed and cheating in his dealings. Eyes as cold as ice, and a dry pockmarked face that seemed as seared as the cruelty of the desert. He had once ordered his wife flogged on the flat roof of his house when she miscarried with a son inside her belly. A punishment for whatever she had done to offend the prophets and cause the loss. He had killed a slave too, in a drunken fit, beating the boy's head in with a piece of firewood one night. Why? Who knew: just because he could, maybe. *And what would he do to me if I dared to present myself as a potential suitor, a lowly slave come calling, and without a dowry to boot?*

There had been a brief interlude in the inevitable after a disastrous plague had swept the region, carrying away both Omar and Shadisa's mothers in the same sickening outbreak: a freeman's wife and female house slave equalized at last by death's cold touch. So many had died that the old ways and social codes had briefly tottered. There hadn't been enough hands to do half the work of the town, let alone bother with the strictures of society. The prices of slaves had tripled, along with the wages of freemen; food had become ever more scarce, with insufficient hands to work the fishing boats or keep the irrigation channels clear of sand. Commercial concerns had gone bankrupt all across the province. With one solitary consolation. The grieving over the loss of their mothers had briefly brought Omar and Shadisa even closer. By then, they were of an age where their presence together would be remarked upon, and the beach had become unsafe as a rendezvous; too much danger of being spied upon by a passing townsperson looking to supplement a barren larder by collecting the last tide's seaweed.

Reluctantly, Omar had abandoned the familiar fan of their palm tree's leaves, trading it for an ancient ruin in the desert. There was a place ten minutes' walk from the town, a failed oasis and its collapsed wellspring. There had been a construction there once, as old as time, now with only seven pillars left to make its presence in the world. Shadisa had called them the 'Pillars of Nuh' after an old children's tale, a little bowl of sand offering the shade of its cracked marble columns to rest in. You couldn't always find it, as the drifting sands sometimes covered it over, before reversing its passage a few weeks later and revealing the dried up watercourse again. When you were inside it, nobody could find you, not unless they stumbled over the top of the basin by accident.

Omar had missed the sound of the sea lapping against the beach and the cry of the gulls, but along with his advancing years, there were other consolations to capture his attention. Like the way Shadisa would flick and curl her golden hair across her soft smooth skin as she gazed up at the clouds, or bump him playfully when he made her laugh with some boast or sly observation. His mimicry of the cooks, gardeners and water engineers working at the great house had been particularly useful in that regard. She would roll about laughing, her teeth flashing as white as the mysterious arched bones they occasionally found jutting out of the dunes, allowing him to pull her close and taste her lips with his. He hadn't even needed to arm-wrestle Shadisa to claim his prize.

But in all lives there comes a time when the laughter must end, and for him that had been one evening after they'd been staring up at a sunset together, the hot ancient peace of the desert interrupted by a woman's wails. He and Shadisa had crawled to the top of the dried-out wellspring to see someone fleeing across the sands, a young woman wearing an ivory scooped-neck *abaya*, her body weighted down with dozens of leather water bottles. Shadisa recognized her first, whispering her name to Omar. One of the staff at the great house, a raven-haired beauty called Gamila. She had been promised in marriage to a water trader, a man of such exceptional ugliness that it was said none of his other three wives could bear him children. Despite his advanced age, or perhaps because of it, Gamila had been promised to the merchant as a cure for his other wives' infertility – hardly an attractive fate for one so young and vivacious. And here she was, sprinting across the dunes in the cool of the evening, enough water sloshing about her person to follow the caravan road all the way to the next coastal town.

He had hardly needed to hear the distant shouts of a pursuit to know that she wasn't travelling with her family's blessing. Shadisa had made to jump up and signal to Gamila to hide with them under the watercourse's crags, but Omar has pulled her back. If they were discovered out together, Shadisa wouldn't have needed Gamila's presence to condemn her in sharing the errant daughter's fate. Shadisa had struggled and kicked, but the days when she'd been a physical match for Omar were long gone. With his fingers clamped over Shadisa's mouth, Gamila sprinted past, following the crescent-shaped mound of a sand dune without spotting the dried-up oasis.

Then she was gone, the shouts of the chase growing louder, men's voices hooting and calling to each other, before passing and fading under the darkening sky.

How Shadisa had cursed and damned him for stopping them going to the girl's aid. He was a fool and a coward and a timid fraud. She couldn't believe he could be so selfish. Shadisa simply didn't see how he'd been protecting her all along, saving her from her own thoughtless, reckless actions. Shadisa's father's temper would have been volcanic if she had been discovered out in the dunes with a male slave, aiding a girl in dishonouring her family's name. Gamila had called her own fate down upon her; every slave knew there was only one crime worse than running from your master, and that was getting caught in the attempt. Shadisa didn't deserve to join the careless house girl in her punishment, and frankly, although he had never voiced it, neither did Omar.

And a wantonly cruel punishment it proved to be. After Gamila had been dragged back to town, the old merchant quickly decided to break off their betrothal in favour of one of Gamila's younger sisters. Her family then paid for a master womb mage – an expert in the honour-sanctions demanded by wealthy families – to travel to the town from the distant capital. The spurned suitor rejected the lighter punishment of giving Gamila two extra arms and sentencing her to a life of hard labour as a baggage carrier. Instead, the womb mage had buried her in the sand up to her waist on the outskirts of town and inflicted a changeling virus on Gamila, twisting and mutating her form into a cactus-like taproot. What had been her arms and head warped into fleshy green pads, the outline of her face barely visible as lumpy veins of spines. No eyes to see, no mouth to scream; Omar had often prayed there wasn't enough sentience inside her barrel-like trunk to feel the cuts of travellers' knives as they sliced wedges out of her body and sucked on the rubbery green flesh for her water. *The desert wastes nothing*, the travellers would mouth, before discarding the sucked-out flesh in the dust and continuing on their way.

But more than Gamila's body had changed that day. Ever since then, Shadisa's attitude towards Omar had cooled. No more walks. No more time together in the old oasis or on the beach. She barely smiled when he approached, and made every excuse to be out of his presence as quickly as possible. Perhaps she was frightened of receiving a similar punishment from her father; perhaps she had seen the price of flouting society's rules and judged the potential cost of continuing to see Omar too high? *Surely she still can't blame me for what happened to Gamila? It was hardly my fault. You would think that given the time we've spent apart, on reflection, she could now see that it is only my quick thinking that saved her. Show me a little gratitude at least. The town's hunters wouldn't have just given up looking for Gamila. They would have kept on searching until they found her alongside us, and there wouldn't now be one body twisted to serve as a taproot outside the town, but three. No, Shadisa's scared, that has to be it. She's seen what happens to those who defy their family and she's fearful.* Shadisa just had to be brought to see the greatness burning within her suitor, the infinite potential, then she'd realize that he wouldn't always be fetching and carrying on a water farm.

'Hey there,' ordered Alim, flicking a pebble of limestone rock at Omar, 'stop mooning over girls too fine for you and open the locks to the next tank. If the fish don't purge soon, you'll have a tank of spoiled water and a school of sick salt-fish.'

Omar nodded and made his way to the lock wheels. The last slave who'd killed a batch of salt-fish had been made to eat the sickening black things for a week and almost died of salt poisoning. *Yes, the arbitrary punishments, just another perk of being a slave in Cassarabia.* Alim helped the young slave in his task, walking down the line of water tanks, twisting the rusting wheels that opened the lock doors, the sloshing water sweeping the fish away to the next stage of the filtering process. The fish were biologicks, of course: the product of womb mage sorcery. Only the House of Barir and the other houses that worshipped the Sect of Ackron, all members of the guild of water farmers, understood exactly how to create and nurture the salt-fish. Adding special vials of hormones to the water supply through their complex life cycle to keep them thrashing and thriving.

Ackron was the fifty-third sect of the Holy Cent, informally known as the trader's face, and those who embraced the sect often prospered as traders and merchants. That was the theory, at least. The rusting wheels on the water farm's tanks spoke of a different reality, though. When the plague had spread through the northern provinces of Cassarabia, it had killed over two-thirds of the House of Barir's people, leaving their coastal water farms undermanned and in the care of the house's slaves and vagabonds-for-hire like Alim. The bones of the house's faded glory were laid out in the sand dunes alongside the farm, a handful of metal arches that had been constructed to hold a water pipeline which had never been completed; pipes for fresh drinking water that should have reached all the way to Cassarabia's capital, bypassing the water traders and the caravans.

It was through the broken arches of the house's half-finished pipeline that Omar noticed the first visitor rising out of the baking sands, the dark silhouette of a scout atop a saddle raising a long spindly rifle in friendly greeting as the chattering of the sandpedes' bony legs grew louder in the distance. The insect-like creatures that made up most of the caravan came slithering out of the desert with the dazzling white enamel of thousands of water butts tied to their segmented bodies, flashing towards the water farm.

'Not good,' murmured Alim.

'They are early, old master,' said Omar, watching the line of water traders coming down the dunes towards them, 'but so are we. We have enough tanks to fill all their butts. The salt is counted and bagged.'

'It was I that bagged most of the salt, Omar Ibn Barir,' spat the old nomad. 'It is not the traders I talk of. Look . . .'

Omar shielded his eyes from the sun and turned his gaze to where Alim was pointing. By the silver gates of heaven, the old nomad still had the keen sight from his desert days. There was a keeper on the dune line – one of the respected priests of the hundred sects – riding a camel, breaking away from the main caravan and threading his way through the pump heads that brought sea water up from the harbour. He was bearing straight for the great fortified house overlooking Haffa's harbour – Master Barir's residence, as well as that of the beautiful Shadisa, of course. Her olive skin, golden hair and wide green eyes be blessed.

'It's just a keeper,' said Omar. *The priests of the Sect of Ackron are always coming and going.* The tithes from the House of Barir were important to the sect, and the holy men that received them no doubt said many prayers for the soul of Marid Barir and his profitable water farms.

Alim rubbed the stubble on his old chin. 'Just a keeper? Have you no eyes to see with, young pup? Look at the green edging around the number fifty-three on his headdress. It is the high keeper of the Sect of Ackron himself.'

An emir of the church, one of the hundred keepers of the Holy Cent of the one true god! What business could he have so far beyond the capital's comforts? There were no politics here, no court, no temples of note. Just the margins of the desert, a sea breeze, a distant fishing town and the house's many water farms.

Omar ran a hand through his dark, slightly curly hair. 'Clearly, my eyes are as perfect as the rest of me. Are you sure it is the high keeper?'

'Yes,' sighed the old nomad. 'I am sure.'

'He probably wants more money.'

'Keepers are sent to demand extra tithes from their flock,' said Alim. 'Not the high keeper himself. This is bad. In a strong wind, an innocent man's tiles are blown off a roof the same as the wicked's.'

'Is that one of the sayings of the witch that used to travel with your clan?'

'It is but common sense,' snapped Alim. 'Even a town-born slave may drink from that well.'

Omar shrugged and went back to opening the rest of the salt-fish locks, leaving the old nomad to mull over his concerns. Yes, that was the only good thing about being a slave. When you had nothing to lose or hope for, you had little to fear. Worries only came, it seemed, when you had property and status to lose; as a slave, there would be a worker-sized dish of food on his table this evening – because when you owned a beast of burden, it made good sense to feed it and keep it working. *And if I am lucky, tomorrow morning might even bring a glimpse of Shadisa's heart-stopping face. Yes, something will come along for me. Fate will surely accommodate the wittiest and most handsome slave in the empire.*

Omar began to hum one of the wild nomad ballads that Alim had taught him.

If he had known what the evening was to bring, he might have changed his tune.

CHAPTER THREE

Jack stumbled to the rail at the front of the stand, his feet constrained by heavy irons and manacles. This was his first time in the middle-court of the Jackelian legal system – his first time in any court for that matter. But even given his lack of experience with such matters, the crowd of illustrators and journalists sitting scribbling away in the public gallery seemed unusually large to his eye. Perhaps if Jack's father had still been alive, he might have been able to offer some advice – he must have stood in a courtroom like this when the terms of the family's bankruptcy had been read out. *Although perhaps not one so crowded.* What was debtors' prison – the everyday ruin of a common family – compared to the greatest robbery that the capital had nearly seen? And one attempted by the forgotten scrapings of its gutters.

'The undeserving poor . . .' pontificated the judge from his high wooden plinth. A light mist of dust fell from his elaborate wig to be sucked into the pneumatic tubes below where the clerks were sending and receiving reports in between tapping away on the keys of their punch-card writers.

There was a chorus of clanking chains behind Jack as the

other members of the gang were pushed to the rail, the public and the newssheet illustrators getting their first look at the felons on trial. The newspapers had no doubt paid a good few pennies to the court officials to ensure that Boyd's crew would stand there long enough for them to make the drawings that would adorn the late editions of the day's newssheets.

'Moral degeneracy . . .' the judge growled.

Jack glanced around for their lawyer, who strode forward towards the advocates' bench. It didn't look as if things had gone well for the gang in the main hearing. The one Jack hadn't been allowed to attend while the learned silks argued back and forth, in case the felons' pauper-like appearance prejudiced the jury. Too many women whose delicate sympathies might have been aroused if they'd been allowed to see the fresh cheeks of the young pickpockets and street thieves who were hauled up in front of the capital's courts.

'All results of the failure of the undeserving poor to accept their duties as citizens of the Kingdom, results which are evident all around us,' sounded the judge. 'In those so feckless that they have wrongly concluded that the poorhouse rather than paid work should be their employer. And for those too worthless to accept even the generous regime of the workhouse, there are always the pockets of their fellow citizens to pick, the windows of good people's houses to lever open!' The judge banged his gavel and pointed it angrily towards the gang. 'The statutes issued by parliament prevent me sending a message to the slums that would be properly understood. Otherwise, have no doubt that, despite your age, I would have all of you standing on the gallows rather than facing transportation to the colonies.'

Jack breathed a sigh of relief. Thank the stars that the liberal-leaning party of the Levellers was still in government in the House of Guardians.

'But!' boomed the judge, his hawk-like nose sniffing in disdain, 'for the ringleader of this foul crime, I thankfully still have available the option of exercising the middle-court's full discretion.'

Jack glanced over to where Boyd was standing defiantly, his large frame bearing his chains as though they had been tailored for him. Unlucky for Boyd. Well, at least the publicity concerning the trial would mean there would be a couple of well-wishers in the hanging-day crowd who would bribe the executioner's attendants to jump up and pull on Boyd's boots if the rope didn't break his neck clean after he dropped through the trapdoor. *Goodbye Boyd, I would say it's been nice knowing you, but I'm not that good a liar.*

The judge lifted up the small square black cap that those condemned to death were forced to wear while waiting in Bonegate jail. 'Bring the ringleader forward to receive his cap.'

There was a murmur of sympathy from among those watching on the public seats, a few women tossing their handkerchiefs through the line of constables keeping order. Jack stared at them with contempt. This was real life, not a romantic tragedy put on for the mob's benefit. Jack's look of contempt turned to astonishment and then to panic as the guards behind him seized his arms and dragged him out beyond the prisoner's stall. Pushing him in front of the judge. *Me? It's not me, you idiots!*

'Jack Keats,' said the judge, glaring down, 'you have corrupted the benefits of your early training at a guild school to foul ends, leading the ill-educated criminal poor of the Sungate slums on a wicked attempt to undermine, nay, to *plunder* the hard-earned wealth of those who have chosen to prosper through work rather than squandering their gifts.'

'I didn't!' shouted Jack, pointing back at Boyd still on the prisoner's stand. 'I wasn't the leader. It was him.'

'Your cowardly lies will not save your neck,' warned the judge, his eyes narrowing. 'The members of your gang have all named you as the leader of this wicked enterprise.'

Jack stared back shocked at the ranks of the gang he had followed into the basement vaults of Lords Bank. The young criminals who had been incarcerated together with the threatening bulk of Boyd, while Jack had been locked in solitary confinement inside a security cell designed for those who might be able to work mischief on its transaction-engine lock. Boyd was gazing back coolly at Jack, while Maggie and the others couldn't even meet his startled eyes.

'Maggie!' Jack pleaded. 'Please, tell them—'

'Silence!' thundered the judge. 'It would be clear to a simpleton which among you had the education, knowledge and skills necessary to break into the vault of Lords Bank. The rest of these gutter-scrapings standing before me do not possess such ingenuity. Dear Circle, man, you're the only one of them that even has his letters.'

'It is clear. To a simpleton,' muttered Jack.

He had been betrayed by all of them, even Maggie. Royally rogered. Jack would have been beaten to death if he hadn't gone along with Boyd on the robbery, but it seemed now as though he was going to meet his maker anyway. *Family, you could only ever trust family.* Who were his little two brothers in the poorhouse going to rely on when he was gone? The thought gnawed at Jack's heart as painfully as his sudden death sentence. People like Boyd, that was who they would fall in with on the streets. *Repeating my errors and ending up in a courtroom like this in a few years' time. Failed them, I've failed them.*

The guards pushed Jack down to his knees, ready to receive the black cap. The whole courtroom appeared to freeze with the unreality of the occasion. What a dramatic scene this would make for the front of the *Middlesteel Illustrated News*. A lone figure, bent down to receive the swift mark of Jackelian justice, the judge in his dark robes like a figure from mythology on his high perch. The judge who was about to pass down the black cap to a clerk's outstretched hand when a court reader stood up to discreetly interrupt him. The clerk was whispering in the judge's ear and pointing to the corner of the public benches where a man was sitting alone. Jack's eyes widened. He knew the man sitting on the bench. He had seen those piercing eyes before. The ginger hair. But not the clothes, a large military-style cloak that hid almost all of the man's body. *Where have I seen your face before?*

'It appears,' announced the judge, 'that in this case the state has elected to exercise its rights under the articles of impressment.' Reluctantly storing the black cap back under his perch, the judge looked over the contents of the scroll that had exited the clerk's transparent vacuum message pipe. 'However,' the judge fixed the ginger-haired man on the bench with a steely glare. 'This impressment order merely suggests the service of the Royal Aerostatical Navy as a suitable sentence, rather than expressly dictating it.'

The ginger-haired man stood bolt upright in anger as if he had been well defied, his cloak a second shadow behind him.

Returning his gaze to Jack, the judge glared down at the young thief. 'There was a time when the RAN used to be a fit service for gentlemen, and you sir, will never be a gentleman. It pains me to see how in this matter, like so many others, times have changed for the worse. It is therefore the express wish of this court that your life impressment is to be served with a punishment battalion of the New Pattern Army. They may be able to flog some of the criminal tendencies out of your hide before you are required to shed your worthless blood in the service of your nation. Now, officers of the court, kindly remove this lowly piece of gutter-scum from our sight.'

Drawn up from their seats, the mob in the court were in a state of near riot at the unexpected turn of events, and Jack was pulled away to the shouts of frantic questions being hurled down at him by newssheet writers, the repeated banging of the judge's gavel, the yells of sentences of transportation being passed on the remaining members of the gang. Jack was almost overwhelmed by the stench of the jostling crowd, some laughing at him, some spitting and shouting obscenities, others calling out encouragement and trying to press small gifts of waxpaper-wrapped food into his hands. He got a brief glimpse of the dark cloak of the mysterious figure who had brought news of this bizarrely unexpected intervention in the trajectory of his decline, and then he was on his confused way down the cold damp tunnel and back to the holding pens.

It wasn't the hangman who would be coming to collect Jack now; it was the army and a death almost as certain, if not quite as immediate.

Jack sat with his back against the cold stone wall of the cell. Before he had seen one, he had always expected a cell to be small, cramped and damp. *Well, one out of three isn't bad.* All the damp you could wish for. But the cell was closer to one of the poorhouse's large chambers where make-work was shipped in – sacks to weave, granite slabs to chip into shape; the whole thing built on an industrial scale to house hundreds of the court's poor and dispossessed 'patrons' while they awaited dispatch to their fate. More permanent cells, transportation to the colonies or for an unlucky few, the hangman's noose. Jack gazed around at the dirty huddled clumps of humanity. The lucky ones still had family or friends outside with enough coins to pay the authorities for a few comforts for their kin – straw to bed down on and coarse hemp blankets, parcels of food to replace the rancid gruel that was slopped out.

There was a time, a few years ago, when I would have looked down on them, blamed them for their own condition. Now I am them. A time when his father still owned land, collected rents rather than debtors' bills and gambling losses. The sad truth of the matter was that there wasn't much that a man wouldn't do to feed himself. When that person had a family with mouths to feed, there was even less. Jack winced as he tried not to think of his two young brothers sleeping in a place little better than this; different only in name and just as trapped. Poorhouse. Jail. Workhouse. Prison. Interchangeable.

A middle-aged man shuffled over, scratching a long silver beard, wispy and yellowed at the edges from smoking a mumbleweed pipe. 'You're the boy who went to guild school?'

'Brotherhood of Enginemen,' said Jack. 'I didn't sit the exams.' *No, our money had run out long before then.*

'But you've got your letters?' He indicated a couple of families crouched around one of the brick pillars holding up the chamber's arched roof. They had a newssheet spread open in front of them. Jack nodded. Wearily picking himself up, he walked over to where they were waiting. How his bones creaked and his muscles ached. A day in this rotten hole and already he was moving like he should be drawing a pension. Picking up the paper he looked at the date on the front. 'It's two weeks old.'

The man thumped at his chest and hacked out a sawing cough out before croaking. 'You think the world's changed much since then?'

'No.' *Although I had so hoped my world would have. My biggest problem should have been explaining where the sudden*

29

shower of gold guineas had appeared from to buy back our estate.

'Have a look for news of the match workers' strike,' said a woman who looked like she might be the mother of one of the families. 'Are they still bringing in blacklegs to break the strike?'

Jack leafed through the sheaf of large sheets, dark ink staining his fingers, imprinting them from the damp. 'No mention of the unions here, lady. It's all talk of a possible war brewing with the Cassarabians.' They looked up at him, disappointed. There were dozens of families in the cell who had been accused of tearing up cobblestones and throwing them at a factory owner. The recent confrontation between the match workers' union and the guards who'd been paid to keep the mill open had filled the holding cells.

Jack pointed to the cartoon on the front of the newssheet. A pregnant woman was stretched across a doctor's table being attended to by a gaggle of surgeons with the faces of famous politicians. A plump young Jackelian boy wearing the uniform of the Royal Aerostatical Navy was jumping up and down in a jealous fit at the sight of a grotesque baby – clearly a Cassarabian – being delivered; the babe also dressed in an opulent airship officer's uniform. 'You have a rival, Jack,' noted the voice balloon hanging over the leering surgeon's head. 'Confound you,' the plump boy was yelling. 'You promised me nary a sibling.'

'A bad business,' said the man.

Jack had to agree. His namesake in the illustration was a Jack Cloudie, an airshipman, and for centuries the monopoly the Kingdom had exercised over the celgas that floated the RAN's four fleets of airships had kept the nation safe from foreign invasion. Now their belligerent neighbours to the south had secured a supply somehow, and a rival aerial fleet had been spotted patrolling the Jackelian–Cassarabian borders along the uplands. A bad business, indeed. And devilish worse when you'd been sentenced to service in the regiments. First in line when it came to being marched into a fusillade of Cassarabian cannon fire. How much could the world change in two weeks? Always for the worse, that was Jack's experience. *Always for the worse.*

The man looked at Jack. 'What did you get, the boat or the regiments?'

'The army.'

'Me too.' There was a wave of weeping from the woman and her children at that. Of course, it would be transportation to the colonies for them. Without their father. Without her husband. 'All my life I've laboured morning, day and evening. We were just standing on the picket line when management's men cleared us out with whips and canes. That's all, just standing there. All my life I've done the right thing.'

His voice trailed off.

At least someone here knows what that is.

'On your feet,' called the court constable, dragging his cosh along the iron bars of the cell. Jack woke coughing, blinking at the fierce light of the lamp in the policeman's hand. There were a couple of hulking red-coated soldiers behind the constable, a sergeant and a corporal, the yellow light of the lamp reflected ominously on the death's heads of their oiled shako hats. The two men fairly strutted along with their left hands balanced on their sheathed sabres to stop them bumping along the damp stone floor. The pair of soldiers might have been Boyd's older brothers judging by the arrogance of their gait and the unvoiced capacity for violence they left hanging in the air around them.

'Is this all you have for us?' said the sergeant, disdainfully.

Jack rubbed the sleep out of his eyes. *What were you expecting? A cell full of smartly dressed officers, expert duellists and marksmen for you to press gang into your suicide squad?*

'Not much to look at,' said the court constable, waving dismissively at the prisoners. 'But we don't feed them a fighting man's rations in here. Give them a plate of gruel and a bayonet and they'll stick someone for you right enough. Most of them already have.'

'On your feet, my raggedy boys,' yelled the sergeant. 'Move as if you had a purpose – and that was to be chosen by the hand of parliament to serve in its glorious army.'

'Come on, come on!' yelled the corporal. 'Jump to it.'

Jack listened to the creaking of his reluctant bones, a product of the damp, as he joined the others in the cell shuffling through the door that had been opened for them, their leg chains still attached to their ankles. Where were his chains to be removed, Jack wondered? Behind the safe, high stockade of some New Pattern Army barracks, no doubt. Jack felt a sting on the back of his neck as the sergeant encouraged him along with a flick of a swagger stick. 'Step lively, now. I've seen more bleeding life in a fella flogged for sleeping on duty.'

Jack's wound smarted like a bee sting and he wasn't the only one to receive some lumps at the hands of the two soldiers sent to collect the convicts. There was an army carriage waiting for them at the other end of the holding cell's passage, a segmented iron-hulled thing with large spoked wheels. Two soldiers stood in front of it, a man and a female officer, both in brown oiled greatcoats. The appearance of the officer seemed to disconcert the pair of brutes dragging Jack into military service and no wonder. The woman had an angelic face, but frozen with a cold superiority that sat ill at ease with her smooth skin and elegant features; wide eyes that should have radiated softness, glimmered with a piercing intensity instead. She was beautiful the same way an assassin's dagger was. You might admire it, but only a fool would want to take a closer look.

The male soldier, a broad-shouldered bear of a man with a forked beard salted white with age, came to attention and stamped his boot on the street's cobbles. 'The prisoners, lieutenant.'

'Very good, Oldcastle,' said the woman.

Both brutes shepherding the convicts into the light halted and saluted back – in what seemed to Jack a rather cursory way – towards the female lieutenant. 'Prisoners of the Twenty-Second Rifles, sir. The Third Penal Battalion.'

'Only so long as they don't escape,' said the lieutenant.

'Ah, you're lucky indeed we caught you two boys in time,' said the soldier the female officer had named as Oldcastle. He banged the side of the armoured carriage. 'This old clunker is fine to hold run-of-the-mill ruffians from Bonegate jail, but not this imp!' His fat fingers jabbed towards Jack. 'Why, the slippery rascal is the same fellow whose clever fingers nearly teased open the vault of Lords Bank. The locks on the back of your carriage are like bread and butter to a wicked clever thief like this one.'

'We have sole custody, sir.'

'House Guards sent us,' announced the female lieutenant. 'The general staff want Jack Keats in a secure stockade cell by the end of the day while they consider what to do with him.'

They do?

'Of course, lads,' winked Oldcastle. 'If you want to keep hold of his sly bones, just write us a little note saying that you wouldn't discharge him across to us. Two strapping fellows like you to look after the pup, he probably won't escape, will he? The general staff will understand. Look at the thin rascal; why, I reckon the smoke rising from a good hot beef broth might blow the scrawny, thieving mischief-maker right over.'

The corporal pulled open an armoured door on the carriage for the convicts to board, but the sergeant reached out to stop him. 'If the boy escapes, we'll both lose our stripes.' A key was produced, slipped into Jack's ankle restraints and the corporal pushed him roughly towards the lieutenant. 'Your prisoner, sir.'

Jack rubbed the life back into his chaffed shins while the corporal looked knowingly at the old soldier. 'Keep your eyes on him. Some of these street rats got a turn of speed on them like you wouldn't expect.'

If you think I can run for it, you've never spent a night in those cells.

'Not a problem, corporal.' Oldcastle unslung a rifle, a cheap-milled brown bess, the army's weapon of choice. 'Why, John Oldcastle could shoot a moustache off this lad's lips at a thousand yards, were he qualified for growing a man's set of whiskers.'

The corporal nodded in satisfaction at the answer and the two brutes pushed the rest of their shackled prisoners into the armoured wagon.

Jack was marched around the corner to where a shining civilian horseless carriage was waiting, the hum of high-tension clockwork making the air shiver and spooking a horse pulling a coal cart along on the other side of the road. It was the sort of vehicle Jack imagined a general might be chauffeured around in, but the old soldier John Oldcastle pulled himself into the driving pit in the front of the vehicle's sloped hull while the woman indicated Jack should climb up into the leather passenger seats mounted in the rear. As the lieutenant mounted the steps, her greatcoat fell open, revealing the white facings on her red uniform. Jack's eyes narrowed in surprise.

'Do you know what the colour means?' asked the lieutenant.

'When you're in an alehouse,' said Jack, 'an army redcoat will drink until he can't fight. Marines always stay sober enough to dish out some mean lumps.'

John Oldcastle laughed from in front of the carriage. 'I told you he would be a quick one, Maya. The lad who nearly broke into Lords Bank.'

The woman's green eyes widened in an appraising stare. 'Marines stay sober by habit, because they operate under the discipline of a crowded airship, where any jostle that sparks a brawl could lead to fatal damage to a vessel.' She looked at her sergeant. 'And Oldcastle, you will address me as First Lieutenant Westwick when others are present.'

'Yes, sir.'

This odd pair and his situation perplexed Jack. *Their uniforms don't even fit them.* First Lieutenant Westwick's was clearly tailored for a man. *This stinks, I can feel it in my bones.* 'Why do you want me . . .?'

'Don't think that I do,' said the first lieutenant. 'You wouldn't be my hundredth choice, let alone my first.'

'Why does the Royal Aerostatical Navy want me, then?'

The first lieutenant laughed, even as her eyes stayed icy and forbidding. 'Admiralty House would have gladly let you hang on the gallows, boy. Maybe that's why we ended up with you. Now, keep your questions to yourself until you've learnt how to salute.'

'I'll take the lad under my wing,' Oldcastle called back from the front of the horseless carriage. 'Keep him on the straight and narrow until he finds his air legs.'

'Yes, you bloody well will. Could we make this any harder for ourselves?'

'Beggars can't be choosers,' said the soldier, throwing the steering wheel about as he directed the horseless carriage across the capital's crowded streets.

'Nothing good will come of this,' muttered the first lieutenant.

Jack said nothing, although his curiosity was still burning. In truth, he couldn't agree with the attractive but flinty-looking woman more. *Nothing good has happened to me for a long time.*

Omar stood on the balcony outside the pavilion that housed his master's office. He could see over the great house's forti-fied walls, look down on the town of Haffa's white flat-roofed buildings, at the sea glinting like an endless expanse of beaten bronze beyond, and the fishing dhows that stayed close to the coast and still landed generous catches. Other slaves might have stood fretting, wondering if the summons to meet the great Marid Barir might auger a beating for some infraction of the house's many rules. But what was the point of that when there was a fine view of the harbour to gaze at? Why, he might even be able to watch one of their large paddle steamers come in to dock. The ships needed fresh water for their boilers to drink as much as the Cassarabian people did – using sea water in a ship's boiler caused rust and eventually explosions when the pressure proved too much.

The guard standing by the master's door opened it, allowing a tall figure in green-coloured robes to exit; the number fifty-three repeated in ornate script hundreds of times across the shot silk of a priestly dress. It was the high keeper of their house's sect, and Omar dropped to one knee to give the neces-sary bow to the great figure. 'Ben Issman be blessed.'

'Ben Issman's blessings upon you too.' The prince of the church stopped to nod at Omar. Omar snuck a glance upwards. *This isn't usual.* Slaves should be invisible to such a great patronage.

'May I help you, high keeper? I am exceedingly clever and talented for my age and would be happy to put my soul to your service.'

The priest was staring out across the sea that had been Omar's distraction a second before. 'I do not think so, my child. I will just stand here a while. There are fish in the sea, and there are men to catch them, all set in place by heaven's will. How long has the town of Haffa been nestled down there?'

'For as long as people remember, high keeper.'

'And perhaps a little longer than that too, eh?'

'So it may be,' Omar grinned.

The high keeper patted Omar's shoulder and walked away as if he was lost in thought. Quite extraordinary. The emir of the church had clearly seen the greatness within Omar where so many others had dismally failed. Omar's reverie was broken by the cough of the master's shaven-headed house manager, who was pointing towards the door, left open for him by the guard.

Marid Barir was waiting for Omar behind the wide sparkling surface of his marble-topped desk, the master's main office silent except for the twisting cooling fan in the ceiling and the cry of the gulls from beyond his massive open window.

Standing up from behind his desk as Omar entered, the short, portly figure brushed his oiled goatee beard while he slowly paced by the window. 'Good evening to you, Omar Ibn Barir.'

'Master,' said Omar. 'We have filled the traders' water tanks and loaded all the salt. They will be leaving shortly.'

'Of course,' said Marid Barir. 'But that is not why I have

brought you here this night. You have been weighing on my mind, boy.'

'I am ever your loyal servant, master,' said Omar bowing and smiling ingratiatingly.

'You make a very poor one.'

'I understand everything about water farming, master,' said Omar, trying to sound hurt.

Marid Barir scowled. 'At least well enough to keep your desalination line ticking along while you find ever-more inventive ways to skive off. We have tried everything with you. But we never did beat you enough. Would you work harder if I had you flogged every morning?'

'I would labour mightily even with the weals on my back, master,' said Omar, trying to keep the smile on his face. 'With the strength of three normal men.'

'You are a poor liar,' said Marid Barir. 'I think I am done with you, boy.' He picked up a rubber tube from his desk, opened it and took out a roll of paper to throw at Omar.

'Master,' said Omar, glancing at the paper as he unfurled it. 'What is this?'

'You were taught to read the panels on your equipment, well enough, boy. What does it look like?'

'My—' Omar looked at the elaborate calligraphy on the roll in confusion '—my papers of indenture.'

'You are a freeman from today,' said Marid Barir. 'The *Ibn* is removed from your name. Struck away.'

Omar fought down the rising sensation of confusion, all his certainties, collapsing around him. 'But why?'

'There was one week, Omar, when you didn't wear that perpetual foolish grin of yours. It was a few years ago when you went down to Haffa's graveyard to try and find the tombstone of your mother.'

'It was not there,' said Omar, remembering. *But then,*

mother had just been a slave. How few there were left in the house to remember her after the plague had struck Haffa.

Marid Barir walked to the window and pointed to the hill at the side of the house. 'You will find her out there.'

'That is the House of Barir's family graveyard,' said Omar.

'I buried the best of them out there, Omar, after the plague. My wives, my daughters, my sons, my brothers. All of them, but one.'

'I—' Omar started.

'It is not fitting for the last of this house's blood to die in bondage, Omar Barir. Not even the foolish result of a dalliance with one of my wife's maids.'

'But . . .' Omar looked at Marid Barir. The great, wealthy Marid Barir, so shrunk by age, by the worries of freemen. *My father*. Omar was rendered nearly speechless. All these years, he had known he was not fated for the life of a slave. But this? He had never imagined this. 'Am I to inherit the water farms, the great house, to lead our people?'

'You misunderstand my intentions, Omar. I have granted you your freedom. I do not intend to shackle you with anything else, least of all running the House of Barir.'

'You do not intend to . . .' The implications of the man's cold words struck Omar in his heart.

'My father,' said Marid Barir, 'your grandfather, was a renowned caravan master, but he left me nothing. I raised the money to lead my own caravan. I parlayed one trade route into twenty, and then multiplied that into enough to buy a seat on the guild of water farmers, to pay for the first womb mage with the guild spells for our salt-fish. I did this by myself. An ancestor's wealth is a gilded cage, a curse you cannot escape. Your grandfather was wise enough not to trap his sons in such a cage. This is the gift I pass along to you. It's a most valuable one.'

'Then I cannot stay on the desalination lines?'

'I could not demean the family's name by having the last son of Barir toiling alongside nomads and slaves.'

'Then what shall I do?'

'What is it that you are always saying? Something will come along . . .'

Omar gawked at his master. *No, not my master. My father. Who would have guessed that freedom would feel so uncertain?*

'Congratulations, my son, you have discovered the joys of independence, the consequence of being a freeman. If I had known it would silence your prattling so effectively I might have done it years ago.'

Omar waved his ownership papers at the man, no longer his master. 'What shall I be?'

'We are what heaven wills us,' said Marid Barir.

'What shall I do? Tell me what I should do now!' Omar begged.

Marid Barir tapped his greying hair. 'Think.' He barked an order and the house manager opened the door. 'And go.'

Omar looked at the scroll of paper in his hand. It had all the weight of a length of steel pipe from a salt-fish tank.

The house manager shut the door as Omar – Ibn no more – Barir stumbled out.

'You managed to remove the grin from his mouth, master.'

'For an hour at least,' said Marid Barir. 'Now then, we must make time to prepare.'

The house manager nodded sadly and began to unfurl documents from the satchel he had with him, laying them across the marble table.

Omar blundered down the corridors of the fortified house, all thoughts of the views the pavilions' windows and gardens afforded an idler forgotten as he struggled to come to terms with his new status. Free. Every certainty of his life broken into pieces. *Is this what greatness feels like?*

Glancing up he saw Shadisa at the end of the corridor, walking serenely with one of the house cooks, an icebox of fish under her bare arm. Shadisa, the most beautiful of all the women in the house. And he was free. Free to marry her. Surely her scowling-faced father could not object now? Why, if anything, he should thank his stars that the last son of Barir favoured his lowly daughter!

Omar sprinted up to her and held out his ownership papers as if they were a talisman. 'Shadisa! I am a freeman. I have my papers.'

She looked at Omar as if he had gone mad.

'Do you not understand? I am not just any freeman. I am the blood of Marid Barir, and he has—' Omar hesitated, about to say, *cast me off.* 'I am my own man.'

Shadisa took the ownership papers Omar was proffering with her spare hand, scanning the contents, and then thrust them back towards Omar as if she was furious at him. 'You are a fool, Omar. It is you who do not understand.'

'But . . .'

'He has not done this for you,' said Shadisa, 'but for himself. It is only to ease his conscience.'

'I may seek your father out now,' pleaded Omar. 'As a freeman.'

Shadisa's full lips pursed and she forced the papers into Omar's hand, shaking her head. 'Go away Omar.' She turned and fled down the corridor, leaving Omar more confused than ever.

'Stay away from the house, water farmer,' warned the cook. 'Blood of Marid Barir,' she grunted. 'After all of this time, to acknowledge you now. Such a fool, such a cruel fool.'

'Where am I to go?' Omar nearly yelled out the words.

'Go back to your wild nomad friend and your stinking salt tanks,' spat the cook, running after Shadisa.

Omar looked at the crumpled roll of paper in his hand and smashed a fist into the wall, shouting a roar of frustration. Free and poor. *Is that why she has rejected me?*

He stalked off in search of Alim. In reality, the old nomad had been more of a father towards Omar than Marid Barir ever had. Old Alim would know what was to be done.

For a second, Omar thought that the water traders had changed their minds and returned to the farm. But there were no water-butt laden sandpedes among the group on the rise of the dunes behind the desalination lines, only camels and tall white-robed figures sitting high and proud in their saddles, the bells of the milk goats they kept with them jingling. Alim was walking towards the newcomers, without even the protection of a rifle.

'Alim! Alim!' Omar cried. The old water farmer spotted the young man and turned back, orange sand spilling down in front of his boots.

'Who are these people?' demanded Omar as Alim drew close.

'My people,' said Alim. 'Tribesmen of the Mutrah.'

'But you said they would kill you if you walked among them again.'

'The family of the chief I duelled and killed are all dead now,' said Alim. 'Slain in another feud. There are new princes of the sands riding under the moon, men who remember me more kindly. I may return to their fold.'

'You can't leave, Alim. I am a freeman. Look. I have my papers.'

'He finally recognized you?' Alim sighed.

Omar stared in disbelief at the old nomad. 'You knew?'

'Any man too blind to look into Marid Barir's face and see his eyes in yours could feel your back and know you for what you are from your lack of slave scars.'

'I can still work with you, Alim. Not here, perhaps, but we can travel to the water farms down south. They are as short-staffed as we are after the plague. They will welcome two expert workers.'

'I am called,' said Alim. 'This is my farm no longer. Wait here, boy. I will speak for you.' He walked back up the hill and Omar watched the old nomad talking to the tribesmen and pointing back down the dunes towards Omar. The conversation became heated and Alim returned, followed by an old crone with a large hump on her back, bent to the side and filled with water – the result of womb magic. Perhaps her own? *Is she a witch of Alim's people?*

'I have spoken for you,' said Alim. 'But you may not come with us.'

'Why would I want to come, Alim? My place is here in the empire – so is yours.'

The witch was shuffling about, looking at Omar from strange angles and he suspected her stance was not just simply due to the weight of water sloshing about her back. *She is seeing into my blood, my very future.*

'Not with us,' sang the witch. 'He must not come with us. His path lies down a different line.' She brushed Omar's arm gently, then seemed to turn feral, spitting at his feet. 'Filthy townsman.'

Omar watched the witch hobble back up the slope to the rest of the clan. 'You would leave the House of Barir to follow that mad old crone?'

'Foolish boy, do you think it is a coincidence my kin have chosen this day to come for me? She had brought word,' said

Alim. 'The whisper of the sands, the storm that is following the high keeper here.'

'What storm?' demanded Omar.

'The Sect of Ackron is to be declared heretic,' said Alim. 'Not enough tithes have been offered by the sect's followers to pay the Caliph Eternal the Holy Cent's one-hundredth annual share. There is a new sect rising, the Sect of Razat. They now have the power in the capital, and they would take their place in the unity of the one true god. They will offer your sect's tithe money instead. They will be the new fifty-third sect.'

'That is just politics,' said Omar.

'Fool of a freeman,' said Alim. 'There can only be a hundred facets of the one true god, not one sect less, not one sect more. When the Sect of Ackron loses its place at the table, its followers will lose all protections under the caliph's law. Everyone in your father's house will be declared heretic. The first to arrive here will be brigands and bandits. Everything of value will be looted and plundered. Every man, woman and child healthy enough to be tied to a camel will be taken as slaves.'

'No,' protested Omar. 'I am a freeman now.'

'Free to die, perhaps,' said the old nomad. 'The bandits and slavers and freebooters are not the worst. All the houses willing to renounce the Sect of Ackron have already done so. Only honourable houses like Marid Barir's have stayed loyal and not shifted their allegiance with the changing wind. The followers of Razat know that anyone who defects at this late stage will harbour hate in their hearts towards them, and they will never allow such vipers to be given sanctuary within the other houses, where they might rise to prosperity again and declare feud in the years to come. The houses that support the new sect will send their troops to Haffa and leave not even the children here alive. Your newly found blood, Omar,' Alim touched the boy's arm kindly. 'It is a poison that has marked you out for certain death.' He made a strange warbling in the back of his throat and one of the riders came galloping down the dunes, holding the reins of a riderless camel.

Alim smoothly mounted the saddle and threw down a thick leather purse filled with *tughra*, the paper notes of the empire's treasury. 'This is all the money I have saved tending the salt-fish with you over the years. It will be more than enough to pay one of the fishermen to sail you north. Travel away from the empire until you see the sands give way to scrublands, then hills that run green. Those are the uplands of the Jackelians. Tell them you are an escaped slave and you will find sanctuary there in the Kingdom.'

'But the Jackelians are infidels,' cried Omar. 'It is said they deny all gods, even the heathen ones. Their cities run dark with evil smoke and dead, lifeless machines.'

'They have a council,' said Alim, 'which they call parliament. Their ships and soldiers hunt all the empire's slavers, for which their loathing is well known. They will protect you.'

'Please, Alim,' begged Omar. 'Let me fetch Shadisa and we will travel with you. We will go to another town where no one knows us.'

Alim shook his head sadly. 'There are family markers in your blood that will be known by any womb mage who chooses to test you, and the assassins that will follow after you will know both your markers and your face well. Whatever happens here, you must never travel across the dunes of the Mutrah, Omar Barir, not unless you are riding with a well-armed caravan. You will not like our punishments for trespassing. If I catch you in the sands after today, I will dig you a pit and bury you up to your waist. Then I will stampede my camels across your head. Filthy townsman.'

'Please, Alim,' shouted Omar, taking a couple of hesitant steps forward. 'In the name of the one true god, Shadisa and I have nothing left here!'

'There is the desert,' Alim called back. 'The desert is always left, and for you the desert is death. Flee, freeman, travel north and fly before the storm.'

Whooping in their strange gargling throat songs, the nomads rode away, Alim among them, without even a backward glance, disappearing into the last tinges of red on the horizon above the dunes. For as long as Omar could remember, Alim had been the one person he had counted as his family, and now he was riding away into the desert. Omar's luck had vanished the moment he had received these papers of freedom: abandoned him just like Alim.

Omar looked back at the water farm, empty now except for him, and then he looked over towards the distant fortress of Marid Barir. *My father is inside there, and Shadisa.*

Picking up the nomad's purse, Omar started to run wildly before the gathering storm.

CHAPTER FOUR

Jack didn't know the name of the airship field the horseless carriage had driven him to, but First Lieutenant Maya Westwick and the soldier John Oldcastle seemed to know it well enough. The portly man threw the horseless carriage around, dodging past the field's massive airship rails and docking clamps, some pulling RAN aerostats into colossal hangars, others holding airships stationary while the craft were regassed and provisioned with fuel, oxygen tanks, supplies and ordnance. There were no airships of the merchant marine here, no passenger and visitor enclosures. Just blue naval uniforms striding about to inspect the work of stripe-shirted sailors hanging off the side of their giant cigar-shaped vessels, repainting the navy's standard chequerboard pattern on the lower envelopes or cleaning cannons that had been pushed through rubber-hooded gun ports.

As his carriage pulled up in front of a hangar with its doors shut, Jack saw there were multiple lines of people queuing behind desks while others stood ready for inspection. First Lieutenant Westwick jumped out of the vehicle and strode across to a line of sailors, men and women standing at ease as an official inspected them. Lifting a sheaf of papers from the officer, Westwick walked down the line, her eyes switching between the records and crew in front of her. She returned to the horseless carriage shaking her head as John Oldcastle climbed out of the driver's pit and motioned to Jack to step down onto the grass.

'Wasters and idlers to a man,' spat the first lieutenant. 'I wouldn't trust them to keep a kite aloft on a windy day, let alone a ship of the line.'

'There are other options,' said Oldcastle, drawing Jack aside and moving him into one of the lines of people queuing behind a desk.

The first lieutenant glanced at Jack as angrily as if she had caught him with his fingers around a knife, slicing open her bag of shopping to catch the dropping food. 'We've already scraped those barrels.'

She pointed to the lounging sailors she had just inspected and shouted to the navy official. 'Send them back to Admiralty House, every one of them.'

John Oldcastle watched her disappear into the hangar and tapped Jack on the shoulder, calling out to the officer manning the desk at the front of the line. 'Just administer the oath for this young fellow, Lieutenant McGillivray. He's in.' He glanced at Jack, before following the first lieutenant away. 'You'll do for now, Mister Keats, yes you will.'

'That's luck,' said an old white-haired man with a wooden leg, waiting ahead of Jack. He rubbed a finger on Jack's dirty torn jacket, his hand clutching a punch card, presumably his state work record. 'Give me some of it, boy. You're in.'

'Yes, but into what?' said Jack.

'The service,' rumbled an odd-sounding voice behind Jack. Turning, Jack saw it was a steamman, one of the foreign machine creatures queuing behind him. 'Into the Royal Aerostatical Navy.'

The people of the metal tended to keep to their own quarter of the capital. *Why would one of them want to sign up for military service?* Did King Steam permit the citizens of the Steamman Free State to sign up in their neighbour's aerial navy, even if the Jackelians were their ally of longest standing?

'You're going to join the RAN?' asked Jack.

'He'll get in today,' croaked the wooden-legged man. 'We all will. Nobody else wants to fly in the *Iron Partridge*.' He pointed to the colossal hangar doors that had started opening in front of them. 'An unlucky ship, aye. That's all anyone has ever said of her.'

Jack looked at what was beginning to emerge from the hangar with astonishment. The vessel had the basic cigar-shaped lines of an airship, but there her similarities with the other airships on the naval field ended. For a start, her hull appeared to be riveted over with metal plates from stem to stern. The top of her hull was decorated with a frill of massive pipes, as if some lunatic had inserted an oversized organ along her spine. Her lower hull wasn't painted with the black and yellow chequerboard of a Jackelian man-of-war either, but streaked with grey and blue angular shapes. The only standard thing about her was the figurehead on her bow dome, a sharp-beaked partridge with a pair of iron fin-bombs wrapped by lightning bolts clutched in its claws. Jack had to cover his ears as the engine cars – double rows of eight along each side – burst into life, the propellers giving her an extra push out of the hangar.

'How can she even fly?' shouted Jack over the noise.

'She flew out of the breaker's yard right enough,' said the old sailor in front of Jack. 'Slow and easy, only a day before they were due to scrap her.'

'Curse my valves, but I will serve aboard her,' the steam-man's voicebox vibrated. 'If it means I can fly, I will take her.'

'She looks like she was designed by King Steam,' said Jack. 'She looks like one of your people with fins.'

'You are closer to the truth than you realize, my softbody friend,' said the steamman.

'Listen to Coss Shaftcrank, he knows,' laughed the wooden-legged man. 'Haven't we been in the signing-on line for months together, waiting for a berth. Me and the old steamer here, every day, without a single skipper in the high fleet willing to give either of us a chance.'

What is going on here? Jack gazed with shock at the unwieldy metal-plated whale bumping out of the hangar. Nobody in their right mind was going to climb inside that monstrosity and risk heaven's command in her. Then the realization struck. Nobody who had a *choice* in the matter.

They had reached the head of the queue and the officer behind the table, his uniform half-hidden by a portable trans-action engine set up to process the recruits, took in all three of them with a sober glance. 'Pete Guns. Has the navy, by chance, stopped paying you your pension, that I have to see you back here in the signing line again?'

'Nobody can tie a fuse as well as I, Lieutenant McGillivray,' insisted the old man, 'as you should well remember.'

'And I have now reduced my weight to within navy board guidelines,' added Coss Shaftcrank. The steamman pointed to the massive craft drawing up behind the desk. 'The final requirement, as you stipulated to me at the start of the week. And kiss my condensers, but you will need engineers with an affinity with machines on board the *Iron Partridge* to fly her through the clouds.'

'Aye, *with* machines,' said the lieutenant, sounding resigned. 'Not *a* machine.' He stared at Jack. 'And John Oldcastle's wee thief. Well, it takes one to know one. You steal from a fellow cloudie's chest on board my ship, laddie, and you'll wish they had given you the rope, you will. Have you got your letters?'

Jack nodded and caught the card that was tossed at him with the oath to parliament printed on it. 'I don't suppose the judge furnished you with a state work record, laddie? No. Too much to ask. These two lubbers have the oath memorized already. Come on, laddie, let's hear it from you, or you can go back to your courtroom and choose the knot for your noose.'

And just like that, Jack found he had a half-honest trade at last. For as long as his strange airship stayed aloft.

Jack stole past the back of the red-coated marine walking down the airship's corridor, slipping into the keel deck's loading station, and, exactly as he had hoped, found the *Iron Partridge*'s hatches still open. Peering through, Jack saw bales of supplies left on the grass of the airship field below. He shinned down one of the crane cables on the lifting gear. Touching down on the grass, which felt slightly damp in the evening air, Jack heard a cough and he spun around.

It was John Oldcastle, his borrowed marine's crimson jacket swapped for the better-fitting but still untidy fabric of a warrant sky officer. The large man was rubbing the side of his dark salt-peppered beard with a mumbleweed pipe and didn't look surprised in the slightest to see Jack trying to go absent without leave.

'The locks I had put on your cabin were the best the navy had to offer, lad,' said Oldcastle.

Jack shrugged.

'But that's not much for a mortal clever fellow like you, I suppose.'

'The cipher on the lock's transaction engine wasn't random,' said Jack. 'It repeats itself every few minutes, if you look hard enough.'

'They always do,' sighed the warrant officer. 'I know you have family in the care of Sungate Board of the Poor. Two brothers is it?'

'They're not old enough to leave the workhouse,' said Jack. 'And I wouldn't have them run from it.'

'It's a hard place,' said Oldcastle.

'You don't even know the half of it,' said Jack. 'Don't try and stop me from leaving.'

Oldcastle slid a heavy bell-mouthed sailor's pistol across the bale he was sitting on. 'It'll pain me to shoot you, lad. But I'll do it for your own blessed good.'

Jack's eyes flicked across the space between the pistol and the old sailor's plump fingers. Calculating the chances he would be able to draw an accurate bead on Jack as he was dodging between the supplies waiting underneath the airship's belly.

'They'll find you,' said Oldcastle, 'if you run. Navy provosts will come after you. They'll stretch your neck, Jack Keats, and then what good will you be to your family? A dead man is no good to anyone but the worms.'

Well, what good have I ever been to my family anyway? What good would he be lying dead in the wreckage of the flying metal folly he had been sentenced to serve on board?

Oldcastle struck a match on the side of a crate and relit his pipe, puffing contentedly with the simple pleasure of sweet smoke. 'I have a friend back in the capital. A Sungate girl herself, once, not that you'd know it to see the fine trim of her bonnet now. She'll look in on your two lads and make sure they don't starve on that poorhouse gruel.'

'I'm nothing to you,' said Jack. 'Why would you do that for me? I don't trust you or your friend First Lieutenant Westwick.'

'She's a spiky one, isn't she?' said Oldcastle. 'As fair a face as ever graced a ship of the line, but don't let that fool you; she's a steel rose, with the petals of a cutting razor. And you're right not to trust me, lad. For I'm aiming to get you killed. But not this evening. And not in front of a Bonegate gallows-day crowd. And my word's gold for your two brothers in the workhouse, and that's as good an offer as you're receiving tonight.'

He brushed the barrel of his pistol to reinforce his words. The warrant officer's veiled threat was interrupted by the appearance of a military carriage that could have been the twin of the one that had arrived to take Jack to the army. A man on foot was chasing it at speed. At first Jack thought it was the mysterious man he had half-recognized in court, but the runner was only wearing the same style of long dark cloak tied at his neck. This officer's face was different: sandy hair flopping above an angular nose that looked too big for the measly pinched face that surrounded it.

First Lieutenant Westwick appeared like a ghost from behind the bales, and Jack wondered if she had been there all along as she glanced irritated towards the carriage and its naval pursuit. She pointed at Jack. 'A little early for him to be helping you.'

'Just two sailors, chewing the fat, Maya,' said Oldcastle

Jack nodded a silent look of thanks to the portly warrant officer. *I could have swung for what I just tried to do.*

Overtaking the armoured carriage, the beaky admiralty naval officer stopped his sprint and pointed accusingly at the first lieutenant. 'This carriage has no business being here.'

'It has every business,' said the woman. 'Unless you have an order from parliament that rescinds our authority over the *Iron Partridge*.'

There was a hum as the carriage's ramp was lowered, and a pair of marines walked down escorting a veritable mountain of a man, seven feet tall, with a neck like the trunk of an oak. His large hands were bound with chains and he was wearing a marine's boots half-covered by the rough cotton robes that Jack well-recognized from the sight of the convicts shuffling around Bonegate jail's exercise yard. Another convict, but this man's face was concealed by a rubber mask.

'A captain of marines must command order on a ship,' spat the admiralty officer, 'not disrupt it.'

'The case,' demanded Lieutenant Westwick, her arm outstretched to receive a wooden medical box that one of the marines had carried down from the carriage. 'You received my original list of staff requests a month ago, Vice-Admiral Tuttle. Every one of the sailors I asked for has become unavailable or has been conveniently reassigned.'

'I demand to see your captain,' barked the admiralty officer. 'Immediately.'

'He's not presently on board our ship.'

'Drunk, gambling, or both?' sneered the admiralty officer. He stared at the man mountain shambling down the ramp. 'You will find there are not nearly enough marines in the naval stockade to crew your pathetic commission of an airborne hulk.'

'Ah, that depends on how wide you cast the net, sir,' called Oldcastle, pointing behind the carriage. Jack turned to see near a hundred horses bearing swarthy riders, curved short-swords hanging from their saddles. Benzari tribesmen! They thundered to a halt in front of the airship's nose and dismounted, chattering approvingly at the sight of the vessel; slapping their thighs in amusement, as if the *Iron Partridge* had been pulled out of her hangar and onto a fairground lawn for their amusement.

The admiralty officer's sharp face was turning a beetroot colour in fury. 'The Benzari Lancers are an *army* regiment.'

'Attached to our ship now, sir,' smiled Oldcastle. 'Courtesy of the fine fellows at House Guards. Always willing to honour a request for cooperation, the general staff, what with Admiralty House being so short of marines for us.'

'You are both a disgrace to your uniforms,' said the admiralty officer. 'And we shall see how this matter is to proceed, that we shall. Your superiors will be hearing from the First Skylord about this outrage.' He stared across at the barrels of expansion-engine fuel stacked below the airship, noticing the supplies for the first time. 'Who ordered this gas here?'

'Was it not yourself, vice-admiral?' asked Oldcastle, in surprise.

The admiralty man shook his head in fury and stalked away, leaving Jack watching the milling Benzari warriors with a mixture of bemusement and uncertainty. Something was deeply wrong here. A first lieutenant and her warrant officer defying a vice-admiral in front of a greenhorn like Jack Keats and a rabble of Benzari warriors. What he knew of the RAN from the aeronauts' alehouse boasts and tales did not include such things in the navy's tightly regimented world.

Westwick reached up to pull the mask off the man mountain she had ordered released from the stockade and Jack saw a mist of green gas escape the mask's mouthpiece, leaving the broken brutish features of the convict underneath blinking like a sleepwalker as she gently pinched his arm. 'You've been sedated, Henry. Wake up.'

'How perishing long?' he mumbled.

'Two years,' she said. 'Floating in the waters of the navy's total security tank. But the captain needs you again.'

'Yes,' said the convict. 'The captain. He always looks after me. Do I know you?'

'Not directly,' said First Lieutenant Westwick. 'But I know of you, Henry Tempest. You are to be our captain of marines.'

'I forget sometimes,' said the brute. 'Me mind and me dreams. What's real and what's not.'

'Welcome back to the world, Mister Tempest.'

The man mountain made to salute the lieutenant, but his arms were pulled short by the chains clanking around his wrists. His dirty blue eyes turned wild for a second, his pupils seeming to dilate as he raised his arms in unison. There was a crack as the iron links were sent flying away across the field, then he dropped his free hands down, one of them stopping by his slab-like brow for the navy salute.

Jack realized he had been cowering beside one of the crates. They must have been old and rusted, the chains. *Nobody has the strength to do that, surely?*

The ship's surgeon had appeared and, taking the medical box from the first lieutenant's hand, he led their new captain of marines up into the *Iron Partridge*, the giant shaking slightly as if he had been smoking too many opiates.

'Find the captain,' First Lieutenant Westwick ordered her warrant officer. 'Search every alehouse, jinn house and gambling house from here to the capital if you have to. We lift with the morning trade winds, before Admiralty House finds a way to reassign our bloody propellers to the board of engineering for maintenance.'

Oldcastle nodded grimly and weaved off through the Benzari regiment.

'Do you trust me?' the first lieutenant asked Jack.

How much did she hear of my conversation with the warrant sky officer before she appeared?

Jack shook his head, and as quick as a snake, Westwick had him by the throat, a tiny razor-sharp stiletto blade in her hand, pressing up against the bottom of his chin. Jack struggled to break free but her grip was granite-strong.

'Do you trust me when I say that if you ever try to desert

my command again, I will slice you a smile from here—' she tapped along his throat '—to here? Look into my eyes, Mister Keats. Do you trust that?'

It was Boyd staring back at him. Boyd at his murderous worst. As if the street thug had been trained by someone and turned into something far more *honed*. She would do it, Jack could see that. In fact, part of her wanted to, just to set an example. Maybe just for her own amusement.

'I do,' coughed Jack.

She dropped him down to the grass. 'Be about it, Mister Keats. You may re-enter the ship by the main boarding ramp, like the loyal skyman we shall make of you.'

Jack heard the snick of the springs as the hidden blade withdrew back into her sleeve. That was the weapon of one of the capital's assassins, a topper, not a lady gentlewoman of the fleet. Circle's teeth, what kind of mess had he landed into here?

Rubbing his throat, Jack staggered up the *Iron Partridge*'s main boarding ramp and back to the airship's keel deck, his mind spinning with unanswered questions, the pain of his neck muscles made a collar – reminding him how near to death he had just come. Reminding him he was just as much a prisoner on board the airship as he had been in jail.

CHAPTER FIVE

Omar ran through the great house's central garden. Everywhere there were gas lamps burning without thought for the cost, people moving about the colonnades and pavilions, some sprinting through the cold night air as the first stars slid across the heavens above.

He nearly ran into the house's soldiers by one of the fountains, dozens of troops dragging struggling men in long black robes through the garden. With a start of recognition, Omar realized that these were learned men, the House of Barir's womb mages. How could these powerful sorcerers be manhandled so? They held the miraculous secrets of creating the salt-fish that generated the house's wealth from mere sea water.

'Stand aside,' one of the soldiers shouted at Omar, and he was pushed back with a rifle butt while the womb mages were hauled into the centre of the garden.

The soldiers carried crates with them that they spilled onto the carefully tended grass, and Omar heard the rattling of copper pages bound with metal chord hitting the ground. He scooped a book up, staring at the metal-stamped lines of characters, a handful of letters, – *A, C, G, T* – repeated over and over again in seemingly random patterns. This had to be one of the womb mages' precious spell books. The sorcery that allowed the creation of such wondrous biologicks as the salt-fish. Omar nearly dropped the book in superstitious dread. It was said that to read such a miracle without a womb mage's powers would cause you to go blind.

A soldier snatched the copper book out of Omar's hands and thrust a glass jug of foul-smelling green liquid at him. 'Pour it all over the pages,' ordered the soldier. 'Splash none over yourself.'

The soldier began to pour the liquid over the crate of spell books, acid turning the tomes into a bath of hissing steam and bubbling fury. Omar emptied the whole flask over a crate and then ran towards Marid Barir's office, turning to see the womb mages flung backwards by the first volley of the firing squad. Bursting into the master's office, Omar nearly tripped over the body of the house manager lying sprawled across the tiles, sending an empty vial of poison scuttling across the floor. Omar was still on his knees when he saw his father's kaftan by the window. A richly jewelled dagger had been thrust into Marid Barir's chest.

'It is not fitting for the last of this house's blood to die in bondage,' whispered Omar, moving closer to the body, remembering his father's words. His father of a single day seemed to be staring peacefully across the rooftops of Haffa below. *I wish I could feel more sorrow than this, but I cannot. You were my master for longer than my father, a good master, but a poor father. Will my sadness serve your soul, as you are lifted into heaven?* 'I will go, master. And I take Shadisa with me. She does not deserve to be a slave. I think she will not care for such a life, even less than I did.'

By the time Omar reached the bottom of the stairs, the

bells were ringing from the top of each of the house's tall corner towers.

'They're coming,' a soldier yelled, pushing a spare rifle into Omar's hands. 'Down the caravan road.'

'Please,' Omar said. 'Shadisa of the golden hair, the kitchen girl, where is she?'

'Down to the town!' ordered the soldier, ignoring Omar's question. 'The women and children have first call on the boats. We will hold the raiders back. All men to stand and hold.'

'I don't know how to use this.' Omar had been about to protest that as a slave he could be put to death for merely holding a rifle. But of course, he was a freeman now, free to die as their house's enemies fell upon them.

Grabbing the rifle angrily out of Omar's fingers, the soldier drew the curved scimitar from the belt by his side and pushed it at Omar. 'Do you know how to swing and cut, idiot?' he shouted, disappearing into the gardens.

Omar went looking for Shadisa, jostled and shoved down the corridors by the running staff and soldiers. The palace echoed with the sound of his boots as retainers bundled past him, ignoring his pleas.

At last someone came towards Omar who looked like he had more on his mind than bundling the house's contents up into sheets, but the scar-faced fellow slapped the sabre out of Omar's hand and grabbed him by the throat, waving a sword under his neck. 'The house's treasury, where is it?'

Brigands were already in the house! They must have scaled one of the outside walls in advance of the main party of looters. Another man came running behind the first bandit, fresh blood staining the front of his robes. 'He won't know,' hissed the newcomer. 'Stick this foul-smelling slave in the belly and let's find someone worth taking back across the sands.'

'I know where the treasury is,' hacked Omar as the brigand's grip tightened. 'My master keeps so many coins down there – towering hills of silver, enough to blind you if you open the doors during high sun.'

'Take us to the treasury,' commanded the brigand who had his throat. 'And your bones may end up on the slave block back in Bladetenbul, rather than within the ashes of this palace.'

'Quickly!' ordered the other. 'We're the first, and we're taking the first's share.'

'You are fleet fellows,' said Omar as he was released. He sped up his walk to a sprint in front of the two bandits. 'But even such master brigands as you will be slowed by the weight of coins I shall lead you to.'

If our house guards hadn't already spirited the money away, of course. Either on their own account or to help the House of Barir's people escape with more than empty pockets and a heretic's fate awaiting them. If that was the case, Omar suspected, he wouldn't be getting to see the capital's slave market. *Please, fate, keep your servant alive for a little longer. I still have many great deeds to perform. I just need a little time to work out what they will be.*

As they dashed down the house's lower central corridor, a group of five or six brigands spilled out from a doorway, struggling women flung unceremonially over their shoulders. One of the women had golden hair and dark olive skin. *Shadisa!*

Omar yelled and was flung against the wall for his trouble, held there by his two brigands while the screaming line of kitchen staff and their new masters vanished up a stairwell at the far end of the corridor. Omar's shout had gone unheard by the rival brigands under the racket of their newly acquired human cargo.

'Adeeba's men,' growled one of his captors.

'Fool of a slave,' the other brigand slapped Omar's head with the buckle of his scimitar guard. 'There are quicker ways down here.'

I have to get her back. Think. 'But the master's counting rooms are yet two floors below us,' said Omar. 'Buried deep in the harbour cliffs. That girl with the golden hair was one of those trusted with the code to the lock.'

'Liar!' accused the bandit who had struck him. 'Who would trust a woman with such a thing? You are trying to get us to save one of your little sweetmeats, eh?'

'No,' insisted Omar. 'She knows. Marid Barir is a clever man. He knew a serving girl would never be questioned for the lock's code.'

The first of the bandits sneered. 'Too bad. Adeeba's men will sell her on the trading block back in the capital like they always do. Such a secret will not be much use to the girl when her new master comes calling each night, eh?'

'We know where to search for the treasury now,' said the other. He drew his sword ready to plunge it into Omar's heart. 'I might waste explosives on the vault door and good water on taking your golden-haired beauty back out across the desert, but I won't waste any water on your stinking carcass.'

'Water for a water farmer,' laughed a voice behind them. 'You might consider investing in this one; who knows what secrets of salt-fish breeding he has been taught?'

Omar's two captors turned, one of them too late, the ball from a pistol blasting into the centre of his chest and carrying him slamming into the wall. It was another bandit, a short stocky man wearing a voluminous kaftan, belts tucked full of guns and knives, a smoking pistol in one hand, a wickedly sharp scimitar balanced in the other.

Omar's remaining captor pointed his scimitar towards the

killer. 'Are you one of Adeeba's men? Have this one if you want him, take him and go in peace.'

'But this is hardly a time of peace,' said the killer, rubbing his bald, shaved head. There were tattoos rising up around his neck that looked like the heads of vipers. 'Is it?'

'Then you can go to hell instead!' yelled Omar's captor, lunging forward and trying to shove the point of his sword into the killer's belly.

Dancing away, the killer easily avoided the brigand's thrust. His cloak swirled out, seeming to swallow the two of them, muffling the repeated sound of wet slapping as his knife found its mark. When the cloak whisked back it revealed the killer crouching like a sand lion over the bloodied ruin of the brigand's body.

'There is money below.' Omar's shaking palms turned outwards to indicate he had no weapons. 'A fortune.'

'Yes, money,' said the killer, wiping his sword clean on the bandit's robes. 'Money and blood. Always.'

As the killer's fist connected with Omar's face, he caught a glimpse of the bandit feeding a fresh crystal charge into his pistol's breech, before darkness descended.

One last reeling thought crossed his mind. *Who would waste a bullet in the head or heart for a slave?* No. Not a slave anymore. He was a freeman. The last son of Marid Barir.

Omar moaned, darkness and sparks of light rolling across his vision. Through the blur of the pain and the fog of his aware-ness – drifting in and out of consciousness – he smelt the burning carnage, flames leaping among the screams. He was slung over someone's back, but he spotted spinning glances of the sack of the town. Men kneeling, their faces bowed while fighters strutted behind a shivering line of captives, blades flashing, sprays of blood, heads dropping to the ground to roll away down a slope. Surreal hideous visions of a painting of hell, a house guard tied between two sandpedes and slowly ripped apart, other men fixed to horses and dragged across the ground shrieking. Silhouettes chasing other shadows through the night, laughs, cries, jeers, challenges and curses, people jumping out of a blazing building. Survivors rolling across the ground beside him, their clothes ablaze. A column of women being chained and made ready for the journey to the slavers' block, a dark-robed womb mage injecting them with a phage to turn them into temporarily submissive zombies, fit only to compliantly march across the desert until they reached market. Less water consumed. Fewer escape attempts. Less trouble.

Was Shadisa among them somewhere? *Don't think of the other possibilities, the brutes who'd carried Shadisa off, what they might do to her.* She could die out there in the desert, a mute stumbling wraith. With her beauty, perhaps she would be lucky to. Before she reached a slaver's platform where fat, lustful merchants would look upon her and reach for the purses dangling upon their plump guts, imagining what sport they might have with their fine new servant. His soul felt as if it was being crushed, his guts crumpled into a burning gemstone of pure grief. The agony of worrying about it was more than he could stand.

'Shadisa,' he tried to yell. All that came out of his mouth was a hollow gargle.

A corpse tumbled past Omar as he was lugged across the ground, the body's leather armour sliced by scimitar cuts. Someone who was foolish enough to challenge the deadly killer carrying him away for the bounty written in his bastard's blood.

Something will come along.

Right now, it was the darkness of oblivion as he lost consciousness again.

Omar came around feeling queasy. Not because of the pain in his nose or the spinning of his head, but thanks to the jouncing motion of the floor underneath him. He had been semi-conscious for some time. Was he on a ship? A fishing boat from the harbour? No, the hissing he could hear had a mechanical quality to it, and there was the smell of oil burning on metal, like the desalination lines just after they had been stripped, cleaned and reassembled.

Omar moaned as he pulled himself up. His hands were chained behind his back and he was inside the claustrophobic confines of an iron room, all pipes and boxes and controls.

Lounging against the wall opposite him on a pile of green pillows was the same killer who had broken his nose in Marid Barir's palace. The shaven-headed man looked up from sharpening his scimitar with a whetstone.

Omar and the killer weren't alone in the confined iron space. There was also a crimson-hooded man seated at the front of the room, his hands on a wheel like one of the ferry pilots that called at Haffa. But the pilot had no window in front of him, just a small flat table with a map under a wire mesh, a pencil locked on a metal arm tracing a vibrating passage across the paper as the room shifted and swayed from side to side.

'Where am I, my new master?' coughed Omar. 'You will not regret sparing me. I will work as hard as ten men for you.'

'Those who serve me know that I do not like to answer questions,' said the stocky man. His gloved hand reached into his kaftan and produced the roll of Omar's papers, Marid Barir's last gift. The boy groaned. *I must have dropped my ownership documents when I was taken prisoner by the first two brigands.*

'You father did not love you very much, I think,' said the killer. 'As a slave you were merely property, and property can be traded between one master and the next. But as a freeman and the last surviving blood of Marid Barir?' He shrugged. 'There is a great bounty to be collected on your head. The Sect of Razat demand the death of all of those that their rise to the Holy Cent have made into heretics, and the higher in the house's ranks the survivors stand, the greater the reward on their heads.'

'You have made a mistake,' said Omar. 'I am just a slave. All of master Barir's children died during the plague years.'

'Perhaps I am in error, then,' said the killer. 'But I was not confused when I saw a gang of freebooters running laughing to their camels carrying the hacked-off head of Marid Barir. They will deny he had the honour to end his own life. When they hand it in for the reward money, they will say that he begged them for mercy and that they sliced off the snake's head as their reply.'

'Do not say that!' shouted Omar. 'Marid Barir was a good man, he was—'

Omar ducked as the killer threw the whetstone at him, the rock bouncing off the metal rivets behind his head.

'You curse like a freeman. Loyalty is not a bad thing, Omar Barir. But your house has fallen and a wise man would learn to hold his tongue and choose his battles.'

From the front of the metal space, the crimson-hooded man turned around and tapped a dial on the wall. 'Pressure is at maximum, we must surface and blow.'

The killer nodded and Omar found himself sliding down the floor as it slanted to an incline. Then there was a jolt as the room righted itself. An iron panel in the front wall lifted noisily to reveal an expanse of endless sands and burning bright daylight outside.

'We are on a dune whale,' said Omar.

'I do not like to attract the attention of competitors,' said the killer.

So, the killer travelled *under* the sands. There was a screeching noise from the rear of the room and Omar imagined he could see the super-pressurized blast of smoke from the dune whale's engine being funnelled through the blowhole above. They would not stay on the desert's surface for long, for that dirty boom would have alerted every nomad and wild desert fighter for miles around that here was a prize worth taking. Omar could just see the corkscrewing nose drill of the dune whale turning at the front of the craft, and then he was swung about as the machine dipped forward and started tunnelling below the fine orange sands again.

'That will be the last venting before we reach the caravanserai,' announced the pilot.

'You must be a rich man to travel this way,' said Omar.

'I will be richer still with the bounty on your head,' said the killer.

'Perhaps I will serve you so well that you will not wish to hand me over to the priests of this new sect.'

The killer walked over to Omar and unlocked his chains, dropping the scimitar onto his lap. 'Start by sharpening that.'

Omar looked incredulously at the sharp blade that had fallen into his care.

'Raise it against me,' said the killer, 'and we will discover what you are worth to the new sect's high keeper with no hands attached to your wrists.'

'What is the name of the man who owns this sword?' asked Omar.

'Farris Uddin. But master will do well enough for you.'

There was something about this man, Omar realized, something familiar: as if he had known him before, perhaps in a previous life. No, his senses must be playing him false – he couldn't have met this deadly force before. *Surely I would have remembered.*

Omar started to draw the whetstone down against the length of the shining silver steel. Sharpening the blade for the man who might be his new master, or his executioner.

It seemed burning hot to Omar, out in the open again after so long trapped in the close shaded confines of the deadly Farris Uddin's dune whale. The dune whale's captain had set them to rest next to a line of similar giant teardrop-shaped craft. There would be no more diving under the desert for Omar and his captor; the deep orange sands gave way to rocky ground from here on in. Omar didn't know precisely where they were, but if he had to hazard a guess, he would say that they had travelled southeast, away from the thin patch of civilization that ran along the coast, across the desert, and towards the great centre of Cassarabia; to where the empire's true civilization was counted to start.

They had reached a caravanserai, a series of windowless buildings connected by rocky palm-tree shaded lanes. Merchants sat outside the crenellated walls selling dates, black bread and yoghurt. Omar could almost feel the cool shade and taste the spray of moisture from the fountains within.

A line of sandpedes emerged from the stables on the side of the caravanserai, the drovers crying commands and cracking their whips against the hundreds of bony legs straining under the weight of their enamel water tanks. Omar recognized some of the drovers – the water sloshing about their tanks had come from Haffa a couple of weeks ago.

Farris Uddin tied Omar's hands together with a length of

leather and bound it to the rail on a stone trough meant for tying up camels.

'I will not run, master,' said Omar.

'No. You won't.' Uddin disappeared into the stables, leaving Omar outside in the beating sun, tied up like an animal with only the half-shade of the palm leaves for shelter.

I suppose I won't at that.

Watching a kestrel circling overhead, Omar's glance fell down to the end of the street where one of the water traders was talking to three men and pointing back towards the stables where Omar was standing. He looked around nervously. There was nobody else here. Just himself, the trough and the stables. A coin was exchanged and the three men began walking purposefully down the line of sandpedes towards him. Omar pulled at the leather thong tying him to the rail. Too tight to slip. Too thick to chew through. Omar tried to keep calm. Perhaps the gang had just been asking for somewhere to stable their steeds? But the hope of that disappeared as they got closer. Three tall rangy thugs wearing crossed belts filled with crystal charges for the rifles strapped to their backs. Caravan guards, or hunters of men?

'There's a pretty parcel,' said one of them, looking Omar up and down. 'Left trussed for us to find.'

'The wrist ties are mine.' Farris Uddin's voice sounded unexpectedly behind Omar, making him jump. The killer moved like a ghost. 'As is the slave that is bound by them.'

'A male slave is worth only fifty altun,' said the thug. 'The bounty on a heretic that served the House of Barir is ten times that.'

'Then I have made a fine profit.'

'A profit like that,' said the thug, licking his lips expectantly, 'deserves to be shared.'

Farris Uddin glanced languidly about the street, as if he

was surprised to see where he had ended up. 'Is this the desert wastes? Is this the heathen borderlands? No, it's the empire, and the Caliph Eternal's law states that taking another's property is theft. That's sharing you can be executed for.'

'There is no garrison here,' snorted one of the thugs. 'And you have not paid for the protection of the caravan.' He tapped his neck, indicating the space where the bronze seal and chain would be if Omar's new master had paid to travel under the immunity of one of the caravan trains.

'A guardsman,' said Farris Uddin, his voice turning low and dangerous, 'does not need protection. He *is* protection.'

'Oh, ho!' The three of them roared with laughter, while one poked a finger at the preposterous Uddin. 'You are a long way from the great palace, then, noble guardsman. Is the court of the Caliph Eternal coming up here to pay for dune whale trips around the town to amuse the great ruler's harem?'

'It is strange, noble guardsman,' said the most sizeable of the thugs. 'For I am sure you have been marked out to me before as Udal the Viperneck; a mere bounty hunter, just the same as us.'

'My name is Farris Uddin,' insisted the killer, pulling his collar down to reveal his bare throat. 'And I have no tattoos on my neck.'

Omar blinked in disbelief. The killer had possessed the tattoos back in the master's palace at Haffa. Omar had seen them. *What is going on here?* All three thugs slid out their scimitars in unison and Omar groaned when he noticed that Uddin was totally unarmed. The careless fool must have left his weapons saddled to a camel inside the stable and he had come out here without his pistols and blades.

'You are a stubby little liar, Udal, or Uddin, or whatever you are called. But we have just the thing to shave another few inches off your height.'

Farris Uddin raised his empty hands in supplication. 'There is no need for that. I can see you are set on stealing my slave. I would not have my death on your heads.' He walked to Omar and untied the leather knot from the long palm-wood rail. 'You are too much trouble to me already.'

'Easy come, easy go, master,' said Omar.

As the three thugs came to seize Omar, Farris Uddin snapped the rail off the trough and jammed it like a spear into the face of the tough on the left, before sliding it around and shoving it into the features of the man on the right. Only the thug in the centre of the trio was left standing, looking on in astonishment as both his friends tumbled to the ground. By the time the man had remembered the sabre in his hand, Uddin had snapped the pole in two over his leg; he used the twin batons to dance a series of rapid strikes across the thug's head and shoulders. With his scimitar falling to the ground, the third fighter crumpled to the dirt under the fierce tattoo of blows.

Farris Uddin moved over the cowering thug and pointed his two makeshift wooden batons towards the man's forehead. 'What is my name? What am I?'

'Farris Uddin,' spluttered the rascal. 'You are a guardsman.'

Omar looked at the two ruffians lying crumpled to either side as Farris Uddin sent the surviving man scampering away down the street with a swift kick from his boot. Their noses had been pushed back into their skulls and both men were dead.

'You killed them, master.'

'Easy come, easy go.'

Had Uddin been telling the truth when he said he was an imperial guardsman? The caliph's guardsmen kept the peace in the palace and served as the ruler of Cassarabia's elite regiment of soldiers. But unless such a man was cast out and declared rogue, what would one of them possibly want with the bounty on a heretic like Omar? No, the killer was just a hunter of men who had been trying to bluff his way out of a fight. A particularly lethal example of the breed. *That is the only thing that makes any sense.*

'I saw a guardsman once,' said Omar quickly, trying to talk away his nerves. 'He was travelling with a war galley that had come into our harbour, and he flew above the galley on a great lizard with wings as wide as this street.'

'A drak,' growled Farris Uddin, leading the way to the stables. 'They are called draks, and the man you saw would have been an officer of the twenty-second talon wing. Draks do not like the open sea and they have to be specifically trained for such duties. The twenty-second has such steeds.'

'Do draks like sand better?' asked Omar, ducking through the stable entrance and entering into a dark space with a mud floor covered with straw.

'No,' said Farris Uddin, rolling up the sleeves of his robes before dipping an arm into a stone tank and lifting out a large, bleeding carcass with four small hooves still attached. 'They like sheep.'

Omar hollered in fear as a head as long as he was tall lashed out of the shadows to lance the tossed carcass on its razor-sharp beak, throwing it up into the air like a cat playing with its prey, before swallowing the carcass in a single sinuous gulp.

'And human flesh,' added Uddin, gripping Omar's shoulders tight. 'When they are permitted it.'

Jack Keats yelled as the rush of air whipped past his face. A thousand feet above the ground wasn't high enough to require the *Iron Partridge* to run pressurized, but it was high enough that no airship sailor would walk away from a fall.

Even hanging upside down, Jack could just hear the reasonably voiced protests of the steamman Coss Shaftcrank from an open gun port.

'I've done it,' cried Jack, the blood rushing to his head. 'I've kissed the ship's nameplate.'

The lumpen face that belonged to the two hands clutching Jack's ankles poked out of the gun port where the cannon's rubber hood had been withdrawn, a brief distraction for Jack from the distant landscape whipping past below at seventy miles an hour.

His answer came back over the roar of the engine cars below. 'You aren't low enough to have done it proper, thief boy. Stretch yourself down.'

Jack felt his body jolt as the hands around his ankles swung him down still lower. As initiation ceremonies went, the Royal Aerostatical Navy's seemed particularly brutal and pointless. At least when he had been running with the flash mob, his baptismal trial of breaking into a warehouse one night had yielded a few pennies of profit.

Pasco, the ship's savage master engineer and self-appointed 'tutor' of the navy's traditions to the new hands, leant further out of the gun port and threw a line down to Jack. At first, Jack thought that he was meant to grab it – extra security now that his ordeal was over – but then he noticed the bulky pair of gloves hanging at the end.

'Put them on, thief,' shouted the master engineer. 'One at a time.'

It had been Pasco's turn to teach the classes that the new recruits were obliged to sit – instructions on ship lore and layout, the navy's rules, regulations, traditions – the thousands of obscure pieces of equipment that an airship sailor's life depended on. Pasco's teaching methods, however, seemed rather more direct than those of his fellow officers.

The gloves swung closer and Jack did as he was bid, discovering a handle inside each of the leather mittens just as the fingers holding his ankles released their grip. Jack screamed in panic, sliding head first down the outside of the *Iron Partridge* until he swung around on the gloves, gravity and the winds tugging his boots as he found himself miraculously clinging onto the side of the massive craft's iron plates. *The gloves are magnetic!* When his hands had contracted inside the gloves, the gauntlets had activated – and releasing the handle inside loosened the invisible bond between man and the airship's hull. Hair blowing in the crosswinds, Jack glanced up at the jeering faces, shouting abuse – or possibly encouragement – from the safety of their gun port.

Down below, the transmission belt running out to the engine car underneath growled at Jack, as if the engine moulded as a lion's head was actually alive; its rapidly turning rotor waiting to carve him into pieces if he lost his hold. He could hardly hear the engine over the sound of his own heart hammering inside his chest. Crying in an unholy blend of rage and fear, Jack released the magnet's activator on his left hand and threw his arm up to fix his glove on the metal plating above his head. Repeating the manoeuvre, using the rivets on the plates below him as barely functional footholds, Jack steadily, desperately, clanged his way back up the airship's outer metal skin and towards the open gun port. There were thieves back in the capital who specialized in running the labyrinthine maze of rooftops and towers in Middlesteel, experts in rattling skylights. Jack was not one of them. *Don't look down. One hand in front of the other and whatever you do, don't look down.*

The young sailor cursed his tormentors with every freezing yard he climbed. Finally, Jack got near enough to the gun deck to hear a commotion inside – which explained where the jeering sailors who had just been observing his progress had disappeared to. Grasping the inside of the gun port, Jack tumbled back onto the airship's deck and fell into the middle of a brawl.

John Oldcastle was wielding one of the flat-headed rammers the gunners used to load cartridge wad and shot as a stave. Two sailors had been laid out cold with its blunt end, and the large officer had Pasco, the master engineer, pressed down on the neck of a thirty-two pounder. His makeshift weapon was held tight against Pasco's throat, choking the man. Coss Shaftcrank was also threatening some of the master engineer's men with a wad hook, his voicebox sounding a warning in case they tried to save their chief.

Coss was still wearing the harness the sailors had used to dangle him out over the hull, none of the cowards wanting to risk the creature of the metal's weight dragging them over the side during his brutal initiation ceremony.

'Ah, there you are lad,' said Oldcastle. 'Me and the master engineer were just having a lively little debate about the use of a safety line during the kissing of the ship.'

'What loss is that thief going to be?' choked Pasco. 'Fresh out of Bonegate jail. Another pressed man. Better the bastard drops now before one of his mistakes kills a real cloudie.'

'I can find a blessed use for him on the upper deck,' said Oldcastle, easing up the pressure on the master engineer's neck. 'And if you try to nobble the lad again, I'm going to take the harness off this old steamer and see if it's long enough to swing you down onto the rotors of one of your own engine cars.'

'You're just a warrant sky officer, the same as me,' said Pasco, angrily rubbing his sore throat. 'You don't get to decide who has the new signings. Maybe the thief'll end up in my engine room, and then he'll know what it is to serve in the Royal Aerostatical Navy.'

'The first lieutenant has already given me these two,' said Oldcastle, indicating Jack and Coss Shaftcrank. 'And we've got our own initiation ceremony up top.'

'You and the first lieutenant,' spat Pasco. 'You've got your tongue so far up her arse it's a wonder you can talk. She's as much a greenhorn as these two. What's this to her? First voyage for some lady noble with more connections at Admiralty House than sense? You and me, Oldcastle, we'll settle this proper when we're back on shore.'

'Well you'd better be prepared to wait a good long while, then.'

Jack saw a dangerous look cross Pasco's face as the engineer realized that the old sailor knew how long they were going to be in the air. 'You know where we're going, fat man? You know what the captain's orders are?'

'I know your rotors are going to need to keep on turning to get us there, Master Engineer Pasco. And that's as much as you need to understand to do your mortal job.'

Jack followed Oldcastle and the steamman as they warily withdrew from the gun deck and headed for the upper lifting chamber – one of two on the airship – its vast space filled with thousands of spherical gas bags secured by netting. The ironically named crew of idlers were busily checking pressure and looking for rodent-teeth tears and leaks that needed patching. Metal ladders fixed inside pipework frames connected the *Iron Partridge*'s upper deck and lifting chamber, but Jack was relieved when John Oldcastle led them to the frame that held the lifting belt – a privilege, he had been warned, usually reserved for officers. After the ordeal of kissing the ship, Jack didn't think he could stand to climb by hand up one of the lifting chamber's vertigo-inducing ladders.

Waiting for one of the wooden steps fixed onto the rotating leather belt to come around, Oldcastle appraisingly looked over Jack and the steamman. 'Master Engineer Pasco knows his engines well enough, lads, but he's a rabble-rouser who's spent time in a stockade for trying to organize the RAN's engineers into a workers' union.'

'And we're the only ship that would have him,' said Jack, remembering the first lieutenant's confrontation with the vice-admiral the evening before the airship launched.

'All we could mortal get,' said Oldcastle, grabbing a handhold on the belt as he swung his boots out onto its wooden step. Jack followed after Coss Shaftcrank stepped on, watching the floor of the lifting chamber drop away as he was carried nearly eighty feet up towards the highest of their airship's seven levels, the upper deck.

'Like our ship herself, perhaps?' said Coss. 'Due to be scrapped, but rescued at the last minute . . .'

'A flying albatross right enough,' said John Oldcastle. 'And when we get to my kingdom under the crow's nest, you'll see quick enough why.'

'I understand the *Iron Partridge* was a proving craft,' said the steamman. 'Built in the air yards of the House of Quest.'

Oldcastle stepped off the belt as they passed through to the upper deck, ignoring the smells and sounds coming from an open door down the corridor where the airship's stock of pigs and sheep were housed. 'Aye, I can see you've done your research before signing on with us, Mister Shaftcrank. But all she proved was that the great industrial lord that built her wasn't quite as clever as he believed he was.'

Jack saw why once the warrant sky officer had led them through a series of narrow corridors past several doors labelled as stores. Nestled between the wooden walls, a short companionway led up to the last thing Jack had expected to see on board an airship – transaction engines! They looked down into a long deep pit filled with the massive calculating machines, and not in any design that Jack was familiar with. Multiple banks of transaction-engine drums slowly turned as steam hissed out of a labyrinth of copper pipes. At the far end of the transaction-engine room was a series of globe-shaped boilers. Two stokers were feeding the furnace, the sweat-soaked skin of their bare chests glowing orange against the flames.

'Sweet Circle,' swore Jack, stretching over the railing to look down at unfamiliar symbols turning on the thinking machines' drums. *This is nothing like the antiquated standard equipment I trained on back in the guild.* 'I've never seen the like – what's it doing here?'

'A folly, Mister Keats,' said Oldcastle. 'A folly that has never worked. And the other reason, besides our blessed armour plating, why the *Iron Partridge* handles like a whale of the air, large and slow-like.'

'The softbody designers intended for these thinking machines to control the airship,' said Coss. 'Using a crew a tenth of the size of a normal ship of the line.'

'Not just the airship, old steamer,' said Oldcastle, pointing up to a rubber-sealed skylight in the ceiling from where the frill of massive mortar tubes was visible outside, stretching like a spine of chimneys across the top of the ship. 'But all the gunnery on this wicked organ of death we're lugging about on our backs, too.'

'And it never worked?' asked Jack.

'Over-engineered,' said Oldcastle. 'Much like the mind of the fool who designed it – too clever for his own mortal good. When the navy realized the vessel's automation couldn't cope, they spent a second fortune redesigning the *Iron Partridge* to work manually with a full crew – and the airship still didn't fly well enough. Our main job here is to make sure that the transaction engines don't get in the way of the crew. The systems still try and come back fully online every now and then, working their automated mischief. These transaction engines were buried too wicked deep into the fabric of the ship for us to allow the boilers to run cold and still their drums altogether. Just enough power to let her tick over and no more, that's what we must be about.' He pointed to a line of hammocks hung up behind the spherical boilers, the sailors' wooden air chests sitting beneath. 'You can bed down there. You'll be glad of the boilers when we're running high and cold. Warmest place on the *Iron Partridge*, so it is. The watch in the crow's-nest dome down the corridor come in here after they've stood a duty, to toast their gloves against our plates.'

Better than the cramped confines of the crew's quarters on the lower deck where Jack had been camped until now, he supposed. Blanket Bay, as the airship's sailors referred to the long swathe of hammocks.

'Is it only us up here?' asked Jack.

Oldcastle nodded sadly, gesturing to the rows of empty punch-card writers and injection desks opposite the boilers. 'There's not many trained enginemen and cardsharps with a taste for the navy's foul food and parliament's meagre pay. Even our two stokers are on loan from the captain of marines.'

Jack nodded. So, was this pit of broken thinking machines the reason the RAN had been so eager to rescue him from the gallows? But then there had been the man in court. Jack knew his face from somewhere. *But where?*

'We might have been the pride of the fleet,' said Oldcastle with a melancholy expression pinching his cheeks. 'Gliding over the battlefield like an eagle and letting enemy cannon fire bounce off our hull while our mortar shells found the foe's helmets as if the very steel in our guns were bewitched. But here we are instead, on another desperate voyage, with cruel fate carrying us far from home. Damn my unlucky stars.'

He looked at the curious faces of Jack and Coss. 'But I mustn't say too much about that. The first lieutenant's orders are the first lieutenant's to keep.'

'You mean the captain's orders?' said Jack.

'Indeed, Mister Keats. Too much heat in here. It dries a man's mind without a little wine to help moisten the thinking.'

'It is clear we are travelling south, warrant sky officer,' said Coss Shaftcrank. 'Every sailor on this ship can read that from the sun and the stars.'

'Master cardsharp, if you please, old steamer,' said Oldcastle. 'A title you would normally hear when saluting the supply clerks of Admiralty House, I admit, but it is mine for this voyage.'

'And the newssheets have been full of talk of war, master cardsharp,' said Jack. 'With Cassarabia to the *south*. Now that they can build ships like ours.'

'Oh, they have always been capable of building ships like these, lad,' said Oldcastle. 'Floating them with a gas that doesn't explode like a grenade when you strike a spark in the lifting chamber has been a trick that's proved a little harder for the empire to master, but one they seem to have got hold of now.'

'Will it be war, sir?' asked Jack.

'Always, lad. There's two cocks-of-the-lane swaggering down the street, and only enough space on the cobbles for one of them. And the caliph has to build a great new temple every century or so, with Cassarabian tradition demanding it be paid for by tribute taken from heathens and new conquests, not by his own people. Booty for his army and supporters, to keep them all on-side and well greased. Yes, there'll be war alright, now that the Cassarabians have airships to take on the Royal Aerostatical Navy. The only question is when. And whatever the answer to that, you'd better hope that we're not on board the ship when it breaks out. Not that you'll hear such a view coming from Admiralty House. They think that because the RAN's been sailing in the clouds for centuries, our tactics and experience will see the Cassarabians off like cheap whipped hounds if they dare to drift across our border with mischief in mind.'

'You don't think we will?'

'I've never been privy to an easy victory, Mister Keats,' said the old officer. 'No, indeed, I don't think I know what one of those even looks like.'

Now Jack could see why the crew seemed so restless on board the airship, pressed men and the scrapings of the barrel, sailing on an unpopular scrapyard vessel towards trouble. Whatever their mission was, it was obvious that Admiralty House hadn't wanted any part of it. And that meant politics. Army interference, or parliamentarians in the House of Guardians ramming it down the reluctant throats of the braided naval uniforms who thought they knew best.

The three of them were meant to ensure that the chamber of thinking machines didn't interfere with the running of the ship. *But who is going to ensure that I return alive to keep Alan and Saul safe?*

Omar yelled as the great winged lizard, the drak that Farris Uddin had named as Quarn, banked and began to descend towards Bladetenbul. Never in all his years as a slave had Omar expected he would see Cassarabia's capital city – and if someone had told him a week ago that his introduction to its immense spill of streets, souks and towers would be from a saddle at a hundred feet, he would have joked that the speaker had been exposed to the heat of the sun for too long.

The light of Bladetenbul is the light of the world, ran the old saying, and from this high up Omar could see why. There was a great fortified wall running around the outside of the seven hills the city sprawled across, and behind the fortifications stood the capital's sun towers, each fluted construction filled with boilers and capturing the reflected light of the thousands of great mirror arrays that circled Bladetenbul. Water into steam, steam to drive the city's machines, and the steam caught again and fed back into the system of reservoirs and pipes – far too precious a resource to waste on the sky under god, as the heathen northern nations were said to.

Light from the mirrors seemed to reflect off the drak's green-scaled skin, dazzling Omar where he sat behind Farris Uddin, strapped above the base of the creature's long sinuous neck. The rushing of the wind and the drumming of the drak's wings made it hard to communicate with Farris Uddin – not that the taciturn killer had much to say to Omar. He really was an imperial guardsman, that much was certain. Sand dogs and bounty hunters did not ride such creatures as this, that Omar knew. As much effort as the womb mages of Omar's old house had put into the breeding and nurture of salt-fish, it was child's play compared to the skill and resources needed to create and raise something as large and complex as a drak.

They whisked lower over the city, low enough for Omar to see the bazaars crowded with canopy-covered stalls selling silks and spiced rice, iced-water sellers weighed down with gas-cooled tanks on their backs, importuning the clients coming out of the great domed bathhouses. The drak followed the line of the stone pipe network that fed the capital with its precious water supplies, flying so near to the ground that Omar winced as they banked around minarets, the breeze from their passage ruffling the robes of the watermen at the major tap-points, officials inspecting the lines of those waiting for any sign of unpaid water taxes.

On the drak hurtled, riding the thermals from the white-washed city below and hardly beating a wing now, gliding up towards the tallest of the hills where the Jahan Palace waited. Not for nothing was this called the *Jahan* – simply, *the world*. A tower-tall crystal dome on the brow of the hill, ruby coloured and surrounded by smaller emerald green domes. World enough for the Caliph Eternal and his court. Sultans and emirs came here to renew their vows and the pledges of their nations to the mighty emperor of emperors, Akil Jaber Issman, blood descendent of the legendary Ben Issman himself, his name be blessed. What chance would the barely freed slave of an outlawed heretic house have when swimming in such perilous currents?

Farris Uddin's massive drak glided towards a series of fortifications sitting watchfully behind the massive central dome of the palace. Embedded on top of a rocky rise, it was the eyrie of the guardsmen that protected the caliph and his realm. Tilting back, the drak used its wings to break, two massive clawed feet touching down on the rock floor of a cave-like opening, then swinging forward to walk them into a hangar where jagged walls were hung with rows of colourful shields. A stableman emerged from a door in the wall and ran a cable through the drak's harness, before receiving Farris Uddin's instructions on the creature's care. As the young stable hand led the drak away, Farris turned to Omar. 'That is Boulous, my retainer. He is a slave, and though his blood is originally of Jackelian stock, his heart has been raised to be as stout as any guardsman that serves the order. I chose him for his keen mind. Let his caution, wisdom and loyalty become yours.'

'I shall be at least twice as loyal as he; you have my word under the sight of god and Ben Issman, his name be blessed. Are they in the palace below, master? The priests of the new sect that had my house declared heretic?' asked Omar.

'Indeed they are,' said Farris Uddin, splashing cooling water on his shaved head from a wall-mounted basin.

'Do not sell me to them, master. I shall work harder for you than a dozen—'

Farris Uddin raised his hand for Omar to stop and pulled out the young slave boy's roll of indenture papers. He pointed to the sigils sitting in the bottom corner. 'Can you read that?'

'It is the code stamp of a transaction engine, master.'

'I know what it is. I asked can you read it?'

Omar traced his fingers across the embossed code of vertical bar shapes. 'It is the date I became a freeman.' Omar ran his fingers across the code again, confused. 'But—'

'Always read the small print, Omar Barir,' instructed the guardsman. 'Your papers as a freeman were drawn up by your father two months ago. Long enough for you to have travelled over the desert with a water caravan and made your way to civilized company on your own. Before, mark you,' he raised a warning finger, 'before the House of Barir was declared heretic.'

'I do not understand, master?'

'A slave cannot serve as the cadet of an imperial guardsman,' said Farris Uddin. 'But a freeman can. And in the service of the Caliph Eternal you become Centless. Those in military or civil service are not permitted to follow any one sect. Your oath is directly to the lawful descendents of Ben Issman, unifier of the one true god, and the empire, his name be blessed. No other loyalties are permitted. Not nation, not tribe nor house or sect.'

'But why am I to be your cadet?' Omar blurted out. *Why did you venture all the way out to the western coast to spare me from a heretic's fate?*

'Because my last one fell off a drak,' said Farris Uddin. 'And because it will annoy the keepers of the new sect endlessly to see the last blood of the House of Barir walking the palace wearing guardsman's robes. And for many other reasons too, but they are not yours to know.'

'What call did my father have on you?' said Omar. 'He sent for you, did he not? That is why you came to Haffa.'

'Call enough,' growled the guardsman. 'Now hold your tongue and save your questions, boy. A cadet calls his guardsman master as well as a slave does.'

'Yes, master.'

'Down there,' Farris Uddin pointed out of the hangar towards the palace, 'under those great domes rules the most powerful man in the world. Sultans from Zahyan, Seyadi, Fahamutla and a dozen other kingdoms come to beg favours, offer tribute and remind the Caliph Eternal what good, loyal clients their countries make for the empire. The high keepers of the hundred sects of the Holy Cent jostle each other aside to shower the emperor of emperors with his share of temple tithes. Womb mages vie for favour and peddle promises of miracle cures and prodigiously lethal new creatures. Viziers plot their way to higher council, while generals and admirals struggle to obtain new commissions and appointments. Courtiers and courtesans are as the grass you will walk on, the sighs of their greed, envies, hopes and ambitions are the breeze you will feel on your cheeks. Down there is opulence without equal in the world, but it is not a safe place. You will quickly come to yearn for a world of simple fishermen and uncomplicated water farming.'

Omar nodded. The waves from that world down below had already lapped out and destroyed his own familiar existence, setting him adrift. There was an irony that of all the places in the empire, the tides of fate should have carried Omar here.

You have a cruel sense of humour, my lady fate. You cut

away my chains and then you steal my world. And here you are now, pushing a sword into my hands. Whatever weapons this killer gives me I shall master, and when I am as great a guardsman as I was a slave, I shall find the people who killed my father and burnt my home to the ground. And one day I will find and free Shadisa, this I swear.

CHAPTER SIX

'Help me,' begged the six-year-old stuck down the claustrophobically tight shaft. 'I can't breathe down here, I'm choking, please—'

But Jack couldn't help. He was running for his life through the vaults of Lords Bank, hissing waves of poison gas swirling at his heels, the shouts and shots of the bank guards and the constabulary whistling around him. Maggie was waiting for Jack at the breached wall, trying to stop him ducking back out into the sewers.

'Go back for them, you can't just leave the boys in there.'

'It's little Tozer,' said Jack, 'he's stuck – we'll all die if we try to pull him out.'

'It's not just Tozer,' shouted Maggie, 'he's in there with your brothers, Jack. Your brothers are thieves now, just like you.'

'No!' screamed Jack, but the bank's wall had collapsed behind him. He scrabbled at the fallen masonry with his nails, digging until his fingers were broken and bleeding.

Boyd was laughing in Jack's ear, shaking him by the shoulders until he felt as if he were rocking on the deck of a ship. 'Leave them to die. Leave all the runts to die.'

Jack gasped as he woke, his cheeks wet with tears. For the boy he couldn't save, or for the two brothers he had abandoned to their fate?

'Damn me for a coward,' whispered Jack to himself, rubbing his eyes as the makeshift bed swung gently. *For that is what I am.* Try as he might, Jack couldn't get used to sleeping in a hammock, the sling of fabric between the boilers permitting its occupant no shifting or rolling from side to side. It was an all-enveloping swaddle that moved of its own accord with the trims and turns of the airship.

As if this alien way of sleeping wasn't enough, there was the noise of the ship: the *Iron Partridge*'s croaking beams, the crackling from behind the closed furnace doors, the rattle and clack of the spinning transaction-engine drums – a constant low rumble even on their reduced-power setting. And now the *Iron Partridge* was sailing through a storm, the rain drumming on the sealed skylight above, the armoured glass failing to soften the whistle of the wind through the forest of mortar tubes running along the spine of her hull.

Groaning at the snores from the two Benzari stokers, Jack swung his legs off the hammock and touched his feet down on the deck, the surface every bit as warm as John Oldcastle had promised in the space between the boilers. But of Oldcastle himself, there was no sign. His hammock lay empty. Over in the transaction-engine pit, Jack could just see the metal skull of Coss Shaftcrank moving through the maze of thinking machines, checking the steam pressure of the dials as he reached up with an oil can to apply lubricant to a bank of rotating drums. Jack walked over to the rail.

'Where's Oldcastle?' Jack asked, low enough not to wake up the pair of stokers.

'I believe there is a game of chance being played down in the surgeon's ward,' said Coss. 'Although the master cardsharp was rather insistent that there would be a degree of skill in its playing, which he believes he possesses in abundance.'

'My father thought much the same,' said Jack. 'That and a couple of poor harvests was enough to lose our family everything we owned.'

'The injection of unnecessary risk into a life is one trait of your people I have never understood, Jack softbody. By my rolling regulators, the great pattern of existence always seems capable of providing us ample dangers without going to the trouble of actively seeking them out.'

Jack leant across the pit's rail and looked up at the rain lashing against the skylight. 'What are you doing here, Coss?'

'I require less sleep than you softbodies,' said the steamman. 'I can function reliably on a fifth of the rest you need. The extra shifts I can complete were one of the reasons, I suspect, why the master cardsharp was so eager to procure my services.'

'No,' said Jack. 'I mean what are you doing *here*, on the *Iron Partridge*? I've seen graspers and craynarbians on the ship, but you're the only steamman on board. I had no choice. For me, it was this or the rope outside Bonegate jail. But I saw you back in the signing queue . . . you were desperate to sign up.'

'It is my destiny, my softbody friend,' said Coss. 'Do you know much about my people and how we are born? Have you ever visited the Steamman Free State?'

'No,' Jack admitted. 'And there weren't any steammen in the debtors' prison or living rough on the streets.'

'Kiss my condensers, but there would not be,' said Coss. 'Our kind cares for each other too well to permit the crime of poverty to be inflicted on our people. Normally, when a steamman is born in the Free State, it is the will of King Steam and the skill of the king's architects that give him life.

A steamman starts life in a nursery body which has been inhabited many times before, and after his education is complete, his intellect is then transferred into his final adult body.'

'You said *normally.*'

'There is another way a steamman can be born,' said Coss. 'Much rarer. The more advanced members of our race can simultaneously distribute their intellect across multiple bodies, their own main body and those of their drones as well. The drones are called Mu-bodies, and are treated as tools, or perhaps as you softbodies might treat a favourite suit of clothes.'

'I've seen them,' said Jack, remembering the time he and Maggie had been picking pockets outside the steammen embassy; a large tracked steamman with a crystal dome-topped head moving past with a retinue of gnome-sized metallic servants surrounding him.

'Mu-bodies sometimes develop sentience,' said Coss. 'Occasionally spontaneously, more often than not as a result of being possessed by one of our ancestral spirits, the Steamo Loas. This is the other way of birth for the life metal. When such an event happens, the intellect is moved out of the drone, into a nursery body, and finally into an adult body when our years of education are complete. But our people feel a degree of disquiet towards those not born from the familiar, comforting designs of King Steam's architects. I, press my unlucky plug rods, had such a birth. The population at large does not trust us, and we are regarded as the mischief of the gods, touched by madness. We are known as *mutables,* a term of little affection among steammen.'

Jack nodded. Maybe the steamman's origins as a drone explained his unusually small size, a stature that was some-what accentuated by a swollen back from which two stubby stacks emerged. Coss was barely five foot tall. He had a flat-plate of a face with a vision plate above a noseless grille, the visor mounted like a mask on a sphere of copper connected by one large neck joint and a smaller piston whose sole purpose seemed to be to raise and lower the mask. His torso was similarly connected to his pelvis by three pistons, three legs emerging from the pelvis unit, two large and one small and spindly, almost a prehensile tail.

'My existence as a drone seems a blurred dream, now. But I remember one thing, the same dream, repeatedly: sitting in a garden in the shade of a tower, watching birds. Always, the birds. Marvelling at how well they flew, tracing the patterns of their flight. Modelling their miraculous ability with mathematics. That was my initial awakening of sentience. It is where my name comes from – the Rule of Coss, pure algebra.'

So that's it. The navy might not have had to send a press gang out for this steamman, but he was as much an outcast as Jack had been the day he'd been scraped from a prison cell and thrown into the care of the navy.

The steamman tapped his skull. 'There's something about the master cardsharp you should know, Jack softbody.'

Jack looked inquisitively at Coss.

'I have seen him in the dream from my previous life. I know his face.'

'You know Oldcastle from when you were a drone?'

'I think so,' said Coss. 'But his face and his name doesn't feel right. I don't think that John Oldcastle is his real name.'

Jack stared at the warrant sky officer's vacant hammock. John Oldcastle seemed sure enough of his name, and the Royal Aerostatical Navy had a place for him on the *Iron Partridge*. If John Oldcastle wasn't John Oldcastle, then who in the name of the Circle was he?

'Are you sure about this, old steamer?'

'It is possible it may be a false memory. Curse my vacuum

91

pumps, there is not much that I am certain of from my existence as a drone, before my true life began.'

'What's the name you think of when you see the master cardsharp?' asked Jack.

'Jared Black is the name,' said Coss. 'I can see his face talking to the steamman I served when I was but a drone. His name is Coppertracks, and he is a great philosopher and scientist of the people of the metal who lives in the Kingdom. Jared Black has the same silver beard, much the same voice, but the master cardsharp was not dressed as an airship officer. I see another uniform. A civilian one, if that makes sense?'

'Civilians don't wear uniforms – unless he served with the RAN merchant marine before Admiralty House dumped him onto a warship,' said Jack. 'They've been short of skymen for years. You and I wouldn't be here if that weren't the case.'

Jack remembered his suspicions about the first lieutenant. Nothing about the deadly woman and the ageing soldier who reluctantly followed her rang true. What business could the officer have had with Coss's ex-master? Whoever the master cardsharp was, whomever he answered to, one thing was true; Jack and Coss were stuck firmly under his command.

'We steammen are usually a grounded people, in all senses of the word,' added Coss. 'All I know from my earliest years was that I had to fly. It was all I dreamed of in my nursery body, and the moment I was granted my adult form, I came to the Kingdom of Jackals and learnt everything I could about the Royal Aerostatical Navy; its traditions, its sailors and ships, its rules and regulations.'

Jack grunted, a smile flickering across his lips.

'Tear my transfer pipes, but I am used to being laughed at,' said the young steamman, his voicebox pitched with a sad vibration. 'My friends back in the Free State say I must have been possessed by Lemba of the Empty Thrusters, the spirit of the sky. They say that he is the Loa that possessed my miserable drone body and blessed me with sentience.'

'I wasn't laughing at your story,' said Jack. 'It's just that if you had left school a couple of years later and hadn't got into the RAN, you might have signed up with the Cassarabian navy!'

'Most amusing. I much prefer an allied multiracial society such as that of the Kingdom,' said Coss, pointing to the iron clock above the entrance to their chamber. 'The master cardsharp asked to be interrupted from his game before six-bells sounds. He also left a parcel that he wants you to deliver below decks, although I suspect he intended its delivery to be made during daylight hours.'

Jack retrieved the heavy waxpaper-wrapped parcel from the stool in front of his punch-card writing station. There was a scribbled note slipped below the string sealing the parcel, its instructions read: 'For the cabin at the end of the middle deck's main passage.'

'I'll fetch the master cardsharp,' said Jack. 'And see if I can drop this off too.' *Better that than listening to those two Benzari stokers snoring away. Perhaps the long climb down the lifting chamber ladder will bring some peace to my nerves.* Coss might have dreamed of sailing thousands of feet across the world like one of his birds, but Jack was just happy to have avoided the six-foot drop that was to have been his courtesy of the hangman back home.

After clambering down the ladder, Jack considered the route, his new recruit's training spinning around his mind. The easiest way to the surgeon's ward in the middle of the airship was to head down the upper lifting chamber's main gantry, then into the gun deck, another climb through the lower lifting chamber, before threading through the corridors of the middle deck.

Jack walked down the central catwalk that cut through the twelve-hundred foot length of the upper lifting chamber, the thin strip of metal bouncing underfoot, its handrail preventing him from slipping into the thousands of ballonets and their network of bracing wires. He was halfway down the gangway when he almost stumbled into the officer, a tattered well-worn cloak half-hidden by the shadow of one of the airship's regassing towers. Jack caught a breath as he recognized the face of the man from the courtroom. Close up, his skin was pockmarked with smallpox scars, but there were the same intense eyes, the same mop of ginger hair. Yes, this was the RAN officer who had so annoyed the judge in the middle-court by saving Jack from dancing the Bonegate jig.

'Mister Keats,' said the half-familiar man.

'Sir.' Jack still felt awkward saluting, every raise of his hand an acknowledgment he was now reluctantly part of something larger than just his own life and survival, with very little choice in the matter.

The officer's cloak was pulled tight like a poncho, so Jack couldn't get a clear look at the man's uniform. Was he one of their ship's seven lieutenants?

'You are up early I see,' said the man.

'The storm was rattling our skylight, sir.'

'Ah yes, all bedded down in the transaction-engine chamber. Never draw a berth on the keel deck or the upper deck, Mister Keats.' He pointed to one of the aluminium spokes radiating out like a wheel, giving the vast upper lifting chamber its strength. 'The noise is passed to the decks at the top and bottom of a vessel through the supports. And we're worse than most airships, the plates on our hull rattling around as if we're some damn armoured knight riding off to battle.' The officer walked briskly along, his swagger stick striking each of the gantry railings. 'A strange bird, this metal partridge of ours, eh, m'boy? A cloud-borne ironclad – don't seem natural. Everything different for difference's sake alone.' The officer pointed at the thousands of spherical gas cells corded together under the lifting chamber's netting. 'Even our celgas is bagged up inside some strange composite rather than plain honest canvas. The genius that cooked this vessel up was off with the fairies when they laid their pencils on the draughting board, alright. I understand that some call that progress.' He spotted the package under Jack's arm. 'Ah, I believe that would be the parcel the commodore promised me.'

'The commodore?' said Jack, confused. 'Don't you mean the master cardsharp, sir?'

'Indeed, indeed. That's just a nickname some of the officers have for him – his manner, d'you see? Although I wouldn't advise using it around the fellow, he wouldn't thank you for it.'

Jack held the package out. 'You have the cabin at the end of middle deck, then, I presume? Do you serve under First Lieutenant Westwick, sir?'

'I think it would be fair to say that ultimately, we both owe our positions on the ship to her, Mister Keats.' The officer took the parcel and removed the string and the waxpaper, revealing a pile of books with a receipt from the stationer's stall where they had been purchased. 'Capital. Just the stuff for a cold evening's reading.'

The tomes in the officer's hand weren't the cheap penny-dreadfuls and lurid fiction that Jack favoured, but rather dry, leather-bound books of military strategy with titles such as *Aerostatical Theory: Classical Practices, Principles and Historical Perspectives*.

'Our civil war, that's the only time we've seen airships raking each other in the clouds. It seems we have to look back to history for a fresh perspective on how to take on the

Cassarabians. All our tactics, all our weapons, are predicated on placing us in the sky and the enemy firmly on the ground. With the exception of warding off the odd mutineer or the occasional science pirate who has managed to cook up some mad scheme to get into the air, our sailors' experience is completely sky-to-ground. Dangerous thinking for these modern times we find ourselves in. Keep up, m'boy,' he said, half a command, half a booming laugh. 'Twelve times around the ship is four miles. That's what a sailor requires every day to keep his mind fresh and clear, d'you see?'

It was the laugh that did it. Deep and boisterous, resounding through the upper lifting chamber just as it had at the – *debtors' prison*! That's where he knew this man from. He had been one of the patients in the fever room of the debtors' prison. Jack's father had led the collection to try to buy medicines and food when the sickness had struck the Five Stones district of Middlesteel where the debtors' prison squatted down by the river. Another of his father's foolish, over-generous impulses in the prison to help everyone except those who really should have mattered to him. The last time Jack had seen this face was when he'd been doling out carrot broth to the inmates who had been separated off into quarantine. Then it had been blotchy and sweating under a coarse charity blanket, but capable of booming out a note of thanks even so. So, the ill man had been a navy officer? Well, they were as likely to be declared bankrupt as anyone else. Someone must have taken care of the officer's debts for him, though, for him to be able to re-enter service with the navy. Jack's recollection was shattered by a savage whistling from a stove pipe-like tube hanging above the gantry, the noise rising and falling like the scream of a banshee.

Jack covered his ears. 'Are we crashing into Jackals?'

'We haven't been travelling the Kingdom's skies for days,'

said the man. 'We're sailing over Benzari territory, and that, Mister Keats, is the general-quarters being sounded. Propellers ho! m'boy. The enemy's been sighted.'

'Are we at war, sir?'

'Benzaral is disputed territory, Mister Keats. The caliph thinks it is his, but we have a couple of hundred marines on board that will swear it is independent and belongs to the free Benzari tribes. And they are our nation's allies. The perfect place for us to do a little fishing.'

'What are we hoping to catch?'

The stocky man reached out and slapped Jack's shoulder. 'An airship, Mister Keats. A nice fat Cassarabian airship, d'you see?'

Men from the night watch were swinging down onto the gantry, stowing their gas-bag patching tools in secure boxes and pulling the lifting chamber netting taut for action.

'You know what to do, gentlemen,' the ginger-haired officer called to them. 'Back to your post, Mister Keats. Keep your transaction engines well and quiet; we don't need the ship pulling at the reins of her own accord for the next couple of hours. Smooth and certain as you go.'

Jack saluted again as the man he had once served soup to inside a debtors' prison sprinted down the gantry, his left hand steadying his officer's cutlass.

'Out of our hair, greenhorn.' One of the lifting chamber crew pushed Jack back towards the ladder. 'You heard the captain. Sharp to it.'

Jack gawped. 'Captain!'

'The honourable Donald Lawrence Jericho himself, lad. Now return to your post before I dirty the sole of my boot on the arse of your fine regulation breeches.'

Jack had barely cleared the climb back to the upper deck when the airship started trembling. Not the crack of a storm, but a different sort of thunder. The *Iron Partridge*'s guns were speaking, and then the airship shook as the enemy's reply sounded in kind.

By the time Jack had stumbled back to his station, the trans-action-engine room was a scene of organized chaos, the two Benzari stokers grunting as they shovelled coal into the furnace, John Oldcastle, chased back by the screech of the general-quarters, helping Coss down in the pit of noisy thinking machines.

'Where have you been, lad?' called Oldcastle over a booming sound echoing off the ship's plates outside. Was that the sound of an enemy shell bouncing off their armour? 'We need you on the punch-card writer up there.'

'I was with the captain, master cardsharp.'

'On one of his early morning walks, lad, to help keep the black dog at bay? A great one for walks, is old Jericho. Well, he'll have his blessed exercise now, running around the Cassarabians!'

Jack sprinted to the nearest punch-card writer, keeping his footing as the deck trembled with the roar of the *Iron Partridge*'s massive thirty-two pounders.

'I have an automated system activating,' shouted Coss, his voicebox on maximum amplification as he read the symbols off one of the engine's rotating calculation drums. 'Kiss my condensers, it's the gas compression on the ballonets. Lower lifting chamber.'

Oldcastle pointed up at Jack. 'Shut it down. If the lifting room crew apply extra pressure to a gas cell that's already been compressed, it'll explode like a wicked volcano under our feet.'

Taking a blank punch card from the tray, Jack bashed out an instruction set to kill the airship's automated system, pushing it into the injection tube and watching as it was sucked out of his fingers.

'It's back under manual control now,' shouted Jack. 'How long is our engagement against the Cassarabian airship going to last?'

'Damned if I know, lad,' said Oldcastle, pointing towards the porthole above the punch-card desk. 'And it's airship*s*. There are two of the blessed things flying out there hammering away at us.'

Jack stood up on his toes to stare out of the porthole. He could see an enemy airship banking to broadside, just a silhouette against the dark backdrop of dawn's first gleaming, spouts of angry orange light and smoke coming from the line of her gun deck as she exchanged fire with the *Iron Partridge*. Where was the other airship? Ah, there she was, a second shadow rising, the stern crossing the upper corner of Jack's porthole.

'One of the enemy ships is trying to climb above us,' said Jack.

'Wicked clever of them,' said Oldcastle. 'Our guns can depress elevation with the best of them, but they don't lift up so well. The RAN fleet was designed to trade blows with regiments on the ground. But the Cassarabians? Their shipyards knew that they wouldn't have the skies to themselves. They'll have built airship hunters, that they will, and we're to be their prey.'

A whistling from the chamber's speaking trumpet called Oldcastle out of the engine pit and he barked a brief exchange of words with the voice at the other end before turning to Jack. 'The Cassarabians don't seem to know what the pipes on our spine are for, Mister Keats, not having seen their like before. We're looking to give them a little flutter of the feathers on our back, but the mortar loading station has locked our boys out.'

Jack grabbed another blank punch card, leafing through the leather-bound instruction manual chained next to his punch-card writer. There were notes in pencil annotated alongside the armoury instruction sets, from a time when the transaction-engine chamber had possessed a full crew of navy enginemen who had hopefully known what they were doing better than the young novice currently manning their station. Jack winced when he noticed the date scribbled next to the notes. Their mortar tubes hadn't been fired in over three years. It appeared as if the mothballed mortars had never been intended to be used again, hampered by a fully automated loading system with minimal manual oversight from the gunnery board down on the bridge. No wonder the airship was trying to shut out the crew from accessing her mortars; sailors had never been meant to manually load its shells. *This is not going to be easy.* Jack's fingers danced nervously across the enamelled keys, each stroke of a symbolic logic icon punching a corresponding hole in the taut cardboard oblong.

'Master cardsharp!' shouted Coss. The steamman was pointing to the skylight. The dark shadow of the second Cassarabian airship was now illuminated by a spill of light from its fully open bomb bays. Was the *Iron Partridge* about to be rained on by explosives? No. Jack swore quietly to himself; cables were falling, human shadows riding the rappel lines down.

John Oldcastle ran to the wall and began to pull on a winch, the iron storm doors shutting across the skylight. 'Prepare to repel borders!' he yelled at the two stokers. 'Mister Keats, today for the mortars would be mighty grand. Mister Shaftcrank, keep to your post. Read our systems off as they attempt to go live.'

Jack finished the punch card, pushing it into the injection mechanism, and the transaction engines began to rumble below, processing his new instructions. Oldcastle and the Benzari warriors were rifling through the air chests under their hammocks, the stokers pulling out sharp curved short-swords and the master cardsharp emerging with a bandoleer of crystal ammunition, three pistols and a short-barrelled carbine. He laid the weapons across the unmanned punch-card station next to Jack and began to break the guns, pushing a shell into each weapon's breech, liquid explosives visibly sloshing about inside the shells' transparent casing. 'Turnaround is fair play, lad. We thought we were going fishing for a Cassarabian ship to find out what makes her tick, but instead it's us that's ended up wriggling on the end of their line.'

Jack hardly heard the old officer. His eyes darted to the abacus-like Rutledge Rotator above the punch-card writer, hundreds of beaded tiles turning and twisting to form line after line of results from his query. His last command had been accepted and processed but— 'We're still locked out!'

It couldn't be. Jack's instructions had been perfect, everything the manual said was needed to crack open the loading station for the ship's waiting gunners; yet here they were, their mortars sealed deadly tight and still inaccessible to the sailors below.

There was a clanging from above the chamber's skylight, iron doors being levered apart an inch or two. Enemy marines were clambering above their room!

'A second attempt if you please, Mister Keats,' ordered Oldcastle. 'Cover the doors' – that to the two stokers – 'they're not breaking in from above. That's storm glass up there, good for gale, bullet or shell. But there are maintenance hatches aft of here that were never meant to be secured against our own boys repairing the hull. That's where they'll pile through. Ah, I'll have a few blessed choice words with our shipwrights when we return back home.'

Jack fought down panic, trying to focus on the keys of his writer and block out the sound of Cassarabian marines scrabbling above them, swarming over the hull like ants. Coss had stopped distracting him by calling out the names of the systems that were interfering with the sailors' tasks throughout the vessel. If Jack couldn't allow their gunners access to the mortar loading station below, then an inconveniently sealed fire hatch here or there wasn't going to make a whole lot of difference to the *Iron Partridge*'s survival.

'Keep your eyes on your task,' ordered Oldcastle. 'Concentrate, now. I've got a warm welcome here for our wicked visitors.'

Jack was still trying to focus on his half-completed punch card when the first Cassarabian marines burst into the room with flashes of scimitar steel and pistol barrels. Their mouths were concealed by rubber breathing masks that made them look like beaked eagles, their black and silver uniforms covered by leather armour stained red with dyes – or the blood of the *Iron Partridge*'s unlucky sailors the invaders had already come across.

'No man may mount a drak as a bonded rider,' called out Farris Uddin, 'unless they are able to kill as well as their drak.'

Omar blinked away the sweat rolling into his eyes. He held out his sword horizontally with his right hand as the shaven-headed guardsman officer walked down the line of struggling cadets. How much longer could he carry the weight of his blade like this, the steel heavier with every second? How much longer could he stand in the courtyard of the palace fortress' middle bailey, exposed to the sun in full riding leathers?

'And a drak,' continued Farris Uddin, 'is bred for nothing else but fighting and killing, which is—' he stared down the line, '—more than I can say for you. It doesn't take much to train as a cadet. I see the sons of generals and rich traders, I see the sons of guild heads and viziers, but I don't see any here fit to mount a drak.' The guardsman officer halted before Omar. 'Is your sword heavy, Cadet Barir?'

No, you old goat. In my hands it is as light as a feather. And one day I'm going to use it to carve apart the people who burnt down Haffa and laid their fat, evil hands on Shadisa. 'Yes, master.'

'Yes, master,' parroted the guardsman. 'It will be a lot heavier when you have been pulling the reins for a day and are given the order to dive down on the enemy.'

'I will dive like a falcon upon your order, master. A falcon with keen eyes and a willing heart.'

'A falcon, well,' sneered Uddin. 'You believe, perhaps, that your training flights qualify you as a veteran? Let the weight of that scimitar sap away your irremediable optimism, boy. If your training draks could talk, the stables would be echoing with their laughter. A falcon must have talons, and most of you have, I fear, proved yourselves to be little more than songbirds kept too long in your perfumed cages. And back to your silk-lined cages you will go when you fail me.'

The guardsman stopped as a covered sedan chair emerged from a round tower in the curtain wall. 'Ah,' said Uddin. 'It is that time. Our songbirds must line up along their perch. *Command.* Sheath your blades.'

Omar didn't know what perch the guardsman was referring to, but he let his aching arm fall down like a rock, glad that the stocky man was not going to make them all move through the twenty-five basic patterns of scimitar thrusts and parries again. They had tasted months of this repetitive grind, and at times Omar felt as if he were training to be one of the dancing monkeys that capered for coins down in the bazaars.

Life back on the water farm had not been nearly so regimented. Here, Omar was up early, to bed early, every minute spent being instructed how to act. How to hold, oil and sharpen a scimitar. How to check a crystal shell's casing for cracks that could cause its liquid explosive charge to leak and shatter a rifle barrel in its owner's face. How to saddle and care for a drak, or strip and clean a pistol; how to communicate silently in the air and on the ground using the hand and finger gestures of the language the caliph's military called 'war sign'. There was never enough time, it seemed, to adequately study all the skills a guardsman was expected to master in the service of the empire. He didn't care. *Every day I get stronger, every day I get quicker with the blade, every day my aim with pistol and rifle grows truer. Each day that passes is a day nearer the time when I will have the skills to track down Shadisa and punish anyone who has dared to hurt her.* He was aching for the chance to go down in the capital and begin searching the slave bazaars for her. Someone down there would remember her, surely. Remember the house that purchased such a beauty and the price she must have fetched.

Well, at least weapons drill made a change from flying practice on the draks. Even as Omar discovered he had something of an aptitude for the task, the actual act of mounting a drak and taking to the air frequently left him dizzy. Belonging to no single rider, the training draks were used to having novice cadets saddle them, and could beat a path into the air, sail around and land back at the fortress with minimal suggestions from a guardsman's stirrups or reins. Sometimes Omar felt like he was just supplying guidance to the mighty flying creatures. But by the silver gates of heaven, their training draks knew how to leave saddle stiffness in a cadet's limbs; the day after his first flight, Omar hadn't even been able to bend down to fold the sheets of his cell's bunk.

Working the water farm's desalination lines had been easy graft in comparison, once you got the knack of moving in rhythm with the salt-fish; always plenty of time left over to rest and contemplate the slow-moving clouds above or the beauty of kitchen girls below. In Omar's old existence, the rituals of his life had been small, insignificant things. Here in the palace fortress all of life seemed a ceremony, the corridors and rooms of the stronghold perching on the rocky peaks as much a monastic prison as a protecting fastness. Omar hadn't even left the confines of the fortress to see the palace below, let alone gaze upon the legendary marvels of the capital's streets on foot. He was free in name, but not in practice.

Green silk curtains along the side of the sedan chair were drawn back by four bearers who had carried it into the courtyard, to reveal an old white-haired man wearing a golden tunic, the dark silhouette of a drak on his chest. Boulous, Uddin's retainer, slipped forward out of the shade of the fortress. Uddin frequently disappeared for long periods of time on guardsmen business, and during such absences the retainer was expected to maintain the demanding schedule of training. Unfortunately for Omar, the young man had a serious manner and a thoroughly studious attitude to how a cadet's timetable should be maintained. Perhaps that came from his northern blood. *Weren't they all said to toil away in dark mills, worshipping money more than god, busying themselves with unnatural practices?* Many of the other cadets had retainers too, the sons of the greatest families and houses in the empire. But in their case, the retainer's duty was to run after the cadets, fetching and carrying and generally kowtowing. Boulous did disappointedly little of this for the heroic future guardsman that Omar was destined to become.

Boulous whispered to Omar, 'That is the grand marshal of the order. We go onto our knees.'

A relative latecomer to the cadet's ranks, Omar saw that all the other cadets along the courtyard were already dropping down on one knee, and Omar followed suit with undignified haste, not wishing to be singled out again for the attention of Uddin or the other tutors. Two of the guardsmen in the courtyard helped the grand marshal out of his sedan chair and up the steps towards the battlements. He was very old, Omar realized. The grand marshal wouldn't have made it as far as the iron finger pillory at the bottom of the wall without assistance. Omar counted his blessings that he hadn't caused any infractions of the order's many rules that would have left him confined in the pillory today, his fingers inserted in the slots of the punishment frame and kneeling like a fool with the undignified sight of his arse presented to the order's master of masters.

After the old man had gained the parapet, the cadets in the bailey were lined up; then the front of the line began to march up the stairs, and Omar saw that guardsmen and the order's staff were marching out onto towers and gatehouse all across the fortress in a courtly fashion.

'Are we to hear a speech?' Omar whispered to Boulous.

'No, no,' said Boulous. 'Today is a holy day, the Dream of the Silver Tree.'

Omar started. *Is it that time of year already?* Inside the guardsmen's fortress, time seemed lost and scattered like motes of dust floating in the sunlight. Omar wistfully recalled the festival back in Haffa, happy cooks and Shadisa bringing out white cheese and fruit to the workers on the desalination lines. Even the grumpy old nomad, Alim, had taken that day off to play draughts with him in the shade of the tanks. *Where are you now, Shadisa? Not enjoying a feast, of that I am sure.* Well, Ben Issman, his name be blessed, might have dreamed of the hundred faces of the one true god under his tree thousands of years ago, but Omar hadn't yet noticed any white cheese, fruit or iced water being distributed, let alone lazy hours playing draughts in celebration inside the corridors of the fortress.

The cadets filed out onto the battlements, a panoramic view of the Jahan Palace sparkling in the afternoon sunlight below them while the white roofs of the city stretched out for miles, encircled by the dazzle of sun towers. A distant rumble of fireworks drifted up towards the fortress, strings of explosives hung between the palm trees, detonating and shaking the streets; sheets of dust filling the spaces between the domes and towers.

'Oh, this is bad,' said Boulous.

It appeared to Omar that the retainer also possessed a naturally pessimistic bent – especially given that his status as a *jahani*, a slave raised from childhood to imperial service, meant he had about as much responsibility to concern him as the birds that made their nests in the cliffs below the fortress walls.

'What is the trouble now?' asked Omar.

'This is the first year that the order has not been required to fly in formation over the city. Instead we can only stand and watch.'

'Watch what?'

Boulous unsheathed the scimitar and passed it hilt-first to Omar as the command to present swords in a salute echoed down the battlements.

'That . . .'

By the prophets!

Omar stared down the length of killing metal he had raised above the fortress parapet, catching sight of the first of hundreds of cigar-shaped silhouettes riding out of the sun, light reflecting off silver writing engraved across their hulls.

They were like the narwhales that dipped in and out of the waters off Haffa, but a school of titans that had taken to the air, long glinting rams made of steel mounted on their nose domes. The drone of engine cars and the blur of propellers vibrated across the curtain wall. Great ribbons of silk had been tied to the crafts' cruciform tails, rippling behind the armada of airships as though rainbow lines were being drawn across the perfectly clear sky above the capital.

'Do you feel pride, Cadet Barir, at this great new show of force?' said Farris Uddin from behind Omar. 'Or do you feel shame that command of the imperial Aerial Squadron was given to the admirals of the caliph's navy, rather than those who already had true mastery of the heavens under god?'

'I believe I may feel both, master.'

'You may indeed feel both,' said Uddin. 'For while nothing may stand against the empire and the new range of our ambitions, I fear that you see before you the ruin of the guardsmen's fortunes. For centuries we trained to fight such machines when only our heathen neighbour possessed them, splashed grenade fire against their canvas and carried propeller snarls crafted for their engine cars. Now we have our own fleet and at best we are cursed to ride in their shadows as mere scouts. What do you see, Boulous?'

'I see a man,' said the retainer, looking towards the grand marshal's place on the battlements with a tear in his eye, 'made old before his time.'

'You are a good and true servant of the Caliph Eternal,' said Uddin, kindly. 'But watch whose ears hear you say that.' He raised his scimitar and shouted, 'Remember Cann-Khali!'

All down the curtain wall the cry was taken up. The greatest battle of the order, where fifty draks and their riders had held off an army of ten thousand Seyadi levies for a week in a lonely mountain gorge.

Their greatest battle, thought Omar, mouthing the cry, their greatest triumph. *But still an eventual defeat that had left every guardsman who fought in it a corpse.*

It took every ounce of willpower for Jack to stop himself glancing behind his back. The shouts and grunts of the Cassarabian boarding party intermingled with the war cries of their two brave Benzari stokers and the thunder of pistols as John Oldcastle calmly discharged one after another across the transaction-engine pit. Concentrate on the punch card he was composing, not allow himself to be distracted by the screams of dying men, or Coss Shaftcrank shouting his tinny curses, or the thud of swords against flesh and the explosions of guns. Concentrate on the punch cards, where Jack was used to bending the calculation drums on transaction engines to his will. And where they wouldn't bend, you could always roll with the drums and see where they took you.

Another yell, closer. The master cardsharp swore and tossed an empty pistol down onto the deck, but Jack couldn't spare the seconds to look around. Not with the door on the mortar-loading station still locked tight against their gunnery deck crew.

A rifle ball ricocheted off the hull near Jack's head, but he was focusing on writing the lines of code for the loading arms that had been decommissioned three years ago: the automated loading arms, with a dumb waiter system that still ran into the magazine buried in the well-protected heart of the *Iron Partridge.* The original repair crew who had refitted her had locked the automated systems down tight. But they hadn't counted on Jack Keats and his clever fingers overwriting their work. Luckily for him, they had done their job in a rush, the ship's ability to automatically fire and load constrained by some basic and strikingly obvious safeguards. *Delete, delete,*

delete. He was almost there, the automation almost back online. He ignored the yell of the stoker being pushed down into the pit, impaled on the bayonets of three Cassarabian marines. Ignored the sounds, as Jack trusted the crewmen in the magazine would be ignoring the live shells being drawn into the dumb waiter system, lifted up and pushed into the breech of their mortars. *Don't you pay those shells any mind, boys. You just let them slide on past without anyone reaching for the manual overrides.* The automated mortars that according to the notes in Jack's manual couldn't hit the side of a barn door, unless, *please*, the enemy's barn door happened to be drifting feet above their mortar barrels. Sometimes, you just had to roll with the drums and see where they took you.

There was a series of hollow metallic thuds as the mortars erupted along the length of their airship's spine, followed by a trembling whine as the tubes back-filled with the cold air from outside, then an answering series of explosions from above them, a line of fire stitched along the belly of the Cassarabian airship hanging above their vessel. Seconds later Jack clung onto his station as a wrenching impact slammed him forward, the remains of a decapitated enemy engine car spinning down on top of the *Iron Partridge*, the rest of the ruined airship just visible through the crack in the skylight. It glanced off their armoured hull with another harsh jolt before continuing downwards on its fiery descent.

From the doorway there came a second explosion. Not a debris strike, but a blast of tumbling Cassarabian marines as Henry Tempest, their recently released captain of marines, erupted into the transaction-engine chamber. His rifle now discharged and empty, the giant soldier was using the weapon like a fighting staff, its butt lashing out and caving in skulls and ribs. The black and silver figures wearing Cassarabian marines' uniforms were sent flying around him, as though they were kites launched into the air, while Tempest's crimson features were distorted into a yell. 'Get off my ship! Get off my perishing ship!'

There were others fighting in the corridor outside, its confines echoing to the clash of hatchets, knives, bayonets and cutlasses. Firearms took too long to reload at close quarters and Jack caught a glimpse of First Lieutenant Westwick entangled in the deadly mêlée of Cassarabian marines and short Benzari tribesmen.

One of the Cassarabian marines came at Jack from the edge of the tumult and Jack grabbed the empty bandolier from the station at his side, swinging it like a whip and catching the Cassarabian marine in the face, dislodging the man's beak-like mask. Propelled by fear and fury, Jack ran at the marine and shoved him over the rail, watching him crumple onto the machinery of the transaction-engine pit below. As Jack turned, a rifle butt slammed into his gut and winded him. He collapsed back; the rifle's barrel fell across his throat and forced him choking down against the rail. It was Henry Tempest, his eyes glinting like tiny marbles as his sweating face bore down on Jack. 'Get off my ship!'

Jack could only snort, his fingers trying to find purchase on the rifle as the seemingly unstoppable force of the soldier crushed his larynx. It was true, then, what the sailors had been whispering about Tempest: that he had been left half-deranged by an addiction to opiate poppies. That he had to regularly slake his thirst on a mixture of drugs and rum just to stay sane.

'He's one of ours, Henry,' the female voice spun out of the darkness that was beginning to envelop Jack.

Jack croaked desperately for air as the pressure eased.

'Drink from your green flask, Henry.'

There was a grunting like a pig feeding and Jack focused

on a green-lidded canteen being slugged back by the marine officer before being clipped down on his belt next to an identical red-lidded canteen. And there, next to him, was First Lieutenant Westwick, severe and proud, a pair of blooded cutlasses gripped tight in her hands.

'Sorry, boy,' said the brute, extending a giant hand and enveloping Jack's trembling arm. 'I was stuck in one of my rising rages, so I was.'

Well, that makes everything okay then.

Jack's eyes slipped across the transaction-engine chamber, dead bodies littering the deck. Benzari tribesmen moved across the room with their short curved swords out, checking for any in the enemy boarding party that might be faking their demise.

'Your leg,' said Jack, pointing to a knife embedded in the captain of marine's limb.

'It's not mine,' said the brute, as if that explained everything, pulling the knife out as though removing an inconvenient thorn.

By his side, First Lieutenant Westwick turned at the sound of Coss Shaftcrank's voicebox, the steamman kneeling over the corpses while he chanted prayers to his ancestors and the Steamo Loas. 'Belay that racket. Pile them up and roll them out the nearest hatch.'

'Wreck my relays, but their people have established burial rites,' protested Coss.

'Those are *my* rites, and those are *your* orders, skyman. Their god can clean them up from the ground below using the vultures as his divine instrument.' First Lieutenant Westwick angrily spun Jack around, jabbing one of her fingers at his face. 'That was a synchronized volley from our mortars. An *automated* volley.'

'The mortars weren't accepting manual control,' protested Jack.

'Do you know how many sailors died in the last voyage this malfunctioning metal hulk made under full automation? If those mortar shells had been loaded fin up and warhead down, you would have caused a full salvo detonating right above the ship's magazine! You, sir, would have blown our bloody remains all the way back to the Kingdom.'

'The lad saved the ship, first lieutenant,' called John Oldcastle, still checking his pistols. 'The Cassarabians were swarming over our top side like ants across a blessed picnic blanket.'

'He gambled our ship and our mission and he got lucky,' spat the woman.

Outside the ship a ripple of fire sounded – not the oak-sawing sound of their cannons, but the whoosh of landing rockets blasting out and the rattle of anchor lines running behind them, then the *Iron Partridge* started to shake from stem to stern.

'Ah,' said John Oldcastle admiringly. 'There's the wild genius of Jericho at work. He's fired our anchors straight into the Cassarabian airship. That one's not in the admiralty rule-book. He's pulling them in. You've got your ship, Maya, if you've got the taste for another game of tickle-my-sabre with their crew.'

'Open the hatches along the engine car repair gantry,' Westwick ordered her hulking captain of marines. 'We'll board them at the broadside.' She seized Jack by the scruff of his striped navy shirt, wiping off the blood on one of her cutlasses against his shoulder. 'I'll deal with you later, Mister Keats.'

'You did the right thing, lad,' said John Oldcastle, watching the first lieutenant sprint out with her Benzari warriors in tow. 'Remember that. Not by the book, but the right thing, nevertheless.'

Jack felt a knot of fear tightening in his stomach.

Back in the unforgiving slums of Middlesteel, doing the right thing was often as costly a mistake as you could make. You only looked out for yourself, and at a push, for your family. Jack's decision, would, he expected, end just as badly. In his world, no good deed went unpunished.

Jack watched the binds being tightened around his wrists, his face pressed between the frame of a fin-bomb rack, the closed bomb-bay doors locked beneath his boots.

'For disobeying a standing order when pressed by the enemy,' intoned the first lieutenant as she read out the charges. 'For cowardice in the face of enemy fire and imperilling the Royal Aerostatical Navy vessel *Iron Partridge* while on active duty.'

'Take this lad,' said John Oldcastle from behind Jack, pressing a cloth-wrapped wooden handle between his teeth. 'Bite down on it, it'll help save your tongue.'

'Skyman Jack Keats is sentenced to ninety lashes.'

'What is this?' the voice boomed from behind the crewmen lined up along the side of the bomb bay, Captain Jericho pushing his way through the press of sailors.

'The maintaining of discipline,' said First Lieutenant Westwick.

'I did not order this!'

'Under the articles of war, I have the authority to—'

'It is customary to inform the captain before ordering a flogging,' barked Jericho. 'And those articles you are suddenly so familiar with allow me to set the number of lashes.' He pointed to the Benzari marine holding the cat-o'-nine-tails, the knotted lines of the whip dangling dangerously by his side. 'The minimum. Ten lashes only.'

'That's far too soft a sentence,' objected the first lieutenant.

Not for my bloody spine, it isn't.

'This is not a flogging ship. You have duties to attend to, first lieutenant. The officers we took prisoner have been made ready on the prize vessel.'

'I see no prize vessel.'

'You will find her firmly tied off against our starboard side, first lieutenant.'

'Read your orders again, captain. We have a very specific objective to accomplish and it does not include losing weeks we cannot afford on a round trip to tow a Cassarabian airship all the way back to the border just so you and your crew can line your pockets with Admiralty House's bounty money.'

That drew furious murmurs from the crew. It was the greatest bugbear of any airship crew that the only time they got to claim prize money was when they helped the Fleet Sea Arm capture enemy u-boats and frigates on the surface of the ocean. Now the skymen finally had an enemy their equal in the air and they had shed their blood to capture one of the foe's vessels. That share of the admiralty's prize money was their right!

'That is not our tradition, d'you see?' said the captain.

'Damn your bloody tradition, sir,' said Westwick. 'Orders trump tradition and the articles of war, both. We'll learn what we can from the prisoners and take what we need from the captured Cassarabian aerostat and then you'll mine her and you'll blow her.'

Her words drew a collective growl from the crew. Whether it was seeing their captain treated like a pet hunting hound by the first lieutenant, or the prospect of losing a sailor's share of a thousand guineas' prize money, Jack couldn't say.

'Master Engineer Pasco,' barked the first lieutenant, 'I don't believe our marine has the height to make a mere ten lashes count. Step forward and take the cat-o'-nine-tails from him.'

Jack groaned as the mean bullying officer did as he had been ordered.

'This is your fault, thief,' whispered Pasco, pulling Jack's shirt up. 'She's only doing this out of spite because you wouldn't take your ninety licks like a man. You've stolen six month's extra salary out of the pockets of every Jack Cloudie on board the ship.'

The marine drummers started the rattle of their instruments and the count began. Pasco had the size to make the lashes count alright. Jack got to seven numbing lashes before he passed out, the biting taste of the saliva-soaked cloth fading from his mouth.

CHAPTER SEVEN

'Where is your mind today?' demanded the cadet master, cutting left and right with the practice sabre as if he was punishing the air rather than Omar.

'It is the day for the womb mages to sample his flesh for a new drak to be grown for him,' called Boulous from the other side of the fencing mat.

The cadet master snorted at Omar. 'Pray you can honour your sword when your drak is ready for you. It is not a womb mage's ritual that is on your mind, cadet. Command. Tell.'

'I was thinking of a girl,' growled Omar, dripping in sweat from the exercise. 'A girl I know who was taken by brigands.'

'Well then,' said the old swordsman, flicking Omar's sword up to guard readiness with the tip of his sabre, the position called third tierce. 'Brigands and guardsmen often meet, and when we do, the business is not much different from ours this morning. Except these brigands will not have Farris Uddin quite so angry at them for running a sword through a cadet's foolish, mooning guts.'

Omar felt anger rise in him at the old man's scorn and

disrespect for his feelings towards Shadisa. Not taking his eyes off the old swordsman, Omar raised his free hand towards the weapons racked by the practice hall's walls – swords of all shapes and sizes: sabres, rapiers, longswords, fencing foils, foreign blades. 'I have mastered your weapons.'

'Have you then, young fool?' sneered the cadet master. 'You are as blind as one of the snake charmers' nobbled pythons down in the bazaar. Those aren't weapons in that rack. Your sword is not the weapon. *You* are the weapon.' Casting his own sword to the floor, the cadet master went over to the rack and pulled away what Omar had initially taken for part of the frame. He came back with two tall polished wooden sticks just shy of his own height, and tossed one to Boulous, throwing the other one to Omar.

'What is this?' demanded Omar. 'Something for the palace gardeners to grow their beans around?'

'A lesson,' said the cadet master. 'My father was a jinn trader and I grew up travelling with him across the infidel lands. Those bean sticks are what you get when you make duelling with edged weapons a crime for hundreds of years. The Jackelians call them debating sticks, and any Kingdom street rat would be able to stick one right up your sorry arse and make you twist around it as though it was one of their Maypoles.'

Omar felt the heft of the thing, deceptively heavy. Had it been weighted inside with lead?

'Come on, boy. It's not a real weapon, is it?' said the cadet master. 'Just a little stick. See what you can do against the commander's retainer. Boulous's blood runs Kingdom-red, even if his heart is as true a guardsman's as ever walked this fortress. Have a little prod at each other. Show me your great mastery of my arts.'

Omar struck out at Boulous with the staff, but the retainer was as quick with it as he was with a practice scimitar, ducking back and not even needing to block Omar's strike. Angered, Omar tried to windmill the staff, turning it and jabbing from multiple angles and directions, but Boulous was able to step around each strike, his boots flowing as though he were dancing. They hadn't even touched wood yet.

'Enough, Boulous,' spat the cadet master. 'Plant the cadet's beans for him.'

Boulous swept his staff around, tripping Omar onto the floor before he could attempt to jump or manoeuvre, the flat end of the staff hovering an inch away from his nose.

'That staff isn't a weapon,' the cadet master shouted at Omar on the floor. 'A sword isn't a weapon, nor a stick nor a stone. The guardsman is the weapon, and in his hands, so is anything he touches.' He waved at Boulous. 'Do I need to press my point, retainer? Shall I show this young fool how to take that staff away from you and give you a few lumps in payment for it?'

Boulous smiled thinly and shook his head. 'I still remember you laughing at me during our empty hand sessions, cadet master.'

'A little shame worked well as a spur with you, retainer.' The cadet master shook his head sadly at Omar. 'But you learn well enough without it, cadet. I don't know why, but being a guardsman seems to run in your lazy, skiving blood. Have nothing on your mind when you train with me. Bring me some foolishness about a woman again and I'll show you where the flat end of the length of infidel wood is meant to be inserted.'

Omar and Boulous bowed and left as the next cadet entered to receive his punishment.

Omar had imagined that his first visit outside the environs of the guardsmen's towering fortress, venturing into the Jahan

Palace below, would have been an occasion to partake of the legendary sensual pleasures of the Caliph Eternal's bounty. Instead, Omar's passage down the monstrous granite staircase that had been carved into the rock face in the shadow of the fortress was filled with dread. It was the retainer's warning that had done it for Omar – that the womb mages who would sample his flesh to create a drak for him were bound up with the Sect of Razat. Omar had escaped the extermination of his house using the last of his slave's luck, and now he had none left to protect him from the dark sorceries of his enemies.

What if the womb mages gave him a deadly disease when they sampled his flesh? Something to leave him gasping and rolling around the cells of the fortress in a week's time, when the sect's involvement in his murder could be denied? Or they might twist and warp his body in revenge for escaping the sack of Haffa. He remembered the work of the womb mages back in his hometown: creating changeling viruses to heal and cure, or curse and kill, depending on whose coin had been taken in payment. How welcome would Omar be among the ranks of the guardsmen if they found him growing a third leg or an extra set of arms one morning?

Omar felt a fraud every step of the way down to the great domes below, the wind whipping his cloak about his black leather armour. Even the presence of the retainer Boulous to lead the way and lend authority to his presence seemed only a salve to the situation.

'A cadet is still invested with the authority of the order,' said Boulous, as if sensing Omar's mood. 'You are a custodian of the Caliph Eternal's law inside the palace.'

'I will be quick to sever the hands of any courtiers I find fighting unlicensed duels,' said Omar. 'What did Master Uddin mean up on the walls when he warned you not to repeat what you said about the grand marshal? It is clear the grand marshal has lived a long life. Who would object to hearing that?'

'It is not his age,' said Boulous. 'It is how the grand marshal came by it – or rather the speed by which he came by it. Until two years ago, the grand marshal was subject to the caliph's bounty, you understand? He was given the drug that blesses a man with eternal youth. The grand marshal might have lived to be three hundred years old, but now its blessing is his no more and his true years advance fast on him.'

'More politics,' said Omar.

'We are not in favour, Cadet Barir,' said the retainer. 'The guardsmen are traditionalists, and we live in an age of progress. That is why the Caliph Eternal's new armada of the heavens was given to the control of the navy's admirals, salt-stained fools who know more about tides and sounding depths than they do of aerial navigation in the face of sandstorms.'

'There was an old nomad I was friends with at home,' said Omar. 'He would have shrugged his shoulders and said such a misfortune must be god's will.'

'Perhaps, but it is also the will of the same sect that saw yours cast down from the Holy Cent,' said the retainer. 'You need to watch your tongue in the palace below. It was not just your father's house and its allies that were destroyed by the new sect's rise to ascendancy. The Pasdaran was dissolved by the Caliph Eternal last year when they were supposedly discovered plotting against the empire.'

The Pasdaran! But they were the caliph's secret police. Even in Haffa just the invoking of the name of the caliph's shadowy torturers had been enough to scare overactive children to sleep. It was said they had spies in every town, spirits in every house listening in for any fool reckless enough to dare speak treason against the caliph.

'They are gone?' said Omar, sounding astonished.

'Their reward for standing against the appointment of the new grand vizier, Immed Zahharl,' said the servant. 'Immed Zahharl is also the head of the order of womb mages and he stands as high keeper for the Sect of Razat. The secret police declared publicly that Zahharl's appointment was contrary to the tradition that a vizier must renounce all house, guild and sect and accept only the Caliph Eternal as his one true prophet. The "treason" among the secret police was uncovered soon after they spoke out against the new grand vizier.'

'I remember when I was growing up,' said Omar, 'I thought the Pasdaran were demons hiding under my cot. I felt such fear. Of course, I was not as brave then as I am now.'

'Oh, oh, there's still plenty to be feared in the palace. But not from the hands of the secret police, nor any more from the swords of guardsmen.' He reached out and touched the back of Omar's cloak imploringly. 'It is not the Caliph Eternal's fault, not when sorcerers whisper in his ear. Sometimes I think the new sect has him half-bewitched, and they will hate you twice over. Once for the house that was yours in your old life, and once for the guardsman's mantle you wear in your new one. When we walk inside the palace, remember, in imperial script there is only one syllable's difference between the word for favoured and the word for executed.'

'Do not fear, Boulous Ibn Jahani,' said Omar. 'You are a servant of the order and the order's sword is here to protect you.'

Omar almost managed to sound as if he truly believed it.

Jack gazed with despair at the small transaction-engine-room pit of the Cassarabian airship, as ruined as his red-raw back. The wrecked room had been adequate enough to give them navigational control of the enemy vessel, but Jack was struggling with the differing standards when it came to symbolic logic, not to mention the fact the enemy calculation drums had been scuttled by her own crew when they realized their ship was falling to the Kingdom's boarding parties. The prize vessel's crew hadn't been very forthcoming so far, but the airship – named the *Kochava Saar* – was slowly revealing its secrets. Unlike the *Iron Partridge*, its main structure wasn't made of the iron-strong paper composite, *carper*, but some light material that seemed to be part bone and part wood, no doubt secreted like silk by one of the twisted creatures given life by the caliph's womb mages. There were other mysteries, though. Such as the non-standard racks in the vessel's bomb bays, seemingly built to hold fin-bombs several orders of magnitude larger than any found on a Jackelian vessel, yet completely empty of ordnance – the pair of enemy airships running light for long-distance patrol. What on earth would fit inside one of those monstrous frames?

'What are we looking for?' asked Jack, running his fingers down the strangely arranged symbols of the enemy punch-card writer.

'Anything that might indicate where these Cassarabian lads are getting their celgas from, Mister Keats,' said John Oldcastle, helping Coss lift up a spilled bank of machinery, the metal casing bent out of shape by wrecking hammers.

'Searching for the source of their celgas is our mission?' asked Jack.

Oldcastle indicated the debris filling the enemy transaction-engine chamber. 'An airship is just canvas and metal with some clever papier-mâché and chemicals all brewed up together. But what the Cassarabians are using to float their 'stats with, lad, that's pure gold.'

'It is neither RAN celgas nor gold,' said Coss, 'that much I am sure of, master cardsharp. I helped our crew tap some barrels of enemy gas on the *Iron Partridge*. Tear my transfer pipes, it had a most unpleasant smell – although it is non-flammable and appears to have a similar lifting capacity to our own airship gas.'

'Get the furnace going, Mister Shaftcrank; we're going to tickle some life back into their calculation drums. Mister Keats, you'll search for anything to do with the enemy gas. Where the Cassarabians loaded it, how much was taken on, and if you've even a sniff of how or where they get it from, you inform me right away.'

'Their writer layout isn't the same as ours,' said Jack pointing to the punch-card machine. *And it looks as if it's been put together by a half-drunk blind man.*

'Best efforts, lad, best efforts.'

Jack was halfway through puzzling out the foreign systems, when two of their Benzari marines appeared escorting a Cassarabian prisoner, a thin-faced man whose sunken cheeks were covered with an elaborately greased and embroidered beard, his tanned skin still marked with soot from the fires that had been burning across the stricken airship.

The marines pushed him roughly down onto the chair and secured him to it.

'Ah, just the fellow,' said Oldcastle, cleaning his engine-oiled hands on a rag. 'You've been fingered to us as one of the clever jacks that used to run this room.'

'I have nothing to say to you,' said the Cassarabian, 'and you will find I am worth no ransom to your people.'

'Here it is, my fine friend,' said Oldcastle, 'we might lock you away for a prisoner exchange later, but we won't sell you, not even to your own side. We're not slavers in the Kingdom.'

'I know what you are,' snarled the Cassarabian. 'I have heard the screams of the others after they were taken away.'

'That would be our first lieutenant,' said Oldcastle. 'She a direct lass, so she is.'

The Cassarabian spat at the master cardsharp's feet. 'I expect no honour from you, infidel.'

'You'll have to forgive our first lieutenant,' said Oldcastle moving behind the prisoner and putting his hands on the man's shoulders. 'Her mother was one of your escaped slaves, crossed the desert to the uplands to get away from the empire. Not just any sort of slave, our good lady officer told me, but a *producer*.' Oldcastle looked at Jack. 'They've got some funny ways in Cassarabia, Mister Keats. All those creatures bred by their womb mages. They come out of the thighs of slaves when they're born. Not a very pleasant job I would say; bottom of the slave pecking order when you draw that duty. The ones that are forced into the trade are known as producers. Most women that draw that wicked straw only last for three years, but the first lieutenant's mother was a tough old bird. She was at it for five years before she escaped.' He patted their prisoner on the back. 'You can imagine the kind of stories the first lieutenant was raised on, can't you? I think that's why she treats her job so mortal serious. But it could be worse for you lads, you could have her old ma here, instead, asking you the questions.' Oldcastle angrily spun the prisoner's chair around. 'So let me ask you, my fine fellow, how much honour is there in your desert brigands having to tie the hands of our upland lasses to stop them committing suicide when they're snatched by you? Or is your honour measured in the number of luckless children the caliph receives as annual tribute from the conquered nations that have your wicked lackeys installed as sultans?'

'I live by the will of heaven,' said the prisoner. 'Ben Issman's name be blessed.'

'And isn't it funny how often heaven's will coincides with the will of all the emperors and their armies and thugs,' said Oldcastle. He leant in close to the prisoner and Jack only just heard what he whispered. 'We're devils, and the woman taking your lads out of your brig one by one, she's the worst of us all.'

He drew his naval cutlass. For a moment Jack thought Oldcastle was about to cut the prisoner's throat, but instead he sliced the ties around the Cassarabian's wrists. 'You've told me plenty, lad. No money to pay for a ransom, you're just a dirt-poor scholar, and you can either help me get your foreign thinking machines working again, or I'll let the first lieutenant have you for her entertainment. You've seen some strange creatures bred in your land, I warrant, but a woman that's half-Cassarabian and half-Jackelian, that's the most wicked unholy animal you will ever see in this life or the next.'

The master cardsharp's cajoling had its effect. Seeming to crumple, the Cassarabian become pliable enough to do their bidding, inspecting the broken transaction engines and helping Coss patch up the damage. Oldcastle had brought over a portable transaction engine configured with translation filters from the *Iron Partridge* and patching it into the ruined Cassarabian systems allowed them to access the data they needed in a format that was intelligible to Jack. Wherever that box had come from, it wasn't standard navy issue, that much Jack was certain of. Coss's warnings drifted back to Jack's mind, that John Oldcastle wasn't who he claimed to be, but someone called Jared Black. Yes. The master cardsharp knew just enough about transaction engines to get Coss and Jack to do his bidding, but he lacked the real expertise that an officer in his position should have had.

'What you were saying about the Cassarabians and the first lieutenant's mother,' said Jack to the master cardsharp. 'That's why there's so few women sailors on the *Iron Partridge*?'

'You've noticed that then, Mister Keats?'

'They have an advantage in the weight tables against most male sailors. I expected to see more of them on board.'

'Disappointed were you, lad? All those bawdy penny-dreadful tales about the airship lasses. Ah, to be a young buck again. As desperate as we were for a competent crew, old Jericho refused every female cloudie that tried to sign up. There are a few people who have a grand old time of it down in Cassarabia, living high on the hog, but you won't find too many of them being women.'

'We have First Lieutenant Westwick on board,' noted Coss.

'The skipper didn't get a choice with her,' said the officer, winking at Jack. 'But then not many of us do.'

Jack knew what the old man meant. *Pity the enemy that thought they had captured her.*

'I have a sister, Mister Keats, every inch as sharp as our prickly first lieutenant. Not that we get on that blessed well – truth to tell, she'd stick me with a dagger as soon as look at me. But mean as she be, if I had any say in the matter and push came to shove, I wouldn't let her within a thousand miles of the empire.'

'This is the softbody concept of male gallantry towards the opposite gender?' asked Coss.

'Not gallantry, old steamer. I've shipped out with some tough old birds in my time and pulled through more than a few tight scrapes with some brave lass guarding my back, and been happy for the privilege. But never down south. Never down there.'

He turned back to the console. To Jack's eyes, their efforts seemed to yield little of interest when it came to the origin or nature of the gas being used to float the enemy's vessels.

Jack showed Oldcastle the admittedly incomplete entries he had dredged from the enemy thinking machine, the results twisting on the abacus-like beads of the Cassarabians' version of a rotator screen. 'There's nothing meaningful about their gas. Just leakage tables and regassing estimates.'

'Don't be so sure, lad,' said Oldcastle. He tapped a series of unfamiliar icons on the top rail of the rotator. 'I would say this is something. Mister Shaftcrank, switch off the translation box and let me view this in Cassarabian.'

All the icons on the beads rotated into patterns unfamiliar to Jack, but they seemed to make sense to Oldcastle.

'So, lad, it's a rising tide that floats all ships.'

'You can read Cassarabian?' Jack asked.

'Indeed I can. This,' Oldcastle tapped the corner of the rotator, 'is the supply chit for the gas they took on. But it's not the caliph's military that signed it over to the airship.' He glanced at their prisoner and gestured at the two marines guarding him. 'Back to the brig with our scholarly friend. This isn't for his ears.' After the prisoner had been removed, the master cardsharp continued. 'This gas came from one of the Cassarabian temples, the Sect of Razat. They're a new crew, all for war and expansion and banging the patriotic drum.'

'Temples?' said Coss from the small transaction-engine pit. 'Unlike the people of the metal, I understood that the Cassarabians allow for the existence of only a single true god?'

'It's the genius of their faith, Mister Shaftcrank,' said Oldcastle. 'One god maybe, but they have as many prophets and competing philosophies within heaven as your steammen have ancestral spirits. Well, a hundred of them, anyway. It's a holy number in Cassarabia. A hundred sects for the hundred faces of the one true god. Anyone can sup at their priests' high table, if they can command enough power and temple tithes and are willing to play by the caliph's rules when it comes to mouthing platitudes about the one true god.' He patted the rotator. 'It's like your transaction engines, Mister Keats. As long as you're inclined to unconditionally accept the operating system and are minded to make your code compatible with it, you can merrily write punch cards and may the best cardsharp's works prosper. Cassarabian myth says there was a wicked sea of bloodshed before the first caliph, Ben Issman, unified the sects down south. Now their faith evolves over the ages without all-out religious war, without the whole wicked empire murdering each other over whether their priests need to demand two or three days' fasting to prove true penitence.'

Jack resisted the urge to touch his aching spine. 'And this new sect wants war?'

'Aye, from what I've heard,' said Oldcastle. 'The hundred faces of the one true god, and this new face is preaching that the Cassarabians have grown terrible soft, easy and complacent over the centuries. Trading silks, jinn barrels and spices with filthy infidels has fallen out of favour. Trading shells and scimitar thrusts is to be the new thing. Paradise will only come from the conversion of unbelievers at the point of a sword. That's a rather traditional view, and I'm mortal unhappy to see it coming back into favour.'

'Infidels,' said Jack. 'That would be the Kingdom, then.'

'Sadly the case. It's been an age since I've travelled south,' said Oldcastle. 'The Sect of Razat is after my time. I'm all for a little ease and complacency myself, but I don't think this new crew are going to allow us much of that. Now, where is this cursed sect getting their mortal airship gas from? That's the question we need answered.'

Jack tapped the information slowly flickering across the rotator. 'Will the information be in their machine's memory?'

'No, lad,' said Oldcastle. 'Because such a secret is too sensitive, and because my unlucky stars are never that kind to these poor, tired old bones. A map with an "X" marking the spot of a newly discovered celgas mine would be too easy for us, not when we could happily sip our grog rations as we sailed straight back home before sending the high fleet down here with enough fin-bombs to wreck the caliph's dreams of glory forever. No, we'll be doing this hard and slow-style. Boots on the ground and sniffing around Cassarabia the old-fashioned, dangerous way.'

Oldcastle laid a hand on the back of Jack's shirt and he winced from the pain of the weals left by his flogging. 'My boots, Mister Keats and yours too. I haven't killed you yet.'

Don't worry, old man. You and the navy, between you, you're working hard on it.

As Omar moved through the imperial palace he saw why those who called it home knew it simply as the Jahan, *the world*. The high crystal geodesic domes protected a universe in miniature, immaculately tended gardens filled with streams and orchards, gently curving brooks and jasmine-scented pools that had been expertly crafted around the luxurious pavilions and ornate buildings. While he and Boulous walked, they were sheltered by the palace's crystal covering, shimmering as it matched opacity with the position of the sun burning high above the capital. Omar revelled in the expensive, luxurious sprays of water on his skin as he watched the calligraphy slowly tracking across the dome's inner surface, an animated scroll from the writings of the Holy Cent. But the mournful retainer Omar was travelling with managed to spoil even the sight of this dazzling world when he pointed out that now, only the visions of the keepers of the Sect of Razat were present in the enchanted march of words, the teachings from the other ninety-nine sects' temples relegated to the evening after the majority of the court had retired to bed for the night.

Omar looked at the courtiers walking around the cool waters, nodding respectfully at each other on their slow circuits of the landscaped paradise, and the knots of officials – some in uniforms, some in expensive silk robes – sprawled across the grass while tiny colourful birds fluttered in and out of the trees. This was the life, Omar decided. Being waited on by retainers with iced jugs of water under the magical shade of the palace's domes. One day he and Shadisa would share it together, of that he was certain.

'What do they find to talk about all day?' Omar wondered out loud.

'Who's up, who's down,' said Boulous. 'Who's in and who's out. Which sect of the Holy Cent is gathering the most worshippers and tithes, which sect is dwindling. Which viziers are to be replaced this year and who is to replace them. Which of our dominions will rebel and who the Caliph Eternal will trust to crush them. It is like a game of draughts with ten thousand players competing on a single board.'

'I could play such a game,' said Omar.

'Yes, yes, but a better question is why would you want to?' Boulous pointed to one of the retainers holding out a tray of delicate steaming kebabs for a small group of men wearing turbans. 'Better to buy your food from a street vendor in the souks below the palace hills. Then at least you will know the true price you must pay up front.'

Why would I want to? So I can bring down the bastards that sacked Haffa and stole Shadisa from me. I can think of no finer game than that.

The two of them crossed the largest of the domes where the palace's pavilions intertwined with numerous waterways, walking under an arched entrance and emerging into one of the adjoining rotunda. Omar noted that when seen from above, standing on the parapets of the guardsmen's fortress, the palace domes' crystal surface appeared to shimmer in a medley of colours, but from inside there was a uniform appearance of a slightly shaded sky – as if the roof hardly existed at all – and god himself was writing the words of the hundred sects' holy teachings across the heavens.

As new to palace life as Omar was, it was easy enough to recognize the domain of the womb mages, the delicate sophistication of bulb-shaped pavilion towers and calligraphy-engraved marble walls giving way to a featureless ziggurat made out of a dull, brooding stone. The building was so out of place it looked as if a squadron of draks might have lifted it out one of the dark, distant provinces of the south and dropped it down onto the hills for the Caliph Eternal's architects to raise a dome about its bulk. Unlike many of the palace's grander buildings, there were none of the caliph's soldiers standing sentry outside. *For who in their right mind would want to disturb the peace of such men as dwelt inside the ziggurat?* The main doorway at its foot was guarded only by the twin serpents from the garden of life, carved in stone above the entrance and intertwined in the shape of a helix, the womb mages' ancient symbol, hung up outside their surgeries in bazaars. Unfortunately for Omar, the inhabitants of this building weren't simple healers, able to encourage a fisherman's finger to grow back after proving too careless with a scaling knife, available to craft a changeling virus to bless a soon-to-be-born child with extra height and strength. Here lurked the guardians of the caliph's private library of spells; secrets that dated back to when Ben Issman, his name be blessed, had led his people into the desert and made life bloom there, rediscovering the one true god who had been lost for so long. Womb mages powerful and dark, trained in the heart of the sorcerer's own city, *Mutantarjinn*, their dark domain scored out of the very rock by the sight

132

of god when the highest of highests' eyes reopened after sleeping for so long.

Even if the womb mages inside the ziggurat hadn't embraced the troublesome new sect, Omar would have avoided them like the plague in the normal course of affairs. Avoided them in the same way people avoided an undertaker; because they touched dead flesh as well as living, and the things they did to slaves, especially women, did not bear thinking about. It was for good reason that when slaves were bred, the slaves themselves prayed for males and the masters – thinking about the resale value of their progeny – prayed for females.

Boulous placed his hand on a glass panel set in the wall and a light appeared as if a lantern had been lit behind the crystal; a short while later, a small iron sally door set within the larger gate opened. A eunuch wearing robes marked with the twin snake helix bade them enter, making a snide comment about having to open the gate to a mere jahani, a discourtesy which the retainer and Omar both chose to ignore. Inside, they were led through stone passages, corridors made an indeterminate size by an ethereal red illumination that revealed little.

'It is dark inside your corridors,' said Omar.

'There are things grown here that would not benefit from brighter light,' said the eunuch guiding them. 'Does it scare you?'

'Me? I am as brave as a sand lion. Besides, I prefer the darkness,' said Omar. 'In darkness all women look beautiful and even the stalest of bread appears a banquet.'

'You will like it here then,' muttered the eunuch.

They travelled further than the length of the ziggurat Omar had seen outside and he realized that they must now be travelling underground, the womb mages' domain stretching to chambers and corridors carved out below the hill itself. Their passage intersected a far larger one and Omar tripped over the first of a pair of metal rails set in the floor when he made to cross the space. As Boulous extended a hand to help him up, the eunuch raised a palm to stop the two of them going any further. A rumbling grew louder in the half-light, a sled-like affair on rail-locked wheels being drawn down the passage by a team of twenty bare-chested slaves. The sled was mounted by a tall glass box, as if the slaves were pulling a giant aquarium behind them; a thick mustard-yellow gas swirled about inside.

Omar caught a glimpse of the glass case's occupant as it passed and nearly stumbled again. It looked like a woman struggling underneath the crush of an albino whale, choking in the yellow stew. But as the mist momentarily cleared he saw it was the woman's own body that curved out into a whale-sized appendage, her lower ribs as large as the archways around the palace pools and hung with rolls of flesh so gargantuan she looked as if she was drowning in her own frame.

Omar grasped the eunuch's shoulder. 'She's suffocating inside there!'

'Don't be a fool,' said the eunuch, disdainfully removing Omar's hand. 'The gas is a nutrient bath. No producer can eat enough through her mouth to feed both herself and her load. The skin of her womb must absorb the food directly. That producer's load is a mine worm. Not quite as large as a drak when it's born, but large enough to need a gallon of food pumped into the producer's tank every hour during her second trimester. Ours is not an easy vocation, it requires both precision and dedication.'

Omar watched the sled disappear down the rails with horror, imagining his mother's face swollen and red, as she choked on the mustard-coloured fumes of her food. 'What will happen after the birth?'

134

'The mine worm will be taken to the mountains at Riyjhi – the Caliph Eternal's prospectors have discovered many new veins of silver there.'

'No,' said Omar, 'to *her*.'

'The producer will be normalized and rested for a month,' said the eunuch as if he was talking to a child. 'You can't keep them breeding constantly. Not unless you want to receive a whipping for a miscarriage.' He pointed to the disappearing sled. 'Lose an expensive load like that and you would be made to feel it. Two thousand tughra. And it will cost the caliph as much as that to raise your drak; remember the cost next time you choose to dive around the sky as if you are flying a five-coin hawk bought for you at the bazaar by your mother.'

What if that's been done to Shadisa, what if that's the life the bandits sold her into?

'Be careful what you say,' Boulous warned the eunuch, 'and who you say it to.'

'I know who the House of Barir is,' sneered the eunuch, looking at Omar, 'or who it *was*. Old money. A manta ray with a modified spleen system and gills that filter salt. Not so difficult. The witches that walk the dunes with the nomads no doubt consider salt-fish quite a feat of sorcery out in the borderlands. Here in the Jahan we are not impressed with such petty trickery.'

Omar and Boulous followed the eunuch down a passage lined with mesh-gated doors, each giving onto a lifting room that appeared to lead deeper into the catacombs beneath the palace. They passed by the doors to the lower levels, however, and the eunuch took out a punch card tied to the end of a chain from under his robes. Advancing with the card in his hand he inserted it into a small injection slot by the side of a door at the end of the passage. His key caused the door to retract upwards into the ceiling. Their shadows fell onto a long gantry, and stepping out, Omar saw that they were entering a cavernous space, the gantry emerging fifty feet up, carved out of stone as if a bridge. This was no natural cavern, though – its walls curving in and out like the surf of a sea frozen solid – the cavern floor and the gantry they were standing on the only flat surfaces to be seen. Down below in the blood-red light from wall plates, hundreds of womb mages sat dotted around circular tables, the copper-plated books they were reading from glinting under table lamps. Shelves had been carved out of the cavern's undulating walls, filled with the same type of book Omar had helped destroy with acid in his father's house at Haffa. There must have been hundreds of thousands of the mages' spell books racked below, even the dozens of stone columns rising up to the cavern's roof were carved with shelves and heavy with books. Standing on the stone gantry pushed out like a mooring into this sea of knowledge, Omar watched shelf stackers on rail-mounted harnesses being lowered and raised by slaves working winches to retrieve requested tomes. The vastness of the cavernous space echoed with a low humming as the seated womb mages repeated the letters of their spells, *A, C, G, T,* over and over again in seemingly random patterns. Committing to memory the structures of flesh that dark sorceries could create, their chanting interwoven with a gentle clicking from the turning copper pages.

'So many books,' whispered Omar in awe. *It would take centuries to study them all.*

'This is the Caliph Eternal's private library,' said the eunuch, his chest puffing out with pride. 'His private wealth. It is very old, but it pales in comparison to the size of the order's own library in Mutantarjinn. There, just the indexing halls are larger than this library.'

136

Omar found that hard to believe, that this colossal space carved out under the palace hills had its equal, let alone its superior, in any of the other cities of the empire. Whatever he believed, its hold over him was disturbed by the throb of a familiar soul calling out to him. It couldn't be *her*, not here. But it was. Omar was thrown into confusion by the sight of the female slave who emerged from an open-caged lifting room at the end of the stone gantry along with two servants girls as companions.

'Shadisa!' *Why didn't I feel her sooner, and her presence here is so faint? What have they done to her?*

The look on her face turned from puzzlement to shock as she recognized the young man standing before her in the leather armour of a palace guardsman.

'Shadisa, in the name of god, what are you doing here?'

'I am in the service of Immed Zahharl,' said Shadisa.

'Thank the prophets! You survived the sack of Haffa.'

'Obviously,' said Shadisa, with no small degree of disdain in her voice. 'We were brought to Bladetenbul and sold. Only the men in the town were executed by the troops loyal to the Sect of Razat. Well, *most* of them. Why are you wearing that ridiculous uniform?'

'Quieten your tongue,' said Boulous. 'You speak to an enforcer of the Caliph Eternal's law, and a slave that speaks with such disrespect will find herself with a finger or two less to do her master's bidding.'

'A slave I may be, now, but I am a slave in the service of Immed Zahharl,' said Shadisa haughtily. 'The grand vizier of the Caliph Eternal, high keeper of the Sect of Razat, grand master of the order of womb mages and keeper of the caliph's spells. You would be well advised to ask his permission before you touch me, little jahani. He is a good master and you may lose more than a finger for violating his property.' She nodded towards the eunuch as an indication of what the retainer could expect as payment for his effrontery.

Boulous snorted. 'So you say.'

Shadisa looked at Omar. 'You are the guardsman I have been sent to collect for the creation of a new drak?'

Omar nodded. She was every bit as beautiful as he remembered, but there was something different about her. Something had altered in her soul.

'Well, how the world changes.'

The eunuch bowed and remained on the gantry, letting Shadisa and the servant girls escort Omar and Boulous into the lifting room, the fenced-in platform sinking towards the floor of the library.

'Did you think I was dead?' asked Omar.

'Yes,' said Shadisa, though with little of the joy that Omar had hoped she might display at finding herself proved wrong. 'Most of the men died. The Sect of Razat's followers burnt Haffa to the ground. We saw the flames as we were tied behind the bandits' sandpedes and taken through the desert. As clouded as our minds were with those filthy drugs they injected us with to march across the desert, we watched the column of smoke hanging above the coast for two days.'

'I tried to save you,' said Omar. 'I was coming for you, I saw bandits grab you in the kitchen.'

'A fine job you made of it then,' laughed Shadisa. 'You protected me as well as you protected Gamila when her fiancé's servants were chasing her across the sands.'

'I shall rescue you now, I *will* free you from this life,' promised Omar, taking Shadisa's hand. 'You were not meant to be a slave – you were born the daughter of a freeman. I will buy out your papers of ownership.'

'Was I free back in Haffa?' said Shadisa, pulling away from him. 'A couple of coins a week to work in the great master

Barir's kitchens? Buying food in the market, salting and smoking meats, cooking, washing dishes, serving the men of the house in the evening; up at five, not asleep before midnight. Do you know so little of what my life was really like?'

'Back in the town, did your father . . .?'

'He died too, I suppose,' said Shadisa, sadly. 'Unless he got out in one of the fishing boats. There were thousands of people in the harbour, fighting our own soldiers for the chance to escape. Begging, cursing, offering money to the boats that remained. Every man I knew is dead but you, Omar Barir. You have your damn father's luck, alright. You could be thrown off a slave galley wearing only chains and you would wash up on some island with your shackles slid off, palm trees for your bed, dates to eat and a waterfall to bathe in.'

'I have whittled my own luck with the tip of a scimitar, my great courage and my epic wits,' said Omar. 'And now my luck will be yours, too.'

'Oh, your epic wits,' laughed Shadisa, opening the gate to the lifting room as it shuddered to a halt. 'Everyone in Haffa knew that the House of Barir had attached itself to a dying cause, that it was only a matter of time until the Sect of Razat replaced our own in the Holy Cent. Your father mistook stubbornness for honour, Omar, and our people paid the price with their blood as we always do. Recognizing you as his kin was just another selfish act, easing his conscience for his last few hours, and it should have seen you dead. We all knew our end was coming, but you, you and your epic wits, were lazing about on your water farm. You didn't know and you couldn't have cared less if you did.'

'You are wrong,' said Omar, stung by her words. 'About my father and about me. I don't know how he did it, but I know he saw me placed with the guardsmen. Now I have no house, I serve only the empire and the Caliph Eternal.'

'Then we are alike,' said Shadisa, leading them through the library. 'For I serve a man who serves only the caliph too.'

'I will set you free, Shadisa.'

'Free to do what?' asked the woman. 'To be the wife of a common guardsman? To sit around on a hemp mat in a fortress cell and cook up a stew for the few days in a year when you're not off with the army campaigning? I have seen another life here in the Jahan, Omar. A life of luxury; of water that flows out of a tap without an hour's walk to a well head; of fine gardens and music and colour and splendour. Here,' she tapped her long ornate tunic. 'Silk, worth twenty times my slave price. Which of us apart from Marid Barir's wives could afford to wear such silk back in Haffa?'

'I would make you free,' pleaded Omar.

'A wife of a soldier, or a servant to the grand vizier,' said Shadisa. 'Which of those is more free?'

'You ask the wrong question,' said Boulous. 'You should ask which of those is the right course under heaven?'

'I have only been a slave for a few months, unlike you, little jahani,' said Shadisa. 'But I have been a woman for all of my life. I know which is the better course.'

Omar reeled in shock at her attitude. This was not the reunion he had dreamed of during the long, tiring hours of sword practice, during the hard days he had spent cleaning pistol barrels and oiling drak saddles. A grateful Shadisa falling into his arms as he beat off the slavers who had captured her was what he had imagined. How could she have fallen in love with the luxury of the grand vizier's service so easily? She had never cared about such things back in Haffa. Plenty of the great house's female servants had made it perfectly clear that a mere slave like Omar could never provide such luxuries and was therefore of no interest to them, but never Shadisa – this was not her. *Has the grand vizier, this Immed*

Zahharl, bewitched her? Had Shadisa fallen under the chief minister's spell as easily as Boulous had implied that the Caliph Eternal himself had?

He lay his fears for her aside and followed the girl. Shadisa led Omar and Boulous to an archway bordered by towering stone shelves, the copper plates of the spell books looking as if they were slicked by blood in the crimson twilight. She bade them sit on a bench cut into an alcove while she went to fetch Immed Zahharl, leaving the two of them under the watchful gaze of the other two servant girls.

'So, your pretty friend serves Immed Zahharl,' Boulous whispered to Omar. 'Immed Zahharl himself – he should not come to personally collect the blood of a drak rider.'

'He wants to see me,' said Omar, speaking softly. 'To observe what an unbelievingly handsome fellow the last son of the House of Barir is for himself.' He nodded towards the two slaves standing sentry over them. 'That pair served in my father's house too. The grand vizier sends us a message with their presence, don't you think, Boulous? That a certain quick-witted hero of your acquaintance who currently wears a guardsman's riding leathers, should really be wearing a slave's robes, or a corpse's shroud.'

'I see that Master Uddin's teaching has not been totally in vein,' noted Boulous, dryly.

'You know the funny thing about playing the fool?' said Omar. 'People ignore a slave who is clumsy and stupid. They do not expect much of him. They don't ask him to achieve anything too complex.'

Boulous grunted, as if in understanding. 'Master Uddin said something to me in your first week at the citadel. He said, "There, Boulous, goes the best actor who will never appear under the lamps of the imperial theatre company. The very best."'

Omar shrugged. 'Have I won your applause?'

'If you can remember where the actor begins and the act ends, I think it will be very wise for a fool of a freed slave to greet the grand vizier,' whispered Boulous. 'Your existence in our order is already an affront to his schemes. Give him a face to match what that slave girl you like so much has probably said about you.'

'Shadisa would never betray me,' whispered Omar. He imagined drawing his scimitar and plunging it into the grand vizier's gut. *Nothing personal – no more personal than unseating my house and supplanting our sect in the Holy Cent.*

Shadisa returned accompanied by a wiry thin man with an intricately oiled and curled beard hanging off his slim cheeks. By the cut of his expensive purple clothes and Shadisa's respectful distance behind him, Omar marked this as the man responsible for his house's destruction. Confirming Omar's suspicions, both the slaves watching them dropped to their knees, Omar followed Boulous's lead in giving a low bow to the man.

'The last son of the House of Barir,' said the man in a purring, silky voice. 'And following such a traditional calling, too: the imperial guardsmen. Nobles, always rushing to push their sons forward for the guards.'

Omar stared into the grand vizier's strangely cruel, calculating gaze. Eyes so wide and intense, but with heavy hoods that looked as though they were trying to press his eyelids down into a sleepy slumber. 'I like waving a sword about, grand vizier. It is easy work compared to what Master Barir had me doing on his water farm.'

'And now you're to wave it about on top of a drak.' Immed Zahharl's lips curled in amusement. 'Down here, everyone prefers to use the title grand mage. Only in the palace above is it grand vizier, or high keeper if I am in one of the Sect of Razat's temples.'

'Truly,' said Omar, letting an almost genuine note of awe creep into his voice, 'you are a great man.'

He seemed amused by this. 'So it seems. My airships have given the Caliph Eternal command of the very heavens themselves. His bounty is merely in proportion to my labours for his glory.'

Zahharl led them to a round chamber. There was a horizontal steel slab as its centre, surrounded by a ring of lamps giving off a more intense form of the blood-red light that seemed to pervade the womb mages' domain. Shadisa and the other two slaves stayed by the door to the chamber. Boulous shifted nervously from boot to boot within the circle of light.

Zahharl looked at Boulous. 'You have seen this done before, jahani?'

'I have, grand mage.'

'You will assist your noble guardsman in training. I would not wish to spill *too* much of his blood this afternoon.'

Boulous ignored the mage's sarcasm and helped Omar onto the metal slab, then secured the leather wrist and ankle ties around Omar's limbs.

'Do not move,' warned Boulous. 'Clean cuts must be made. Struggle and you will bleed greatly.'

'A pity that your father was not more progressive in his vision,' said Immed Zahharl, moving behind a lectern-like bank of machinery at Omar's feet and twisting at controls hidden from Omar's angle of vision. 'You could have had a commission in the new Imperial Aerial Squadron.'

'Do they serve good food, grand mage?' Omar coughed, trying to keep a look of panic from his face as a metal globe started to descend from a recess in the ceiling above. 'To be frank with you, the rations up in the fortress are foul.'

'In the years ahead they'll be dining on the fruits of many victories,' said Zahharl. He twisted the controls and a series of sharp razored tools and syringes pushed out of the iron ball. 'But this is time for the old ways. Flesh of your flesh, blood of your blood.'

Omar flinched and the sphere swept down and jabbed painfully at his restrained arms, cutting an incision on his biceps.

'Your flesh must be blended inside the arnay ball with the essence of the drak we are to create for you. Too little human flesh and the producer's womb will reject the drak embryo. The drak will be you, Omar Barir, and you will be your drak. Is that not a fine thing? That is our magic.'

Omar yelled as one of the syringes on the globe found a vein in his leg and the arnay ball drank from him.

'Too much of it, and well . . .' the grand mage shrugged. 'That would be unfortunate. Are there any body parts you don't use much?' The globe glided up towards Omar's groin and he saw the metal arm bolted into the back of the cutter machine quiver as if in anticipation.

Don't think of the blade, think of the drak that will be born mine from this ritual. A drak, fine and strong, a drak which might allow guardsmen to mount him, but will only fly like the wind for me, its mind and mine as one creature as we soar. Don't think of the blade. A flying war machine. Unstoppable, invincible.

'Your slave, Shadisa,' Omar's voice came out in a tremor. 'I would buy her papers of ownership from you.'

A knife-like thing on the globe nicked his skin in surprise, Zahharl standing like a wraith at the other end of the bench. 'This is an ancient and hallowed rite, last son of Barir. It is said that Ben Issman himself created the first drak on this very table millennia ago, and during this most blessed rite, you wish to haggle over a slave girl with the second most wealthy man in the empire? Is this a souk?'

'Thank you for my drak, grand mage, but I would have the girl too. I would have Shadisa for my wife.'

'Thank the Caliph Eternal and our foolish traditions for your drak,' said Zahharl. He glanced back at Shadisa. 'Do you know this dolt of a farm hand?'

She nodded.

'And would you marry him?'

She shook her head. 'Our time finished many years ago. Everything that was mine in that life ended for me when Haffa was razed to the ground.'

Shadisa, you fool, what are you doing? You can't choose a slave's life with him over me. What foul magic has he used to cloud your mind? He has done something to you, that's why I couldn't sense your soul until you were right under my nose.

'In this matter, I think my slave is far cleverer than her perspective suitor.' He played with the controls and the sphere dug into Omar's thighs, the young man shouting in pain through clenched teeth.

'A pound of flesh for your drak – that's an old bargain. But for this finely formed and highly intelligent slave, I'll take twice my weight in gold as her price.'

The globe retracted back into the ceiling and Boulous undid the arm and ankle restraints, one of the three slaves coming forward bearing a tray of bandages that the retainer used to staunch the cuts and wounds on Omar's body.

'Unfortunately for you, the days when a guardsman could earn such booty during a campaign are in the past,' laughed the grand vizier. 'The future belongs to others, last son of Barir. The old days are never coming back. That's a lesson you should learn from Shadisa here.' He snapped his fingers and Shadisa and the other two women from Omar's hometown followed him out and left Omar and the retainer alone in the chamber. Her departure from his life again was almost more than he could stand, an abscess stabbing in his soul. *How many more times am I going to have to lose her?*

'A little too good an actor,' said Boulous, tightening the compress around Omar. 'A little too good an act.'

If I play the fool so well, it is only because she makes one of me every time she stands close to me.

'I have agreed a price,' said Omar. 'And I have kept my life to earn it, and I have the man who would see me dead walking away thinking that I am a fool.'

'He is not the only one,' whispered Boulous. 'There is something you need to know about Immed Zahharl, but not here. I will tell you back on the surface when we are safely out of here. Now that you have met him, there is a dark secret that you must be told . . .'

CHAPTER EIGHT

Jack watched First Lieutenant Westwick walk across to where he and Master Cardsharp Oldcastle were waiting on the brow of the rocky slope, standing sentry over the Cassarabian prisoners on the floor of the valley below along with the other sailors from the *Iron Partridge*. She stood for a second silhouetted against the pall of smoke, the boom of explosions from the mined vessel crackling away just out of sight. The empire's remaining airship had been scuttled beyond repair, and gone with the *Kochava Saar* was any chance of the crew collecting the prize money that should have been their due from her capture. *Is she the most hated person on the airship now, I wonder, or is that still me?*

'Keep an eye on the prisoners, Mister Keats,' said the first lieutenant.

'They're licked,' said Oldcastle. 'Good and proper.'

'They know what's waiting for them,' said the first lieutenant, pointing towards the Benzari warriors whooping and hollering as they approached to take custody of the enemy crew. 'Tribal hospitality with the slim hope of a prisoner exchange or someone

147

back in the empire making their hostage price. Men without hope are men without fear.'

Westwick walked down the slope to greet the lead riders and Oldcastle muttered, 'I think they know who to be afraid of here, lass.'

Jack saw the prisoners at the head of the column shy away from the female lieutenant, jostling back towards the marines' bayonets rather than staying close to Westwick at the foot of the slope. The first horsemen to arrive began galloping wildly around the enemy sailors, singing a fierce whistling song and shooting their rifles into the air. Their Benzari marines started waving their navy carbines in response until the giant captain of marines cursed them for savages and they quickly fell silent. Jack had noticed the wiry little marines were treating Henry Tempest like their own god now, a god of war given flesh. His commands were no longer orders, they were the word of tribal scripture.

'Ah, that's bad,' said Oldcastle.

'The marines seem to be learning navy discipline fast enough,' said Jack.

'Not our marines, lad,' said Oldcastle. He pointed to the wildly circling riders. 'Them! Look at their guns. Brown Bess pattern rifles, freshly minted, and no doubt right off the back of our Corps of Supply's wagons. If we're openly supplying Benzaral with army rifles, that can only mean one thing.'

Jack was about to ask what, but Westwick returned with a sun-faded copy of the *Middlesteel Illustrated News* under her arm.

'It's begun then,' said Oldcastle.

Westwick nodded and handed the newspaper to the master cardsharp to read.

'Ah, this is a week old,' said the officer, flicking through the pages. 'Parliament imposed a wave of import duties on Cassarabian goods. The first traders that came up north along the caravan road refused to pay our taxes. A temperance movement mob attacked their jinn traders in the upland towns, took axes to their barrels and burnt the mortal alcohol in the street, and then they sent the empire's merchants scampering back over the border tarred and heathered. Our newspapers are calling it the Great Jinn War. Great for their wicked sales, not so good for the poor devils who'll be doing the dying and the bleeding for their stories.'

Behind them, the anchor cables holding the *Iron Partridge* above the hill-line started to vibrate as her engine cars tested their propellers before launch.

'Then we were already at war when we engaged their two airships,' said Jack.

There was a strange hissing sound from the armed sailors on the slopes as the news of hostilities spread, the kind of ugly noise a Jack Cloudie would make when whistling through clenched teeth.

'Stop that disgusting sound!' the first lieutenant shouted down the slope. She drew her pistol. 'Captain of marines, any sailor you find making that foul noise is to be arrested and held for flogging.'

'What is it?' Jack whispered to Oldcastle. 'Why are they doing that?'

'In times of war,' said Oldcastle, 'Admiralty House triples the prize money for a captured vessel.' He nodded towards the waves of heat and smoke rising up from behind the hills. 'We've just blown up a small fortune, Mister Keats. If you can find me an unhappier ship in the navy right now, I'll crack the blessed shell in your gun's breech and mix the charge with tonight's rum ration.'

The hissing from the crew was subsiding, like an angry snake sliding away to bide its time before coming back during darkness to strike.

'We're going to war with Cassarabia over some spilt drink?' Jack said in disbelief.

Oldcastle clapped Jack on the back. 'Now I know you've been in a tavern before, lad. All the finest fights start over a spilt drink. No need to play gently in Benzaral's disputed acres now, lad. We're heading over the border and sailing for Cassarabia proper. Into the bloody empire for some bloody action.'

Oh, fine. No prize money, but plenty of chances to die in action. They might as well appoint the first lieutenant as our morale officer. Jack stared at the downcast enemy sailors trudging away surrounded by Benzari horsemen. As prisoners of war their position seemed miserable, but at least they had survived. It seemed that the master cardsharp was going to have plenty of opportunities to make good on his promise to get Jack killed in action.

A whole war full of them.

Jack's dreams were normally shapeless, formless things; flashes of memories and movement like treacle, and this one had started no differently. But clarity, terrible clarity, was coming, like sunlight streaming through parting clouds – his father on his sickbed in the debtors' prison, telling Jack in between hacking coughs that the burden of being head of the family was going to be on his shoulders soon. All thoughts of his son's engineman training forgotten, the fever running so high, Jack's father was no longer aware that the farm and its lands had long since been sold off – trying to make Jack promise that he would find good positions for his two younger brothers when he took over management of the estate.

His brothers so young they had come to look on the four high walls of the debtors' prison as home. Their bewildered looks as the three of them were cast out of its gates – the family's debts annulled after the funeral. Then long weeks of being moved on by shopkeepers angry at finding the three of them sleeping in the doorway, running from the constables of Middlesteel, one step ahead of the vagrancy laws and the brutal, enforced care of the poorhouse. They were falling away from him, Jack's deathbed promise to his father stretched paper-thin by circumstance. Every job he tried to take on paying just pennies when the cost of life was measured in shillings and crowns. It was like being back on the farm when it all started to go wrong. Failed harvest after failed harvest. Debts. His mother and father arguing about having to let the tenant farmers go.

Fewer hands. More work. Their clothing growing frayed, the paint peeling from their house, fences on the land unrepaired and then the fields unploughed. Their mother dying of an old age arrived early, buried by worries. Not enough to feed all of them, going hungry for his brothers' sakes, a little more tired and weary every day. Until he was falling, falling out of the airship and tumbling through a sky without ground. They were gone.

'Alan! Saul!' Jack yelled, his clothes whipping in the wind, the air fierce and angry as he fell. He raised his hands towards the distant shadow of the airship, but there was no help, only the distant jeers of Master Engineer Pasco. *Thief. Thief.*

Spinning through the air, the storm playing with him. No mercy, only the black mote of an eagle growing larger and larger, talons outstretched. But as it got closer Jack could see this was no bird – it was all steel and spikes, a moving machine of wings and razors, twice as long as Jack's falling, flailing body.

'Do you know me?' hissed the machine, a beak of reinforced steel needling closer towards Jack as it spoke.

'You are a Loa,' said Jack. 'One of the steammen gods.'

'Not just any mere Loa,' hissed the machine as it looped

about the falling boy. 'I am Lemba of the Empty Thrusters, the spirit of the sky.'

'Save me,' begged Jack, tumbling wildly as the Loa darted after him. 'Pull me back to the airship.'

'Why should I, little godless softbody? You who trespass into my realm in your ridiculous bags of lighter-than-air gas. And now there are two of your kind's nations in my heavens, flinging iron balls at each other and filling the skies with smoke and noise. How am I to choose which of you to cast down? Maybe both, maybe both shall be my choice.'

There was blackness below the sky's blue: icy blackness rather than ground. He was pitching towards his oblivion. 'Save me,' called Jack, 'and I will help you.'

'Help me, then,' said the Loa, rolling in the gale and clamping a hold on Jack's body with its hard, biting metal manipulator arms. Tighter and tighter. Jack yelled in agony, as he was pulled out of the dive and accelerated upwards towards his airship.

'I wish to hear music.'

'I have no instrument to play,' cried Jack.

They were travelling so fast Jack's eyes had difficulty opening against the wall of wind driving into his face.

'Oh, but you do,' said the Steamo Loa, opening its manipulator talons and letting Jack arc out. He was above the *Iron Partridge* now, sailing down towards its frill of mortar tubes and the vessel was blasting out a tune like an organ grinder.

'Play,' the Steamo Loa called as Jack tumbled towards the mortar tubes. 'Play!'

There was a tiny glint of light in the darkness of the tubes, the light of – Coss Shaftcrank's vision plate staring over him as he jerked upright in his hammock. He was in the transaction-engine chamber, waves of pain streaming down his back from the flogging he had endured.

'You were just dreaming,' said Coss. 'And calling out in your sleep.'

Jack rubbed at his temples. 'I never normally dream.'

'Everyone dreams,' said Coss. 'Even my people. It's probably that you don't normally remember them.'

'I wish I hadn't remembered this one.'

Coss listened to what Jack recalled of the dream, the steamman's vision plate juddering in surprise as the young sailor described his meeting with Lemba of the Empty Thrusters. 'You have described this Loa just as he appears to my people, Jack softbody. Truly, the Loas are walking your dreams.'

'He must have been aiming for your noggin and missed,' said Jack.

'Kiss my condensers, but the spirits of my people's ancestors are not sponges tossed at a village mayor's face in a summer fair,' said Coss. 'Loas do not miss; Lemba of the Empty Thrusters only crosses the threads of the great pattern with purpose.'

'If it was giving me a headache to go along with the stripes on my back, he may consider his purpose achieved.'

'This is unprecedented,' said Coss. 'I have never heard of one of our gods visiting a softbody as if he was a steamman throwing his cogs at prayer.'

'It's just a dream, old steamer. They never make sense.'

'This one makes more sense than you seem to know. If you had taken the time to read through my newssheet cuttings concerning the air-yard trials of the *Iron Partridge*,' explained Coss in irritation, 'you would know that one of the unnecessary flourishes this vessel should be capable of is playing the Jackelian national anthem using air drawn through her mortar tubes.'

Playing music . . . Jack looked at the steamman in astonishment. 'You are joking?'

'I am entirely serious, Jack softbody. The *Iron Partridge* failed to do it, of course. One of the writers watching the vessel's trials described the ship's wailing in their newssheet as the cat-o'-nine-tails' song, but a far better show than her gunners' accuracy.'

'That's one song I've had enough of,' said Jack, his spine burning at the thought of the flogging he had received. He rubbed his throbbing temples in annoyance. Whatever music the steamman gods had in mind for Jack Keats, they would have to sing along to it without him.

Now he was awake, Jack was glad to be out of the hammock; even the thin hanging fabric was rubbing raw against his back. But the start to the day's roster of duties was swiftly circumvented by the appearance of the master cardsharp, who bore a more pressing appointment for Jack.

'I need you, lad,' wheezed the old officer. 'It's Captain Jericho – he's feeling poorly and he's holed up in his cabin and not in a mood to come out.'

'Do you want me to fetch the ship's surgeon for him?'

John Oldcastle shook his head. 'It's not that sort of malady. It's the black dog chasing him, a mood as dark as thunder. When he's up he's up, and when he's down he's down. I've been trying to rouse the skipper out of his moonless humours for half an hour, but he won't even come to the door of his cabin for me.' The old officer saw the look on Jack's face. 'He'll come to the door for you, Mister Keats. He still feels bad about you taking your stripes. The ship needs its captain and he just needs a little winding up to get him started. A few laps of the lifting chamber will see him set back on the mend. We'll do it mortal discreetly, won't we – no need to spook the rest of the crew.'

Jack did as he was bid. The gods of the steammen wanted him to make music and the master cardsharp wanted him to coax the captain out of his dark humours – everyone on the ship had something for him to do, it seemed. Jericho might, as the master cardsharp had intimated – and their recent improvised engagement proved – be a genius at the art of commanding a war vessel, but the flame of his genius was flickering erratically.

In many ways, their skipper was as broken as his vessel, and this was just the first of many times that Jack was sent down to bring Jericho out of his cabin. And always the captain came, shambling and ill shaven, and getting him out and ready to command the vessel was much as the master cardsharp had described it – a matter of slowly winding the captain up. Engaging Jericho in talk through the cabin door, getting him to open it, easing him into his uniform and walking him to one of the vessel's two massive lifting chambers, where he would pace his way towards some sense of normality. Jericho would walk out his moods along the lifting chamber, marching the carper walkways between the gas cells as if the very act of driving himself forward and counting the rails along the walkways, would drive out the demons that haunted his mind. They worked too. Each mile driven forward stiffened the man and filled his uniform with command authority, until the doubting miserable wreck was replaced with a towering ship's captain, his voice able to boom commands and direct the *Iron Partridge* with the skill of a fencing master directing a rapier.

This, Jack came to realize – perhaps even more than his talent with the ship's transaction engines – was why he had been fished out of a hangman's noose at Bonegate jail by the master cardsharp and the menacing first lieutenant. Perhaps it was why Westwick had been so insistent on enforcing her whims upon the skin of Jack's spine – to make sure Jericho would come to the cabin door when Jack needed to call.

Patching up their broken ship and patching up their broken captain.

'What else do you have to tell me about Immed Zahharl?' demanded Omar as soon as he and Boulous had reached safety.

'I can see how powerful he is. Grand mage of the sorcerers' order. The high keeper of the Sect of Razat. A grand vizier with the ear of the Caliph Eternal. Making an enemy of any one of those positions would be enough to crush me twice over. What couldn't you tell me about him back down in the palace?'

Boulous walked beside Omar, as they climbed the stairs back up to the guardsmen's fortress in the crags above the palace.

'It is his dark tastes,' said Boulous. 'That girl you are so fond of is a bigger fool than you are, if she truly thinks that Immed Zahharl is a good master. He brings in many female slaves to his household, and when he tires of their novelty, he drags them to his bed and he strangles them with a silken rope he leaves hanging there.'

'You are wrong!' said Omar. The retainer had to be mistaken.

'The whole Jahan knows of his depraved pleasures,' said Boulous. 'I have lost count of the women he has purchased who have vanished from his bedchamber. He fills his personal court with killers and sadists just like himself; men who share his evil tastes. He uses some of his victims' flesh in his rituals, for the biologicks he creates – the rest of their remains he dissolves in the secret vats of the womb mages. The slaves are never found or seen again.'

'You are wrong!' Omar repeated.

'Slaves talk among themselves, Omar Barir, you remember that, don't you?'

'The Caliph Eternal would not tolerate such a thing.'

'Zahharl is the high keeper of a sect, he is grand vizier, he is grand mage,' spat Boulous. 'Never has a single man wielded such concentrated power within the empire. I told you, the Pasdaran saw him for what he was, and when they tried to remove him from office, it was the secret police that were toppled, not Immed Zahharl.'

'Shadisa!'

Boulous grabbed Omar's arm and restrained him from running back down the fortress steps. 'Why do you think I waited until now to tell you this?'

'I have to warn her, tell her about Zahharl,' said Omar. 'She must run away, leave him.'

Boulous shook his head. 'Did you not hear her words, cadet? She doesn't want anything to do with you.'

'I shall warn her,' said Omar. 'Shadisa loved me once and with or without me in her life, she can still live. With my warning she will at least know to watch out for him.'

'She will never accept you,' said Boulous.

'You do not know that.' *I'll save her, then she'll have to know what I feel for her.*

'Of course I do, I am a jahani,' said Boulous. 'I was raised as a slave in imperial service. Without tribe or house or sect, we are seen as a clean pair of hands, owing everything to the state. Jahani have gone on to command armies and fleets for the Caliph Eternal; as administrators we hold power throughout the empire – but no matter how high we rise, how much money and power we accumulate, no daughter of a respectable freeman would ever want to see their blood tainted by a marriage to someone such as me. It does not matter that your position is now reversed with hers. You were once a slave and she was once the daughter of a freeman; she can never forget that.'

'I have made myself worthy of her. I am a guardsman, not a slave.'

'Whatever you do in the future, you cannot change the past,' said Boulous.

Omar threw his hands up in despair. 'If that is how it is to be, what can you hope for?'

'I will end up as an administrator in a nice fat province like Seyadi or Fahamutla, where the local sultan will know I am one of the empire's eyes and will tread carefully around me,' said Boulous. 'I will grow old and fat and the province's courtiers will elbow each other for the privilege of dropping dates into my senile mouth as I lounge in the shade of a fountain.'

'No, anything is possible,' insisted Omar. 'At the start of the year I was tending the tanks of a water farm as a slave; today I have the grand vizier himself whisking my blood in his sorcerer's cauldron to create a drak fledgling for me. In such a world, what is winning the heart of a woman like Shadisa, when there is a fellow as handsome and cunning as me ready to fight for her?'

'You will see. That is, if Immed Zahharl doesn't create a drak for you that is so sickly and blind it flies into a cliff on your first outing.' Boulous pointed to the sun setting over the capital. 'Zahharl will be back in his pavilion inside the palace now.'

'Then the grand vizier's staff are lucky, for they will have an extra guardsman to patrol their corridors tonight!'

'This is no skirmish for you to be fighting in,' Boulous pleaded. 'When Immed Zahharl begins his war against the Jackelians, he will use the Imperial Aerial Squadron to consolidate what little military power he doesn't already control into his hands. When that happens, he won't be the grand vizier of the empire, he will *be* the empire. That is what we must fight. What is the life of one fool of a slave girl against such an outcome?'

Omar pointed down towards the palace as he started to run back down. 'The Jahan.'

The world.

'I can't cover for your absence too long,' Boulous shouted down. 'You damned fool.'

But even as he said it, he knew it was the sort of foolhardiness that the guardsmen had once been famous for, from an age when they drew their blades first and only calculated the odds afterwards.

Boulous called out again, 'When you get to the grand vizier's pavilions, ask to speak to a slave woman called Nudar.'

'Who is she?' Omar shouted back.

'A better woman than the one you are going for. I pray that she will be able to save you from yourself long enough for you to come to your senses.'

Boulous watched Omar disappear from sight; the last glint of the sun's gleaming falling upon his scimitar.

The old days were coming back after all.

John Oldcastle stood up from where he was helping Coss and one of the Benzari stokers patch a line of boiler pipes, noticing Jack's limp as he entered the transaction-engine chamber. 'Have you slipped in the lifting chamber, lad?'

Jack shook his head. 'I was walking down a corridor on the lower deck with that upland lieutenant.'

'McGillivray,' said the master cardsharp. 'He's a charmless dog, alright. Tosses his grog ration over the side every night and frowns on gambling. If he were walking the decks as the blessed captain, we'd all be sailing on a dry ship. Did he give you a kick for my sins, Mister Keats?'

'No,' said Jack. 'I was passing by the rudder room and the lieutenant was walking the other way when a cannon ball came rolling down the corridor – an incendiary round, unsecured – we both had to jump out of the way and it staved in the bulkhead. I almost twisted my ankle trying to jump over it.'

'The magazine is three decks up from where you were,' said Coss looking up from the boiler's pipes, his voicebox quivering with surprise. 'Vault my valves, but what was a round doing rolling loose down there?'

'Ah, you won't find that trick in any of those manuals of official airship service you bought from the stationer's stalls back home,' said Oldcastle to the steamman. 'It's called "rolling shot"; a brutal little prank an unhappy crew likes to play on their officers to draw attention to their grievances. Someone was trying to play skittles using you as their mortal target. We're sailing close to a mutiny here, lads. I had better let Jericho know. He's respected well enough by our Jack Cloudies, but if the crew are rolling shot at the likes of McGillivray, we're in for a choppy ride on the other side of the Cassarabian border.'

Jack watched the master cardsharp leave the transaction-engine chamber and wondered whether the sailors' rolling shot had been aiming for the upland lieutenant. Jack was unpopular enough with the crew himself, that brute Pasco spreading the tale far and wide that the loss of their prize vessel was the result of the first lieutenant's pique at Jack avoiding the full ninety lashes during his flogging. Mutiny. *That would do for us all. Wouldn't it be ironic to travel all this way and end up on the wrong end of a hangman's noose after all?*

'As if we didn't have enough problems,' said Jack. 'A whole empire full of hostile airships waiting for us and we've got to pick a fight among ourselves too.'

'By my rotten regulators, that's not our only problem, Jack softbody,' said Coss. 'There's a good reason why our boilers are presently in such a bad shape up here.' The steamman led Jack to the row of punch-card desks overlooking the transaction-engine pit and indicated a long stream of paper tape that had been printed out. 'Read that. We were drawing too much power during the battle. The pipes and boiler were over-pressurized. We should have throttled the engines up to full power rather than running them cold; we're lucky we didn't blow half the chamber away the way we were holding back the calculation drums.'

Jack picked up the paper output and began leafing through it. 'But we had the automated systems completely nailed down. We shouldn't have been pushing anywhere near our capacity or tolerances . . .'

'Nailed down, yes,' said Coss. 'But it was as if all the

automated processes were running anyway, even though they weren't connected into the physical flight mechanisms of the ship. I have never seen anything like this, Jack softbody.'

'I think I have,' said Jack, leafing through the tape. 'Back in Middlesteel there was a horseless carriage that used to drive along the streets outside where I lived, one of the big expensive ones, with a driver taking a child to school every morning. The boy would sit in the back and pretend to steer it. Every day he would come past, working his imaginary controls.'

Jack didn't say how much he had envied the child, still going to school, instead of running through the streets, thieving and robbing for enough money to eat.

'The child . . .' said Coss.

'The *ship*,' said Jack. 'She was meant to fly and fight under full automation, and that's what she was trying to do during the battle. She was working the controls even though she wasn't connected to them.'

'But the *Iron Partridge* never worked,' said Coss. 'In all her original proving flights, her automation consistently failed. The crew always ended up having to assume control and many of them were killed trying to take back manual command. Yet the results on that tape indicate a perfect flight, at least in simulation.'

Jack fingered the thick manuals chained to the punch-card desks, before delving back into the rolls of tape. *Yes, there is a mystery here.* Page after page in the manuals detailing the work the navy's engineers had carried out re-rigging the automated systems for manual control. None of the automated systems had worked when the ship had first been tested in the air – yet here they had been during the battle, ticking along in simulated parallel with the crew's manual handling of the vessel and seemingly running without fault.

'Look at this,' said Jack leafing down to a line of gunnery

tables and trajectory plots on the tape. 'After I opened up the magazine to the mortar tubes, our transaction engines were plotting a firing solution. Here are the orders to load another twenty shells and here's the firing solution, right on top of the prize vessel's lid. We would have opened up the Cassarabian airship's spine if the mortar tubes had been running under the ship's automated control.'

'I can show you the original naval board's report of enquiry,' said Coss. 'It's in my air chest. During the test flights our engine-controlled gunnery proved as good as random. Some of the *Iron Partridge*'s shells even dropped back down on her own hull. If they had been filled with explosives rather than target paint, I doubt we would have a ship to serve in now.'

'And yet here they're perfect,' said Jack. 'It doesn't make sense.'

But, Jack realized, it needed to, and fast. If their ship was becoming unpredictable, if she was undermining the navy's extensive manual jury-rigging, then Jack, Coss and John Oldcastle had to make themselves the masters of the *Iron Partridge* by the time they sailed into their next combat. Failure to do so was going to leave the sun-bleached ribs of the airship as a memento protruding out of the Cassarabian sands.

CHAPTER NINE

Omar returned to the palace. There was a chiming noise resounding through the palace accompanied by an almost carnival atmosphere among the courtiers and staff moving around the wooded grounds. Two silk-robed courtiers came laughing arm-in-arm towards Omar, one of them spilling the contents of an iced cup as he stopped them to ask what they were celebrating.

'Even the palace knows,' laughed the nearest of the courtiers, pointing to the new script flowing along the dome's inner surface. 'It is war.'

'War?' said Omar.

'The heathens in the north,' said the courtier. 'The Jackelians. They have finally provoked the righteous might of the empire.'

'You should be pleased,' said the man's friend. 'There will be many opportunities and promotions for everyone. You will fight for glory and when it is done, we will step in to the new provinces to run them as the Caliph Eternal wills.'

Omar remembered the words the old nomad, Alim, had once uttered when he was cleaning his knife in the shade of the water farm. '*All fights start with two victors. All fights end with one proven right, and one proven dead.*'

'Yes,' whispered Omar, watching the happy pair jump across a water channel to join a group of revellers on the other side of the lawn. 'When it is done.'

The start of a war. What more perfect time for Shadisa to disappear from the palace? When every sinew of the caliph's civil service and the court and the military was focused on victory over their heathen neighbours to the north. No time to look for one of Immed Zahharl's servants disappeared from the grand vizier's devious clutches; perhaps not even time enough to notice she had gone missing – until it was too late.

Following various courtiers' directions towards the pavilion of Immed Zahharl, Omar found himself heading towards the very centre of the Jahan. Protected from the elements by the almost magical dome high above, the buildings here had none of the practicality of old master Barir's great house. No need to keep out the fierce winter storms that would roll off the sea and smash into the harbour town nestled against the lee of the cliffs. The memory of it almost made Omar wistful for his old life. How he would go to sleep listening to the screech of the gulls and wake up to the crack of lightning, watching the great dark storm front sliding in across the ocean. There was no need inside the Jahan for protection against lashing rains coming from one direction and drifting sands from the other. Here, the pavilions were made of crystal-blown walls engraved with flower motifs and stylized borders; curves of glass with just the occasional columns of marble to anchor the onion-topped towers.

Made oblivious to the structures' beauty by familiarity, the staff of the court at least gave some semblance of business-like efficiency. Officials, some in military uniforms, strode about with papers and plans rolled under their arms.

Commissions for the coming hostilities? Plans of supply, perhaps? Farris Uddin had lectured at great length about the logistics and supplies needed for any successful military venture. An army that was not provisioned adequately would quickly lose more men to sickness and disease than to the rifle fire of any enemy column. The organization that went into such things was the empire's greatest weapon, a secret weapon, almost, given how the tedium of such detailed planning made it easy for incautious warriors to ignore it in favour of the glory and fury of a full cavalry charge.

Remembering the name of the slave Boulous had suggested he seek out, Omar asked a gardener tending a bed of orchids outside the grand vizier's pavilion if he knew a woman called Nudar. The gardener nodded and duly went off, returning with a woman so short that Omar at first mistook her for a child. There was no mistaking the lines of her ancient weathered face, hair faded to silver and tied back in tight buns – and judging by her features and pale skin, another slave with Jackelian blood. Taken together with her tiny size she looked as if she might have been born old, but this, Omar suspected, was only his imagination at work. She must have grown old in service.

'Boulous told me that I should seek you out,' said Omar to the old woman. 'He said you were to be trusted.'

'He said that, did he, guardsman?' muttered the old slave, her knowing eyes appraising him. 'Well, he is right enough. Old Nudar was once wet nurse in the jahani academy and as much a mother as he and hundreds of other jahani ever had. My boys, my darling boys. All grown up now and scattered across the empire. No little jahani to bounce on my knee now. How is Boulous, little Boulous, so quick and clever?'

'Not so little now,' said Omar.

'No, not so little. He'll make old Nudar proud one day.

He'll rise further than them all.' She grasped Omar's hand suspiciously and turned it over in her fingers.

'Can you read my future from my palm?' asked Omar.

Her response was a gurgle like wet laughter. 'No, but your past I find puzzling. Your hand is far too tanned to be that of a nobleman's son and your sword practice calluses are new, yet formed across such skin as you only develop from years of manual labour. An aqueduct line worker?'

'Water farmer,' said Omar. He looked at the woman with a newfound respect. She was as canny as a witch, but could she really be trusted when the colour of her skin suggested she had come from Jackelian stock?

'I was not taken by force from Jackals by slave traders,' said the woman, seeing the direction of Omar's gaze and running a prune-like hand along her chalk-white cheeks. 'I was found on the slopes of a mountain by a caravan, abandoned as a baby, when they took pity on my cries. Oh yes, it's not only our nomads that do that. Uplanders like big strapping sons to carry on their crofts too. Old Nudar was lucky, as are you, I think. There are not many ex-slaves among the ranks of those who patrol the palace – you are the first I have seen.'

'There are few men in the guards with my prodigious talents.'

'Well then, prodigiously talented one, what do you need my assistance for?'

Omar told her the story, or as much as he dared. Of his and Shadisa's origins in the far-off town of Haffa and how he had to find Shadisa again to tell her the truth of how her wicked new master really treated his slaves.

Nudar shook her head in astonishment that Omar would risk so much for another slave. 'I don't know who is the bigger fool, a guardsman who would want such a woman, or a woman who would not want such a man?'

'You will take me to her?'

'Old Nudar knows a little more than Boulous in this matter,' said the old woman. 'The girl you seek is already as good as dead.'

'I saw her this afternoon and she was as alive as you or I,' protested Omar.

'Those who would enter the grand vizier's inner circle must first prove their loyalty to him,' said Nudar. 'It is not just the guardsmen who have an initiation ceremony, although I am sure yours is far more honourable than Immed Zahharl's. The rite is murder and I have heard that a new initiate stands willing to take his place in the grand vizier's retinue. The slave you would help escape, Shadisa, is to be the sweetmeat the brutes will toy with tonight in the library of the womb mages, and when they are done, her corpse will disappear into one of their acid vats and all you will be left with are your memories of her.'

Shadisa! How could she have ever thought that the grand vizier was a master who meant well for her? Who would care for her better than I could? Is she such a fool?

'What is the name of the man who would do this to her?' demanded Omar.

Nudar shrugged. 'I do not know. It is not wise to inquire too closely into such things, not in a court where even the secret police's killers can be made to vanish without a trace. I can try to find out for you . . .'

'Do so, and take me to Shadisa,' said Omar.

'Even if you find the man and deal with him, there will be other initiates,' said Nudar. 'The only female slaves who are safe in this place have faces that have seen as many seasons pass as mine.'

'She will not die tonight. I will see to it.' *I saved her before, that evening in the desert outside Haffa, and she did not thank me for it once; let's hope history doesn't repeat itself. It doesn't matter, I'll save her a hundred times if I have to, and carry her away from her murderous rich master screaming and kicking.*

The woman laughed her wet rasping laugh again. 'Well, why not? It's been a long time since I saw such recklessness committed for a motive other than personal gain. Follow me and act as if you are assigned to the pavilion. Swagger, don't waddle like a water farmer trying to conserve enough energy to get through a day's labouring.'

Omar followed the old woman into the pavilion, a series of chambers and courtyards, walls inlaid with abstract frescoes in the traditional style, channels running with water threading through the corridors before veining out to opulent fountains that flaunted the grand vizier's wealth. Omar wondered how Shadisa would react to his presence here. *She has to listen to me this time, doesn't she?* Once he explained the true nature of her duplicitous owner, surely she would feel some gratitude towards him? Trust him enough to spirit her away from the wicked designs of Immed Zahharl?

Omar's thoughts were interrupted by a ripple of awareness that seemed to pass like a breeze through the courtiers and staff in the courtyard he was walking through. Before he could question Nudar as to its cause, he caught his first sight of a phalanx of seven-foot-high grey-skinned giants advancing down a side corridor towards them.

'The Caliph Eternal,' hissed Nudar. 'To your knees, boy.'

All around the courtyard, the staff were dropping to the floor in reverence, and Omar followed their example. Two of the giants were carrying a sedan chair, the windows on either side covered by purple curtains. The other grey-skinned creatures formed a bodyguard marching in a protective square around the ebony-black carriage. The caliph's august presence was heavily concealed, which was just as well, as the stories of those commoners who had lost their heads for staring upon him were legion.

A green-robed courtier marching in front of the sedan chair banged a jewel-headed staff on the marble tiles, making the courtyard echo. 'Make way for his most esteemed majesty, Caliph Eternal Akil Jaber Issman – Emperor of Cassarabia, thunderbolt of heaven, immortal prince of princes, eternal sword of the Holy Cent and protector of the hundred faces of the one true god.'

The caliph's bodyguards might have been dressed as guardsmen in their golden yellow armour, but their phenomenal size and lumpen ugliness indicated they were anything but. Their eyes swept over the courtiers around them as they marched. As well as their swords they carried crossbows so large they wouldn't have looked out of place in the outer circle of a city siege.

Suddenly it came to Omar where he had seen such hides before. Such ugliness briefly surfaced on the waters around Haffa in the hour when the town's fishermen threw the spoiled share of their day's catch back into the harbour. The harbour thrashing with the grey muzzles of . . . 'Sharks!'

'Quiet!' whispered Nudar furiously.

One of the creatures broke away from the caliph's bodyguard and loped towards where Omar and Nudar were kneeling. The shadow of the huge creature fell over them as Omar felt the monster's hand land on the guard of his scimitar, drawing it out an inch as if to check it was genuine. The two nostril slits along the side of its muzzle sniffed at the nape of Omar's neck, warm fetid breath blowing against his hair. The creature made a low grunting noise, as if satisfied, and loped back after the retreating sedan chair.

Omar watched the back of the column disappearing deeper

into the pavilion. 'What was that *thing* doing sniffing my hair?'

'Your sweat,' whispered Nudar, her eyes glancing up from where they had been fixed to the tiles with such intensity that he might have believed the secrets of the world to be engraved on the floor. 'The beyrog was checking that you were a guardsman and authorized to carry a weapon in the palace, not an assassin waiting to attack the Caliph Eternal.'

'How could it know that from my sweat?'

'Your rations up in the fortress carry hidden ingredients,' said Nudar. 'That is why you are confined there for so much of your training. It takes time for your body to begin to sweat like a noble guardsman, giving you command of draks other than the beast that is born from your own blood. Beyrogs can smell steel and the charges of a gun, they can smell poison, and some say that they can smell treason itself. If it had smelt such a weapon on a mere slave like old Nudar, it would have torn me apart.'

That's why my training draks became more compliant the longer I stayed at the citadel. And I thought they were just getting used to me.

'Biologicks,' said Omar, not able to hide his distaste of the dark magic. 'I was not daunted by them, do not think that I was, not even for a moment.'

'You should be, they are the caliph's hand. And who else would you trust if you were the emperor of emperors, ruling for eternity across the ages? Men can be corrupted, even guardsmen like you. Beyrogs are created by the caliph's womb mages to be loyal only to his person. Beyrogs have no family that can be kidnapped to force them to break their vows, they have no desires or lusts other than to serve the caliph, and they obey no orders other than those which comes from his mouth. And why not? Is the Caliph Eternal not the lawful seed of Ben Issman, his name be blessed? It is his wisdom that makes the deserts bloom with crops and keeps the people safe and fed.' Nudar pointed towards the archway through which the beyrogs had disappeared. 'Only the grand vizier's personal servants are allowed into the inner pavilion. Old Nudar can go no further.'

'And guardsmen?'

'The Caliph Eternal's law knows no boundaries, and neither do his guardsmen,' said Nudar. 'At least, not officially. I have heard that the slaves to be murdered are made to await their fate in the hanging garden at the pavilion's centre. Look for your fool of a girl there.'

'Thank you, Nudar.'

'Boulous needs a good friend to keep him safe,' said the old slave. 'If the grand vizier's men catch you with this girl, you will both die and my poor Boulous will have one friend less.'

'He has a good friend who is a legend with a scimitar,' said Omar. 'And I will not die today.'

The old woman nodded and walked away muttering a prayer to Ben Issman's name: a slave's humble prayer.

Omar plunged into the lion's den.

Jack was on the bridge, about to hand a list of automated systems they were having problems suppressing to the captain, when the signals officer received a communication from the crow's nest and picked up the telescope to confirm the sighting. 'Propellers ho, bearing forty degrees to starboard at ten o'clock.'

'Confirmation on her silhouette?' barked the first mate.

'Smaller than fifty feet, she looks like a launch – Jackelian lines.'

'Light her up with the helioscope,' ordered Captain Jericho. 'Standard fleet code. Confirm our name and ask for hers.'

Jack strained for a view of the approaching vessel through the bridge's forward canopy. Confirming their own name was just a formality – there could be no mistaking the lines of the *Iron Partridge* with her strange spine of mortar tubes.

One of the sailors picked up the speaking trumpet and transmitted the captain's orders to crewmen standing duty in the h-station below – the small keel-mounted dome holding a gas-fired helioscope to exchange messages between airships. There was a minute's delay as the communication was flashed across to the approaching airship and her reply sent back.

The signals officer turned in his seat. 'Reply given in well-formed fleet code. RAN *Searcher* requesting dock. Vice-Admiral Tuttle on board.'

Jack winced but didn't give voice to his thoughts. That was the same arrogant arse that had threatened to stop the *Iron Partridge* leaving the airship field back home.

One of the sailors had the fleet list book out on his control desk. 'The RAN *Searcher* is an admiral's packet, sir, attached to the RAN *Trespasser*.'

'The flagship of the Fleet of the South,' said Jericho.

A murmur sounded around the sailors on the bridge and Jack realized why. *A vice-admiral doesn't have the authority to countermand the written admiralty orders held in the captain's safe, but a fully flagged admiral does.* Would their unpopular sorties into Cassarabia soon be over?

The captain nodded thoughtfully. The same notion must have occurred to him. The skipper pointed at Jack and two of the other more junior ratings on the bridge. 'You three with me to the boat bay. Do you know how to pipe a vice-admiral on board, Mister Keats?'

'Master Cardsharp Oldcastle taught the new hands during one of his lessons, sir,' said Jack, falling in behind the captain.

'Then the rascal's probably taught you the tune from some

stockade ditty,' said Jericho. He winked at Jack. 'Lucky for us that Vice-Admiral Tuttle is an inky-fingered Admiralty House politician who normally flies a desk. He'll hardly recognize the difference.'

There were already two stocky Benzari marines standing sentry outside the boat bay hatch, rifles shouldered, when the captain and Jack arrived. The marines' presence around the ship had become a lot more conspicuous after the master cardsharp informed the captain about the shot-rolling incident that had nearly seen Jack and Lieutenant McGillivray scattered like ninepins. Five more marines came trotting along to form an honour guard, while Jack helped a pair of sailors wind open the bay's starboard hangar doors. There was plenty of room inside, the frames of their own three boats – in reality, small semi-rigid pocket airships that could carry up to ten crew in their gondolas – racked and packed on shelves with their small expansion engines, ready for assembly and independent action in less than ten minutes when they were needed to land crew or marines, act as scouts, or exchange sailors between vessels.

Each of the sailors had clipped a line to their belts as they entered the boat bay. Some small protection against an unexpected shift in position and a sudden tumble through the wide open doors, wind whistling in, setting the envelopes of their boats' racked fabric rustling noisily in the blow.

'Prepares for lines,' Jericho shouted over the wind.

'Beware the lines,' called one of the boat bay men.

A second after the warning shout, a lead-weighted line was cast in from outside the *Iron Partridge*, hitting the wooden target against the hangar wall with a bull's-eye. Jack and the other sailors ran in, catching the line before it could tumble back out, carrying the heavy head to a mechanical winch where it was locked in place and the equipment activated.

Her rotors stilled, the vice-admiral's launch was drawn inside the boat bay, still bucking in the sky against the crosswinds outside. Her crew was bustling about the open gondola of the pocket airship, the flash of the vice-admiral's blue uniform visible between the sailors' canvas rain cloaks. Jack and the other two ratings held their whistles at the ready as the launch was winched in. Just as the pocket airship was being tied down, First Lieutenant Westwick joined the reception party, looking about as happy as Jack felt.

The ratings' greeting trilled out as the step-like doors of the small launch dropped to the boat bay floor, Vice-Admiral Tuttle walking down triumphantly, ignoring the red-coated marines shouldering arms with snap-lock precision. He at least had the courtesy to return Captain Jericho's salute.

'So, the evasive captain of our elusive *Iron Partridge.*'

'We weren't expecting company quite so soon, vice-admiral,' said Jericho.

'If you mean how did I find you,' said the admiralty officer, 'we've been bribing those sharp-eyed little devils from the Benzari tribes below to send word to our embassy of every airship they've spotted in the sky. Although I could probably have simply followed the trail of wreckage you've been leaving strewn across our ally's mountains.'

'A successful action,' remarked the first lieutenant.

'Really, my dear lady?' said the vice-admiral. 'An intelligence mission that measures its success in seizing, then burning enemy prize vessels? What a curious notion. Your friends back on the State Protection Board will be *so* pleased.'

Westwick's eyes flashed angrily at the vice-admiral's indiscretion. So, the Jackelian secret police were behind their voyage into Cassarabia. *Does that explain a first lieutenant who seems to think she is the vessel's commander, helped by a master cardsharp who swaps uniforms as easily as he produces the credentials to have me released from custody and press-ganged into the navy?*

'The nature of our mission is sealed as secret and this vessel is still operating under independent command,' said the first lieutenant.

'As inconvenient as it must be for you, I'm afraid a state of war trumps even the favours your board called in across parliament,' said the vice-admiral. 'I carry orders for the *Iron Partridge* to rejoin the Fleet of the South along the Southwest Frontier.'

'This mission is vital,' insisted the first lieutenant.

Captain Jericho nodded in agreement.

'Your mission has been superseded by events, captain. Admiralty House doesn't care two figs where the Cassarabians are finding the celgas to float their vessels. It is enough that they have it, and the point will be rendered moot when we take their fleet on and pound them out of the clouds.' He raised his fingers archly to indicate the boat bay. 'If this clanking carbuncle of a vessel and your crew of press-ganged misfits managed to bring down two of their airships, wholly unsupported, I don't think the entire high fleet will have too much trouble seeing off this Imperial Aerial Squadron of the caliph's.'

'Even Admiralty House can't be so blind,' said Jericho. 'We need to know if they've found a natural vein of celgas to mine or if they've synthesized it, d'you see. At the very least, we need to know if the caliph has enough gas to sell to other enemy nations in an attempt to open up a second front against us.'

'Irrelevant, irrelevant. Superior skymanship, captain, will always win out. We'll certainly discover where they're getting their celgas from the wretches we drag out from the empire's crashed, burning hulls. Finding an airship that can float is one thing; finding hundreds of years of fighting tradition in the men that serve in her is quite another.'

'Only an admiral can countermand my orders for independent action,' said Jericho.

'I'm sure your loyalty to the first lieutenant's paymasters on the board is quite commensurate with the amount they paid to buy you out of debtors' prison,' sneered the vice-admiral. 'And as ironic as I find the sight of a maverick of your notoriety pettifogging on regulations, I took the precaution of making sure I was carrying the admiral's written orders with me.' He flourished a wax-sealed envelope. 'Besides,' he raised a thumb at the two armed sentries posted on the boat bay, 'I am sure that the members of your crew who aren't mercenaries or scraped out from gutters, prison cells and stockades would relish the chance to pick up enemy vessels that are left intact enough to earn prize money. There should be enough of those in the next week or so to keep the poorest of your Jack Cloudies in rum and beer until next winter sets in.'

'And if we join the Fleet of the South,' said Jericho, 'the first two kills of the war go against the admiral's name; I take it our engagement was the opening action of the war?'

'And I was told you could only be relied on to ignore admiralty politics,' smiled the vice-admiral. He looked at the first lieutenant. 'Don't worry, my dear, you'll be able to get back to the normal run of bribery, assassination and skulking around in the shadows soon enough. We'll slip the *Iron Partridge* in the rear of the line of battle and you'll get your chance to see what a direct action looks like. A hard pounding or two and the empire will soon fall back to their natural boundaries. A clean pair of heels, that's what we'll see from the caliph's sand-trotting lackeys.'

Jack watched the look on First Lieutenant Westwick's face

as the vice-admiral stalked out with Jericho in tow. She was clearly thinking about putting that hidden sleeve dagger of hers in the vice-admiral's back, and calculating the chances that she would be able to get away with rolling his corpse off the ship and claiming him lost overboard in a storm. But that wouldn't wear now. Not when the sailors in the boat bay started spreading word of what the vice-admiral had offered. Which the vice-admiral had obviously intended. The chance to ride into battle in their armour-protected tortoise at the back of a squadron. The chance to take the fleet's share of the prize money and sail back to the Kingdom as rich men.

And to be honest, the prospect of such a deal was lifting Jack's heart as much as any man in the boat bay. A quick victory and back to Jackals. Alive, pardoned and with enough money to take his two brothers out of the poorhouse and pay for a new start for the three of them. Only the nagging words of the master cardsharp sounded a warning deep within his mind. *I've never been privy to an easy victory. No, indeed, I don't think I know what one of those even looks like.*

Jack soon dismissed the words. In that, he was wrong.

It was cool and shaded in the grand vizier's inner pavilion, full of shadows in which Omar could hide, avoiding contact with any courtier or servant who might question his presence. Well, the caliph's law knew no bounds, and Omar was meant to be its hand inside the palace. Murder, even of a slave, was against the laws laid down by the Caliph Eternal.

Eventually the shadows of the passages gave way to the light of a central courtyard, and Omar found himself on the first terrace of the hanging gardens the old slave Nudar had sent him towards. A maze of paths wound through trellised walks bounded by orchids as tall as Omar himself, vines and creepers hanging like a curtain over the side of the terrace.

Flicking away a bright blue dragonfly that had drifted in front of his face and peering upwards, Omar counted five more terraces laddering up to the open sky above. On the central courtyard below was a slab of marble the size of a bed. The mist of water from the nozzles at its four corners partially enveloped Shadisa's green silk-robed form. Her wrists and her ankles were tied to each of the nozzles and she was lying soaking like a human starfish fixed to the slab's centre. Her eyes were shut and her face peaceful, as if she had chosen to sleep in the middle of this garden fountain. *But she is alive – she has to be.* Beyond being tied down there were no signs of violence upon her beautiful body. Surely nothing that looked so serene could be dead? He extended out his senses towards her. The same senses that had served him so well back in Haffa. Yes, she was alive, but the differences within her he had sensed under the palace were heightened – a drug? Perhaps, but it was more than that. Deeper. Her soul felt wrong. What had that devil Immed Zahharl done to her? *What can change a soul?* He begged the heavens that it wasn't love. Not for the grand vizier.

Omar grabbed one of the thicker creepers and, using it as a rope, shinned down towards the courtyard. He stopped, hidden in the tree, as the sound of boots on one of the marble paths grew audible, two columns of men emerging, their faces completely covered by golden masks except for their eyes and mouths.

Omar would have recognized the man at their head by his malicious hooded eyes, even without the robes of the high keeper of the Sect of Razat. Leaving the grand vizier standing above Shadisa's head, the two lines of men split off in opposite directions and slowly surrounded the slab where their victim was bound. The caliph's law would be enforced as they were engaged upon their crime, with no excuses possible as Omar leapt down among them and slashed apart the first man to try to take Shadisa's honour and her life. He would run his steel through as many as he could before they fled like rats and the grand vizier would run away, not daring to tell anyone that he had been part of this evil gathering.

The man Omar had marked as Zahharl intoned, 'Which of those is last among us?'

One of the golden masked figures stepped forward. 'I am last.'

'Then it is upon you to prove you will follow our true way,' called Zahharl. 'The Sect of Razat calls for blood, and from this maiden's flesh will it be spilled.' He pulled out a long silver syringe from under his priest's robes and plunged it into Shadisa's arm, filling it with the unconscious woman's blood. 'You must prove yourself to me and you must prove yourself to the will of the one true god.' He lifted up the filled syringe as if it was a sceptre and the golden-masked figure stepped forward to receive it. The grand vizier indicated Shadisa's prone body. 'This slave's name is Shadisa and she shall die. It is for you to prove yourself upon her body. As we honour progress . . .'

'As we honour progress,' intoned the circle of figures, 'she shall die!'

Omar was flexing his legs to propel him into the leap down from the tree when the tiles below began to shake. A stomping sound echoed from the corridor the grand vizier had entered through and the first of a company of giant beyrogs emerged into the hanging garden from the pavilion. Ben Issman be blessed, Boulous must have told the guardsmen what Omar was about to do, and they had informed the Caliph Eternal. Here was the ruler's bodyguard, come to arrest the grand vizier for his crimes. The caliph using the excuse, no doubt, to remove a thorn from his side who had grown over-powerful and dangerous. The sedan chair borne into the hanging garden by the beyrogs dropped to the floor behind Zahharl and a figure to the left of the grand vizier removed his mask, revealing a face that Omar had to suppress a gasp upon seeing – a profile familiar from any coin stamped in Cassarabia. It was the Caliph Eternal standing beside the grand vizier, Akil Jaber Issman himself, his immortal youthful features looking not much older that Omar's own!

'Take her,' ordered the Caliph Eternal, and at the sound of his voice the shark-faced beyrogs came alive and lunged forward, ripping off Shadisa's restraints and pulling her off the slab.

'Careful, you wretches,' called the Caliph Eternal to the beyrogs, pointing towards the masked man holding the syringe of blood. 'The woman does not require her skin bruised as if she is an overripe banana. Prove your loyalty to progress and the Sect of Razat: this slave shall die this night by your hand.'

Omar watched in shock as the Caliph Eternal's hideous bodyguards tossed Shadisa's comatose form inside the sedan chair. The masked initiate who was to kill her stopped with one boot on the chair's step as the grand vizier passed him a cork-stoppered vial of green liquid. 'Use this to wake her up,' laughed the grand vizier, 'before you start with her.' The initiate nodded and took the vial, entering the chair's box.

The Caliph Eternal himself is a member of the grand vizier's wicked sect. A man who should have commanded the loyalty of every sect of the Holy Cent as the voice of the one true god on earth. No chance of invoking the caliph's law and trusting to the empire's justice here. The only law now was the depraved whims of Immed Zahharl. Any one of the beyrogs would be a match for a dozen guardsmen, and Omar wouldn't get more than a step towards Shadisa's body before the caliph's bodyguard cut him to pieces. He had to bide his time. Save Shadisa later.

Omar kept as still as a leaf in the foliage. The Caliph Eternal's monsters would slay him if they scented him up here. Back in Haffa, Omar had heard a story once about a salt-fish farmer who had escaped a nest of sand vipers that had been tracking him by rubbing a salt-fish against his skin to disguise his scent. Omar quietly plucked one of the oranges and sliced it against his scimitar, squeezing its juices against his face, arms and legs.

'I want no trace of her left,' ordered the grand vizier. 'Carry the chair to the lowest level of the womb mages' library and do it there.'

No. NO!

Concealed inside the sedan chair, Shadisa and the initiate who was to be her executioner were carried away by the beyrogs, a couple of their number standing sentry outside the archway, the gold-masked figures of the sect striding solemnly behind the procession.

Shadisa. Omar had failed her again – a guardsman with a scimitar at his side, trained to hack apart her would-be killers, and he had been every bit as helpless to intervene as he had been during the sack of Haffa.

Omar's self-recriminations ended as one of the beyrogs turned and sniffed the air suspiciously, growling like a wolf.

'Stop,' ordered the caliph.

Immed Zahharl turned. 'What is it?'

'There is someone else here,' said the caliph. 'My beyrogs' senses are never wrong.'

'Move on,' the grand vizier called to the departing sedan chair and the masked figures. 'Seal the garden behind you.'

'Find the intruder,' the caliph ordered the beyrog as it loped howling straight towards Omar's orange tree.

* * *

Jack was helping Coss with a broken regulator on one of the transaction engines when a banshee-like wailing began sounding about the chamber and the two of them halted their work.

'General-quarters,' said Coss.

Jack was puzzled. 'This close to our rendezvous with the Fleet of the South?'

John Oldcastle leant over the rail into the engine pit. 'The bridge wants a check on the navigation drums, they need to confirm our blessed position.'

Jack saw why through the porthole when he went back up to the punch-card desk. There were dunes below – known as the great southern desert to the Jackelians, the northern to the Cassarabians – but the orange sands were covered with smoking debris and bodies. In the air clusters of gas cells drifted through the sky attached to scraps of burning carper, like corpuscles bled from the airships' veins and set astray to wander the heavens.

'There are no airships left intact,' said Jack, injecting his query into the punch-card reader.

'Aye lad,' said John Oldcastle, looking out of the next porthole. 'And unless both sides blew each other to bits, that's the remains of one fleet while the victors have had it away on their heels.'

Results for Jack's query began twisting away on the beads of his abacus-like screen. 'All our compass points have been tracked correctly. Our navigation drums are turning fine. These are the rendezvous coordinates the vice-admiral gave us for the Fleet of the South.'

The master cardsharp reported the results down to the bridge and returned to Jack's station a minute later. 'You and the old steamer can get your tools. We're to report to the boat bay and go down there – sift through the wreckage for anything resembling a ship's record drums – Jackelian or the caliph's.'

Jack couldn't tear his eyes away from the sight outside the porthole.

Coss came out of the pit to take in the sight too. 'How could one fleet wipe out another so completely in a single engagement?'

'Perhaps the vice-admiral was right,' said Jack. 'Superior skymanship will out.'

'Ah, that strutting popinjay,' whined John Oldcastle. 'If he's right, there's a first time for everything.'

If the *Iron Partridge*'s skipper had been looking to find the remains of a captain's log among the dunes of the Southwest Frontier, then Jack hoped Captain Jericho wouldn't be too disappointed. There was enough of that to go around for everyone. While the figures sifting through the wreckage – John Oldcastle, Coss, Jack, their brutish captain of marines and a handful of his soldiers – had yet to find anything resembling a transaction-engine register in the ruins left scattered across the desert, there were enough bodies wearing the torn, burnt uniforms of the RAN to speak of which side had flown away victorious. So many ships' names on the caps – the *Audacity*, the *Guardian Kirkhill*, the *Javelin*, the *Parliament Oak*, the *Swiftsure* and the *Ultimatum* – and not a single Cassarabian sailor among the bodies strewn half-buried among the shifting sands.

Dirty rolls of smoke threaded across the sky for miles, hiding the hundreds of circling carrion birds. Pieces of smouldering carper jutted out of the desert like a field of thorns, and the saltpetre smell of matches from the residue of liquid explosive charges lingered in the air. The *Iron Partridge* must have missed the battle by no more than a day – or the desert would have reclaimed the scene of carnage, covering the wreckage with sand after scavengers had stripped the carcasses of the fallen to their bare bones. No need to post sentries here to guard against looters; only the vultures had turned up to avail themselves of the war's bounty.

'Nothing,' Jack called across to Coss, poking an arch of a girder emerging from the sand as if it was a whalebone trapped on the bed of an evaporated sea. *What in the name of the Circle happened to our airships out here?* Apart from a few melted keys from a punch-card writer, Jack hadn't found anything even approaching useful. There were thousands of tiny scraps of blackened material on the ground. Not paper, but more like a very fine cloth that had been burnt close to ashes. Jack picked up a brittle leaf of the burnt material. Nothing he recognized. Too thin to be the canvas of an airship envelope, but it had been left blowing all over the battlefield.

'Kiss my condensers, but this wreckage is all wrong, Jack softbody,' said Coss.

'Too right it is,' said Jack. 'These are all our people. If we'd made the rendezvous any quicker, this would have been you and me lying here as vulture fodder. How are we even going to bury so many?'

'You misunderstand,' said the steamman. 'I mean this wreckage is too small.'

'You've got a good set of vision plates in your skull, old steamer,' said Oldcastle. He had abandoned the search and was sitting on a piece of hull, shading his eyes from the high sun and gazing up at the reassuring armoured bulk of the *Iron Partridge* floating overhead. 'You saw how much was left of our prize vessel after we burnt her down to her bones. And we did that with charges laid on the inside. This—' he waved a hand across the sands '—wasn't a normal battle. It was a slaughter.'

'Something new,' said Coss.

'Aye,' said Oldcastle. 'Something new in the very old game we've been playing against the caliph these last few centuries. Something new come along to disturb an old man's rest, curse my unlucky stars.'

Jack turned away from the sight of the sailors' mutilated corpses in disgust. 'Their faces . . .'

'A tradition of the caliph's army, lad,' said Oldcastle. 'They present their officers with sacks of ears and noses severed from the bodies of the fallen to prove the scale of their victory. It leaves little room for exaggeration of your triumph. It's a wicked hard thing to be an infidel in this land.'

'Yes, a hard thing.'

Was it just the dead and fallen, or were prisoners and wounded fair game too, Jack wondered? *Alan, Saul, you've never seemed so far away.* How he wished he was back with his brothers now – it didn't even matter that he had failed to raise the money he needed to rescue them from poverty – even the grime and relentless destitution of a state poorhouse was better than picking through the terrible litter of this battlefield.

A call sounded out from over the rise of the next dune and one of their Benzari marines appeared waving a rifle to indicate he had found something of note. Wading through the fine orange sand alongside the master cardsharp and Coss, Jack saw that the marines were pulling what looked like a white blanket off a man-sized canister jutting out of the sands. Captain of Marines Tempest was running down towards his men and cursing them for fools. Something glinted below the white sheeting, two glass hemispheres filled with liquid, separated by a thin membrane.

'You perishing idiots,' yelled the marine office. 'There's enough explosives sloshing around in there to blow you back to your barbarian mountains.'

Jack took in the find as he warily approached, the captain of marines shoving his men back. The object they had discovered looked like one of the shells the *Iron Partridge*'s gunners loaded into the breeches of their cannons, but a hundred times larger. And the material they had pulled off it resembled white silk, connected to the canister by guide lines, an oversized version of the sail rider chutes sailors would use in a last-ditch attempt to abandon a wrecked airship.

'This canister was floating in the air,' said Jack, pointing at the silk-like material. *Dear Circle, this thing was designed to fly!*

The master cardsharp pushed Jack's hand back down. 'Careful about it, Mister Keats.' He pointed to a crown of metal spikes circling the canister's rim. 'Those are contact detonators. The ones on its side lying against the sand have been sheared off by a shockwave, which is the only reason this wicked contraption didn't blast itself and half an acre of desert away when it hit the ground.'

'It's a mine,' said Jack. 'An aerial mine!'

'The racks we found in the prize vessel's bomb bays . . .' said Coss.

'Too big for standard fin-bombs,' said Jack, 'just the right size to mount these.'

'Just waiting to be loaded for war,' said the master cardsharp. 'Hindsight makes wise men of many a blessed fool.'

'You could only release such a weapon into the air if you were following the wind down onto an enemy squadron,' said Coss.

The master cardsharp took the tool chest out of Coss's hands and stepped towards the mine, waving away the captain of marine's protests as he used a screwdriver to lever off a metal plate above the transparent explosive chamber, revealing a throbbing layer of yellow-furred flesh beneath. 'A fair wind,

Mister Shaftcrank, and the foul touch of their womb mages to guide its sails. Those great big flying lizards that their scouts ride can follow the scent of carper to track down an airship and I'll wager these wicked things can do much the same.'

'Those bleeding little Cassarabian sand monkeys,' growled the captain of marines. 'I'd like to get my fingers around the necks of the ones that did this to our boys.'

'Here's mortal progress for you,' said John Oldcastle. 'Our ships are racked with fin-bombs to see off their nomads and bandits, while theirs are racked with ship-killers like these. Get the master bombardier down here, Mister Keats. We'll drain out the charge of this beastie and then load her onto the boat.'

'How can we possibly defend against something like this?' Jack asked.

Oldcastle pointed up to the *Iron Partridge*. 'The answer's blowing in the wind, Mister Keats. An iron skin to cover our carper guts. This spiny floating chandelier of the caliph's is all blast – fine for ripping apart a soft-skinned vessel, but you need to shape an explosive charge if you're to pierce armour plate properly. Still, I wouldn't want to risk a cloud of these mines – they could blow off our engines cars and woe betide the skymen with their faces pressed against a porthole when one went off.'

Jack nodded in understanding. Their oddity of a vessel was so different from the rest of the fleet, it was the one thing that the Cassarabians hadn't planned for when designing their weapons.

Omar's heart stopped as the monstrous seven-foot-high beyrog sprinted towards the orange tree he was hiding in, ready with the blade of his scimitar to slash down when the creature came clawing up towards the foliage. But it never leapt, crashing instead into the bush beneath Omar's feet and emerging a second later clutching a small slave boy, a belt around his waist hung with gardening tools.

'Everyone was ordered out of the gardens tonight,' said the grand vizier.

'I arrived late for my duty after supper, your eminence,' pleaded the boy dangling from the beyrog's grasp. 'I never spoke to the master of the gardens, I didn't know . . .'

'What did you see here tonight?' demanded Zahharl. 'What did you hear?'

'Nothing, your eminence. I saw nothing.'

'A wise young slave, who sees no evil and hears no evil.' The grand vizier turned to the caliph. 'You know what to do.'

'He is just a child,' said the caliph.

'You too must prove yourself to me this night.'

'I cannot,' begged the caliph, trying not to look at the struggling slave's face.

'Then have your beyrog do it.'

'That would be the same as if I had done it myself.'

'You are right,' sighed the grand vizier. He grabbed the slave by his rough gardener's robes, lifting him out of the hulking beyrog's grasp. 'And if you must do these things, they are better done by your own hand. Then you know they shall be done properly and efficiently.' He took the boy's head and thrust it down into an irrigation channel next to the path. 'Hear no evil, see no evil, and now, speak no evil ever again.'

Omar watched in disgust as the boy's legs spasmed and jerked while the grand vizier drowned him. The murder done, the grand vizier stood up and pointed past the foliage of the orange tree where Omar was hiding. 'The poor lad. He must have slipped from the terrace up there and landed unconscious in the water where he drowned. A good thing he is of no account to anyone.' Zahharl indicated the beyrog, standing dispassionately on the other side of the path. 'Order your hound away.'

The caliph did so and Zahharl marched behind the beyrog, shutting the garden's doors behind the bodyguard and the other sentries standing outside. As he returned towards the caliph, the grand vizier's right leg lashed out and caught the empire's leader in the gut, doubling him up.

'I asked for one simple thing to prove your loyalty and you failed me.'

'Please, don't,' coughed the Caliph Eternal as the grand vizier's leg lashed out again, catching him between the thighs and sending him sprawling across the slave's corpse.

'You are too weak,' said the grand vizier, advancing on the figure whimpering against the tiles of the hanging garden. 'And if you want to see progress done, you must be strong, as strong as our brave new age demands. You want a strong empire, don't you?'

'Yes,' begged the caliph, raising his arms up to ward off any more lashes from the grand vizier's boot.

'That is good,' said Zahharl. 'For that is what I want also.' He removed his boots and sat down on the slab where Shadisa had been tied down, soaking his feet in the water channel at the slab's base before pushing his soles out towards the caliph. 'Rub my feet for me, and then dry them on your clothes. Show me how much you love me. Then I shall reward you.'

Omar watched in silent horror as the empire's ruler of rulers prostrated himself before Immed Zahharl, massaging the killer's feet before rubbing them dry with the silk of his own robe. The Caliph Eternal could cry out in a second, call in his bodyguard of beyrogs outside and have them rip the limbs off this sly, devious murderer, one by one. Yet here he was, supposedly the most powerful man in the empire, bowing down before the grand vizier as if he was no more than a slave from one of the capital's many bathhouses. *What sort of devil is this grand vizier, that he can turn Shadisa against me and treat the Caliph Eternal like a hound to be whipped on his whim?*

'Kiss them now and I shall give it to you,' said the grand vizier, and as the Caliph Eternal moaned and pressed his lips against the feet of his advisor, the grand vizier brought out a syringe filled with a blood-red liquid. 'Stay still,' commanded the grand vizier. He leant forward and shoved the needle into the base of the caliph's neck, pushing the plunger down and releasing the substance into the ruler's body as he lay down moaning. 'Aren't you glad I'm here for you,' cooed the grand vizier. 'Someone to look after you and protect you.'

'Yes,' wailed the Caliph Eternal. 'Yes.'

'Well, then,' said Zahharl, tossing the empty syringe into a bush, 'get to your feet now. We have a war to prosecute and the Imperial Aerial Squadron will bring you victory after victory. In the end, even you may begin to tire of accepting the triumphs that are to come.'

Once the caliph and the grand vizier had departed the hanging garden, Omar dropped to the ground beside the forgotten corpse of the gardener. He lifted the dead boy out of the channel and rolled him onto the path leaving him with as much dignity as he could.

'I'll send the ones that did this to paradise after you,' whispered Omar. 'You are of account to *me*, and that is my promise to you.'

Omar walked over to the bush by the side of the orange tree and carefully pulled out the syringe that had been used to inject the caliph. There were drugs of a thousand hues available inside the palace, served to its courtiers on trays like iced sherbet, but what drug could be so powerful that the grand vizier was using it to make such an utter vassal of the caliph? How addictive would such filth have to be? Omar didn't know the answer to that, but there were chemists inside the capital who might be able to produce an antidote to it and restore some semblance of a ruler able to stand up to the grand vizier's ambitions. Omar pocketed the empty syringe. The proof was mounting up against Immed Zahharl – the trick would be to stay alive long enough to use it.

Omar climbed back up the tree and used the vine to retrace his steps to the next level of the hanging gardens. He had other steps he had to retrace, too. One of the grand vizier's murderous disciples was taking Shadisa down to the lair of the womb mages and Omar knew the way there – the lifting rooms by the library's entrance burrowing all the way to its lowest levels. There was only one victory that mattered to Omar. *I'm coming for you, Shadisa, I'll follow you to hell and back.*

He ran back towards the exit. Shadisa wasn't dead yet.

Standing at the end of the wardroom, Vice-Admiral Tuttle indicated that he was finished with the ground party's report on the caliph's deadly new innovation – the aerial mine. Their find was, Jack supposed, one scrap of small comfort for the admiralty politician, his name now attached to one of the greatest naval defeats the Royal Aerostatical Navy had ever suffered – and at the hands of their enemies to the south, mere novices in the trade of airship flight. Jack could imagine the uproar when news of this defeat started circulating at home. The newssheets would send mobs flailing at the doors of parliament, demanding heads roll for this fiasco. The grim nodding faces of the *Iron Partridge*'s officers seated around the table indicated they concurred with what Jack was imagining as their reception back home.

At least the vice-admiral would have an example of the enemy's secret weapon to present to the fleet's airship yards for their engineers to try to devise a counter-defence. Jack had already heard some of the wilder ideas of the crew on the subject – everything from protective nets, using rotors to blow the mines off course, or launching lead weights on miniature chutes to set the mines off early.

'This is a devious innovation,' announced the vice-admiral, 'but one that will be easily exceeded by the navy's air yards. We will carry the defused mine back to the Kingdom and present it to the admiralty with all haste, so that our next engagement can be made on more equal terms.'

Seated at the table of officers, First Lieutenant Westwick leapt to her feet. 'We will not. Without the admiral's presence to countermand our orders, the *Iron Partridge* is back under independent command.'

In the absence of a séance, Jack judged it unlikely the admiral's ghost would be countermanding anyone. *Was his corpse one of those I was poking through on the sands below?*

'Under whose command, my dear?' the vice-admiral laughed, pointing at the captain's vacant chair. Jericho was in his cabin again, struck by his dark humours and refusing to come out. 'Yours? Your naval commission is caught somewhere between being a mere formality and a high farce.'

'The source of the enemy's celgas is more important than ever,' insisted the first lieutenant. 'The loss of the Fleet of the South has shown the failure of conventional tactics against the empire. We need to raid deep into Cassarabia for answers.'

'This vessel is under the command of the Royal Aerostatical Navy, not the State Protection Board,' the vice-admiral raised his voice. 'I am a vice-admiral of that navy, your superior officer, and by my order we are retuning to Jackals.'

'I heard you were a coward, sir,' said the first lieutenant.

'Always to be found at the rear of a squadron, as far away from danger as your position could afford you.'

'You will not offer such vile insubordination to me!' yelled the vice-admiral.

'Marines,' shouted the first lieutenant towards the two Benzari guarding the door, 'arrest the vice-admiral and place him in the brig.'

The two marines advanced on the vice-admiral and seized his arms to an uproar from the officers around the table, some protesting the arrest of a senior officer, others supporting the principle of independent command in the absence of a living ranked flag officer to countermand it. Jack was pushed back against the wall in the mêlée. *If only Jericho was here to call order on the riot.*

Oldcastle clearly had the same idea. 'Run to the skipper's cabin, Mister Keats, Mister Shaftcrank. Rouse Jericho from his black dog and bring him here even if you have to shove a pistol in his blessed back to do it.'

Jack and Coss were attempting to leave by the wardroom's exit hatch when the door swung open and a mob of sailors clutching cutlasses and marine carbines burst in. Master Engineer Pasco was at the head of the table, waving the rabble in.

'Shut it down,' yelled the burly engine master over the ruckus, his men fanning out down the sides of the wardroom, shoving Jack and Coss against the officer's table with their rifle butts. The two Benzari marines were overpowered and pushed to the floor, the vice-admiral struggling to his feet.

'This is mutiny, Mister Pasco,' spat the first lieutenant.

'So it is, my dear,' answered the vice-admiral. 'But it is not being committed by the master engineer and his men. You have chosen to go against the written orders of a flagged admiral and disobeyed the lawful orders of a superior officer and it is you that is to be charged with mutiny. I am relieving Captain Jericho of command, and you and your minions are to be brigged pending a court martial. Jericho will be confined to his cabin under guard for the rest of the voyage.'

'You're out of line,' protested the master cardsharp. 'On what basis are you relieving the master and commander of this vessel?'

'Gross dereliction of duty,' smiled the vice-admiral. 'He burnt a Cassarabian prize vessel rather than handing it over to the admiralty as he was required by regulations to do. If we had properly examined the enemy airship you had captured, we would have discovered its aerial mines and the Fleet of the South would not have been lost!'

Jack groaned. The duplicitous navy politician had found a way to scapegoat the captain for the loss of the Fleet of the South after all.

'There were no mines on board the prize vessel,' called Jack. 'Their bomb bays weren't even loaded – the ship was rigged light for long distance patrol.'

'Shut your mouth, thief,' said Pasco. 'You're only on this ship because you were in the pokey with Jericho. We all know it. Nobody checked the prize vessel properly; she was burnt as fast as your Benzari wild boys could lay charges inside her.'

The vice-admiral shook his head sadly. 'The word of a pressed criminal; well, at least we still have some real navy personnel left on this ship. Mister Pasco, do your duty. Westwick and her secret police lackeys are to be held in the brig. I want a loyal sailor with small arms on every station as we set a course for home.'

There was a cheer from the mob of armed sailors and Pasco's men grabbed Jack, Coss and John Oldcastle, pushing them after the first lieutenant, the female officer surrounded by a ring of jeering armed mutineers. They would be lucky if they made it to the brig without being hanged first.

'Not the brig for the old steamer,' said Pasco, pointing at Shaftcrank. 'Escort him up to the transaction-engine chamber. We need someone to prevent this albatross of a ship from killing us all on the way home.' Pasco turned to Jack as he pushed a cutlass under the master cardsharp's nose. 'I told you, boy, and you, fat man, the day would come when we'd settle this proper.'

That day had arrived.

CHAPTER TEN

Standing in the corridor that led to the great library cavern, Omar could hear the clacking echoes of the womb mages' copper-plated spell books turning under their fingers as he frantically inspected the buttons on the lifting room's wall panel. Where would you go to assault, murder and dispose of a slave? Deep, that was what the grand vizier had told the initiate. Deep to hide the crime, deep to dispose of Shadisa's corpse.

Omar had a name now for the golden-masked would-be slayer, courtesy of Nudar. *Salwa*. A name accompanied by a warning, for Salwa was reputed to be a keeper of the Sect of Razat, a priest who had already proved himself by questioning and strangling many of the men captured in Haffa by raiders. Men that Omar would have known of old. The priest's murderous actions towards those who had been cast out as heretics should have already proven his loyalty to the grand vizier, yet here this devil Salwa was, about to snatch the greatest love of Omar's life away from him.

Well, Salwa the priest is going to become Salwa the dead when I catch up with him. And if he had harmed so much as a hair on Shadisa's head, then he would become Salwa the man who welcomed death on the day his fate crossed paths with a certain guardsman's. If only Omar's luck held until he caught up with them. Omar had already seen the sedan chair and the bodyguard of massive beyrogs exiting the womb mages' lair, the chair held noticeably higher by its two porters now its occupants had been deposited somewhere below. *Why set me this fate, god, why make a guardsman of a slave if you don't mean for me to rescue her?*

It was as if the heavens were blessing Omar's plans, trying to restore the balance of justice here in the Jahan. Guiding him to alcoves to hide in and ledges to crouch on unseen while the sorcerers passed by. The fear of their craft among the people was both their strength and their weakness. They were so sure that nobody would dare to poke their nose in a sorcerer's business, that they didn't even require guards to watch their gates.

Standing in the lifting room, Omar pressed the button for the lowest level, and shuddered as the gate shut off the corridor and the room began to sink. There was a smell inside of chemicals that reminded Omar of the bleaches he had used to clean the water farm's desalination lines out after their pipes clogged up with crusted salt. Omar's heart was pounding as he tried not to think of what would happen if he were too late. It felt as if his guts were being wrung tighter and tighter as the lifting room descended painfully slow. When the gate finally opened again, the surprise of it almost made Omar jump. *Focus, I have to focus. Remember the advice in scimitar practice. Master yourself before you master your opponent.* As he walked the crimson-lit corridors the many different doors and passages seemed to create a maze. He picked one route and stuck with it, ducking into an alcove as a column of womb mages came marching down the corridor. He heard them before he saw them, each of the men humming the letters of a different spell. It was as if they were in a trance, their faces fixed on the bare concrete floor. They wore not the usual robes of the womb mages, but voluminous white garments. Matching white skullcaps covered their heads, while small gauze masks protected their mouths like the filters nomads wore when hunkering down during a sandstorm.

Silently following the procession at a distance, Omar passed an alcove railed with freshly laundered clothes in the same style. He slipped one of the robes over his guardsman's uniform and donned a white mask, scented with a chlorine tang. It was an easy enough thing to join the back of the procession, muttering the same limited hum of letters in an order as random as those in front. If Omar's spell was nonsense, none of the womb mages – focused as they were on their own sorceries – noticed.

The chanting line passed a glass window as tall as five men. The long chamber on the other side was stacked with large, gas-filled aquarium-like tanks, producers and their loads veiled by the yellow gas pumped in through long coiled pipes joining each tank's roof from the chamber's ceiling. The pipes had a glistening organic quality to them that made them resemble umbilical cords. Womb mages in their all-enveloping white outfits moved about the tanks, tapping dials on banks of machinery at the front and noting measurements down on clipboards. Glancing across, Omar couldn't even see the end of the chamber, just cage after cage. How many biologicks were being grown through there? How many slaves inside, their bellies swollen like whales, hatching the womb mages' creatures? Draks for the guardsmen to fly patrols on, beyrogs to march in the caliph's bodyguard, sandpedes to bear the loads for the empire's trading caravans. How many creatures whose creation spells were racked in the great library above;

how many slaves who had given their lives bearing such biologicks into existence? *Poor devils, I can't save you. Only Shadisa. Forgive me.*

Omar left the chamber behind and continued following the chanting womb mages. The teachings of the Holy Cent might have told of how after mankind had been cast out of the gardens of paradise, when Ben Issman – his name be blessed – was shown how to lead the tribes to prosperity in the deserts by casting down the thousands of false deities, moulding them into the one true god. How to pluck his own flesh and cast it down upon the sands to make the dunes bloom with plants and gardens, gardens filled with creatures that would serve mankind after god's wrath had stilled their old machines. But their salvation came at a price; a price that could be avoided by most freemen, as long as they averted their eyes in fear and superstition when womb mages passed. A price that was paid by slaves and the conquered from all the subject nations of the empire.

As Omar walked the underground passages, he saw sights that he could not begin to understand. Another glass-walled chamber contained a tall, sloping wall divided into shelves and squares like a giant bookshelf. Each compartment was covered with about an inch of what looked like jelly. Womb mages pushed ladders along a rail to reach the different compartments, scraping off the gel with white swabs and depositing the residue into Petri dishes. They resembled worker bees intently busying away on the face of a honeycomb.

Another chamber could be observed through long armoured glass slits rather than a floor-to-ceiling window. On the other side was a spherical area where a womb mage was mounted on top of something like a cannon on a pivoted arm. Bursts of lightning flew from its needle-like barrel and forked around the chamber before striking a ball on a plinth in the centre of the space. The bottom hemisphere of the ball was plated with copper, the top half transparent and filled with viscous fluid. Omar watched as another womb mage walked out to the sphere to inspect its jellied contents with a thin metal instrument. Dissatisfied with the results, he made a sign towards the womb mage riding the cannon. As soon as the inspector had cleared the chamber through a vault-like door, the cannon began lashing the contents again with an angry discharge.

'Animating dead flesh,' whispered Omar as he noticed the procession of mumbling sorcerers branching off down a corridor. *Are there no depths these demons will not sink to?*

His way lay down another passage, however. He could sense that Shadisa had passed down there. Omar halted and glanced intently around the crimson-lit corridor. He was getting closer to Shadisa, he was sure of that, yet her presence was getting weaker – that couldn't be, unless . . . an image jumped into his mind. Of Shadisa struggling as Salwa's greasy fingers closed around her neck and he choking her struggling body to silence.

Throwing subterfuge to the wind, he began sprinting down the passage, desperately trying to sense where Shadisa had been taken. *There.* One of the heavily riveted iron doors, identical to a hundred he had already passed on his journey down here. Omar drew his scimitar from under his robe, threw the door open and had a second's glimpse of a small narrow room divided in two by a metal mesh, two womb mages turning around to see who was bursting in on them. Omar smashed the nearest of the white-masked sorcerers in the face with the guard of his sword, sending the man stumbling back into a counter covered in scalpels and other instruments that might have been the tools of a womb mage, or a torturer.

The second womb mage tried to get to the counter, his hands diving down for one of the blades, and Omar kicked him in the side, overbalancing him, then took out the back of his legs with a second kick. As the womb mage went down, Omar slammed the man's face into the blade-littered surface, before running to the mesh dividing the room.

On the other side was a circular pool filled with bubbling acid, its fumes drifting across a figure naked except for a wrap of cloth around his waist. He was kneeling down by the side of the pool dropping in blood-soaked items of clothing, each of them swirling away in a smoking hiss. He held in his hands Shadisa's ornate silk tunic. The one that she thought had marked her out for the grand vizier's attentions – and it had, but not in the way she had anticipated. This was Salwa. Salwa the killer, his taut muscular body covered in sweat and blood from his work.

'Shadisa!'

Please, god, I have followed the fate you have given me. Don't do this. Let her be alive. Give me a miracle, is that so much to ask? Too late. By heaven's silver gate, he had failed her. Shadisa, beautiful Shadisa who had been the only girl he had loved. He had been too late when she needed him. Too late to save her from the grand vizier's evil sect and the perverted initiation rites that had been demanded of this devil, this dog, this beast, Salwa.

The man stood and turned, looking at Omar through the mesh wall. Shadisa was gone, all sense of her soul had vanished from his heart.

'You killed her!'

'Yes, I believe I did. Who are you behind that mask?' asked the killer.

'The man who's going to slice you into pieces!'

Salwa picked up something, a tray of human flesh bobbing

in a darkening pool of blood. In his other hand was the golden-faced sun mask he had worn to conceal his face in the grand vizier's hanging gardens. 'I have a mask too.' He tossed the tray of human remains into the pool of acid, a terrible stench emanating from it as it flamed away, then he pulled the mask down over his face. It was slicked with blood. *Shadisa's blood.*

Omar grabbed the handle on the door in the mesh partition and yanked at it to no avail. It was locked tight.

The murderous priest laughed and pointed to a transaction-engine lock with a blood-testing spike mounted against the wall on Omar's side of the mesh. 'Only those whose blood has been entered into the sect's records can gain admittance into the inner sanctum. And you're not on it. You're not even a womb mage under that mask, are you?'

'Open the door and find out!'

'It doesn't matter,' said Salwa. 'Our sorcery is strong. You'll have left some part of yourself down here – hairs, skin. We'll find out who you are, my troublesome friend, and then you'll be silenced.'

'Come and find me now!' yelled Omar. 'I'm right here!'

'Stay there, save me the trouble of hunting you down, then,' laughed Salwa, walking towards the mesh. 'You can wait while I summon the entire Sect of Razat.'

Omar kicked over a table filled with connected glass vials, the sound of their smashing mingling with his cry of rage as the killer stepped through the mesh door and clanged it shut.

The young guardsman was already running when the alarms began to fill the corridors of the womb mages' lair.

Jack was pacing the small box of their cell in the brig, ignoring the snores of the master cardsharp and the dangerous, brooding silence of the first lieutenant. John Oldcastle might be able to lie down and sleep through their predicament without a problem, but every time Jack tried to close his eyes, all he could see was the fate waiting for him back in the Kingdom. The best he could hope for in front of a board of enquiry orchestrated by that slimy toad Tuttle was a dishonourable discharge that would see him handed back to the judge in the capital's court – and a short walk to an even shorter drop on the scaffold outside Bonegate prison. The alternative was a charge of mutiny and the only difference there would be the location of the rope, this time hanging in the naval stockade at the fortress city of Shadowclock. He imagined his brothers weeping when they heard of his death in the poorhouse, the shrugs from the underpaid functionaries of the Board of the Poor at the news. Hanged as a mutineer or hanged as a thief. The result was inevitable, wasn't it? A bad apple, from the same barrel as his father. *I'm sorry, Alan, I'm sorry Saul. We always seem to let you down, don't we? First father and now me. That's it, perhaps I'm just carrying on the family tradition. I drew some bad cards in this game of chance we live, and I've thrown our lives away.*

It was easy to listen to your own thoughts in the brig, swim in your worries insulated from the noise and vibrations of the airship by their position at the centre of the middle deck. No rattling beams or creaking hull. The only thing that Jack had felt of late had been the jolt of the landing anchors being discharged, one of Pasco's henchmen only too glad to inform the prisoners that the Benzari marines had been left on their home soil on the vice-admiral's orders, crowing about their marooning as he slipped stale rations through the cell door's metal slit. At a stroke, the vice-admiral had repatriated the one contingent of the ship's crew whose fierce loyalty to the ship's captain was without question.

Jack heard clanking at the iron door and as it opened, three armed sailors threw the captain of marines, Henry Tempest, onto the floor of the cell. It looked as if he had taken a pistol whipping from their rifle butts, and the giant was shivering despite the controlled warmth inside the airship.

'Henry,' said the first lieutenant, on her feet immediately, inspecting the soldier's wounds. She ran to the cell door, speaking through a thin grille. 'His flasks, where are his two flasks?'

There was a laugh from beyond the door. 'Hanging up outside here. You didn't think we'd leave them with you, did you?'

'Too much green,' whispered the shaking marine officer. 'I need the red. They tricked me, dosed me good.'

'Give them to me, you bastards; send the surgeon down here to administer them.'

There was no reply. Their captors had left the prisoners alone in the brig to rot again. John Oldcastle had been roused by the commotion and it took all three of them to drag the shivering marine to the cell's solitary bunk.

Jack looked out of the cell's viewing slit. There was a pair of canteens hanging on the back of an empty guard's chair. 'He won't be chasing the poppy powder any time soon.'

'The big lad isn't an opiate addict, Mister Keats,' said Oldcastle. 'That's just scuttlebutt the crew has been spreading.'

First Lieutenant Westwick flashed Oldcastle an angry look.

'What's it matter now, lass?' sighed Oldcastle. 'Our cover's blown. The navy's as likely to hang us all before the State Protection Board ever gets a chance to spring us.'

'I know that you two aren't real naval officers,' said Jack. 'You're agents of the secret police.'

'Don't wish that terrible trade on me, I'm not even that,' said the master cardsharp, sadly. 'Just a poor unlucky old fool the State Protection Board has blackmailed into acting as a pawn in their great game. My real name is Jared Black although my friends call me the commodore.'

Jared Black. That was the name that Coss had remembered from his pre-sentient dreams – the steamman had been right about the master cardsharp all along. And the commodore was the nickname that Captain Jericho had warned Jack not to use in front of the rest of the crew.

'In the flush of my youth I used to be a royalist rebel, in the days when the cause was given mortal succour by the caliph,' said the prisoner. 'Arms, explosives and money – anything for the fleet-in-exile if it meant pulling parliament's nose. Real boats, lad, submersibles, not these gas-filled sausages the RAN float about the sky; the roll of the ocean beneath your feet and the spray of water coming across your face in a blessed conning tower as you recharge your air. The years I spent in Cassarabia and the contacts I made down south are the only reason I'm here.'

Jared Black: John Oldcastle. The commodore. From traitorous rebel to stooge of the state. It seemed when it suited him, the old man changed names and identities as easily as he did uniforms.

Jack looked at the woman. 'But nobody blackmailed you into making this voyage.'

'I'm an officer of the state,' said Westwick, 'just the same as I was before, and that's all you need to know about me, boy.'

'What about him?' said Jack, pointing at the shivering giant.

'Ah, the big lad's navy, alright,' said the commodore. 'He wanted to get in so bad he volunteered to take a potion the admiralty's chemists had developed a few years back; a fearful formula to create the perfect marine. It worked, in a manner of speaking; took some stick-thin sickly cripples they'd scraped out from the nearest hospital of the poor and turned them into the kind of brute you see here. But the formula left its test subjects' bodies and minds twisted – one minute in a raging fury, the next as placid as a lamb. The only way they can control their humours is by using the flasks. Green to calm down, red when they need to fight, and either a coma or a stroke if they don't sip from the bottles at all.'

'He joined the service he always wanted to,' said the first lieutenant, protectively. 'It wasn't his fault that fate made him into something else. He needs to drink from the red flask now. They've overdosed him from the green bottle – the mutineers must have beaten the surgeon into telling them why he needs his drinks, then slipped the green's contents into his rations.'

Maya Westwick seemed curiously sympathetic towards their captain of marines, as if something in the brute of a soldier had found a vein of softness in the deadly, dangerous woman that Jack would have been hard-pressed to locate otherwise. Jack went to the cell door to see how close the two flasks were and was startled by the sight of Coss slipping into the brig's guardroom. The steamman raised an iron digit in front of his voicebox to indicate that Jack wasn't to make a noise, then gently shut the door behind him. He slipped over to the room's speaking trumpet, lifted it off a copper plate on the wall and began a brief whispered conversation with someone at the other end. A second after the trumpet was set back on the wall, there was a strange whirring noise followed by a series of thuds as the bolts in the cell's door withdrew into the floor and ceiling. Jack tentatively pressed the door, and finding it unlocked, pushed it open. Outside, the drum on the lock set against the cell was rotating so fast there was smoke spearing up from the oil on the drum's gimbals.

'You've not come to hang us, then, Mister Shaftcrank?' asked the commodore, pushing his way out behind Jack. 'Not come to carry out whatever sentence the navy's scheming vice-admiral has cooked up?'

'No, master cardsharp,' said Coss, making way for the first lieutenant to scoop up the two flasks before re-entering the cell.

'Then it's a grand old counter-mutiny you're running?' asked the commodore. 'How many men do we have loyal to the captain?'

'Just myself, sir, that I know of,' said the steamman, before correcting himself. 'Well, the ship and myself. Rot my regulators, but the crew knows the vice-admiral's reputation for ruining the reputations of those who cross him – there aren't many on board willing to take the captain's side now he's been relieved by a senior admiralty officer.'

The ship! Jack looked at the slowing drum on the transaction-engine lock and it suddenly dawned on him who the steamman had been whispering to using the speaking trumpet.

'The ship, she's like you!' said Jack.

'It takes time to come to full consciousness,' said Coss. 'The ship was never broken, it's just taken time for her intelligence inside the transaction engines to develop to full self-awareness. The ship had to take the final steps on the journey herself, after her creator disappeared halfway through her construction.'

'She's alive . . .' said the commodore.

'Yes,' said Coss to Jack and the commodore. 'Her systems went up to full throttle when the two of you were imprisoned and weren't around anymore to help me shut her down, and that was when she began communicating with me. She is like I was when I was taking my first steps in my nursery body. The proving flights, all that has gone before, the ship can only remember them as a dream.'

A *dream*. That was what the steamman god had been trying

to tell Jack. And when the *Iron Partridge*'s gunnery systems worked in perfect simulation offline during their engagement against the two Cassarabian airships, they hadn't been becoming dangerously erratic – they were functioning as they were meant to for the first time! Lemba of the Empty Thrusters had heard the ship's song in the sky, the song of her burgeoning intelligence, and had chosen to answer it.

'If the ship's on our side, old steamer, can we use her to turn our trumped-up charges of mutiny into real ones against the vice-admiral?'

Coss shook his metal skull unit. 'The *Iron Partridge* wasn't built for that. The majority of her systems are external facing – the engine cars and rudders and gunnery. She needs a crew – not one as large as ours, and certainly not with manual overrides crippling her – but she still needs a crew inside her nevertheless.'

'The mission,' said the first lieutenant appearing in the doorway with the captain of marines limping by her side, semi-restored by the dosage from the red canteen.

'The ship's mission is why I am here,' said Coss. 'Just as failure is an orphan, success has many fathers. You must succeed in carrying out the ship's original orders if a board of enquiry is to find in your favour and against the vice-admiral. I have discovered a way to get to the boat bay without any of Pasco's men observing you.'

The commodore looked askance at the prospect of abandoning the safety of the vessel.

'You always knew we'd have to go in on the ground in the end,' said the first lieutenant. 'It's why the State Protection Board put you here.'

'Boots on the ground, lass,' said the commodore. 'I just wished they weren't mine.'

'The skipper,' said the brute of a marine from Westwick's

side. 'I'm not leaving him behind on any ship filled with perishing mutineers.'

'His cabin will be too well guarded,' said the first lieutenant. 'And even if we break him out without killing half the crew, by coming with us, Jericho would be siding with escaped mutineers. If he can even make the charges stick, the worst the vice-admiral can do for the destruction of a prize vessel is have Jericho cashiered. If Jericho comes with us and we don't succeed, they'll hang him for sure. You don't want to see Captain Jericho led to the scaffold by the vice-admiral, do you?'

She might be telling the truth of it, but Jack caught the whiff of dissembling in her argument. *She doesn't want Jericho along with us in case he becomes struck down again by one of his dark humours.* A genius in the air would be no use to the pitiless woman on the ground.

'You won't be able to come with us either, I fear, Mister Shaftcrank,' said the commodore. 'There aren't any blessed steammen in Cassarabia, not even as slaves.'

Jack thought he saw the steamman's vision plate pulse with relief. As the only creature within hundreds of miles with any idea of the process the nascent intelligence of the ship was going through, the ship was in his charge now, and he surely wouldn't want to abandon her.

'Don't concern yourself with my fate, master cardsharp,' said Coss. 'I doubt if Pasco's men will suspect me of helping you. They see me a simple soul, a loyal machine for them to command like one of their tools – and as far as they're concerned, I haven't left the transaction-engine chamber.'

And when Coss led them outside, Jack saw why. The door to the ship's magazine was open, exposing the automatic loading station. Coss had ridden the shell-loading mechanism all the way down from the upper deck, unseen by any of

Pasco's mutineers, and they could travel up to the boat bay the same way. Jack knew who they would blame for the cell break, even without the tools of his old trade to hand – the thief who had nearly broken into the vaults of Lords Bank. Master Engineer Pasco would be only too glad to be proved right in his opinion of Jack.

Even woozy on his feet, the captain of marine made short work of the two sailors on duty in the boat bay with his pile driver fists. As they lay unconscious Jack held open the heavy hatch so the first lieutenant could access the bay's cargo hold. She climbed down into the ship's guts and re-emerged a minute later with a nondescript-looking crate. This case, the commodore informed him, contained the supplies the State Protection Board's quartermaster had made available for covert infiltration into Cassarabia. Next, Coss helped Jack and the commodore winch open the bay's doors as the first lieutenant and Henry Tempest prepared the vice-admiral's pocket airship – still assembled with her envelope gassed – for launch. Jack watched his friends raid the other boats' provisions for enough expansion-engine fuel for a long-range expedition. This was one flight where they couldn't expect to be resupplied by the navy.

Coss pointed out of the hangar towards the peaks of the Benzaral Mountains passing below. 'I have asked the ship to arrange a distraction inside both the crows' nest and the h-dome when you launch. You'll have enough time to conceal your aerostat behind one of the peaks until we have flown out of sight. I doubt if the vice-admiral will waste much time trying to search for you. He is eager to present his account of the loss of the Fleet of the South before any possible survivors beat him to it.'

'Thank you, old steamer,' said Jack. 'The last people I thought were my friends saw me tossed to the hangman back in the Kingdom to save their own necks, and here you are risking yours to rescue me from the noose.'

'Vault my valves, but it would be an unlucky executioner who tries to hang a steamman,' said Coss. 'Besides, we are serving members of the Royal Aerostatical Navy, you and I, and that is what shipmates do – they watch out for each other.'

'Only the good ones, Mister Shaftcrank,' said the commodore. 'Look after your metal skin and see to the ship and her skipper as best you mortal can.'

Jack shook Coss's cold iron hand. Here was a steamman who dreamt of flying and an airship that dreamt of being a steamman. As dangerous as continuing into the enemy heartland to prosecute the ship's mission with just the four of them might prove, it was the lesser of two evils. Coss was right; success in the mission was the only way for Jack to escape a mutineer's fate. A handful of Jack Cloudies against the oldest, most powerful empire on the continent. *What hope will we have out there, just the four of us?*

'I will pray to Lemba of the Empty Thrusters for our Loas to watch over you,' said Coss.

'Let's be on our way, Mister Keats,' said the commodore. 'They can't hang us if we're killed in action, and you have your promise to me to keep.'

Jack boarded the airship and a moment later it was flung into the uncaring sky.

The priest Salwa bent on one knee before Immed Zahharl, who was raging at the courtiers scattering before the cushion-lined pool where the great man had been lounging up until a couple of minutes ago.

Their fear of his temper was all the greater because the pool was located beside the caliph's torture garden, where the bodies of his enemy's had been twisted into tree-like shapes twenty feet tall; their mouths sealed or removed by the mages, so their agonies could offer no disturbance to those who were invited to walk the gardens.

Some of the twisted forms were older than the oldest tree – life-prolonging drugs were mixed with the water the gardeners used to keep their victims alive. After all, there was no memory of betrayal longer than that of the Caliph Eternal. The grand vizier, it was known, liked to do his thinking here – among the contorted bodies of those who had fallen from grace and favour. Perhaps to look into the eyes of those he had manoeuvred into the garden; perhaps as a reminder to himself of the price of failure. Many of the empire's great and good were summoned to meander through the grounds and witness the punishment meted out to those who rebelled against the empire, those who lost wars against Cassarabia, those who were found in the palace kitchen trying to add poison to the Caliph Eternal's meals. Visitors could usually be counted on to draw the obvious lesson, with many cases of treasonous thoughts that never then progressed into action.

The grand vizier flourished the results of the blood-code test that had established the intruder's identity beyond doubt – skin cells scraped from the broken-nosed face of one of the womb mages who had tried to stop the intruder. 'And how was this wretch Omar Barir allowed simply to roam around the library's lowest levels as if he was a senior womb mage? Are we to hold picnics down there outside our breeding vats and invite along every slave in the palace?'

There was no answer from the chagrined staff as the grand vizier pointed down at Salwa. 'If the last son of Barir knew enough to follow you down there, if he knew enough to attempt to rescue his precious Shadisa, then the chances are he also knows the Caliph Eternal is bound to the Sect of Razat.'

'I am sorry, master,' said Salwa. 'This is my fault.'

The grand vizier waved the keeper's apology away angrily. 'Barir, always a Barir. His father was a thorn in my side; continually agitating for trade rather than war, and his mongrel idiot of a bastard son is no different. Well, as Ben Issman once turned the wastelands of the world to gardens, I shall turn the guardsman's interference into victory.' He waved the cowering priest up from the floor. 'I trust some of Shadisa's blood and flesh is left?'

'A little, master,' said Salwa.

'Remove a corpse from the library's mortuary that matches Shadisa's height, weight and age. I will change the body to be an exact match of the slave girl. After the corpse's face is smashed in, we will leave enough trace of Omar Barir's flesh on the body to ensure that he is identified as her murderer. We will let the guardsmen themselves jump to the obvious conclusion when they investigate.'

'The flesh from his drak breeding . . .' said Salwa.

'Yes,' said the grand vizier. 'And how fitting that his drak will be the last one we need to grow for any guardsmen. Those meddling sons of the landed gentry, always bleating about tradition while holding back the empire from its greater destiny. It is time for those dogs to join the secret police among the ranks of the traitors to the empire, and Barir's crimes have provided me with the provocation I need to act. In fact, a delicious idea has just occurred to me. The last son of Barir's blood will come in useful for far more than just Shadisa's murder.'

Salwa knew better than to press the grand vizier on the nature of his notion; the ambitious monster was never more dangerous than when being pressed. 'We will need to find guardsmen who will confess to their order's corruption, master.'

The grand vizier pointed to a figure the size of a cedar tree on the other side of the pool, a torso grown as hard as stone while the victim's arms splayed out in a fan of thousands of bones, eyes staring wildly above a sealed mouth. 'They always confess to something, Salwa. Just unsew the mouth of the head of the secret police, if you do not believe me.'

Omar looked as if he was having to resist grabbing Boulous and pushing him aside. 'I must see the grand marshal of the order.'

'Wait until Master Uddin returns,' said Boulous. 'We need his counsel on what to do next.'

'He disappears for days and weeks at a time,' said Omar. 'Do you even know how long he will be gone this time, or where he is?'

'On the guardsmen's business,' said Boulous.

'This is the guardsmen's business!' shouted Omar, pushing the empty vial towards Boulous. 'The Caliph Eternal has been made a slave with whatever drug was inside here. Our oath is to him, we are his justice.'

'You are letting your anger over the girl's death cloud your decisions,' said Boulous. 'The guardsmen's position is precarious and this tale of yours will carry far more weight if it comes from the lips of Master Uddin. He is senior in the order, he might even be in the running to become the next grand marshal.'

Omar pushed past Boulous and opened the door to depart Uddin's cell in the fortress. 'I am going to face the present grand marshal and he will listen to my words. They are the truth and he will believe me. Are you with me?'

Boulous hurried out after Omar. 'Hasty,' he whispered. 'Too hasty.'

Boulous had never seen Omar so angry. Normally he was as languid as a lizard lying on the sand, content to be still and drink up the sun. Now he was the force of a sandstorm that would send lizards scurrying away to their burrows, scouring the whitewash off the capital's minarets below. No good would come of this, Boulous was certain. He hadn't even needed the note of warning that old Nudar had sent up to him from the palace below to know that. This was a time for subtlety and nuance, the cold calculations that the grand vizier specialized in, not blundering about like a shell-blinded drak in battle.

Unfortunately, the last son of the House of Barir didn't seem to practice subtlety, despite all of Boulous's attempts to open his eyes to the machinations within the Jahan.

Getting to see the grand marshal was every bit as difficult as Boulous had anticipated. The jahani who administered the commander of the guardsmen's diary ran his fingers over the pages, rubbing at a small pair of spectacles as he inspected the evening's business, tutting as he read.

'Not tonight,' said the diary keeper, glancing up from the desk to look down the corridor that led to the stairs up to the grand marshal's offices.

'Please,' said Boulous, 'just ten minutes with the old man. You know me, Jizan, and you know the favours I have done you in the past.'

'Indeed I do,' said the diary keeper. 'And my memory is not so short that I have forgotten their existence over the last hour.'

'What do you mean?' demanded Boulous.

'I mean I already have officials of the guardsmen furious at me for allowing you two an unscheduled appointment earlier this evening; that was his last slot of the night. You can go away now.'

Boulous felt a sinking feeling in his gut. 'We did not see the grand marshal earlier.'

The diary keeper shrugged his shoulders. 'It is time for final prayers. It is time for food, and there is a campaign that must be planned from scratch. You have heard that there is to be all-out war, haven't you? Come back tomorrow Boulous Ibn Uddin and stop wasting my time.'

But Omar had already pushed past the two sentries on either side of the corridor and was sprinting towards the spiral stairs at the other end. The diary keeper shouted for reinforcements from the guardroom down the corridor. Boulous threw caution to the wind and ran after the sprinting sentries, their ceremonial knives jingling on their belts as they pursued Omar.

Boulous gasped as he crossed the threshold. The grand marshal's frail body had been stabbed through the chest with his own scimitar, pinned vertically against a bloodstained tapestry between two firing slits in the wall. He looked like an insect stolen by a collector, pinned to the fabric for display. Omar had stumbled over two dead guards sprawled across the floor, their throats cut, and the two pursuing sentries had seized the young guardsman from behind even as he took in the horror of the slaughter.

Boulous felt the cold metal of the diary keeper's pistol jamming into his neck before he could even turn around. 'What have you done, Boulous, and why in heaven's hundred names did you come back here? You should have run, you two treacherous devils. You should have run.'

Boulous watched hopelessly as Omar struggled in the grip of the two burly guardsmen as they laid into him. 'Yes, I believe we should have.'

Nuance and subtlety. Omar had barely understood how the game inside the Jahan was played. *But the grand vizier does.*

* * *

Omar could feel the blood running down his face as he regained consciousness. The painful swelling around his eyes blurred the sight of Boulous sprinkling him with dirty water from a puddle. Then he remembered the questions being fired at him, over and over again. Why did you kill the grand marshal? Who paid you to join the guardsmen? Which satrapy was he working for, which client state within the empire? Had the grand marshal of the order accused Omar of the crime of murdering one of the grand vizier's servants, before Omar killed him to silence the old man? Had he and Boulous been plotting treachery with the grand marshal? Had they been trying to force Shadisa to put poison in the grand vizier's food, or were they trying to assassinate the Caliph Eternal through the grand vizier's office? Why had Omar killed the slave girl? When had he murdered her? Where was Farris Uddin hiding?

No sleep; lights, being drowned over and over again in a foul-smelling cistern. At least the physical pain distracted him from thinking of Shadisa's blood-soaked clothes being destroyed by Salwa, of what her last few minutes must have been like at the dog's murdering hands. He tried not to sob at the thought. Omar had been kept on his own for what seemed like weeks, but here he was – back with Boulous at last. They would escape together, and he would have his revenge on that savage Salwa and his dark-hearted master, the wretched grand vizier. Revenge, that was all the last son of Barir had been left as his legacy. Fate had taken Shadisa from him as a reminder of that.

'It's raining,' spluttered Omar, watching rivulets running down the firing slit into their prison cell, darkness and a lashing wind outside.

'This is not the rain season, it is an omen,' said Boulous.

'Good or bad?' asked Omar, sitting up and feeling the bite

of his empty stomach, before trying to rub the agony out of his temples. 'What a headache.'

'It is the drugs they injected into your neck,' said Boulous.

'Truth drugs?'

'The sort that will make you agree with anything your interrogators suggest to you,' said Boulous.

'I will not have told them anything. My mind is too strong for them.'

'It hardly matters,' said Boulous. 'The pain was to break us, to make us tell them what we knew; and all they found out was that we knew nothing. They are not interested in the truth now, if they ever were. Some of the ones questioning us were from the Sect of Razat.'

'I did not murder the grand marshal,' insisted Omar, as if it was the retainer he had to convince.

'Nor I,' said Boulous. 'There are assassins that are said to serve the Caliph Eternal. It is whispered that their flesh has been changed by the womb mages so they can alter the features of their bodies and faces at will. Such creatures murdered the grand marshal, although I have no doubt it is traces of your blood the womb mages will have found on the sword sticking out of the grand marshal's chest.'

Omar moaned in despair. 'Immed Zahharl, this is his doing.'

'Now he has everything he wants,' said Boulous. 'A war to consolidate his hold on the empire, the whiff of booty and glory to buy the loyalty of the last of the admirals and generals who opposed him, and for the coup de grâce, the grand marshal cut to pieces and unable to oppose his ambitions.'

'Not quite everything, jahani,' said a voice through the bars of their prison cell.

Omar threw his aching body towards the door in fury. 'Salwa, you filthy murdering cur!'

The man indicated the insignia on his shiny new

guardsman's uniform in amusement. 'You are still a guardsman, at least in name. Do you have no salute for your order's new grand marshal?'

'Come through this door and I'll carve you up like you did Shadisa!'

Salwa smiled sadly. 'I did you a favour, guardsman. The silly girl's beauty would have faded in the end and where would your lusts have wandered then? I've saved you the heartache of growing apart as she slowly became a crone, the expense of acquiring and feeding younger wives.'

Omar gripped the bars on the door so tight his knuckles went white. 'I will repay your favour in kind, you filthy murdering dog.'

'We must all prove our allegiance,' said Salwa. 'You have proven where your loyalties lie. You have chosen the past.'

'How many men did you murder from Haffa?' demanded Omar.

'Heretics,' said Salwa. 'They were declared without Cent. I made their end painless. A silk rope to twist around their necks. They lost consciousness long before they died. I am not a cruel man, Omar Barir. My nature is merciful. I did not invent the rules of the game in the palace, but even you must admit I play them better than you. You cannot bleat about it after you have lost.'

'You have no honour,' said Boulous.

'Perhaps I can afford none.' There was a rattle at the lock as the cell door was opened. 'You know what the laws of the imperial guardsmen demand from traitors to the order?'

'Tied to a pair of draks,' said Boulous, 'and torn apart.'

'One drak for your hands, one drak for your legs,' said Salwa. There were six men waiting in the passage for them with rifles. Not guardsmen, but marines in the new black and silver uniforms of the Imperial Aerial Squadron.

'A merciful man,' spat Omar as the sailors dragged him and Boulous out and pushed them down the corridors of the fortress.

'In this instance, the grand vizier asked that your ancient traditions be honoured,' said Salwa, almost sounding as if he felt genuine regret at their fate. 'But I will instruct one of my airship officers to put a ball through your brain before the pain grows too intense.'

They emerged onto an open parapet, the lashing rain whipping across the top of the fortress, the coloured lights of the palace dome shining from below like luminescent fish beneath the glowing sea, and in the air above them a squadron of airships escorting in the strangest-looking aerostat Omar had ever seen, metal-clad, her armour sparkling in the lightning dancing around her hull.

'A Jackelian ship,' said Salwa. 'The *Iron Partridge*. Admiralty flagged, a magnificent prize. We captured her without a shot being fired. The vice-admiral commanding her was a coward.'

'They will not all be so,' coughed Boulous in the cold rain. 'The guardsmen have flown into action against the infidel's airships often enough to tell you that.'

'Times are changing,' laughed Salwa. 'Locked in the cells you won't have heard the news. We destroyed more than a quarter of the Kingdom of Jackals' combined fleet in a single action. You know how many airships the empire lost? None, not a single vessel. The Imperial Aerial Squadron is already back rearming with supplies and ordnance. When we fly north a second time, we will bring the empire such a victory as your friends in the order have only dreamt of. Your kind is no longer relevant, little jahani. You are fading into history.'

As Omar and Boulous were pushed forward on the parapet, Omar saw that hundreds of guardsmen were lined up in the courtyard below, their leather armour shining in the rain and the lightning.

Salwa looked back towards Omar as he mounted a firing step on the battlements. 'I am not a cruel man, last son of Barir, but I fear necessity has made the grand vizier otherwise. He commanded that you see this and told me to inform you that this is what the march of history looks like.' Salwa turned towards the ranks of guardsmen assembled below. While he was speaking, Omar and Boulous were shoved down to the stone and spread out, their arms and legs tied with thick rope to two pairs of training draks, the large flying creatures jostling the troops holding their reins, spooked by the squall. The draks were never normally expected to fly in such dirty weather.

'Two days ago,' Salwa shouted down, 'I asked for riders to volunteer to join the Imperial Aerial Squadron as scouts – and I see before me the answer to my request. A regiment of cowards who would rather patrol the safe gardens of the Jahan than throw themselves into action alongside the fleet.'

Hisses of outrage rose up from the courtyard in answer.

'I am your grand marshal, you dogs!' Salwa roared at them.

Calls echoed back. 'You wear his corpse's cloak.'

'Send us into battle as guardsmen, not navy lapdogs.'

'We don't send traitors into battle,' Salwa yelled down. 'Before he died, the previous grand marshal was uncovered plotting treason against the empire. These two—' he waved dismissively at Omar and Boulous, '—were leaders in his plot, leaders who tried to save their necks by silencing the grand marshal when they realized that the Caliph Eternal had uncovered their treachery. By your act of cowardice in refusing to fight, you have raised your colours along their side. The order of the imperial guardsmen is therefore disbanded. By command of the Caliph Eternal, emperor of emperors, your regiment is declared heretic!' As his hand dropped, marines of the Imperial Aerial Squadron rose up from behind the parapets of the fortress, rifles pulled tight against their shoulders, and there was a horrendous crackling as if a hundred blocks of oak were splintering. Smoke drifted out across the sky as guardsmen screamed below, scattering and falling and dying, rifle balls buzzing like bees in the air.

Omar screamed in rage at the betrayal, Boulous struggling by his side, even as his legs began to be drawn taut, the drak at the other end of the parapet struggling against the sailors holding it, driven to take flight and seek combat by the sounds and sights of the slaughter occurring below.

'The grand vizier wished for you to see the end of the guardsmen,' Salwa said to Omar. 'And he instructed me to make you this offer. Renounce the order now; join the Imperial Aerial Squadron as an officer. Act as an example that even the grand vizier's most implacable enemies may prosper through shifting their loyalties away from the past and embracing the future and our glorious sect in the name of progress.'

Omar gritted his teeth and silently shook his head.

'I was told you were a lazy fool who would always choose the easy way,' said Salwa. 'Choose the easy way, guardsman. Do it.'

'There isn't a drak in the fortress strong enough to pull my legs out of their sockets.'

Salwa shook his head sadly and motioned a sailor forward, raising his rifle towards Omar's head. 'Well, at least the foolish part is true. Being on the wrong side of history brings with it a savage burden. One it seems you must carry to your grave . . .'

CHAPTER ELEVEN

Jack rubbed his brow, half covered by a turban and sweating in the arc of the high sun. The relative ease with which the four of them had transformed themselves into citizens of the empire still seemed inconceivable to him. The skins of the three men had been darkened by dyes which the first lieutenant, with her half-Cassarabian parentage, hadn't needed. They wore the local clothing that Westwick had pulled out of her supply crate, the lining along the hems of their robes sewn with silver coins stamped with the caliph's head – legal tender throughout the empire. But then, the empire – as the commodore had explained – wasn't a homogenous nation, but rather a civilization composed of disparate nations, all ruled, however unwillingly, by the Caliph Eternal.

Jack did as he was told and repeated whenever he needed to the fiction that he was a slave from the sultanate of Zahyan, loyal servant to the commodore's spice merchant and his new wife, just married to seal a trading alliance, and travelling with their mute colossus of a bodyguard – the contents of his two flasks now hidden beneath his robes.

Having crossed the desert the locals called the Empty

Stephen Hunt

Quarter, in their pocket airship, they had deflated the stolen aerostat and hidden the open boat-like gondola under the cliff of a gorge in the wilds. They had landed a couple of miles outside a small village that the commodore entered before returning with four camels tied together. He had been muttering about parting with good money for the rangy, flea-bitten, bad-tempered creatures, and after a few days on the road with them, Jack came to see why. Jack's camel was always grumbling; deep-throated complaints at being mounted, dismounted, ridden too close to the other camels, or just protesting against every flick of the rider's crop needed to keep the beast pitching forward.

Along with their reluctant steeds, the commodore led them into the hill town of Sharmata Sarl in the south-western corner of central Cassarabia, a couple of days travel from the coastal towns where the royalist fleet-in-exile had docked in his younger days. It was a trading hub for the various caravan roads that crossed the empire, a place where the people that the four of them were impersonating should feel at home – and more importantly, where some of the commodore's old contacts were located.

The commodore had used the spare time travelling to Sharmata Sarl to drill Jack and Henry Tempest in the mannerisms of the locals. Jack found there was as much to learn as there had been when the airship's officers had been tutoring them back on board the *Iron Partridge*. Firstly, there were all the little things, such as how locals would usually refer to the country as the empire, never as Cassarabia; how the caliph was never just the caliph when you talked of him, but the Caliph Eternal. And then there were the bigger things – matters completely alien to the mindset of a Kingdom-born man – such as how locals would always bow when a priest of one of the hundred sects of the Holy Cent passed, and the hours of the day when they were required to supplicate themselves for at least ten minutes if they passed under the shadow of a temple.

'It's the small actions that will give you away,' the commodore had warned, 'never the large.'

Small actions such as the need to fake indifference towards biologicks, the bizarre breedings of the empire's womb mages.

'It might be considered bad form in the Kingdom to have your body reshaped by a womb mage, but here in the empire it is a matter of blessed survival,' noted the commodore. 'Nomads with water-filled humps on their backs to see them through a dried-up oasis or two, or transparent eyelids so they can travel through wicked sandstorms without going blind.'

And there were enough of the twisted creatures tied up against the white-walled buildings of Sharmata Sarl. Caterpillar-like things as tall as a shire horse but seven times the length; carts pulled by pairs of sharp-beaked birds with human eyes, caravans guarded by gold-masked warriors with tails swishing behind them. 'Nothing like growing out your prehensile tail for balance,' explained the commodore. All the great scimitar masters should have one. It was, he explained, considered bad art to blend too much human flesh with the panoply of creatures whose templates the sorcerers borrowed from, although biologicks with human flesh were the easiest to be birthed by the swollen-bellied slaves who acted as the empire's living factories.

'I've never heard of this Cantara woman,' said Westwick, looking at the door of the house that the commodore had led them to.

There had been camels stabled lower down in the town. Narrow, tall streets, steeped in shade now hemmed them in, while laundered items of clothing swayed on lines close to their heads. Further up the hilly incline, a group of old men played draughts in the street while thin hounds lay by their feet, noses laid out across the dusty white cobbles.

'Ah, and that's as it should be, Maya,' said the commodore, his hand lifting a knocker shaped like a bat on the door. 'Your dour friends in the State Protection Board are fine for winkling out the caliph's agents hiding on Jackelian soil, but here in the empire the great game is played by the Pasdaran's rules. Or at least, that's how it used to be, back in the day.'

An old hook-nosed woman wearing a silk head-covering opened the door, her eyes widening in surprise at the sight of the commodore and the other three disguised Jackelians. 'I see an old soul wearing the face of a young man I once knew.'

The commodore's head bobbed knowingly. 'Still in the house, Cantara, after all this time.'

'It's not easy to leave the house,' said the woman. 'As you must have noticed, the neighbourhood is quite different from the old days. Come in, come in you old rascal, come in for some yoghurt and sherbet.'

Jack walked in after the commodore, followed by the hulking captain of marines and First Lieutenant Westwick, her eyes surveying the street suspiciously for any sign that their entry had been watched.

'Are your companions also tradesmen?' said the old woman to the commodore, ushering them into a wide, awning-covered courtyard and bidding them to sink onto the cushions placed around a rectangular pool in its centre.

'Of sorts, Cantara,' said the commodore. 'Tradesmen of sorts with the rival firm, whose wicked employ, I have to admit, has finally found my old bones too.'

The old woman nodded, humming thoughtfully. 'Not so like the old days after all, then. You have heard from afar, I suppose, about how poorly our house has fared of late.'

'Many of your servants have scattered?' said Westwick.

'Most have passed away,' said the old woman. 'Very sad, very sudden.'

'Say it's not all of them, lass,' said the commodore. 'I have travelled a blessed long way for a reunion. A few faces from the past to chew the fat with, that's not much to ask for now, is it?'

'There's a few left,' admitted the old woman. 'Mostly in service with the neighbours, you understand.'

'It would be good to see them,' said Westwick.

The old woman hummed again. 'Travel can be dangerous.'

'Life can be dangerous,' said Westwick. 'You never know when you will have to serve a new master, one who may turn out to be most unkind.'

'That is why there are a hundred faces in paradise,' said the old woman, 'so that we may always find at least one to smile upon us.' She looked at them. 'And which of the sects smiles upon you?'

'I'll take the fifty-third,' said the commodore. 'The old one, that is, although I'd say the new one if it was soldiers doing the asking.'

Remembering the cover story that they had agreed, Jack nodded in agreement. *I just hope that I can get out of this land without the cause to pray to your gods.*

'A good choice for a salty trader and his two servants,' agreed the old woman, leaning over to finger Westwick's kaftan. 'And wearing the sash of a newly wed, which of the sects did your house before marriage support?'

'The Sect of Jabal, the seventy-seventh cent,' said the first lieutenant.

'Known for its fidelity and dependability,' smiled the old woman. 'Good, good. Very believable. If I didn't know better, I would take you all for locals, rather than travelling tradesmen.' She pointed at Jack's turban. 'Better you had been a jahani, with such hair – even concealed, but still . . .' She seemed to make up her mind. 'A reunion after all, then. We shall talk about business old and new.'

'Tradesmen always find something to talk about,' said Westwick.

'There's a lot of business about, my dear,' said the old woman. She clapped her hands together and a thin young slave appeared. 'Rooms for our guests, and I shall have to see if I can arrange for a few more visitors to arrive. Udal Lackmann. Yes, I shall send for Udal Lackmann.'

The commodore nodded in thanks as the old woman withdrew.

'You know this Udal Lackmann?' asked Jack.

'Of old, lad, yes,' said the commodore. 'The caliph never supported the royalist fleet directly, but he used men such as Udal – a smuggler – to channel his aid. That way if the caliph was caught, he could throw up his arms and say, "Ah, what wicked criminals there are dealing with these foreign scoundrels." Udal was the one I dealt with, always good for a torpedo or two, as long as they were being put in the water against parliament's shipping and fired a deniable distance from the empire's shores.'

'Pasdaran?' asked Westwick.

'If he wasn't, he was their creature,' said the commodore. 'Much as I am yours.'

'I am flattered that you believe so,' said Westwick, without a trace of irony in her voice.

'Your old friends may not know about Cassarabia's sudden leap forward when it comes to the caliph's airships,' said Jack.

Westwick shrugged. 'I wouldn't be too sure that the airships are the Caliph Eternal's, boy. There's been an unbalancing of power here. Yes. The Pasdaran are down, but they aren't quite out yet. They'll know something, count on it. If the empire is the foot that is kicking us, then the Pasdaran is a fungus attached to its sole. Even after you rip it out, the roots are still left buried deep in the flesh.'

'You'll tell me when you want me to try,' said Tempest.

'Not yet, Henry,' said Westwick. 'Your time will come, as soon as we find out where their celgas is coming from.'

'Is he really immortal?' asked Jack. 'The Caliph Eternal, I mean.'

'It's how the empire controls all its client nations,' said the commodore. 'The velvet glove slipped over the iron fist. The caliph's private drug, lifelast, is doled out to all the ruling families who keep their loyalty to him true. I've seen men down here who are over two hundred years old and still sprightlier than my creaking old frame. They say the caliph keeps the good stuff for himself and only gives out his diluted piss-water to his cronies. Maybe he will live forever.'

'They also say that the caliph's touch can cure sickness and that he can resurrect the dead with a drop of his blood,' sneered Westwick, 'and that only the one true god himself decides when a caliph's reign is over, striking him down with lightning and calling forward a new member from the blood-line of Ben Issman.'

'Don't let your mother's hatred for this land and what they did to her blind you, Maya,' said the commodore. 'I've seen some mortal unexplainable things during my years down south.' He looked at Jack. 'Next time you're in Middlesteel Museum, have a look at the oldest coins they have from the empire. They're from before the cold-time and the face on those coins is the same blessed one you'll find on the silver loose change sewn into your robe.'

Westwick snorted. 'Go into the town's flesh bazaar, boy, any womb mage there would be able to give you the same face if it wasn't a crime to do so. Tell us what you know of this smuggler, Jared.'

'His mind is as fast as anyone's I've ever known,' said the commodore. 'He's a striking fellow right enough, with skin as dark as ebony and a presence that's large enough to fill a room. His men told me once that he's an exiled prince from the Red Forests in the deep south – one of the empire's disputed satrapies – and he'd fallen in with the machinations of the forest people's politics. He came riding out on one of those great bulls they ride down there, with just the clothes on his back and a single lance, so the story has it. He started off running contraband through the forest, between the empire and the Skirrtula. Now there's not much that moves illegally in the harbour towns that Udal doesn't have a hand in.'

'Then he must be Pasdaran,' said Westwick.

'What can't be stamped out must be controlled,' agreed the commodore. 'That's the caliph's way, alright. Always the long game, down Cassarabia way.'

'You're looking mournful, lad,' said the commodore to Jack as the young sailor sat by the second-storey window looking down onto the street – taking his turn on the sentry duty that First Lieutenant Westwick had insisted on.

'I just realized,' said Jack, 'that I haven't thought of my brothers for days. How they are doing, how they are being treated . . .'

'And now you are feeling guilty for how wicked selfish you've been?' said the commodore. 'Ah, you've discovered the terrible secret of why people take to the great game like a drunk holds to his bottle. You're never so alive as when you're walking with death by your side, and we're cowards all.'

'Cowards?' said Jack. 'We're in the middle of the enemy's territory wearing false clothes that would have us hanged as spies if that old lady downstairs takes it into her head to hand us in.'

'Does that make us brave, Mister Keats, or mortal fools? Brave is waking up every morning and trudging into a mill or the fields before the sun is up, worrying about feeding your family, worrying about whether your children will get an education, food on their plate, or survive the next winter's round of whooping cough. Worrying about whether the crops will fail or your manufactory will have enough work to be able to hire you on for the following month. That's real fear, Mister Keats. Living an ordinary life takes real bravery. Letting danger chase that away from your mind is one escape, travelling on a u-boat and seeing a different shore every week is another; drinking yourself insensible or a pipe stuffed with mumbleweed are more. I've tried them all, lad, and the great game is the best by far.'

'But the State Protection Board forced you to come here,' said Jack.

'It looks like it, doesn't it?' said the commodore. 'And that's what you tell yourself. They've found me. I'm too blessed old to run away and start a new life with yet another name. So it's just one little favour, and then another. Run some cargo here for them off-manifest, no questions asked. Pick up a man on your boat in some far-off port; drop some documents off in another. Avoid the men-of-war hunting your boat; dodge the assassin in the shadows; draw your sword for a game of tickle-my-sabre when you can't. And all the time while you're doing it you never think about the sister who won't talk to you for getting her son killed, or the wife and daughter who've moved along the Circle before you.'

'I won't be like that,' said Jack. 'I'm getting back to Jackals to see my brothers; to buy them out of the poorhouse.'

'Perhaps you will at that,' said the commodore.

Down in the street there was a commotion, the sounds of running – a group of black-uniformed men with red cloaks and strange silver facemasks sprinting after a solitary runner. The commodore pushed Jack back from the edge of the window so they wouldn't be spotted watching from above. 'Nothing down there for us, Mister Keats. Keep your head down.'

The runners caught up with their victim just under the safe house, kicking him to the ground and then dragging him away as he yelled in horror.

Jack shielded his eyes against the sun as he risked a quick look outside at the figures pulling the prisoner away up the hill. 'Were they priests?'

'No, town police,' said the commodore. 'The masks are based on the face of Salofar, the twelfth sect of the Holy Cent. The face of righteous justice, which as you've just seen, runs mortal swiftish in Cassarabia.'

'The man they grabbed . . . a thief?'

'A merchant,' said the commodore. 'The silver sash he wore bore his bazaar trading licence. He must have been caught cheating his customers. Poor devil, they practice *menshala* in the empire.' The commodore saw that Jack didn't know the word and continued. 'It is the will of the one true god that the punishment must always fit the crime. When I was with the royalists in one of the empire's harbour towns back west, I saw a baker who had been caught adulterating his flour with sawdust. The local police baked him to death in his own oven. No judges or courts or juries here. Just menshala.'

'Barbarians.' Jack shook his head in disgust. *And here we are, right in the heart of their land.*

'Don't be so quick to judge,' said the commodore. 'Back in Jackals you can spill seed potatoes onto a field of weeds and most years you'll pull some spuds out. You've seen what the heart of the empire is like. Dust and sand and rocks. Here, you can break your back all year long, then a single neighbour two hundred miles upstream can divert the irrigation and kill your entire livelihood within a day; or a band of wild brigands can turn up, and in one hour steal a year's labour from you at the point of a scimitar. A hard land breeds hardy people and if you don't have hard justice to go along with the land, then you have the rule of the gun and the blade and the club, and no civilization at all that's worth the blessed name.'

'We're here to fight them,' said Jack. 'And it sounds like you admire them.'

'Not so, lad, but I do understand them. Because it's the way of the world. In bright, fertile waters, the fish you see are as shiny as rainbows and swarm in schools as large as clouds. But run your u-boat deep and into the dark barrens, and the fish are tough, bony-looking things, few and fierce. That's the empire. The Cassarabians are warriors. Their land made them that way and they've rolled up all the plumper, richer nations that lady fortune tossed down for them as their neighbours. All but one, Jackals in the north, protected by our floating walls . . . the Royal Aerostatical Navy.'

'And now they have their own navy.' *The Circle preserve us.*

'So they do, Mister Keats, and we must get to the bottom of the whys, hows and wherefores of the Imperial Aerial Squadron's celgas. Because unless we can, they're going to be swimming in our waters. And as you love Jackals, as you love your two fine young brothers, trust me, you don't want to see the Kingdom ruled as a satrapy of the empire.'

When Udal Lackmann did reach the safe house, Jack was not on sentry duty, so it seemed to him that the smuggler had arrived as if out of thin air. The first thing that Jack knew of the smuggler's presence in the building was when he noticed their safe house's aged host whispering with a newly arrived traveller by the entrance to the courtyard and pointing towards the group of Jackelians. Commodore Black got up from the game of cards he had been trying to teach Jack and Henry Tempest, and approached the man with what seemed to Jack a touch of uncharacteristic apprehension. The traveller's white robes were grey with dust, a sand filter hung off his neck, and a single curved dagger was tucked behind his crimson waist sash.

'*Al-salaamo alaykum*, Udal Lackmann,' said the commodore.

'*Wa alaykum e-salaam*, Jared Black,' said the smuggler, flashing a smile as white as the shine on the courtyard's four pillars. 'It has been many years since you were a visitor here.'

'Many years for me, Udal Lackmann,' said the commodore. 'But they've been a mortal lot kinder to you.'

'My life is full of little blessings,' said the smuggler. 'They help me hold to a path that fills its travellers with vim and vigour. I had not heard that your u-boat was back in port.'

'I walked here on my dusty boots,' said the commodore, 'like a true son of the desert.'

'There is not enough iron in your soul to be that,' said Udal, 'yet a little too much to make your merchant's garb believable, at least to one who knows you.'

First Lieutenant Westwick appeared in the courtyard and

the smuggler gave a small bow with one hand held against his heart.

'The face I saw watching upstairs in the window,' said Udal. 'Tell me that you are not truly the wife of this old seadog?'

First Lieutenant Westwick raised the hem of her dress, revealing a brace of throwing blades strapped to her calf. 'That's not the point of me being here.'

'Delightful,' said the smuggler. 'And a half-blood too, with a face exotic on both sides of the border. I shall buy you. How much for her, Jared?'

Henry Tempest leapt to his feet. 'You touch a hair of her head and I'll twist yours off your flaming neck!'

Udal laughed. 'Sit down, giant one; it is too hot for such jokes. The price to be paid for such as she is paid in steel, not gold, and I have no wish to put to the test the accuracy of those deadly little blades.' He looked at Jack. 'And one not much younger than you were, Jared Black, when you first came visiting these shores.'

'Aye, well age does funny things to memory,' said the commodore. 'Like the way I remember you so much the same, you might as well have just walked out the room all those years ago and strolled straight back in.'

'I heard the royalist fleet met its end at Porto Principe,' said the smuggler. 'I raised a glass in toast to you and your friends.'

'They were good ones,' said the commodore, 'in different times.'

'It's always different times,' said the smuggler. 'Are you bringing things in, or bringing things out?'

'Ourselves in,' said the commodore. 'As for what we'd be taking out, my new wife here has a passion for airships. She finds them endlessly fascinating, especially the bit where they get floated off the ground. Isn't that a miracle? All the weight of such a grand large hull, filled with all those sailors and fin-bombs and supplies, then you pack its cells full of gas, and up it goes, as long as a battleship and as high as the clouds.'

'She should switch her temple tithes to the Sect of Razat,' said Udal. 'They find such matters endlessly fascinating, also.'

'That's what I heard,' said the commodore. 'And I thought to myself, I need a man of means, a man who gets about and will be able to introduce me to the right people. Why, my old friend Udal, he'll do, that's what occurred to me.'

'I have very little against the Sect of Razat,' said Udal. 'For keepers and priests, they seem eminently practical people.'

'A smuggler needs borders to cross, lad,' said the commodore. 'Without borders and taxes to avoid, you're only in the haulage business. *One continent, one empire* makes a nice political slogan for the Caliph Eternal, but it'll be wicked hard on your bottom line.'

'To be an honest businessman,' smiled Udal. 'I long for such days. But perhaps not quite so soon.'

'We can help you postpone them indefinitely,' said First Lieutenant Westwick.

'The followers of Razat are a very insular sect,' said Udal. 'But I know one man who can help you with what you wish to know. We will need to travel towards the capital to meet him.'

'May the light of the world shine on you,' said the first lieutenant, in what sounded like a quote to Jack. 'And all who are under this house.'

'The light of the world has been burning a little too brightly lately for those under this roof, pretty lady,' said Udal. 'And you will do well to remember that the road to the capital also ends in the road to the Caliph Eternal's torture garden.'

*   *   *

Jack could feel the throbbing sun above him like a living organism pulsing its heat down upon his neck. The constant scurrying noise of their sandpedes' tiny-clawed feet across the dusty surface of the road provided a counterpoint to the noise of crickets that came from the marshy grasses next to the river. Jack hadn't asked what cargo was strapped to the multi-segmented insect-like beasts of burden by Udal's smugglers, and nobody had volunteered the information. *How can riding in this heat be so tiring?*

They were following one of the empire's more out-of-the-way tracks towards the capital, accompanied by the twisting, turning River Hahran, thrilling-sweet and rotten. There was not much traffic along the road, but they passed plenty of locals from the waterside villages. Women sat in the shade of palm trees like little knots of black crows, weaving clothing while they sang songs with throaty voices that rattled and hummed. Many of the village buildings had wheel-shaped minarets, ornate constructions holding circular rotors that spun into action when the breeze picked up, supplanting the mechanical power being supplied by turning watermills pushed out into the river. Dhows in the water took advantage of both the wind and the drift of the river, their decks piled with large pots containing their cargoes: fish, vegetables and meat from the flood fields along the riverbank, all heading for the great souks of the capital.

Greasy spiced mutton seemed to be the smugglers' staple diet, leavened by tiny salted fish as small as a child's fingers. They would stop and consume them in mud huts erected along the roadside for weary travellers to rest their legs.

When they were on the move again, Jack had to watch that the sling of his camel's saddle, ornately frayed at the bottom, didn't catch in the chitin of the sandpedes, the armour of each bony section clacking in and out as the caravan undulated over the dips and rises of the riverside route. The smugglers acting as drovers would walk alongside the pistoning legs, just out of reach, and crack the chitin with rhino horn-handled crops crafted specially for driving sand-pedes. They would use the crops liberally, striking in the soft spot between the armour and the lashed-down cargo every time the sandpedes appeared as if they were slowing down, yelling out something that sounded to Jack like, *'Jebbal Kallgoa!'*

First Lieutenant Westwick rode under the cover of an umbrella-like sunshade, and would demurely turn her head when the fishermen and farmers along the way called out in her direction – wishing her luck in her marriage or other, cheekier, greetings. It was easy to believe, Jack realized, in the lie of their deception. Just humble travellers, slowly journeying through the heart of the empire at a merchant's pace as they went about their innocent business. It was only when the jarring sight of an airship passed by, distant against a cloudless sky or a jagged mountain range, that reality intruded. Not a Jackelian 'stat, but the alien serrated vessels of the Cassarabians, incongruous both in design and location in these exotic climes. Then the deadly weight of the young sailor's mission rose like bile in his throat. Four Jackelians, disowned by their own side, dressed up like desert nomads from the cover of some penny-dreadful, sedately wandering through the heart of the enemy's territory in search of the source of the power driving the most dynamic sect in the empire. And who were the four of them trusting to guide them? Criminal dregs, the beholden creatures of a foreign secret police force that had already been routed by the enemy.

'You thinking about home, boy?' asked Henry Tempest.

I was thinking about my brothers. If only they could see

me now. They wouldn't believe it. Jack nodded. 'Don't you?'

'A marine carries his home with him,' said Tempest, swigging from one of his canteens – just water to ward off the heat, rather than one of the two chemicals he needed to bring some semblance of balance to his mind. 'It's the decking of your airship, the lay of your hammock, the company's colours and the crew you serve with.'

'Yes, but the ship's gone,' said Jack.

'The ship's mission is here,' said Tempest, 'and so are we. Captain Jericho is depending on us. We find the enemy's celgas and the skipper will be covered in glory. We fail and it won't matter one perishing way or the other.' He gestured to the marshy reeds waving in the river breeze. 'It's better than the four walls of the stockade, and that's where I'd bloody be without the old man. Floating in a maximum security isolation tank with a plug up my nose.'

'They'd have hanged me without him,' whispered Jack.

'So I heard,' said Tempest. 'They tried to hang me once, after I got into one of my rages with a provost. The rope didn't take.'

Tempest was as rugged as the mountains in the distance. The wind didn't touch the captain of marines. The sun didn't burn him. The impossibility of their task didn't faze him. He was a rock in the sea, waiting for the ocean to beat him with her fury; and the rock just sat there and took it – knowing no dread or doubt.

'Didn't you feel *any* fear when they put the noose around your neck?'

Tempest's slab-like brow furrowed as if the thought had never occurred to him, as if the act of considering it now was bringing him pain. 'No. It wasn't a very scary rope. I should feel more things, I know I should. But they took it away from me when they gave me my strength. I think I was frightened before I was strong, I think I can remember what it was like.'

'Maybe you're better off not remembering,' said Jack.

'They made me into a man-of-war,' said Tempest. 'That's what they call our airships and that's what they called us. I'm the last of them, that I am. And I'm not done yet. Captain Jericho always says that when he comes to the stockade for me. You're not done yet, Henry Tempest. Did you really break into the vaults of Lords Bank?'

'Yes,' said Jack.

'Well, bugger me. It's true, then. They would have tried more than two ropes on you outside Bonegate if your weight had flaming snapped your noose.'

From the reeds on their left a series of shouts rose from the wading fishermen. 'Soldiers! Soldiers!'

There was a cloud of birds in the air, but as the wheeling, diving creatures drew closer, Jack saw that his eyes had been deceived by perspective. They were far larger than any bird he had ever seen, more like giant lizards, virtually dragons, with human riders saddled behind their long sinuous necks.

'Those aren't scouts,' Jack shouted back towards the commodore. All around him, the smugglers were running towards the sandpedes, lifting long spindly-barrelled rifles out from under the bundles of contraband, breaking the rifles and pushing fresh crystal charges into their breaches.

There was no doubt as to where the creatures were headed. The caravan of smugglers was their target. This was no innocent over-pass. The smugglers raised their rifles, but they didn't point them at the fast-approaching dragon riders. The four Jackelians on their camels found themselves surrounded.

'Ah now,' whined the commodore at the smuggler's leader. 'Is this how you're being eminently practical these days?'

'It is for the best, I think, Jared Black,' said Udal.

'The best for who?' spat Jack.

Henry Tempest was half laughing, half gargling as he poured the contents of the red-lidded canteen down his throat.

'Henry!' shouted the first lieutenant. 'Stand down. There's too many of them here!'

'Is that it?' yelled Tempest. 'Is that all you've got? A bunch of lancers on those flaming flying snakes, they couldn't take a RAN airship even on our worst day.' He reached down to the pair of smugglers covering him with their shaking rifles, seizing the tips of both barrels and bending them around into a u-shape. 'No polish on your brass, no bayonets.' The captain of marines twisted in his saddle, dismounting and kicking out at the same time, the two smugglers with the crushed rifles collapsing back from the force of the blow. He reached out with his left hand and tore off the leather saddle straps from his camel, grabbing the saddle and using it half as a shield, half as a mace, to lash down another two smugglers running at him with their curved belt daggers. Contemptuously, he kicked one of the fallen jewelled daggers, sending it arcing away into the reeds. 'I wouldn't clean my bleeding teeth with that toothpick!'

The smugglers had seized the reins of Jack's camel. He wasn't armed – no slave in the empire was allowed to wear a scimitar or carry a rifle, not even in his supposed merchant master's name – so he lashed out with his boot, but one of Udal's men clutched his ankle and pulled him off, others seizing him before he'd even hit the ground. A rifle butt connected with his skull and bright light flared across his vision, followed by a spinning darkness encroaching from the edges of his sight.

Just as he lost consciousness, Jack thought he saw Henry

Tempest with his hand around a drak's harness, swinging the giant lizard like a fairground ride, other riders swooping down to cast large nets across his massive form.

The giant's voice faded into the black. *'I'm not done yet!'*

Salwa glanced over at a group of Imperial Aerial Squadron officers coming out of a turret towards the execution party before he turned back to Omar. 'I do hope these four draks are strong enough to rip you and your friend apart, as they are the last ones left alive in the fortress.' Salwa turned his attention to a half-full spherical container being lugged over by the sailors. 'Why do you still have poison left inside there? The womb mages calculated the precise dosage to wipe out the guardsmen's entire stable.'

'Apologies,' said the lead officer, raising his face from under his peaked cap. 'Your men weren't thirsty enough to drink any more.'

Omar's eyes widened at the sight of Farris Uddin's face. There was a sudden exchange of bullets between the guardsmen dressed as marines and Salwa's men, the rasp of steel being drawn and the confusion of crashing blades. Omar was rolled about, the draks thrashing around in confusion amongst the mêlée, the troops controlling them having abandoned the reins for their weapons. His cry of relief at being reprieved from execution by Salwa turned to one of agony as his limbs were twisted beyond their natural tolerance.

Omar felt a burning pain lash across his arms and legs as the severed straps of the chords that had bound him to the drak whipped across them. Rolling to his feet he caught a scimitar tossed from one of the disguised guardsmen. Boulous rose to his feet beside him, then Omar ducked reflexively as a shadow buzzed overhead, the wind of a passing drak ruffling the hairs on the back of his neck. He barely had time to register a whole talon wing in the air before a series of detonations from the battlements on the other side of the bailey filled the air with dust and flying rock fragments.

One of Salwa's men came sprinting towards Omar, his steel blade twisting in an intricate pattern in the air. Omar ducked down and kicked out with both his legs, going under the arc of the scimitar and sending his attacker flying. He rolled along the ground and pulled up into a guard stance to be greeted by the sight of Farris Uddin plunging his blade down into the man's chest, swift and sure, as merciless as an executioner.

Omar yelled in frustration as he saw Salwa retreating back into one of the battlement's turrets with a handful of his men.

Farris Uddin's hand fell heavily on Omar's shoulder as he made to sprint after them. 'Let them go.'

'But he's murdered half the guardsmen in the fortress!'

Farris Uddin pointed down to the corpse-strewn bailey. 'Look closer.'

Omar did as he was bid and noticed something strange about the guardsmen's bodies; their arms were locked behind their backs by ropes, a line of cloth tied around the mouth of each corpse.

'The only guardsmen down there were volunteers,' said Farris Uddin. 'To make enough noise that the Imperial Aerial Squadron wouldn't notice we had already captured the marines they had waiting outside. Salwa was firing on his own men down in the courtyard.'

'You knew the guardsmen were going to be dissolved!'

Farris Uddin held up the empty vial Omar had seen the grand vizier use to make the Caliph Eternal beg like a whipped dog. 'I intercepted this, along with the grand marshal's murdered body and the grand vizier's men charged with disposing of the evidence. The grand marshal was killed by a poisoned needle thrust into the back of his neck – an assassin's kill. Everything else, your blade through his gut, was for show. The grand marshal would have known what this vial meant as well as I. Its existence meant that our demise was inevitable.'

'They have the Caliph Eternal addicted, master,' said Omar. 'I saw him bowing and grovelling before the grand vizier, as if the ruler of rulers was no more than a slave . . . The Caliph Eternal, himself.'

'He is not an addict,' said Farris Uddin, 'and you saw something very different.'

Omar started to speak, but Farris Uddin silenced him. 'Later, boy. There is one truth here. We are now apostate – as rogue and rebellious as any bandits of the Empty Quarter. Boulous, back to the stables. Mount up and follow the talon wing out of the capital. All of you, go, two to a drak if you have to. Any who stay here will be hunted down by the grand vizier's men and silenced.'

'Where will we go?' asked Omar.

'We regroup and we run,' said Farris Uddin. 'That is our duty now, just to survive.'

Omar was glad to be off the drak when it landed, the creature's tail thumping the ground in irritation, resentful of Omar supplanting whoever had been its blood-bonded guardsman. Probably one of their brave volunteers, lying dead in the inner bailey of the fortress. Stable hands came running forward to take the reins dangling from the drak's snake-like neck, dust from the ground under its four stubby, sharp-clawed feet rising up like a veil of mist around its green scales.

Omar followed after Boulous and Farris Uddin, vacating the open clearing outside the hundreds of tents so more riders could land. Everyone who had survived the guardsmen's betrayal had regrouped here – all the planning for a campaign that they had never been called on to execute now put to use in fleeing the capital as fugitives. How long could they survive as a rogue army in the field, raiding for supplies after their stores ran out? That was the question. And how long before the shadow of the Imperial Aerial Squadron's new airships passed over them with their bomb bays open?

'How long will we be here, Master Uddin?' called Omar, catching up with the guardsman commander and his retainer.

'We have a period leave of grace,' said Uddin. 'The grand vizier likes to announce victories, not defeats. He was set to announce the dissolution of the guardsmen, not their flight intact from the capital. Perhaps the dog will try to claim we have been sent into the field against the Jackelians after all.'

'The grand vizier just has to wait for our supplies to run out, master,' said Boulous, miserably. 'An army of foot soldiers might be able to live off the land, but with draks to feed we need the wagoneers of the army supply corps to stay in the field.'

'Your grasp of logistics does my teachings credit,' said Uddin. 'Although watch the impact your words might have on the morale of our people.'

'The grand vizier will wish to finish us off out of sight,' said Omar. 'He does his work in the shadows.'

'Quite so,' said Uddin, walking up to a large collection of tents covered with netting the same colour as the barren rocky ground they were pegged into. 'But we have enough supplies to last for one battle – we will just have to choose that one battle wisely. You have heard the old adage that my enemy's enemy is my friend?' He opened the flap to the tent. 'Meet your enemy's enemy.'

Omar stared in amazement. Inside were four prisoners tied up against the tent posts: a shaven-headed giant of a man wrapped in tight chains; a statuesque woman with the look of both beauty and danger – one who might almost have passed for a Cassarabian; an old salt-bearded fellow; and a young man who looked about Omar's age. The faces of the men mottled where skin dye had been rubbed off to reveal a skin as light as a jahani's, like Boulous.

Omar caught a movement out of the corner of his eye – from Farris Uddin. The guard commander's skin was changing colour, darkening to ebony. It moved and flexed as if parasites were rippling under his cheeks and forehead. Omar stepped back in astonishment, the guard commander raising a hand to calm him. Astonishingly, Boulous seemed unconcerned by the changing features of Farris Uddin, as did all the prisoners except the youngest of them, whose look of horror must have mirrored Omar's own.

'So, Udal the smuggler and Uddin the soldier are one and the same,' said the salt-bearded prisoner on the floor of the tent. He laughed and looked towards Omar. 'What's the matter, lad? Didn't your officer tell you that he's a shape-switcher and an agent of the Pasdaran to boot?'

Omar found the scimitar in his hand, drawn and pointing at the man-thing. 'Who are you, what are you?'

It was Farris Uddin's voice answering, but with an uncharacteristic tone of amusement. 'Everything he said, everything that you know, and more.'

'Ah, they're the only Pasdaran who made it through the recent purges,' said the bearded foreigner. 'Those who were buried deep in the guards and the army and the jahani, with other faces and identities to hide behind.'

'How perfect,' snarled the woman, in a tone that indicated she considered it anything but. 'A smuggler and the guardsman who is meant to catch him, poacher and gamekeeper, both rolled into one.'

Omar remembered the snake tattoo he had seen on Farris Uddin's neck when he first saw him that had vanished by the time they had journeyed away from Haffa. He looked accusingly at Boulous. 'And you knew, all this time?'

'Do not be too hard on Boulous,' said Uddin. 'I told you when you first arrived at the fortress, I picked my retainer for his discretion.'

Omar's head was left spinning by the implications. *All this and more.* But this man was still the officer who had taken his oath as a guardsman, who had travelled to Haffa Township so as to save him from the fall of the House of Barir. What did it matter if his face could flow like melting candle wax to take on the guise of others? The other faces were still *him*. A thought leapt unbidden into Omar's mind. The nagging feeling that there had been something familiar about Farris Uddin when they had first met. Was it possible that Farris Uddin had been in his father's house before, wearing someone else's face, or perhaps using a face that would fit in there. Had he been one of the house's retainers – perhaps even Alim, the rascally nomad turned water farmer who had helped Omar tend the desalination tanks?

No, he couldn't have been a permanent fixture, Omar realized. A guardsman might have to travel the length of the empire on the caliph's business. So might a smuggler or a bounty hunter. But Farris Uddin couldn't have spent years labouring on the house's water farms, could he?

'And what will you get for handing us over to the caliph?' asked the large, bearded prisoner. 'More of your blessed immortality drug? You haven't aged a single day since I left the empire.'

Farris Uddin held up the empty vial that Omar had seen the caliph inject himself with. 'The Caliph Eternal is not the man he used to be – which, ultimately, is why you are here and why we are here too.'

'You're too old to be a philosopher, Udal.'

'I'm too old to be anything else,' said Farris Uddin.

'You told me back in the fortress that it isn't a drug,' said Omar. 'But I saw the Caliph Eternal begging the grand vizier to be given its needle.'

'Not something that will make an addict of a man, although the Caliph Eternal sorely needs it.' Uddin looked at Boulous and nodded at the prisoners. 'Cut their ties and let them stand free. Not the big one, though, his temper runs hot.'

Farris Uddin named each of the prisoners in turn, for the benefit of Omar and Boulous.

'You flaming unchain me,' spat the giant Jackelian the commander had identified as Henry Tempest, 'and it'll take more than some nets dropped by your flying bloody salamanders to stop me.'

'I am quite sure of that,' said Farris Uddin, his features twitching and changing back to the face of the guardsman that Omar recognized. 'You are a piece of inferior work; substantial, but inferior. Your bones and muscles are so dense that your own glands cannot cope with your form without making an amateur chemistry set of your blood. Our womb mages would not have made such elemental errors with your flesh.' He tossed the empty vial across to the woman he had named as First Lieutenant Westwick. Boulous was keeping a wary pistol barrel levelled towards the prisoners.

'What do you think our Caliph Eternal is "addicted" to, sweet lady?'

Westwick dipped a finger inside the syringe, touching the residue to her tongue. 'Blood!'

'By Lord Tridentscale's beard,' whined the commodore, 'is that the secret of the Caliph Eternal's long life? He's made himself into some sort of vampire?'

Uddin smiled. 'I presume the Kingdom's State Protection Board has some insight into the inner workings of the empire

– we always catch a few of your agents every year on our side of the border. They haven't all been shopping for bargains in the souks, have they? Why would the Caliph Eternal need regular injections of blood?'

'He's not the caliph!' said First Lieutenant Westwick sounding astonished.

'Very clever, your price has just risen,' said Uddin. 'The grand vizier has installed an impostor on the throne. Only the true Caliph Eternal knows the secret of the blood engineering which bonds his regiment of personal bodyguards to him. A very useful protection, don't you think?' As Uddin spoke, his features began to warp again, this time reforming into an exact match of the young man that Omar had seen in the heart of the palace. The caliph, ruler of rulers, Akil Jaber Issman himself. 'I can mimic the Caliph Eternal like this, but if I dared to trespass into the Jahan, the beyrogs would rip me apart the moment they saw me. They would know the difference between me and their true master.'

'But how did they get to the Caliph Eternal?' asked the woman. 'We've known of your womb mages' ability to breed shape-switchers for centuries. Jackals has safeguards against them in place and we don't even have a full understanding of the processes you use to create them. Your defences must be superior to ours.'

'Yes, there are tests that can detect such assassins,' said Farris Uddin, 'and of course, our tests are a lot more proficient than yours, but there is one secret you have not had access to – and that is the true nature of the Caliph Eternal's title. His immortality doesn't come from lifelast, although he imbibes the drug too. The drug extends a man's lifespan no more than three hundred years. You die looking as if you are in your third decade, but die you eventually will.'

'Then he is a wicked vampire,' whined the commodore.

'No,' said Farris Uddin. 'The caliph is what we call an *enculi*, although no one outside of the ruler of rulers' inner circle should have heard of that word. It is a form of womb magery. You take the flesh of a man – even a corpse's flesh will serve – and use it to give birth to a child, one so alike the original flesh-giver, that he or she is identical, beyond even a twin's likeness.'

'Your people's blessed resurrections,' said the commodore. 'The oldest son of the sultan of Hakaqibla died falling off his horse on a hunt, and the caliph bought him back to life.'

'Yes, the new son would have been an enculi,' said Uddin. 'It is one of the carrots that is dangled in front of the empire's satrapies to ensure our friends' loyalty. If a loved-one dies, we can bring them back, at least in resemblance.'

'That's the Caliph Eternal's immortality . . .?' said Westwick.

'At any one time,' said Uddin, 'the Caliph Eternal has seven enculi cast from his own flesh and raised in secrecy at the heart of the Jahan, within the womb mages' lair. There they are reared and taught in isolation from each other, waiting for the Caliph Eternal to pass into paradise.'

'Seven of them?' said Omar.

'The healthy body of an enculi can be guaranteed,' explained the guardsmen commander, 'but each mind is unique; even raised with shared tutors, given identical lessons, the same food and training. Some enculi cast from the Caliph Eternal's flesh will grow to be wise, some will grow to be fools, and some will grow to be indolent or insane. When the Caliph Eternal is dying he is given the current seven enculi's test results and the cleverest and strongest of them is chosen to continue as the light of the world. Their tutors strangle the other six and their bodies are destroyed. Before he dies, the passing Caliph Eternal gives his chosen child the secret of the blood sorcery that grants him absolute control over the beyrogs and the other biologick servants of the Jahan.'

'A grand vizier who is also the head of the order of womb mages,' said Omar, the realization of their predicament dawning on him. 'He would have been involved in the destruction of the six spare enculi.'

'Yes, he was,' said Farris Uddin. 'And it is now obvious that filthy wretch Immed Zahharl only destroyed five of them. The weakest and most pliable of the six he had installed on the caliph's throne as his puppet; the Caliph Eternal's chosen one must have been spirited away soon after his recent succession, before he could consolidate his power, kept prisoner and milked like a cow for the secrets of his own blood. How grateful would you be to the grand vizier, saved from destruction and installed on the throne as the true Caliph Eternal, your ability to command the beyrogs solely dependent on a regular infusion of your own flesh-brother's blood?'

'Where is the real Caliph Eternal?' asked Boulous. 'If they need to milk the ruler of rulers for the magics that are within his blood, where are they holding him prisoner?'

'The surviving agents of the Pasdaran used the time the grand vizier's men spent torturing you to good effect,' said Uddin. 'We matched their interrogations with a little questioning of our own. It was easy enough to kidnap one of the grand vizier's inner circle when we knew what to look for, what questions to ask.'

'I wish you had grabbed that bastard Salwa,' said Omar.

'The new grand marshal of the guardsmen?' laughed Uddin. 'A little too obvious.'

'Where is the true Caliph Eternal being held?' asked the Jackelian woman.

'Where else, the Forbidden City itself,' said Uddin. 'Mutantarjinn, the stronghold of the womb mages, where the grand vizier and his disgusting new sect first rose to prominence.'

'Say that isn't so,' groaned the commodore. 'That's a free city, owned and sealed as tight as a drum by the order of womb mages; crawling with your dark-hearted sorcerers and full of sicknesses and twisted abominations that should never see the light of day.'

'It is also where the grand vizier and the Sect of Razat's womb mages are producing the airship gas you have been sent to locate.'

'You're lying to me, Udal,' said the commodore. 'Another lie to go along with your damned false faces, just another wicked lie to get old Blacky to head down to that dark, terrible place and save your undeserving ruler.'

'It is the truth,' said Farris Uddin. 'My agents were already investigating the strange new source of the grand vizier's aerial power when the Pasdaran were declared heretic. The airship gas is not from a natural gas mine such as that which your people guard so jealously. Our gas is a product of womb mage sorcery. I do not know how, that is still their secret, locked away deep in Mutantarjinn, but I know it stems from the grand vizier's position as the head of the order of womb mages.'

'Don't trust him,' warned the young Kingdom sailor, Jack.

'I told you that I would take you to a man who could help you,' said Uddin, 'it just happens that *I* am that man.'

'And why should we assist you?' spat the commodore.

'Our agents once backed your royalist friends' fight to try to restore your true king back to power in Jackals,' said Uddin. 'It is only fitting for you to help me restore our emperor to his throne. Now, as before, your enemy is our enemy, and together we might bring him down.'

'You want us to fight alongside Jackelian heathens?' said Omar, more than a little shocked by the idea.

'We have been declared traitors,' said Farris Uddin, 'so we may as well act like traitors. And your guardsman's oath was given to the real Caliph Eternal, not the weakling enculi that the grand vizier has sitting on the throne.'

'And why should we trust a word you say, many-faces?' said Westwick.

'Because,' smiled Farris Uddin, 'as a token of good faith I am going to give you back your airship – the same one that your fool of an admiralty officer surrendered intact to the Imperial Aerial Squadron without firing a single shot in anger.'

Omar could see that Farris Uddin was smugly pleased by the consternation the news of their ship's capture caused among the four prisoners.

CHAPTER TWELVE

The grand vizier angrily sent a goblet spinning across the secret gardens at the heart of his pavilions. Salwa cowered as the caliph's chief minister digested the last of the news concerning the flight of the guardsmen. 'They knew of our trap – they knew!'

'It is so,' Salwa insisted. 'They had clearly been forewarned of the order's dissolution. Most of our men who entered the fortress were ambushed and led to the slaughter dressed as guardsmen. The guardsmen's supplies, their draks, were already departing even as we believed that we were surrounding them.'

'It might have been bad luck,' suggested one of the grand vizier's retinue. 'The guardsmen could have been preparing for the war – if they were mobilizing anyway, they could have just left when they saw our marines arrive.'

'Fool!' yelled the grand vizier. 'The guardsmen had no orders to join the campaign and there is no such thing as luck. Someone within our own ranks informed them that we were coming, someone loyal to the old regime. Which of you warned them?'

There was a loud chorus of denials alongside protestations of loyalty from the toadies surrounding him.

'We are loyal to you,' protested Salwa, abasing himself on the floor of the pavilion. 'How can you doubt us? All of us have undergone the initiation ritual, all of us have shed blood in your honour, in the cause of progress!'

'I should ask those Pasdaran bastards I have planted out in the torture gardens,' snarled the grand vizier. 'There are still a few of the secret police's cancerous cells left in our flesh, I warrant.' He jabbed a finger towards Salwa. 'You are meant to be the grand marshal of the guardsmen, what will they do now?'

'What can they do, master?' said Salwa. 'They are detached from the army, with only the supplies they carried out of the fortress. They will avoid an engagement, practice banditry in a guerrilla war against us.'

'That would be the rational thing to do,' agreed the grand vizier, his eyes narrowing. 'But they are not rational creatures. They are proud men. They could have abandoned the fortress and fled before we even turned up, but they wanted to give us a bloody nose before they left. As if to say, we are guardsmen, this is our palace, and we choose to leave here on our own terms. They used to be the caliph's elite troops, a strike force of well-trained killers. And what does a strike force do? It strikes!'

'They will not dare to take on the might of the Imperial Aerial Squadron,' said Salwa.

'Their soldiers have trained for centuries to disable and fight Jackelian airships,' said the grand vizier, 'I would not be so sure of that. Yes, I believe they will want to take a prize worthy of a song or two before they die, before their supplies run out and they slide into becoming just another band of bandits, scavenging for booty to stay alive.' He pointed furiously at a clump of officers in the black and silver uniforms of the Imperial Aerial Squadron. 'Recall four squadrons to reinforce the capital's defences and recall another six squadrons to protect Mutantarjinn and the airship yards outside the city.'

'But that will require the bulk of our invasion force to be pulled back from the north,' said the senior officer.

'Let the Jackelians stew for another month or so then, you dolts,' shouted the grand vizier. 'What will it profit us to gain another satrapy for the empire, if the Imperial Aerial Squadron returns back here to find the Pasdaran's new choice of candidate sitting on the throne? How kind do you think the secret police and their guardsmen friends will be towards you if they succeed in mounting a counter-revolution?'

The men bowed in fear at his temper.

'We will carry the day,' said the grand vizier. 'We will carry it because if we fail, we will all die together. Ensure our marines and sailors are billeted in the airfields outside the capital without leave to enter. We do not want them getting sick.'

'Sick?' said Salwa.

'Yes,' laughed the grand vizier. 'Because you are going to have our womb mages release a plague inside the capital's central souk. Use a milder variant of the one we used to depopulate the House of Barir and their allies along the coast. I need a plausible excuse to move our tame caliph out of the Jahan and south to the safety of Mutantarjinn's walls for a while, and a little summer plague will do nicely. Nothing so virulent that the local womb mages won't be able to cure it after a month or two. I don't want mass casualties and wage levels creeping up again, not with a major war to prosecute.'

Salwa nodded and the grand vizier bent in close so only

Salwa could hear his next words. 'Our enemies are not stupid. When the guardsmen come, they'll be coming for my head and the caliph's – our little pet, or the real Caliph Eternal, perhaps both at once. And they'll be coming for your head too, Salwa, last grand marshal of the guardsmen!' He leant back and clicked his fingers, speaking loudly again for all to hear his commands. 'Ready my personal packet for the journey south.'

Salwa allowed his heart to swell in hope. South, to the heart of the Sect of Razat's powerbase, the Forbidden City of Mutantarjinn, the city of sorcerers, where those who entered without the ruling womb mages' permission were struck blind.

Not even the guardsmen would be foolish enough to strike against them there, surely?

Jack walked alongside the young guardsman Omar as the draks were inspected. There had been a lot of contemptuous talk of the Cassarabian household guards and their flying biologicks among the sailors back on board the *Iron Partridge*. The only weapon the Kingdom's ancient enemy in the south possessed that was actually capable of taking to the skies against the Royal Aerostatical Navy. But all talk of human-lizard hybrids and crude jokes about ham-fisted lancers on 'sallys' – naval slang for salamanders – appeared very hollow when confronted by one of the forty-foot long flying monstrosities in the flesh. They might not have seemed much of a threat when viewed at a distance from behind an airship cannon's rubber hood, but up close its sinuous neck could whip around to take a bite out of you with its pointed alligator face in a second.

'This is my drak,' said Omar Barir, indicating his creature with what Jack thought was more than a touch of pride. 'His original rider died. Normally we would put him down as a kindness, but we are short of steeds and every drak is precious to us now.'

The thing looked to be staring at them from the corner of its eerily human eyes – a cunning gaze that Jack recognized from the shire horses back on his family's lost lands. A pernicious look that said, *'Use me at your peril.'*

Jack sighed. The whole plan seemed reckless to him. Hoping to pick up the trail of the *Iron Partridge* and its companion airship from the Imperial Aerial Squadron transporting the Kingdom crew as prisoners towards the testing facilities at Mutantarjinn. Assaulting both airships with the guardsmen's legion of flying biologicks, attempting to capture the two 'stats intact enough to continue their journey and infiltrate the enemy stronghold under the guise of being a prize vessel. The commodore's secret police contact seemed sure enough of the guardsmen's ability to pull the mission off. They would utilize the four Jackelians' knowledge of the best way to board the *Iron Partridge* and fight off the prize crew, hopefully with the assistance of the skeleton crew of prisoners of war being kept on board to assist with the foreign systems. But even if the ruse worked, sneaking into the Cassarabian den of sorcerers was one thing; getting out alive was quite another, let alone getting out with evidence of how the Imperial Aerial Squadron was manufacturing its airship gas. Did Jack owe the Kingdom this? Impressment into the navy was bad enough, but mounting one of these hideous hybrids on a suicide mission – he hadn't exchanged his court sentence for that.

But there was Captain Jericho, who had gambled on pulling his poorhouse friend's son off the gallows and into the service. What did Jack owe Jericho, hopefully still alive on a prison hulk heading for Mutantarjinn? What did he owe Coss Shaftcrank, who had risked his life to save Jack from the trumped-up charges of mutiny? Or the commodore, who seemed determined to drag Jack along in his trail, trying to keep them both alive despite the hard hand that lady fortune had dealt their party of intelligencers?

The young guardsman appeared to mistake Jack's pensive face simply for reticence to mount the drak. 'You have nothing to fear, Jack Keats. This bull drak may not be the steed that I was destined to ride, but by the hundred smiling faces of god, he will know the finest flyer in the guards is in the saddle when he feels my stirrups on his flanks.'

'I was thinking more about the act of boarding and taking two airships in flight before they can be scuttled,' said Jack. 'It'll be flash work up there.'

'My strategy is sound,' said Omar. 'The Imperial Aerial Squadron are cowardly curs who need the protection of canvas and cabin just to brave the reach of the heavens. They won't know how to operate your strange metal airship and will have their hands full with the prisoners they have made of your people. We shall swoop down on them with our claws reached out, like a flight of eagles taking a pair of fat pigeons.'

'I thought the strategy came from your commander of many faces?' said Jack.

'Master Uddin values my advice,' said Omar. 'He asks it many times, recognizing the wisdom that I hold within me. Besides, the duty for all loyal guardsmen can be found in our oath to the ruler of rulers – this impostor Caliph Eternal must be toppled and the rightful light of lights returned to his throne to rule.'

Jack nodded. The oath a man makes. And what of the promises Jack had made to his brothers in the poorhouse, to come back for them with enough money to free them from that dirty, squalid place for good? To be together again as a family? *I can only keep them if I live through today.*

There had been a touch of iron in the young guardsman's

voice when he mentioned his oath. The kind of iron the leaders of the street gangs used back home when discussing which properties and marks to target for a robbery.

'But there's more than your oath at stake here,' said Jack.

'You are correct in that,' said Omar. 'The dogs who plotted this treason, the grand vizier and his minions and his precious Sect of Razat – they burnt my home and destroyed my inheritance and killed everyone I knew, everyone I loved. They have left me with nothing except my life among the guardsmen. Tell me, Jackelian, what would you do to such people as did that to you?'

What would he do?

'Whatever I had to,' said Jack.

'And you will live to see it, Jack Keats,' said Omar. 'You will live to see the day I plunge my steel into their leaders. This I swear on the blood of my father.'

A pair of guardsmen emerged from the side of a tent holding long curled horns and blew a bugle-like summons, a haunting, echoing call. Everywhere around the camp, the draks' riders appeared, guardsmen running towards the reins of their chosen mounts. Jack followed Omar to his creature, the sinuous neck rearing eagerly against the reins of the stable hands holding them, the young guardsman mounting the double saddle just behind the base of the neck first, extending a hand down to Jack to mount up behind him.

The stable hand reached up to pat the saddlebags beneath their feet. 'All the grenades we can spare,' he said, and tapping long dangling weaves of rope, added, 'as well as propeller snarls for their engines.'

Omar raised his hand casually, as if to say, all this he already knew and did not need to be reminded of it.

'Do you have the day's smoke colours?' asked the stable hand.

'Yes,' said Omar. 'But I only need two of them. Red smoke for "dive and attack", and green smoke for "release boarders".'

'May the Caliph Eternal's blessings light your way. Tails up!'

A beating noise sounded, low at first, then louder and louder, like wet sheets being shaken out to dry, and Jack realized it was the talon wing of draks taking to the air. They were starting from the other end of the piece of land wedged between the hills, like a ripple of scaled flesh erupting down the valley. T-shaped silhouettes broke for the sky, pushing higher and higher as they curled around each other and filled the firmament with their din – the noise of their beating wings swelling as if a thousand angry spears were shaking in warriors' mailed fists. On the rear of the saddle, Jack felt himself rock as their drak started to bound forward, its wings angling back as it built up speed, the ground shaking out dust with the weight of its charge. Omar was shouting something down to it, cracking his reins, but Jack was too terrified to make sense of the foreign-sounding cry, his knuckles white on the pommel of the double saddle. The ground below had almost disappeared in the mist of dust being driven up off the hard valley floor. The drak's long neck was tilted down like the straight edge of a lance, and they were running through the kicked-up, wing-beaten powder of the draks who had taken off seconds earlier, now lost in the haze.

Jack willed himself not to bite his tongue. How did these monstrous creatures sense each other well enough not to pile into each other within such a damn soup? Omar shouted something back to him, and Jack was just hearing it as '*Hold on!*', when the drak threw itself up and, still charging, fanned its wings out as though they were sails.

The first beat was followed by a second and a third as the drak angled up over the dust, the heads of its fellow flyers arrowing out behind them. To Jack, they resembled serpentine sea beasts emerging from the ocean on monstrously powerful wings. After four minutes, their drak gained its cruising altitude. Not so high that they would have needed the dangling breather masks Jack had seen being packed into the drak's saddle bags, and well within the operating height of a pair of airships crossing clear skies over what they no doubt regarded as friendly territory. Now all of the guardsmen were in the air, the draks had formed into a double 'V' arrangement. Omar and Jack's drak was towards the centre of the inner V's left-hand wing. Such a formation, flying high, would resemble a flock of migrating birds to observers on the ground, with no way to scale the aerial legion against the cloudless, cerulean sky.

Omar pointed to the riders to their right with one of the big leather riding gloves he used to guide the reins. 'There is your friend, the big one with a eunuch's tonsure.'

Jack nodded. Henry Tempest. If the details of the pre-flight briefing he had attended still held true, all four Jackelians should be riding somewhere on the inner 'V'. It was Jack and the commodore's job to peel off and take back the *Iron Partridge* – the easier mission, with her guns theoretically silenced by the absence of her gunners and a foreign prize crew trying to keep control of the handful of RAN sailors they would have manning the airship's stations. The captain of marines and Westwick were taking the harder task of assaulting the well-manned prison ship.

Jack's mind went into a fugue as they flew for hours and hours, hypnotized by the cold winds and the beating sun above. The monotonously regular ground passing below like a backdrop painting from a stage set.

Eventually a faint spume of white smoke went up from the head of the formation – *enemy sighted*. The flight of draks began to wheel and climb and Jack was finding it harder to breathe. Each intake of air into his lungs felt as if two strong hands were pushing down onto his chest, restricting his muscles from working. Jack leant forward to tap Omar on the shoulder, indicating the saddlebags, and croaking: *'Masks?'*

'No,' Omar called back, flicking the long reins up to the drak's vicious muzzle. 'Enemy airships – running – semi-pressurized. Breach board will – be – our advantage.'

Our advantage. Jack was grateful they weren't facing a fighting Jackelian crew – an experienced crew who would try to tire an attacking wing of draks by climbing further. Instead, it was the guardsmen who had taken up position at a higher altitude and, ready for a dive. Did the Imperial Aerial Squadron's airships have their own version of a crow's-nest dome topside and an h-dome on the bow, manned by experienced spotters with telescopes? And how diligent would they be flying over 'safe', friendly territory?

Then, there they were, below and ahead, two airships – the familiar glinting silhouette of the *Iron Partridge*, and to her port, the profile of a Cassarabian 'stat, matching the tortoise-like speed of the heavy prize vessel.

Red smoke fanned out from the head of the flight – the sight that every Jackelian sailor dreaded. Omar shouted something to Jack, just before the drak turned downwards and drew in its wings. As their monstrous steed plummeted, Jack realized he had called for 'snarls' – propeller snarls. He reached down to the middle of the saddle, where the long weapons were dangling – sticky white fronds like hundreds of pieces of string bound in the middle by a leather circlet. RAN lore had it that the material was secreted from human-hybrid spiders kept scuttling about in some womb mage's dungeon – but whether that was true or not was irrelevant to the effect they would have when impacting upon an airship's rotors.

'Port, forward!' yelled Omar as the drak's velocity increased still further, pointing to the *Iron Partridge*'s front engine, which grew larger with each second they plunged. 'Throw – on the – brake.'

The wind was whipping the propeller snarl in Jack's hand, the dull metal hull of the *Iron Partridge* rising up fast – a trick of the angle, as if the drak was stationary and it was the airship and ground being hurled up at them.

They began banking left, Jack's spare hand clutching the saddle pommel tight as he pushed down into the stirrups with his boots, struggling to keep the propeller snarl level enough to hurl. Seconds away from the engine car and the drak's wings cracked open, slowing and throwing them to one side. Jack hurled the propeller snarl and let the velocity of their fall carry it into the blurred disk of the engine car's blades. Jack hardly caught the explosion of white chords in his wake, another drak's flank coming close enough to theirs that he could have struck a match on the beast's scales. They were manoeuvring through the diving press of the rest of the talon wing so fast that it felt as if his body had turned to lead, his weight doubled. As another drak banked off, clearing his view, Jack saw they were wheeling under the iron belly of the *Iron Partridge*. Her guns were silent, as were her engine cars, the lion-headed motors trailing oily smoke as their traction belts tried vainly to rotate her badly jammed blades.

Then the drak was out from under the airship's shadow, and Jack saw that the Cassarabian aerostat was putting up more of a fight; a few puffs of cannon fire from the rubber-hooded ordnance along the hull aimed at the cloud of draks corkscrewing around her length. Riding a thermal, their drak soared up past the starboard plating of the *Iron Partridge*, angling around to pass the crow's-nest dome.

There were fighters atop the hull and their drak angled itself to swoop down and trace a hull-scratching landing in the lee of the frill of mortar tubes. *Just as agreed*. Jack dismounted, landing heavily on the top plates as Omar cut the saddlebags containing the boarding gear to slide down next to him. As soon as its baggage was cut, the drak went scrabbling off the side of the airship to catch another thermal, clearing the space for the next landing.

It wasn't easy to see the boarding party scurrying around the top of the airship with the sun floating directly astern, but there was one figure Jack would know anywhere – the commodore with his rolling mariner's gait. He bustled over to Jack, a tinted pair of guardsman's brass goggles strapped over his salt and pepper hair. 'Tell me you've got the fuses, lad?'

'I have,' confirmed Jack, hefting the saddlebags.

'You've come on a fair wind, then,' said the commodore, puffing for breath at the altitude. He took the saddlebags and rifled through its contents as he walked. 'I nearly had to put a gun to the head of the guardsmen's armourer to get him to part with enough of his precious explosives to force our hatch. I told him that Jericho had our ship reinforced and sealed down as tight as a drum after that pair of Cassarabian birds used the hatch to board us, but the fool wouldn't listen to me.'

Guardsmen were tying up rappelling lines around the mortar tubes – another of the commodore's ideas. 'The guns, lad,' he'd said back at the camp. 'They'll be expecting us to come through the top hatches, and we'll give them some fireworks there to suit. No, the rubber hoods of our thirty-two pounders are where you'll guarantee finding an empty deck – for what skipper would put his men to guarding prisoners who could touch off a broadside against their sister ship? Our gunners will be chained up on the Cassarabian transport, and the skeleton crew they're keeping will be console men and engine-room stokers.'

The truth of the commodore's conjectures was about to be proved in the field by an experiment in demolition. Jack stripped the fuses as the commodore got back to the job of shaping the putty-like explosive substance around the sealed maintenance hatch on the hull.

'While there's pleasure to be had teasing open a transaction-engine lock,' the commodore wheezed to Jack as he worked, 'this is the other side of a cracksman's art. And look at the mortal cheap rubbish they've given us to work with. Sweating tears in the sun, volatile enough to split the drak that carried it here in half.'

'I know locks,' said Jack. *I had enough practice back home. If I hadn't, I might not have ended up here.*

'Nothing to learn from old Blacky, eh? If I'd been there with you in the vaults of Lords Bank we wouldn't have come away empty handed. There's a time for the cerebral game, and there's a time for the physical game, and a little fun to be had combining the blessed two.'

'They were pumping in dirt gas,' said Jack, 'and the bank's guards were coming at us from above, with the police down in the sewers.'

'That's what this paste is for,' said the commodore, running a finger down the explosives pushed into the wedge of the hatch beneath them. 'Not too much. Not too little. Seal the vents and let the bank's guards drink their own soup. Seal the sewer tunnels and make sure the only rats Middlesteel's finest catch are the furry four-legged variety. That's the problem with training just on transaction engines. Give a fellow a hammer and every problem starts to look like a nail.'

'And what did I look like to you when Captain Jericho sent you to get me from prison?' asked Jack.

'Like a diamond in the rough, Mister Keats. In need of a little polishing.' The commodore drew one of the matches he usually used to light his pipe. 'And now let me show you what just enough looks like.'

He lit each of the four fuses pushed into the corners of the hatch and there was a dull thump as the hatch jumped up out of its hinges. 'And that's what you get when you ask that incompetent sod Mister Pasco to seal a hatch.'

At the sound of the hatch being blown, the guardsmen who'd fixed their lines to the mortar tubes began rappelling down both sides of the airship, the soldiers standing behind Jack and the commodore pulling at the broken hatch and lifting it out of the hull plates.

Drawing his pistol, Jack made to move forward, but the commodore laid a hand on his shoulder as the guardsmen piled past. 'And here's your last lesson, lad. Never be the first into the breach. That's what the army calls the forlorn hope; you need a taste for death to accept that poisoned chalice.'

The dying followed quickly enough, the sounds of shouts and the rattle of pistol fire echoing around the enclosed corridors only seconds after the guardsmen stormed below.

'Second wave, lad,' said the commodore, making for the maintenance ladder revealed by his demolition art. 'We don't want our drak-riding allies thinking we're yellow.'

As they had anticipated, resistance from the prize crew was as light as the numbers on board the vessel, a handful of corpses in the uniforms of the Imperial Aerial Squadron marked the deadly passage of the guardsmen. With their dark leather uniforms oiled against the elements, bandoliers of shells, grenades, knives and aviator goggles, the guardsmen looked like the aerial pirates from some cheap Jackelian penny-dreadful, their manners as fierce as the edges of their blades.

Jack felt like an impostor as he followed in their bloody wake – wearing the tattered Jackelian Royal Aerostatical Navy uniform that the party had secreted in their baggage during their travels through Cassarabia in the vain hope that changing into it if they were close to being captured would save them a spy's fate. *'We'll go back on board our ship like fine Jackelian gentlemen,'* as the commodore had boasted.

The pair of fine Jackelian gentlemen followed the boarding party into the transaction-engine chamber just in time to stop three guardsmen from testing their scimitars on Coss Shaftcrank, the steamman fending them off with a stoker's shovel while another two guardsmen finished off the sentry who had been watching over the room.

'He's one of ours, the metal lad!' shouted Jack. 'Coss, belay your shovel!'

Coss warily lowered his shovel as the guardsmen withdrew to clear out the rest of the airship. 'Those are the caliph's own guardsmen, Jack softbody. Kiss my condensers, but has the world turned upside down while I have been chained up inside here?'

'I think that would depend on which caliph you are,' said Jack.

'Explanations later, old steamer,' said the commodore. 'Anyone in drak-riding leathers is on our side. Anyone in Imperial Aerial Squadron uniforms you can clump with that old coal shovel of yours. Now, would you know if there's anyone resembling a womb mage on board the *Iron Partridge*?'

'There is such a one in the surgeon's bay,' said Coss. 'Or at least so I heard from our cabin boy who has been topping up my water supply.'

'Prize crew and prisoners?' asked the old officer.

'There's around twenty of us and fifty of them on board the *Iron Partridge*. All the officers and the rest of our men are chained up on board an escort vessel.'

'Is Jericho alive over there?' asked Jack.

'Indeed he is,' said Coss. 'Along with our cowardly

Loa-cursed fool of a vice-admiral. Tuttle softbody surrendered the ship as quick as he could strike our colours when we ran into five enemy vessels along the edge of the Empty Quarter.'

'Ah well, the only battles that ever counted for Tuttle were the ones fought around a dining table in Admiralty House,' said the commodore. He looked over at the boilers, cold and shut. 'What happened to the blessed ship? How's she doing?'

'The Cassarabians don't trust our automatic systems. They think they're cursed. We've been flying like a brick on full manual control ever since we surrendered.'

'We'll fire her back up later,' said the commodore, leaving for the exit. 'Right now we need to get down to the surgeon's bay before their wicked womb mage realizes there's been another change of ownership on board the *Iron Partridge*.'

Jack and Coss ran after the commodore and into the narrow corridor outside, the sulphur smell of weapons discharge hanging in the air.

'Why the surgeon's bay?' called Jack.

'Because we need a womb mage's blessing, lad,' said the commodore, cryptically. 'Because we need his blessing.'

What's he planning, the old dog?

When the three crewmen reached the doors to the surgeon's bay, they found they weren't the first to have tried to enter. A fatally wounded guardsman was rolling in agony outside the open doorway, a puddle of acidic green liquid sizzling across the carper planking by his side.

Jack unclipped one of the spherical grenades topped by a small clockwork timer to detonate the explosives inside, but the commodore stopped him from tossing it through the doorway. 'That's a little too much.' Black quickly leant inside the bay and fired the single charge of his pistol, the crack of the weapon answered by a yell inside. 'And that's just enough.'

Jack and Coss followed the commodore in to find a womb

mage slumped across the surgeon's operating table, an uncracked vial of the green acid still clutched in his dead fingers. The commodore's single shot had taken him in the chest through the heart, the blood of the wound like a marks-man's bull's-eye on a paper target.

'Tear my transfer pipes, but if you had hoped for a blessing from him, master cardsharp,' said Coss, 'I believe your shot would have been better aimed towards a less vital organ than his heart.'

'Not so, he's left his blessing behind, Mister Shaftcrank,' said the commodore, walking to the womb mage's case, aban-doned under a cabinet of drugs and medicines that had clearly been broken into and rifled through. The commodore unclipped the case and lifted out what looked like a perfume bottle, complete with a rubber bulb to squirt out its contents. There looked to be dozens of similar bottles inside the bag. 'Just the thing to lift a curse.'

Picking the bottle up, he sprayed the content in his eyes, and beckoned Jack over for a squirt of the same.

'It's itching,' Jack said as the moisture burned angrily on his face.

'No rubbing there, Mister Keats. Everyone who goes into Mutantarjinn will need a dose of this – even our draks, although you can leave the old steamer here off the list.'

'This is not scent,' said Coss, examining the bottle.

'It's not just a wicked legend that anyone who enters Mutantarjinn without the order of womb mages' permission goes blind,' said the commodore. 'They circulate a sickness in the air around the city that attacks your eyes. There's a virus inside this spray that changes your eyeball in a manner that makes you immune to their curse. Your vision plate won't be affected, old steamer – which is one of the reasons why the Cassarabians don't trust your race. Trust only flesh, is an old saying of the womb mages. Trust only that which their sorceries can twist.'

Jack blinked the tears out of his eyes.

'They are not a kind people,' said Coss.

'Aye, they're many things, but that they're not.'

They were to see more evidence of that throughout the ship. Not a single Imperial Aerial Squadron sailor had been taken prisoner. The enemy captain they wanted alive for his knowledge of the route and any codes they needed to gain admittance to the city of sorcerers. The rest of the crew was a hindrance the guardsmen couldn't afford to trust during the infiltration of the enemy stronghold, and the rival sailors met a savage end.

With the foe's crew eliminated and word received that the Cassarabian transport airship had fallen – albeit with a higher price paid in blood – Jack went with Coss back to the transaction-engine chamber to help the steamman restart the *Iron Partridge*'s boilers.

'The empire is fascinated with the Kingdom's machines,' Coss explained as they walked. 'But they do not understand them. The master cardsharp is correct, they trust their ability to pervert the weave of flesh, but not our transaction engines and even less the life-metal such as myself.'

'We saw their sorcerers' work in their cities after we left the *Iron Partridge*,' said Jack. 'They don't have trees to burn in their boilers, let alone coal. The creatures they breed inside slaves' wombs are the one natural resource they can depend on.'

'They had to put a gun to my head to get me to turn off the vessel's transaction engines,' said Coss. 'Before we were captured I got to understand the ship. Kiss my condensers, but turning the boilers off on the *Iron Partridge* is like turning off my boiler heart – it is a little death for the ship's mind.

I don't know how she will react to being rudely reanimated on our whim.'

'You didn't have a choice,' said Jack. 'No more than I did when I had to jump ship.'

Jack explained all that had happened to the marooned Jackelians during their absence from the *Iron Partridge*, their unexpected alliance with the guardsmen and the existence of two caliphs – the false one sitting on the throne, still dependent on the blood of the true ruler of rulers being held prisoner by the grand vizier.

Coss in turn explained how there had nearly been a second mutiny on board the *Iron Partridge* after the vice-admiral had given the ship up when they had been confronted by a flotilla of Cassarabian airships, showing more consideration for the preservation of his own skin than the welfare of his crew or his oath of duty. With the vessel already in disarray, her captain relieved of command and guarded in his quarters, the *Iron Partridge* had proved easy pickings for the Imperial Aerial Squadron.

Back in the chamber, Jack acted as both stoker on the boilers and cardsharp on the punch-card writers while Coss went down into the vessel's small but perfectly formed transaction-engine pit and spun up the drums. Jack's striped sailor's shirt was soon soaked with sweat as he shovelled high-grade coke into the furnace of the high-pressure system in between feeding the punch-card injector with initiation routines.

Slowly, they coaxed the ship's systems back into life, and Jack saw that the steamman's reflections about the nascent artificial mind held on the drums were well founded. The systems were acting with all the jittery nervousness of a hound that had been kicked and banished from the hearth, then reluctantly allowed to slope back into the house. All this time everyone had been treating the ship like a piece of malfunctioning clockwork, but she was closer to one of the guardsmen's draks – a creature of free will that needed coaxing and coaching.

Jack must have spent an hour on the restart, his voice growing hoarse from calling out system details to the steamman in the pit and acknowledging all the processes they were teasing back into life.

Their labours were interrupted by the commodore, returning to the transaction-engine room with his pipe lit; a sure sign that there was quiet on the rest of the vessel.

'We're for the boat bay, lads – the rest of our crew has been ferried over from the transport vessel and the skipper wants a word with everyone.'

Jack dropped the punch card he was forming. 'Jericho's on board!'

'That he is. The Imperial Aerial Squadron killed a few of our boys out of spite before the guardsmen took the ship, but we've a crew and a ship and we're back in the game.'

'I must stay here, master cardsharp,' protested Coss. 'The *Iron Partridge*'s boilers must be fed, or I fear we'll never return the ship to her intended operation.'

'You mind our jerry-built iron lady, then, old steamer. Mister Keats and myself will have to do.'

Jack and the commodore were passing by the engine room on the lower deck when a piercing yell split the air. Jack's hand slipped down to his pistol holster by reflex, but the commodore just calmly tapped his pipe out against one of the corridor's walls as First Lieutenant Westwick emerged from a hatch. She had taken part in the assault on the Cassarabian airship and was still wearing borrowed guardsman's leathers that fitted her like a second skin.

'That sounded like a familiar voice, lass,' said the commodore.

'Vice-Admiral Tuttle has resolved his predicament by taking the honourable way out,' said Westwick. 'The hatches to the engine cars were left open while we cleared the propeller snarls off the blades, and when he spotted the gap, he chose to jump.'

'People will always surprise you,' said the commodore. 'He never seemed the mortal jumping type to me.'

Westwick just smiled her dangerous smile and Jack pretended not to notice as she checked the knife strapped to her arm was secure again.

The commodore clapped Jack on the back. 'Lucky for us, though, Mister Keats. All those foolish accusations about the loss of the Fleet of the South can be put to bed, along with the court martial Tuttle would have faced for striking his colours in the face of the enemy. All you need to do is complete our mission, and you'll have the crowds back home stand you free drinks for the rest of the year when they see the name of the *Iron Partridge* standing proud on your blessed cap.'

All? A couple of airships against an empire. That sounds like an expensive round of drinks to me.

Westwick blinked her eyes in an exaggerated way at the commodore, who nodded happily, as if all was well with the world.

'We're good Maya. And there's enough spray for the crew on both ships, and our guardsmen allies with their mortal flying pets besides.'

The boat bay was full of the *Iron Partridge*'s crew, their uniforms dirty and the men and women unkempt from days of confinement by their captors. Among them was Captain Jericho with his mop of orange hair and piercing eyes, a lightning bolt moulded into human form.

His booming voice cut through the hubbub like fire, as if his confinement on the prison transport had been the closure of a furnace door, the heat of ignoble defeat inside him left to grow sun-hot until the guardsmen had released him back upon his crew of misfits. 'This, given the choice, is not the ship you would have chosen. This mission, given the choice, is not the one you would have accepted. This crew is not one that has fought together and the only mention of the *Iron Partridge* on the rolls of the navy is on the very short list of vessels that have surrendered to an enemy power.'

The crew shuffled their feet, embarrassed, many too ashamed to look their captain in the eyes. 'And your failure is m'own failure, the failure of those set to lead you. The same complacent assumption of victory that left the Fleet of the South scattered across the sands of the enemy and our brothers and sisters to be picked over by carrion and dune beetles. That failure will not happen again! *I will not fail you again.*' He moved down the centre of the boat bay, taking one of the fire hoses from the wall and unfurling it towards the hangar doors to create a line. 'Our mission was originally launched at the behest of parliament and its agencies, rather than the admiralty. Now we must make common cause with regiments of the enemy, guardsmen who we have known only as our most implacable enemy. We must strike directly at the heart of one of the empire's cities. Not just to discharge this vessel's orders, but to wipe the stain of her surrender from our logs. I will take only volunteers with me from here on in. Those who wish to go, may take the *Iron Partridge*'s launches back to the border and pass on word of what has happened here. Those of you that stay, you should know that your chances of returning are slight, and, in actuality, this is why Admiralty House gave us a vessel they did not want and a crew they expected to fail. But there is one thing I will not fail in, and that is m'duty. I stand here . . .' The captain moved to the right-hand side of the line down the deck he had made. 'Those who would follow a captain to war, follow me now . . .'

There was an almost imperceptible ripple through the crowd of aeronauts as, nodding grimly, the commodore stepped across the line after the captain, followed by First Lieutenant Westwick and Jack, then the other lieutenants. Soon the torrent of movement became a soundless flood, though if determination had a sound, then the boat bay might have echoed with the thunder of it.

They had been written off by their own side, shamed and used for fools by Vice-Admiral Tuttle, a coward who had struck the airship's colours just about as fast as he could drop them when faced with a superior force. They were Jackelians – and old and young, they could remember the pride they had felt when first taking the Royal Aerostatical Navy's oath. There was only one way to remove the stain on their honour. Within a minute there was nobody left on the other side of the makeshift line, even Pasco's truculent enginemen had all slipped across.

They might have been flying through the heavens, but now they were following a course for the gates of a Cassarabian hell. And it didn't matter a jot anymore, because there was nowhere else they'd rather be.

The glass portholes of the wardroom on board the *Iron Partridge* gave onto an appropriate backdrop as they sailed towards Mutantarjinn alongside the captured Cassarabian vessel – great forks of lightning illuminating the clouds off their port, the night flickering as if the long scuttled sun was now a gas lamp being toyed with by a child. There was some mineral in the mountains of the deep south of this realm that agitated the storm fronts when they rolled off their peaks, and the land in their lee was known as the Abras Arkk – or the angry ground. It seemed to Omar a fitting territory for the Forbidden City of the womb mages to be located.

Farris Uddin was sketching the layout of the city on a sheet of paper for the council of war that had been convened: himself, Boulous and Omar, Jericho – the captain of the strange Jackelian vessel – and the four spies who had been prisoners of the guardsmen, Commodore Black, Jack Keats, Henry Tempest and the beautiful but deadly First Lieutenant Westwick.

How fitting that fate should send me a woman as heart-breakingly beautiful as Shadisa was to help me avenge her death. Heathen northerners. Strange allies, but it doesn't matter. I would fight alongside a legion of devils if it means bringing down the dogs who killed her; I would let the fires of hell singe my boots to lead the charge against the grand vizier and Salwa's forces.

'Mutantarjinn is a sealed city,' said Farris Uddin. 'Movement in and out is strictly controlled. The caliph's rule is administered by the order of womb mages, much like sultans rule a conquered province.'

'How high are its walls?' asked Jericho. 'And what is the disposition of their defences?'

Farris Uddin tapped the table. 'Their walls are high, but not in the direction you might expect. They start at the ground and run downward. Mutantarjinn is built into the floor of a circular chasm, scoured out when Ben Issman, his name be blessed, caused the eyes of god to reopen. Those chasm walls are three hundred feet deep.'

'That's a mortal powerful gaze,' noted the commodore. 'Although I have an archaeologist friend of my acquaintance who swears that Mutantarjinn was built over the ruins of an underground city that preceded it.'

'The Cassarabian people were shaped by god, Jared Black, not descended from ants,' said Farris Uddin. 'What fools would want to live underground? There are lines up and down the chasm's walls – lifting rooms – and creatures designed by the womb mages for porterage. More pertinently for this vessel, there are hundreds of anti-airship bombards mounted on fortifications that ring the chasm. Big ugly steel toads designed to spit out shells that would test even your carper's resistance to flame. Shells filled with a substance that burns brighter as you toss water over it.'

Jericho shrugged. 'If your plan works, we won't need to test their defences.'

'We have the signal codes to enter the city,' said Farris Uddin. 'As long as they are accurate . . .'

'I believe I convinced the Imperial Aerial Squadron officer who held them to pass me the correct codes,' said Westwick. 'Eventually.'

'That I believe you did,' said Farris Uddin, sketching out more detail to represent the centre of the city. 'And if the signal codes work, the good news is that we will be sent onto here, the Citadel of Flowers.' He drew in a building that resembled a five-leaf clover at the centre of the city. 'The heart of the order of womb mages' power and the repository of all their knowledge and secrets. We would be expected to dock at its central tower and offload all the Jackelian sailors from the prison ship and prize vessel.'

'What would happen to m'crew inside there?' asked Jericho.

'They would be induced to surrender all their knowledge of the operations of your vessel,' said Farris Uddin. 'Afterwards, when they have no more information to reveal? Well, there is always an appetite for human bodies among the womb mages for them to hone their art – a demand that not even all of the empire's slave traders can satisfy.'

'The true caliph is being held within the citadel?' asked Omar.

'Yes,' said Farris Uddin. 'The grand vizier's man we snatched believes he is being kept somewhere well out of public view, in their lower levels alongside their vats and their experiments and their most treasured spell books.'

'Two parties, then,' growled Captain Jericho. 'One to locate your caliph, one to complete the ship's mission and locate the source of the grand vizier's celgas.'

Master Uddin seemed to agree. 'We will time the attack of the guardsmen talon wings on the city for shortly after we dock at the citadel. The grand vizier is nobody's fool, and he will be expecting us to act against him. We will give him the attack he expects, as a distraction for a subtler feint he doesn't. They will be looking to the walls and the city defences and we will already be inside the Citadel of Flowers.'

Uddin looked across at Omar and Boulous. 'You and I, Omar Barir, will have to bear the stench of wearing Imperial Aerial Squadron uniforms, while Boulous, I think, with the addition of a striped shirt and trousers, will make a fine Jackelian prisoner for us to escort.'

'As he should,' said the commodore. 'For as a babe the lad would have been a Jamie or a Donnel, before he was snatched from an upland cot by some camel-riding raider.'

'I am a jahani!' protested Boulous. 'My loyalty is to the guardsmen, whatever the source of my blood.'

'Being of Jackelian stock isn't a taint, lad, it's a windfall. You trace the roots of the word back far enough, and you'll find Jackelian means lion-hearted in one of the ancient tongues.'

'Nobody will doubt the bravery of anyone's heart who enters the Citadel of Flowers,' said Farris Uddin. 'Whether they be counted as guardsmen or Jackelian sailors. We must keep the raiding parties small – only the best fighters from our two forces. Speed and surprise will be our allies – for there are creations of the womb mages inside the citadel that *I* would not face. We shall trust in the one true god that we shall carry the day and return to the two airships in dock before the hive we are dipping for honey is fully roused.'

'Ten rounds a minute, sir,' said the brooding giant who was the vessel's captain of marines to Jericho. 'That's what I'll put my trust in.'

'The crew and the ship and our allies. We needs must trust in them all, eh Mister Tempest?'

A flash across the sky outside the porthole caught Omar's eye. They were sailing through a fury, but Omar would tempt far worse to reach the grand vizier's home; just for the chance to reach inside the heart of darkness and see if he could squeeze the life out of it.

'Is this my fate, father?' Omar whispered to the shade he imagined hanging in the skies outside.

He heard the echo of his father's words. *'We are what heaven wills us.'*

CHAPTER THIRTEEN

Captain Jericho leafed through the ship's dispositions in his cabin as he listened to Jack's report about what he and Coss had discovered of the nascent intelligence turning on the drums of the ship's transaction engines.

'Well, well, m'boy,' said Jericho, glancing up, 'a pity the industrial lord that designed our vessel vanished years ago. I would have a few words with him about his notions of airship design.'

'We're doing our best with her, sir.'

'Just rein the transaction engines in, Mister Keats. You and our steamman rating can coddle her, and whisper sweet nothings if that's what it takes. Grease her drums as if you were combing the burs out of a mare's flanks. Level flying until we reach Mutantarjinn – we'll save her final gallop until our slippery pair from the State Protection Board have discharged the ship's orders inside this dark den of the womb mages.'

'Why am I here, captain?'

'Have you anywhere else you would rather be?' The captain raised an eyebrow before continuing. 'A gentleman always discharges his debts, Mister Keats. Where he can, eh?'

'Yes, sir.' *What do I have to pay with, but my blood?*

'Your father was a good man in hard times. He always tried to look after people in the prison he didn't need to. That's how the navy's patronage system is supposed to work, too. The skipper who saw me into m'first ensign's position did it as a favour for m'family when he really didn't need to. I think he saw something in a young lad just starting out that nobody else had noticed; that I needed what the Royal Aerostatical Navy had to offer, as much as the service needed me. Such lines of loyalty run up and down, crisscrossing the fleet as the invisible netting that binds our vessels and crews together.'

'Does your old skipper sit on the board of the admiralty, sir?'

'No, Mister Keats, Captain Taylor was luckier than that – he was promoted to the officer's cemetery outside Middlesteel. But I stand for him, as do many others who were once ensigns and who are now captains and commanders and vice-admirals, as one day you will stand for me.'

'The truth, sir, is that I just want to go home and take my brothers out of the poorhouse.'

'An ensign's pay will allow you to do that, Mister Keats, and a lot more reliably than chancing a second attempt at forcing the vaults of a bank or rattling the skylights of rich widows. Anyone who can fathom those damned machines inside the transaction-engine chamber can pass any board exams the navy has to set.'

'Yes sir.'

'The navy won't abandon you, Mister Keats. You are the service and the service is you. We may kill you, but you have m'vow we will never leave you. Even after you're pensioned out, your blood will sing every time you feel the shadow of a RAN vessel drift over your cottage. Give it sixty years and some young pup barely able to fill his dress uniform will be weeding you out of the hiring line at what passes for an airship field.'

There was a knock at the door, and when Jericho boomed 'enter', Jack saw it was the hulking form of Master Engineer Pasco, bearing news of his teams' labours in bringing the engine room back to full capacity.

'Smartly done, Mister Pasco,' said the captain, congratulating the engineer on his people's work. 'When the time comes, I will need our iron-feathered bird to fly like a hawk out of the enemy city.'

'We'll soak the traction belts with ballast water and run the loops so fast the cook will be able to bake the ship's biscuits in the engine cars' back draft, skipper.' Pasco hesitated.

'Is there anything else, master engineer?'

'When the time comes, Captain Jericho, you can count on us.'

'That I believe I can, Mister Pasco. Dismissed.'

'How can you trust what he says?' Jack asked when the door to the cabin had been shut again, and the engineer had left. 'He led a mutiny against you for the vice-admiral.'

'Vice-admiral Tuttle was a politician, m'boy, and a politician is an expert at promising the world, even when it always keeps on turning ever the same.'

'I wouldn't trust him,' said Jack.

'Then you would be wrong. Never judge a cloudie without knowing their history, Mister Keats. Pasco was on the *Resolute* when she experienced an engine-room fire. A barrel of contaminated expansion-engine gas had made it onto the ship and blew half her engines away. Pasco was the engineer who received the captain's order to lock the room down to starve the fire of air while they climbed high enough to put the blaze out properly. There were a quarter of the engine room's hands still inside when Pasco sealed it down.' The captain nodded grimly, as if the memory had been his, rather than another officer's. 'Pasco had to listen to his crew burn and suffocate every foot of that journey. The *Resolute*'s captain killed them to save hundreds more. It transpired that the barrel of bad gas was loaded by a convict labour crewman working on the field who would have been hard pressed to tell the difference between expansion-engine gas and the brass tank a Middlesteel lamp lighter carries on his back. I would have ordered the engine room locked down myself in the same circumstances. No choice in the matter, do y'see? He doesn't like pressed hands, he doesn't like officers, and for a long time he didn't even like himself. A battle-hardened man like Pasco will follow you if you prove yourself. I did it by giving him and his crew another chance rather than the gallows for mutiny, but you had better be damned sure you know where you are leading him.'

Jack saluted. 'I believe I will follow you too, sir.'

'Too blasted right you will, m'boy.'

'You have our report, sir. Is there anything else I can assist with?'

Jericho gestured mournfully towards the letter he had been writing on his desk. 'Not unless you have enough skill with penmanship to explain to Admiralty House why the probable last action of one of their vessels is cooperating in an attempt to free the enemy head of state of a nation we're at war with, while fighting alongside the navy's oldest foe in the air.'

'I would write that the two officers of the State Protection Board on the vessel insisted you follow that course of action, captain.'

'Very good. Ingenuity under fire. Those ensign's bars are already half yours, eh Mister Keats?'

Jack could almost feel their dangerous weight as he left.

*   *   *

284

Even at nighttime, Jack could see from the transaction-engine chamber how easily Mutantarjinn had earned its nickname the Forbidden City; there was little about the city that did not look forbidden or forbidding. From the black rocky plain veined with blood-red crystal that sparkled with an evil patina when the lightning storms forked their violence down – a glamour that made it look as if the land beneath the *Iron Partridge* was running with rivulets of blood – to the sharp blade-roofed towers rising out of the canyon floor of the ugly circular chasm scoured out of the ground. It was obvious why the commodore's archaeologist friend thought something ancient had preceded the Cassarabians' presence here. There was an otherworldly nature to the city that went beyond the womb mages' administration of the place. *I would sooner live in the desert under a nomad's tent than down there.* The towers on the chasm floor resembled a series of bone-like spikes that had rained down and landed on top of each other. Many were topped with strange constructions of blades that turned and twisted in the gusts scouring the city, acting as windmills and storm conductors. Gazing on the vista was like watching a thousand erratic, insane carousels summoning bolts of lightning down from the thunderhead sky.

Alongside the *Iron Partridge* a great crack of lightning revealed the chasm drop to be swarming with six-armed creatures, the race of man made into spiders, dark net bags tied around their backs. They were stirring around even larger creatures – beetle-shelled things the size of houses carrying pagodas of passengers up and down the chasm wall.

Jack's eyes moved ahead. There in the centre of the city, rising above all the other towers, was the core of the womb mages' power – the Citadel of Flowers, though if flower it be, it was a decaying swamp lily. It was composed of five rounded wings, each a jutting ziggurat in its own right, pinned to the chasm floor by a massive spire in its centre. A rotating crown of blades encircled the spire's rise every hundred yards, generating a hum audible even on the distant airship. Glinting light spilled from open hangars in between the rotating blades, small courier packets coming and going bearing the empire's lifeblood of information. Nearby were the full-sized gantries for the larger vessels of the Imperial Aerial Squadron, although no other warships seemed to be docked at the moment.

If this was truly where the Cassarabians' one true god had been wakened, burning a hole for the foundations of the Forbidden City to be laid, then he must have been an irritable sleeper. Through the porthole Jack could see the reflection of the ship's helioscope running along their iron plates as they communicated with the ground, and he felt a twinge of uncertainty, beseeching the fates that Westwick's methods of obtaining her information proved every bit as rigorous as she had suggested they had been. *What if our stolen codes are old, or the enemy officer falsified them to get Westwick killed?*

Finally, there was an answering flash from the fortification along the rim of the chasm, then the *Iron Partridge* nosed further over Mutantarjinn. *Thank the Circle. Still alive.* Alive for the most suicidal mission any airship in the navy had ever attempted.

There was a cry from behind Jack, and turning, he saw Coss lying on the bottom of the engine pit, the steamman's metal limbs shaking as if he had been taken by a fit. The commodore was away on the bridge with Jericho – *no time to get him back here.* Jack slid the ladder into the pit, and pulled Coss away from the rotating drums of the transaction engine, saving him from rolling under the lowest one and getting his arms or legs crushed. *What's the matter with him?* The diminutive steamman was shaking, a vapour leaking out of the joins of his body, as if his rivets were sweating a fog.

Jack gawped as the fog seemed to form into a skull-like machine face, then, as quickly as it had formed, it disappeared into the oil-scented air of the transaction-engine chamber.

'Coss, can you hear me? What's the matter?'

'I have been ridden by the Loa, Jack softbody,' Coss warbled through his voicebox. 'The spirit of my ancestor spoke to me – Lemba of the Empty Thrusters.'

The flying spirit from the steamman pantheon of the gods I glimpsed in my own dream. 'Did the Loa speak to you about the ship?'

'Vault my valves, it is more than that,' said Coss. 'This is a turning point in the weave of the great pattern. If we fail here, then the empire of the caliph will become the world. We will all fall – Jackals, the Free State, Quatérshift, all of the nations of the north. Your flesh will be their flesh, and for my race, after an age of hiding like beggars in the Mountains of Mechancia, the people of the metal will finally be exterminated.'

'Did your Loa suggest how we might avert that?'

Coss slowly shook his head. 'He did not. All he left me with was the feeling of power in this land. Great energies that were once released here, long before the caliphate. They have faded; but while I was possessed, I could smell their residual half-life like the scent of diseased meat.'

Jack helped the steamman back to his feet, his head dizzy with the bleak implications of his crewmate's words. It seemed the fate of the entire world rested on the success of their mission. *And the world really should have picked a better champion than the old steamer and me to stand up for it.*

Coss had just recovered enough to return to his post when the commodore appeared at the door of the transaction-engine chamber.

'Time for you to make good your promise to me, Mister

Keats. We're a couple of minutes away from docking at the womb mages' lair. Poor old Blacky – my unlucky stars have left me washed up on some bad shores before, but none as foul as this place. But at least I have misery for company this time, eh? For the grand fellow who was foolhardy enough to poke his nose into the fortified vaults of Lords Banks, this terrible voyage should be a rowboat across a sunny lake.'

Jack nodded grimly, his stomach bunching up with fear. *Right now, I'd take a bank job back in the Kingdom any day.*

'Unholster your pistol, lad. We're meant to be prisoners of war now, and prisoners don't sport shooting irons. Keep the drums turning here, old steamer, for when we return, we'll as like have every devil of the six levels of Cassarabian hell hot on our tail . . .'

The timing of the guardsmen's attack on the defences of Mutantarjinn was every bit as precise as Jack had expected it would be. Sirens inside the great tower's airship docking ring howled into life as the guardsmen and the Jackelians – the former wearing their stolen Imperial Aerial Squadron uniforms, the latter in their soiled crew uniforms – stepped out into the main hangar. There was confusion among the Imperial Aerial Squadron ground crew in the harbour. Jack had to turn to see the first gobs of fire arcing out of the shadows of the distant chasm wall through an open hangar door, the attacking draks rendered invisible by the darkness until a lightning flicker silhouetted their wheeling forms against the sky. Like the other Royal Aerostatical Navy crewmen, Jack's hands were bound behind his back with leather ties, but using a cunning knot of the commodore's devising they could be pulled apart with a twist of the wrists.

Something about the hangar appeared to be angering the guardsmen's commander, Farris Uddin. Jack caught Omar's eye – the boy just a little too gangly for his purloined marine's jacket.

Omar indicated the walls of the Cassarabian script engraved across the walls of the hangar. 'The hundred sects of the Holy Cent have been torn down and replaced by only one – the Sect of Razat. It is blasphemy of the worst kind.'

'We've an old saying in our uplands,' noted the commodore. 'Find three Cassarabians and you'll find two believers and one heretic.'

'You should not bespeak the hundred faces of the one true god, old man,' warned Omar.

'Perhaps I shouldn't at that, lad. We need all the luck we can get in this terrible place.'

An officer who looked as if he might be the master of the harbour came running past the new arrivals and Farris Uddin grabbed him to halt his rush. 'I have the officers from the prize vessel here, and the rest of the enemy sailors as prisoners inside.'

'You are Captain Darwish? In the name of the blessed Ben Issman, get those infidels out of my way. And keep the ones on your transport ship chained up. Can you not hear the city's call to war?'

'Who attacks?' demanded Farris Uddin. 'Who is foolish enough to attack Mutantarjinn?'

'The thrice-cursed imperial guardsmen,' said the harbour master. 'Our own men, our own draks. The grand vizier has just passed us word that they have rebelled against the Caliph Eternal.'

'What, the grand vizier is here?'

The officer thrust a finger towards one of the larger pocket airships resting inside the chamber. 'His vessel arrived before yours. There is plague in the capital. The Citadel of Flowers is the Jahan now – we protect the Caliph Eternal!'

'Not just one caliph, then,' the commodore whispered to Jack. 'A pair of birds in this dark bush, and one of them a cuckoo.'

'What can we do to assist?' asked Farris Uddin. 'What are our orders?'

'None from me,' said the harbour master, 'nor anyone else at the moment, running around like headless chickens. Just keep the filthy Jackelians out of my hair and pray for the guardsmen to be struck blind by the hand of god for their treachery before the fleet arrives.'

Jack felt the ripple of tension running through the party as Farris Uddin's eyes narrowed. 'The fleet?'

'The fleet is returning from the north to defend the Caliph Eternal. We'll catch these dirty rebels in the scorpion's pincer – the city walls in front, and the hammer of our airships behind them. Then we'll teach them the price of their treachery.'

'A price that is much on my mind,' said Farris Uddin as the officer ran off, barking orders at the ground crew scattered around the chamber.

Just behind the guardsman commander, Captain Jericho was looking as perturbed as everyone else at the sudden shocking turn of events.

'You could see the true caliph freed,' said Jericho, 'and we can learn the source of the grand vizier's airship gas. But it'll avail neither of us if your guardsmen are slaughtered outside and we're both left stranded here, bottled up by the entire Imperial Aerial Squadron.'

'It is said that no plan of engagement survives a battle intact, captain,' said Farris Uddin. 'What do you suggest?'

'Your transport ship, sir, should be left here for the withdrawal of both parties. I will take the *Iron Partridge*, warn the guardsmen attacking the city, and then proceed to engage the enemy.'

'One vessel against the bulk of our new fleet,' said Farris Uddin. 'How much time can you buy us?'

'That remains to be seen, commander, but we shall at least have the element of surprise on our side,' smiled Jericho.

'I find this war of ours a funny sort,' said Farris Uddin. 'For the more I fight, the harder I find it to tell the sides apart. Tell the guardsmen that half the talon wings are to stay and harass the city's defences, the other half are to accompany you in assaulting the grand vizier's fleet.'

Jericho nodded, then glanced over at the commodore. 'And for a ship in action, I will need more than Mister Shaftcrank manning that infernal calculating pit some fool of an airwright saw fit to drop into m'vessel.'

'The master cardsharp's skills are required here,' said First Lieutenant Westwick. She held up the bag of supposedly looted booty from the wardroom she was carrying, silver plate and cups concealing the spies' small, efficient transaction engine – the same one that Jack and the commodore had used to crack the enemy vessel they had boarded under the skies of Benzaral.

'Well, there it is then,' whined the commodore, looking at Jack. 'The cold, grey wretches of the State Protection Board had their claws sunk into me long before they made me exchange my sea legs for air legs. My business it seems is here, which means, Mister Keats, that yours needs to be on the *Iron Partridge*.'

'You haven't got me killed yet, sir,' said Jack.

'I believe we'll both get ample chances to make a go of that, lad,' said the commodore. 'You on the ship, and I here. Poor old Blacky. Alone, always alone. Well, they say that you go out of the world much as you come into it – on your own account.'

'Don't worry, old man,' said Omar. 'We have blades enough to keep you safe.'

'Tigers to guard me from hyenas, so it is,' said the commodore.

'My place is by your side too, captain,' the hulking Henry Tempest spoke up from within the party of officers masquerading as prisoners.

'A captain of marines on board the ship, with all our marines left marooned back in Benzaral by the vice-admiral?' Jericho shook his head. 'Your place is here with our mission. Keep our two shadowy servants of the state alive. And Henry . . .?'

'Sir?'

'Try not to get yourself in the stockade again back home. I might not always be around to get you released. You may have your men escort the boy and myself back to the *Iron Partridge*, Commander Uddin. First Lieutenant Westwick, the command here in the citadel is yours – although I suspect in reality, it probably always was.'

Westwick shrugged almost imperceptibly. 'Sell yourself dearly, captain.'

'The Royal Aerostatical Navy knows no other price, m'dear.'

Farris Uddin started shouting commands behind them. Ordering the local ground crew to release the *Iron Partridge* and let their precious ironclad prize vessel sail to the safety of the landing fields to the south. Demanding that the torturers who had requested the presence of the Jackelian prisoners present themselves and lead the party to whatever hell-damned cutting rooms and cells they had ready.

The commodore waved sadly towards Jack, as Omar and another solider walked Jack and the skipper back down the harbour passageway, towards the vessel's port walkway hatch. Whether the commodore was more concerned about Jack's fate or his own was impossible to tell.

'You and Jack Keats are very brave, captain,' said Omar.

'When you engage the grand vizier's fleet, I believe you might almost be considered as courageous as me.'

Jericho shrugged off the praise. 'Thank you, guardsman. Although to be that brave, I'd say I might have to mount one of those flying monstrosities you sally about on, d'you see, and if truth be known, I still suffer from air sickness after all these years.'

Omar cranked open the hatch door to the *Iron Partridge* while he and the other guardsman pushed down Jack and Jericho's heads to enter, allowing them to slip their wrist knots as they entered the airship.

'I shall keep my vow to my father's shade, now, Jack Keats,' pledged Omar. 'If the grand vizier is inside the citadel, then so is that beast Salwa. And I will see them both suffer for what they have done to the woman I loved, to my people and my house.'

'I'll ask that god of yours to see you through to success,' said Jack. *If he'll listen to a Jackelian heathen.*

As the hatch closed, Captain Jericho called out, 'A word of advice, guardsman, passed down from an old soldier. The trick isn't what you do when you're fighting; it's more often what you do when you're *not*.' He turned back to Jack as the door clanged shut. 'An honest hard pounding, Mister Keats, trading shots vessel to vessel. A lot better for us than all that skulking about in the shadows that the State Protection Board's agents seem to enjoy so much, wouldn't you say?'

'The transaction-engine chamber will stand ready, sir.'

'I trust that will be the case,' said Jericho. 'And Mister Keats . . .'

'Sir?'

'I don't have any living descendents. When waterman's sickness claimed m'wife, it took m'poor boy too. Before we left the Kingdom, I took the liberty of bequeathing m'navy pension to your two young brothers. The admiralty's generosity verges on the skimpy, but it will be enough to secure them both means outside the workhouse.'

Jack felt his heart beat fast within his chest and for a second he did not know what to say to this mercurial, flame-haired officer. *My captain.*

'Thank you, truly.' *It doesn't matter if I die, now. Saul and Alan will have a future. They're free! Whatever happens here, they're free.*

'To your post, boy. Run. No dawdling now. Keep m'calculation drums turning and our course true, and we shall see what fashion in tactics these late additions to the party have to bring to our little soirée.'

Jack felt the deck lurch, as the connector arm to their nose lock was set free. The skipper was already down the corridor, his booming voice barking commands and banging on hatches.

However imperfectly crafted, the *Iron Partridge* had been manufactured for war.

Now, finally, she was to have one.

Omar, Boulous, Farris Uddin and the six elite guardsmen fighters in their party had concealed their pistols and scimitars under stolen womb mages' robes. Along with the white face-masks they had tied over their mouths, the disguise was completed with the addition of a small paper skullcap to tie down their hair.

Omar could not contain his triumph at having discovered the womb mages' robing room, which had also furnished disguises for their Jackelian friends who had since set off on their own mission, and come up with the suggestion of arranging their raiding party to resemble the mumbling line of sorcerers he had seen in the womb mages' lair under the palace.

'You are a little too eager to march down into the citadel, Cadet Barir,' warned Farris Uddin as he adjusted the robes over his uniform. 'Remember that we have come for the true Caliph Eternal. His freedom is our victory – nothing else. A little hatred keeps you alive, too much will make you dead.'

But it's not a little hatred I feel towards Shadisa's killers. I burn with it. My body is filled with it. My soul is a sea of it. 'And which of the many men that you have been coined that saying, Master Uddin?'

'All the uniforms I have worn across the years have been in the service of the Caliph Eternal,' rebuked the commander. 'As have all my faces. Although not quite as many as the hundred faces of the one true god, for that would be a blasphemy.'

'You have my sword, Master Uddin,' said Omar. 'May the hundred faces of heaven smile on me when I sink it into those who deserve it.'

'I have always had your sword,' said Farris Uddin. He dipped his scimitar out from under the womb mage's mantle. 'For the true Caliph Eternal and the empire. Are we sworn to it?'

The others raised their swords and joined them in a circle of shining steel.

'For thousands of years the bloodline of Ben Issman, his name be blessed, has ruled as Caliph Eternal on the throne of empire. Let us see what manner of man Immed Zahharl is, that he thinks he shall be the power behind the throne.'

'Shall we seize a senior womb mage, Master Uddin?' asked Boulous. 'Tickle him with our sabres until the dog tells us where the Caliph Eternal is being held?'

'There will be few within the citadel privy to the secret of his existence,' said the commander. 'In this matter, we shall have to follow our noses.'

Omar hesitated before speaking, 'I think I know where he

is. I saw the false caliph back in the palace. I can sense him here in the citadel – I can sense both of them, the grand vizier's pet and the true caliph.'

'A tracker's ability?' said Boulous. 'That is a strange trait for the son of a water merchant to possesses.'

'Do not be so quick to judge. Our people's bloodlines have twisted and turned for hundreds of generations,' said Farris Uddin. 'Mixing and becoming intermingled. There is many a young emir who has suddenly found himself growing a wild nomad's water hump as he reaches his adult years and is sent, running in tears, to the womb mages to be cleansed of a great-grandmother's indiscretion. The question is, can your senses distinguish between the false Caliph Eternal and the true?'

Omar shut his eyes and tried, but when he opened them he shook his head sadly. 'No, I can feel no difference.'

'It will be subtle,' said Farris Uddin. 'Subtle and composed of a hidden reworking of the genes – blood engineering passed down from the Caliph Eternal to his chosen successor. For if it were not, everyone would be able to seize control of the beyrogs and the caliph's private stables, and that would hardly do. Luckily for us, I possess a subtle nose.' As he spoke, his nose began to grow longer, becoming muzzle-like. As if he were a wolf, Farris Uddin sniffed the air and grinned fero-ciously. 'You are right; it is very hard to tell the difference. If you did not know there were a true Caliph Eternal and a false one, you would miss it completely. But I have the slight advantage of having met the real Caliph Eternal.' He opened the door to the robing room and pointed down the citadel. 'This way . . .'

'Now,' said First Lieutenant Westwick while she adjusted the settings on their tiny portable transaction engine, watching as the commodore fiddled with the cables hanging from a bank of the womb mages' engines, 'would be the ideal time for your young cardsharp friend to be in our company.'

'This is a walk in the park compared to the calculation drums back home,' said the commodore. 'We stamp our art out in steel and steam, the Cassarabians write theirs in flesh and blood. But I don't have to tell you that, eh?'

Henry Tempest gave a gentle whistle from the door leading into the womb mages' transaction-engine chamber, indicating someone was coming down the corridor, and the pair briefly halted their noise until the officer thumbed them the all clear.

'Keep the connection and their calculation drums turning while I get down to this,' said Westwick.

'Are you going to try and crack deep into their systems, lass?'

'I would never attempt something so dangerous,' said Westwick. 'But you know how you can tell which chest a house's really valuable silver is hidden in?'

'Ah,' said the commodore. 'I see the board's training is worth something after all.'

Westwick inspected the results on their portable transaction engine. 'Here it is. The level of the citadel with the strongest data encryption.'

'So we'll follow the trail of locks, then,' said the commodore. 'Right down to their strongest, and let's see how they stand up against the genius of old Blacky. Ah, it sounded such a slight little favour when it was asked back home. Just find out how they're floating their airship's envelopes, Jared. That's all. Your old Cassarabian friends will remember you kindly, won't they? Winkle out the secrets of their airships' gas for us. And here we are in the Forbidden City, the three of us against an empire full of enemies while our best chance of escape is sailing towards her end. Not even a drop of RAN rum to wet my lips while I sweat under these wicked robes. You see how cruel fate is to me, Maya?'

'That is the nature of fate,' said Westwick. 'It runs, as our allies here would say, as heaven wills.' She looked over at the captain of marines. 'Sup from your green canteen, Henry. You need to stay calm until we get to the lower levels of the citadel.'

'I've been taking too much green, tonight, first lieutenant,' complained the officer from his watch post. 'I'm going to bleeding sleep over here.'

'Think of it as the milk that lines the stomach before the beer,' said Westwick. 'You'll have your thirst quenched before we leave the citadel, that much I guarantee you.'

'Does it taste good, lad, that blessed soup of yours?' asked the commodore, as if the thought of its quality had only just occurred to him.

'No, master cardsharp,' said Tempest. 'It's just what you need, not what you want.'

'A cruel fate, like I said, a wicked cruel fate.'

Jack had already received the order to ready for battle stations when the transaction engine's main communications pipe began to whistle like a kettle coming to boil.

Another request?

He and Coss had just been warned by the runner from the crow's-nest dome that three enemy vessels forward of the main fleet had been sighted, acting as a pathfinder squadron, each a match for the *Iron Partridge*. They and the drak-riding guardsmen accompanying them would soon have a quarrel on their hands.

Jack could almost hear the commodore's comment on their situation. *'A little appetizer for you lad, before the main course is served.'*

Coss got to the communications pipe before Jack could slide the punch-card writer to lock and the steamman called across. 'Captain Jericho for us, with an urgent request.' The steamman switched the pipe to public address, the captain's booming tones echoing over the sound and heat of their rotating, rattling calculation drums. 'Bridge to the transaction-engine chamber. Check the archive of the ship's schematics and see if we have a detailed specification for that exotic composite our celgas is bagged up in.'

'Sir?' said Jack. *What's he up to now?*

'It's been said that the fellow who designed the *Iron Partridge* was the cleverest man in the Kingdom. It strikes me that if he replaced canvas with that peculiar cloth of his on our gas cells, there might be a reason for it, eh? Tensile strength, gentlemen, pressure per square inch. I require a swift lift for the vessel. I need to know if I can order our regassing tower crew to double the density of the cells – if we'll hold or if we'll burst.'

'Double our celgas density over what time period, captain?' asked Coss.

'A minute, Mister Shaftcrank.'

'Sir,' protested the steamman, 'there's only one vessel that has ever attempted such a manoeuvre and she—'

'I'm quite aware of what happened to the RAN *Hotspur*. Bring up those schematics from the engines' archives,' roared Jericho. 'I'm going to play a little variation on the game of rock, paper, scissors. I call it carper, canvas, and iron – and I'm playing iron as m'hand.'

The captain's voice faded from the chamber and Jack began working on dredging the dustiest corners of their records for the airwrights' specifications. 'He's planning on ramming them, old steamer.'

'By the copper beards of my ancestors,' moaned the

steamman. 'The Loas preserve me from the mad schemes of you rash fast-bloods.'

'The Cassarabians poked about on board when we were a prize vessel,' said Jack. 'They know we fly low and slow. Their ships are going to climb for height, and the skipper wants to bounce us right up into their bows.'

Jack gritted his teeth even as he said the words. They might dig up the tensile strength of their gas cells from the archives, but there wouldn't be a solitary number on record to indicate whether the oddly crafted *Iron Partridge* could survive ramming a single Cassarabian airship, let alone three of them.

What was war anyway, but a collective, consensual madness between two nations? And they were under the command of an officer whose lunacy had been weighed by an admiralty that had judged him and run scared, leaving him marooned on the half-pay list. Only the next few minutes would reveal whether that was to make the *Iron Partridge* the deadliest ship in the fleet. Or the deadest.

Omar stopped at the door to read the elaborate script that had been traced on a copper plate by its side, but Farris Uddin did the job for him for the benefit of all the guardsmen disguised as womb mages, the commander's tones inflected with a lisp-like quality by the length of his hunting nose.

'Let only those womb mages of the Sect of Razat, or accompanied by the Sect of Razat, set foot beyond this boundary,' said Farris Uddin. 'And a saying from the twelfth book of Ben Issman, his name be blessed. "Let the efforts of your flesh be dedicated to progress, for in progress shall you be elevated."' Farris Uddin shook his head in anger.

'Only the trusted may enter,' said Omar. *We are getting close.*

'Is this a warning or a call to heresy?' asked Boulous.

'One sect to control everything under god,' said Farris Uddin. 'This is the grand vizier's vision – the destruction of the Holy Cent. He thinks he makes the empire stronger? He will tear us apart in ancient schisms by his perversions of the scripture's holy word.'

Grimly, they pressed on through a series of narrow corridors, the end of the last corridor leading onto a gantry flanked by railings that crossed above a vault-like chamber perhaps a hundred feet high. The gantry branched out into smaller walkways to allow the womb mages access to the tanks below; hundreds of glass cases filled with every sort of creation the womb mages' craft could call into existence. There were some creatures that looked to be related to the familiar biologicks that Omar recognized – the guardsmen's draks, as well as the sandpedes the caravans used to cross the dunes – but the majority of the beasts were completely unfamiliar. Four-legged things the size of horses but with black armour carapaces, overlarge versions of the fighting beetles that Haffa townsmen used to set against each other while they laid wagers; water-filled tanks where dwarven oil-furred humanoids twisted and cut through the liquid – their child-like eyes staring out beseechingly; another creature man-sized, but lurching about, all exposed white bones with chords of muscle, as if someone had made a scarecrow by tying together dozens of bundles of sticks. With so many raw animal smells rising up in such close confines, Omar had to work not to gag through his womb mage's mask.

The guardsmen stared uneasily at the howling, squalling, scampering mass of flesh beneath their boots. Even Omar felt the superstitious hackles rise on the back of his neck.

In an attempt to reassure the raiding party, Farris Uddin pointed down to the copper-plated pages of the spell books chained to each tank. 'A flesh library. I have heard of such places. This is where the womb mages attempt to advance their craft. They alter their spells slightly to see what new creatures emerge from the wombs of their producers.'

They pressed on across the vault, windowless and dim except for a series of crimson lamps buried in the far wall. It was as if the flesh library had been made as a larger womb to store the children of the sorcerer's craft. Boulous was the first to notice the ripples across the shadowed ceiling of the vault, pointing up and shouting a warning. What Omar had taken for tiles detached themselves in a black cloud and began wheeling down towards them.

'Bats!' shouted one of the guardsmen, sweeping his scimitar overhead as if swatting mosquitoes.

The creatures were the same size as bats, but their bodies were formed as bony flutes and they appeared to be eyeless and blind. They spiralled down and wheeled around the raiding party, keeping their distance from the brandished steel while emitting ear-piercing whistles. The occupants of the hundreds of tanks below started screeching and caterwauling in response.

'They're not attacking,' called Omar. 'They're acting as a tripwire!'

Boulous wheeled around, looking at the circling creatures.

As if waiting for the word *tripwire* to be said aloud, the lights in the flesh library grew brighter, all the dim shadows banished – the trapped creatures howling in even greater panic.

'They know!' growled a guardsman, waving his pistol. 'They know we are not of the Sect of Razat. We were warned . . .'

'Quiet!' barked Farris Uddin. 'Lower your weapons. Even my hunter's nose cannot detect what faith lies within a man's heart. Make for the library's exit.' They sprinted forward, any attempt to resemble a muttering train of womb mages thrown to the wind. The doors in front rolling open matched the rumbling of the doors behind them sealing shut.

Waiting for them was a group of womb mages, including a familiar face that set Omar's blood racing. *Salwa!* The murderous dog's hood could not disguise his effeminate, sneering features. The womb mages parted to reveal a company of soldiers advancing. But these were no ordinary soldiers. Their flat, stone-like features were reminiscent of beyrogs – but squeezed down into a normal human-sized frame. Each of the beasts wore a round metal helmet that fitted so tightly it might have been part of its skull, a pair of iron spikes rising from each helm's edge like curling horns.

'How appropriate,' Salwa called down the gantry. 'The Caliph Eternal's old elite guard of soldiers meets their replacements. We call them our claw-guard. A new guard for a new age of glory. Do you like your replacements? Unlike you, their loyalty to the sect is imprinted. No antiquated notions of honour to get in the way of serving the empire.'

'Serving *you*,' shouted Omar.

Salwa shrugged. 'They are one and the same.'

'The Caliph Eternal's new guardsmen,' scoffed Farris Uddin. 'If you think those stone-faced monkeys of yours are guardsmen, then you've forgotten to give them a songbird each for them to call their draks!'

As he spoke, talons extended from the paw-like hands of the claw-guards, each as long a short-sword. Loping forward and snarling, the grand vizier's vision of progress charged to meet the steel and war cries of their predecessors.

Sprinting through the raiders, Omar yelled in fury, seeing only an obstruction between him and the target of his scimitar. *Time for me to feed you my blade.* 'Salwa! *Salwa!*'

CHAPTER FOURTEEN

Omar dodged aside as a miniature beyrog-like monster slashed at him with its talons. It was even wearing a guardsman's riding leathers. *That dog Salwa is intent on perverting our traditions beyond the limits of all endurance.* Dipping its head down, the thing tried to skewer Omar with the twin spikes of its helmet and Omar beat it back with the curve of his sword. There were ridges under its clothes that it moved to intercept Omar's thrust, bone as hard as armour. If this had been a normal guardsman, he would have been slowly bleeding to death from a dozen cuts by now. Omar's sword managed to fend off its talons again, as the creature moved them with all the skill of a born fencer – or a sorcery-created one. The real guardsmen had already discharged their pistols into the charging horde, and with no room to break them and load second charges, the fighting had switched to close quarters – talons clashing against steel. Killers who had been trained as the Caliph Eternal's finest, versus slayers who had been born to it.

Omar's opponent was joined by two more claw-guards, and he felt himself separated from the main press of the clash.

He was pushed to the side against the railings as the mob of skirmishing fighters moved backwards, away from the exit and towards the sealed doorway his friends had used to enter the flesh library.

All three of the claw-guards came at Omar – not in a coordinated way, like real guardsmen would have done, but as jostling wolves pressing their prey for the first choice of meat. Covered in a sheen of sweat, Omar lunged and thrust his scimitar between them, keeping the beasts at bay – barely. They were hissing back at him in wordless fury as if they were serpents. Maybe the grand vizier only required obedience from his new elite, not conversation?

Then, suddenly, there was another guardsman by his side – Boulous. Two blades against three sets of talons. From the corner of his eye Omar noted that the other guardsmen were being pushed even further back down the gantry, but somehow brave Boulous had fought his way through to Omar's side, leaving the pair of them as a little archipelago of resistance separated from their comrades.

'They fight like savages,' shouted Boulous, feinting forward and turning a taloned hand with a subtle twist of his wrist.

'They are more handsome than you, Boulous.'

Boulous kicked out with a boot, landing a blow on a kneecap that would have left any human guardsman limping with a broken leg.

As the struck claw-guard stepped back, its brother charged at Boulous and the retainer moved sideways, using his womb mage's robes like a matador's cloak, confusing the monster as he speared the creature through its ribs. Boulous tried to slide his scimitar out, but something had clicked in the wounded, dying thing's body, and the weapon stayed stuck. As Boulous was trying to retrieve his blade, the limping claw-guard returned, lowered its twin-spiked helmet and charged, catching the retainer in his gut and sending both of them sprawling back into the railing.

Omar yelled, smashed back the third of the trio, near-decapitating it, then turned around and hacked at the exposed neck of the claw-guard that had struck Boulous. It collapsed and Omar pivoted and unbalanced the last creature, sinking his scimitar through the false guardsman's uniform and piercing its heart. Swivelling, he pulled off the dying claw-guard that had rammed Boulous, flipping it over the gantry and sending it plummeting towards the flesh library below.

'I can't see them patrolling – in the Jahan,' wheezed Boulous, as he fell back against the railing, twin pools of blood soaking his womb mage's robes. 'No style. Give them a guardsman's – cloak – and they'd probably – put it on the floor and shit on it.'

'Get up, Boulous,' urged Omar. 'The Caliph Eternal needs you.'

'The Caliph Eternal,' coughed Boulous, his eyes rolling in his head as if he was trying to find the empire's ruler. 'I want – a governorship – from him – Omar. A nice fat – little province.'

'You'll have it.'

'Somewhere – shaded – with trees.'

There was a bewildered howling down the gantry. The claw-guards were falling back, confused, while in front of them the womb mage's robes that a second ago had been worn by Farris Uddin appeared to be worn by him no more. There was a new face inside them barking orders at the creatures. The grand vizier's face!

'Don't obey him, you fools!' screamed Salwa. 'It's a Pasdaran trick. Use your noses, mark his scent. It's not the real grand vizier!'

The claw-guards were still retreating down the gantry, and

when Omar gazed down at Boulous, his friend had passed away.

'A forest kingdom for you, Boulous, if heaven truly rewards the deserving.'

As Omar glanced up, he saw Salwa flanked by his claw-guards working the controls of a console, his efforts rewarded by a cry from one of the raiders as the gantry began to retract into the wall behind the guardsmen. There was an open space growing between the citadel's claw-guards and the raiding party, a space getting wider as the gantry pulled back. Omar's friends tried to force open the sealed doorway to their rear but it was no good. The floor beneath them was vanishing foot by foot, until the surviving members of the raiding party spilled into one of the tanks below. Its occupants, a troop of stunted monkey-like things, hurled a primitive tirade of abuse at the interlopers. The guardsmen were trapped – even standing as a pyramid they couldn't scale the tank's tall glass walls.

'New blood is always welcome here,' laughed Salwa as his hideous claw-guards loped affectionately around him. 'Especially when we don't have to pay a slave trader's head price.'

Omar rose up from Boulous's corpse, pointing his scimitar towards the murderous cur. 'Face *me*, Salwa! Set your half-sized beyrogs to one side and face me like a man, alone.'

'That would be a hard thing to do, guardsman,' said Salwa.

'Your steel against mine – show me what the guard's newly appointed grand marshal is good for!'

'Ah, Omar Barir. How little you know me. It would be a hard thing for me to truly face you as a man, for deep inside I am not. Do you really not know your Shadisa . . .?'

'Shut your mouth about Shadisa. You killed her, you dog. I saw you washing away her blood down the drains of your filthy lair!'

'The blood of a womb mage's sorcery – a changeling virus as the female parts of my body were twisted into new forms or fell away. Shadisa was my old name – as much a slave name as the Ibn you once sported. Salwa is the new name the Sect of Razat has blessed me with. An identity created and circulated by the sect, associated with dark deeds before the female "victim" received the sect's blessing and assumed his mantle.'

'No!' shouted Omar. *Salwa will say anything, any lie, to save himself from my scimitar's edge.* 'You are lying! You murdered her!'

'Ah, my proud, vain little Omar. You are still a slave, a prisoner to the way of thinking you were raised with. I let the old Shadisa pass away, so a new one could rise up and take her place as a power in society – not an adornment.' Salwa shrugged. 'The Sect of Razat doesn't sacrifice women, *it frees them*. We are the half of Cassarabia that has been forgotten and overlooked and abused. You should appreciate us, Omar, you should applaud the Sect of Razat, for we are the first true slave revolt that the empire has experienced in over a thousand years.'

Omar dropped his scimitar to the floor. The words had to be false, but he had reached out, grasping for the spark of Shadisa that had once fired his love – and there was something there, deep, hidden within Salwa, now that he knew what to search for. An image of the girl his heart had once quickened for, faint and indistinct – the twisted reflection of a chromosome.

Salwa laughed again, a little more gently this time. 'I asked you to join us, Omar. Become part of the Imperial Aerial Squadron. You of all men know what it is like to have been chattel. The half of the empire that is untapped is about to be freed, and then we will be unstoppable.' Salwa pointed to the cloud of bat-like creatures circling under the vault of the flesh library. 'You should have brought a woman here with you, Omar, or one of the sect, and then the creatures would not have sounded an alert. For you and your friends, all the guardians of the old order – the secret police and the guardsmen – you have been outmanoeuvred by *mere* women. How does that feel, last son of Barir?'

Squatting on the floor by Boulous's corpse, Omar could find no words, no boasts. Only tears dropping down through the metal grille into the tanks below. Now it made a terrible, sickening sense. No wonder he hadn't been able to sense Shadisa in the palace until she was right under his nose. She had already begun the treatments to change into this thing, this monster. Sacrificing all that she was, and for what? Shadisa, his beautiful golden-haired Shadisa, remade as this horrific, ugly, power-hungry creature – as much of a traitor as the grand vizier. *Of course, the grand vizier is another one of them too.*

'Kill her,' Farris Uddin shouted from below. 'In the name of the heavens, Cadet Barir, you must kill that abomination.'

Omar barely even felt the paws of the claw-guards, their talons retracted, as they grabbed him and dragged him away.

I am dead. You have murdered me, and you didn't even require a scimitar to do it.

By the time Jack returned to the bridge of the *Iron Partridge* with all the calculations of their gas cells' tensile strength, the three enemy vessels in the pathfinder squadron were already manoeuvring for advantage against the RAN airship.

Jericho was standing at the fore of the bridge with his personal telescope extended, shouting commands back to the signaller on the pipes station to relay across the ship. 'Master gunner to run out our thirty-twos and have all quarter gunners starboard and port on short-fuse readiness, master bombardier to stand ready. Helioscope, flash the guardsmen talon wings to support on our forward quarter, I don't want their draks getting raked in our crossfire.'

'H-station reports flash from their forward vessel. Shall we flash the squadron some of the enemy codes we used to gain access to their city?' asked the signaller.

'Time to fly under our true colours,' said Jericho. 'We'll leave the skulduggery to our State Protection Board friends. Flash the squadron this in Jackelian open signal: We are happy to accept your surrender. Please advise.'

A minute later the enemy responded, the signaller reporting the reply. 'Enemy captain's suggestion involves the use of our seats of ease, sir,' he said, referring to the circular room where the ship's officers exercised their bowels.

'Jolly good, that's all the usual formalities dispensed with. Lieutenant McGillivray, sound general-quarters. All hands make ready to give and receive fire.'

Jack moved forward and the captain noticed the young sailor in the reflection of the viewing port. 'Their three pathfinder commanders are going for glory, Mister Keats. See now, they're launching packets from their boat bays, no doubt headed back to the main fleet with word of our presence. All three of their vessels are coming for our throat.'

Jack looked out: three airships visibly growing larger, silhouetted against the moonlit sky with their running lamps burning, a little triangle-shaped constellation cutting through the night. *They'll be on us soon enough.*

'They're fast studies, m'boy. We call that formation the tricorn hat, the best disposition for a squadron of three against a single enemy. Now – m'gas cell envelopes . . .'

'Mister Shaftcrank and I believe the cells will hold, sir.'

'*Believe?*'

'Our specifications were incomplete, captain,' said Jack. 'We had to extrapolate their pressure potential from the other properties that were on record.'

'Well then, you and the steamman strike me as bright sorts. Double or quits it is to be, quite literally. Across to the pipes station with you. Tell the yeoman of the cells to increase the pressure per square inch of our celgas spheres by a factor of two.'

Jack hesitated. *You expect him to listen to me?*

'You're acting master cardsharp now,' said Jericho. 'A warrant sky officer. I couldn't issue a battlefield commission for Mister Shaftcrank; the First Skylord is a terrible stickler about allied nationals and promotions. I've already entered your temporary field commission in the ship's log. If the ship were running under full automation, you'd be of equal rank to the first lieutenant. No hesitation, now. The yeoman of the cells will listen to you and take your commands, or damn his eyes, I'll want to know why.'

Jack sprinted back to the communications station. The ship's weight was about to lighten, but his own had already increased. Picking up the speaking tube to the gassing stations, Jack gave the order to the increasingly incredulous sounding yeoman of the cells at the other end.

'We'll be running the cells fit to burst!' the man spluttered over the fizzing line.

'Does he like it, sir?' the captain barked.

'He does not, sir,' called Jack. 'But he's obeying the orders anyway.'

'He's quite correct, Mister Keats. Gambling is a terrible sin,' laughed the captain. The airship's master sounded like a boy in a sweet shop who had been given a guinea to spend. 'And now, an order which no captain of the RAN has to m'knowledge ever been required to issue. Pipes, the engine

311

room if you please. Tell Mister Pasco to run up his engines for ramming speed!'

Commodore Black watched the last of the symbols on the door's transaction-engine lock rotate towards the open position, the little portable transaction engine supplied by the State Protection Board cracking their encryption with smooth efficiency.

'This is it, lass,' the commodore said to First Lieutenant Westwick. 'We've followed the trail of locks, and the cipher on our door here is as tough as any I've seen inside this dark place.'

Henry Tempest returned down the corridor, having just dragged away the bodies of the womb mages who had the misfortune to challenge the three of them. 'I stuffed the little perishers in a supply room.'

Westwick nodded. 'Take a sip more from the red canteen, Henry.'

'It's a mortal clever little thing,' said the commodore, patting the small device. 'I could have made mischief with this in the old days, I could. When old Blacky was in his prime and the locks of so many vaults and prison doors needed opening. It's a hard thing to see your mortal genius replaced by a little box of tricks strung together by some engineman in the pay of the board.'

'Your box still needs people on the ground to take it where the state requires its use,' said Westwick.

'That it does, Maya. A poor, creaking old fellow like Jared Black who should be resting in well-earned retirement back in Middlesteel, not sneaking through the empire's terrible shadows wearing an ill-cut RAN uniform under some stinking robes.'

'You're still good for the great game, old man,' said Westwick.

312

There was a clack as multiple bolts in the door withdrew. Pushing it open revealed a long dark corridor. Feeling along the wall, the commodore found a switch to activate the lanterns in the ceiling, and as they flared bright, the wall on the right was revealed as a length of smoked glass, and their corridor a viewing gallery for the chamber below. In the middle of the chamber lay a figure covered by a white gown and hooded by a large metal helmet. Coiled around the length of the body was a knot of tubes that seemed to be extracting blood while feeding in liquids and chemicals from dozens of archaic-looking machines that surrounded the figure.

'Poor devil,' said the commodore. 'Like a fly caught up in a cobweb of the womb mages' dark arts. But one man isn't acting as the factory for the entire stock of the Imperial Aerial Squadron's celgas.'

'It is the Caliph Eternal,' hissed Westwick. 'The real caliph. They're extracting what they need from him to inject into the grand vizier's pet.'

'It could be anyone under that helmet, Maya,' said the commodore. 'Some poor wretch the grand vizier has taken it into his mind to punish.'

'It's the true caliph,' insisted Westwick, pointing to a door in the glass wall that led to a set of stairs down into the chamber. 'Crack that lock and get him out of there.'

'This isn't our mission,' said the commodore. 'We're here for the source of the empire's blessed celgas, not the devil that sits on their throne. Are we to expect gratitude from him if we set him free? The gratitude of kings is a poor, beggarly thing, lass. Take it from one who has served a few.'

'The Caliph Eternal could end the war . . .'

'Or he could continue the whole wicked affair,' said the commodore. 'Once we break him out we have to get him back to the airship – we'll have the whole empire after us and no more chance of a quiet infiltration in search of their celgas.'

Their argument was interrupted by the clamour of distant bells.

'For us?' asked Henry Tempest.

Commodore Black shook his head. 'No, big lad. I think our allies have been discovered. But if the grand vizier knows there are rats creeping about his citadel, he'll surely be sending sentries down here to check in on his prize guest all the same.'

'Just crack the damn door,' commanded Westwick. 'Now! That's an order.'

Commodore Black began to patch their cracksman's box of tricks into the door that led down into the chamber, but he had hardly started the work when the floor started to shake. He looked up to find the end of the corridor, filled with huge beyrogs, accompanied by charging, human-sized cousins squeezed into replicas of the guardsmen's uniforms.

'Slake your thirst, Henry,' shouted Westwick, drawing her pistol with one hand and her sword with the other. 'Drain the red flask. Keep at the lock, Jared!'

She knelt and shot one of the charging beyrogs through the skull as Tempest charged past her. With no time to reload she shoved the pistol back in her belt and drew a knife with her free hand. Somewhere behind the enemy column, a voice was commanding the beasts on.

The commodore urged his box of tricks to its work, cursing it for a charlatan's lock pick. Focus on the job at hand. Not the thud of Henry Tempest's fists as they made a drum of the nearest beyrog's chest, or the wet snick of Westwick's dancing blades. Not the screams of the dying beasts in guardsmen's uniforms. Not the captain of marine's rising rage, his temper tracing the chemical arc of the filthy medical soup he had just downed in a single swig. No time to look at the wild bulging eyes and muscles twisting like snakes under his skin, or listen to the hot-tempered abuse he was hurling at the beasts as they beat at him, trying to overwhelm this wolverine in human form that had unexpectedly flung himself into their ranks.

Finally, the commodore's desperate work was rewarded by the clunk of the cell door's locks retracting into the walls. 'Maya, Henry!'

'Fall back!' ordered Westwick.

Their captain of marines had his hand around one beyrog's throat, smashing it into the corridor's narrow walls while his boot lashed out at another, the giant beast already doubled up in agony from a previous blow. 'I'll hold 'em here, first lieutenant. The little granite-faced goblins will be all over us like bleeding flies if we all fall back at the same time.'

'That wasn't a suggestion, captain of marines!'

'He's right, lass,' called the commodore. 'Circle help us, but he's right. Run for it and we'll see how they value their impostor's milk cow with a knife held to his throat.'

Westwick came running back towards the cell door, while the captain of marines single-handedly fought the beasts' advance to a halt behind her. Westwick and the commodore had just gained the inside of the caliph's cell when the front ranks of the advancing beyrogs parted to reveal more of their number bearing the only projectile weapons that would fit their ungainly fists – crossbows the size of brace supports torn out of an airship. They began to loose bolts into Henry Tempest, the first three missiles catching him in the chest and sending him stumbling back, yelling in pain and anger.

'Is that all you've got?' roared the captain of marines. He pulled two of the projectiles out and charged the front of their ranks, impaling the bolts into a beyrog, even as the next line opened up on him with their crossbows. 'Who taught you dirty sand-footed abortions to shoot? Your bloody aunt?'

He grabbed a monstrous hand coming at him with an over-sized scimitar, twisted it round, and stuck the sharp end into another beyrog as six more bolts thwacked into him. 'You eat a man's round of roast beef and drink a quart of beer, then you'll fight like proper soldiers.'

The first line of crossbow-wielding brutes had reloaded and they put a third volley into the captain of marines, enough of them in the fight now to keep up an almost constant barrage of independent fire.

Commodore Black and Westwick were halfway down the steps of the caliph's cell when the door slammed behind them, their view of the uneven stand-off restricted to their angle of sight through the viewing gallery window. Little flecks of blood struck the glass in between each roar of Jackelian defiance from outside.

There was a thump against the glass as a dying beyrog was shoved up against it, another thump as the beast's twin appeared on the right, and then in the middle, Henry Tempest appeared, a human pin cushion, juddering and twitching with each fresh bolt finding its mark in his spine. 'Perishing – little – sand – monkeys.'

All three bodies slumped off the glass leaving trails of blood. They could hear the feral roars of the enemy's victory through the locked cell door.

'We only have as long as it takes them to key open that wicked door,' said the commodore, moving to pull the cables out of the prone figure's body.

'Poor Henry. You died as you were designed to, as you were fated to by your creators.' Westwick struggled with the visorless helmet, lifting it off the prisoner's head to reveal the ageless features that could be seen stamped on the face of any Cassarabian coin. *The Caliph Eternal*. The rudimentary machines around him whined in protest as their charge was freed.

'Aye now, let's see what their precious ruler of rulers is good for.'

The caliph was still lying down, eyes blinking against the light and groggy from being pulled from whatever sustenance they had been pumping into him to keep him unconscious.

'Up with you, lad,' urged the commodore. 'You've two guardian angels to thank for your wake-up call.'

'Two Jackelians?' coughed the ruler. 'The almighty of almighty's sense of humour has not improved for the better, then.'

There was a banging at the top of the gallery as the door was unlocked and opened.

'And neither has the sight of the grand vizier and my surplus flesh brother.'

They turned to see the caliph's twin in the doorway, with a thin-faced man the commodore took to be the emperor's chief of ministers. Commodore Black had his pistol out and pointed to the back of the caliph's head. 'How long can your impostor survive without the blood of the Caliph Eternal, and still pull off his royal act?'

'Quite long enough for Akil Jaber Issman to abdicate in my favour,' said the grand vizier. 'After it is miraculously discovered that my veins also flow with the blood of Ben Issman.'

'A miracle indeed,' said the true caliph. 'The kind the order of womb mages specializes in.'

'You have slept through the start of a glorious war,' said the grand vizier. 'The sort of war your recently departed flesh father would have loved to have masterminded, little enculi. Plunder and land enough to make sure the only question the empire's generals and admirals and sultans ask is, "How much of what we take is mine?" Their loyalty has been well purchased.'

'Put your gun down,' Westwick ordered the commodore. 'They know you're bluffing.'

'I'm not bluffing, lass.'

Westwick raised her own pistol, pointing it at the commodore's head. 'I gave you an order, Jared Black.'

'Ah, well here's the thing,' said the commodore. 'I'm not quite ready to take my mortal orders from a Pasdaran double agent. Why do you think the State Protection Board really sent me along with you, lass? They've had their doubts about the Cassarabian section for a long time. I didn't even need the proof of us ending up here to save the caliph rather than inside their wicked celgas rooms where we were meant to be – the board knew that the Sect of Jabal was the recognition word being used by the Pasdaran cell inside the Kingdom. The same word you traded with my old friend back in the safe house at Sharmata Sarl to let her know you were one of them.'

The grand vizier laughed from the top of the stairs, his beasts in guardsmen leathers snarling in front of him. 'Ah, the Pasdaran. They are like the knotweed that strangles a garden. So hard to pull out, although heaven knows I have tried. I find it strangely reassuring that the Kingdom has much the same problem with them.'

'Unless your parliament has ordered my assassination,' said the true caliph, 'I would rather everyone put their guns down.'

'This is war, your excellency,' said the commodore. 'That makes this medals, not murder.'

'Not my war, Jackelian.'

'Put your weapons down,' barked the grand vizier. 'Who knows, perhaps I will let you live a while longer.'

The commodore sighed and slowly lowered his gun. 'Well, there it is then, curse my unlucky stars. I suspect I will come to regret this.'

The grand vizier's beasts in guardsmen's uniforms swept down the steps towards the caliph and his two would-be rescuers. 'Bind their hands and gag the caliph's mouth. We don't want the beyrogs getting confused by contradictory orders. So, the Jackelian State Protection Board has taken an interest in the methods for floating my airships? I shall have to involve you all in the process, then.' His cruel laugh cut across the chamber. 'I shall involve you *very* directly. Since you have come such a long way, it is the least I can do.'

There was a lurch as the *Iron Partridge* pulled violently up, the deck slanting and the pilot on the elevator station fighting his rapidly rotating wheel as the upper and lower lifting chambers near-instantly doubled the amount of gas in their cells. Jack could hear the drone of the engine cars, a nasal complaining whine from the rotors as they struggled to match the viciously strong pull of their transmission belts. Alarms were sounding throughout the airship; anything not tied down was rolling and breaking now, from the pots and pans that belonged to the ship's slushy, to the far more dangerous shells that hadn't been tied down by the gunners.

'Vent ballast water tanks, rear only,' barked Jericho. 'I want level yaw for m'broadside when we cut their centre.'

Jack clutched onto the side of the pipes station as the *Iron Partridge* began to level out. *Hold*, he begged the gas cells. *Just hold on a bit longer without bursting. Circle, but we're rising fast.* The pit of his stomach was falling towards his feet.

'Hold us regular – hold us regular,' urged Jericho, his eyes fixed on the view outside the bridge. 'Quarter gunners, ready cannon hoods for movement.'

There was a brief moment of silence, the sense that they were suspended in time as well as the dark night sky, then

Jericho yelled, *'Fire!'* and the airship shook with fury. Even with their cannons rail-mounted on turntables, pneumatic shock absorbers cushioning the recoil, Jack could feel every inch of the anger of the *Iron Partridge*'s guns through the shaking decks.

From a porthole Jack caught a fleeting glimpse of two of the enemy pathfinder vessels which had been caught unawares by the massive ironclad's sudden turn of speed and lift. The enemy's gun decks had been left completely mangled, undischarged ordnance detonating, their crew in air masks just visible in the light of the fires desperately trying to seal rubber hoods that had been torn to shreds. *Such carnage. Men pulling off the remains of their cannons from the remains of their friends. Fires and death and burning. Sailors no different from us trying to cope with it. When will it be our turn?*

Jack marked the wheeling draks and their guardsmen riders, like vultures rather than hawks, closing in to finish off the carcasses this giant iron beast had left in her wake. He only had a second to stare in astonishment at the devastation of their cannonade.

'Pipes!' roared Jericho. 'All chambers, all stations. Brace! Brace! Brace!'

They were heading for the last vessel and about to tear the top off the tricorn hat.

Omar struggled against his bonds, but he was tied to the chair too tightly. Not that he could have achieved much against the line of claw-guards formed up behind the prisoners' chairs. Farris Uddin, Commodore Black and First Lieutenant Westwick were all tied to their chairs, not to mention what looked like the true Caliph Eternal. The bound and gagged ruler of rulers seemed to hold a strange fascination for the grand vizier's pet, who kept peering around Salwa for a better look at his flesh twin. Despite his obvious curiosity, he held back from touching the true Caliph Eternal, as if to do so might negate his own existence in a sudden flash of sorcery. *I can sense the difference between them now I'm so close, much good may it do me.* He had to work hard not to sob at the thought.

They were inside a dim, dark chamber, facing a mirrored wall. The grand vizier motioned to Salwa to open a large womb mage's chest and he – she? – withdrew a set of blood-filled vials, making the case ready for the grand vizier. Now Omar knew the truth of what had happened to Shadisa, he could hardly stand to look at the creature of sorcery that had subsumed her body. *How could she do this to herself? How could she do this to me?* She had swapped her beauty and her soul and her honour for this? Power, the chance to follow the grand vizier around like a lapdog.

'It is always good to know who you are dealing with,' said the grand vizier, pacing the room. 'I believe it was the fourth book of Ben Issman that said that no one should rise to heaven with a lie in their heart or a falsehood on their tongue.'

'You dare to treat the Caliph Eternal like this,' spat Omar, 'the blood of Ben Issman himself, and then talk of the *truth*.'

'The blood of Ben Issman?' laughed the grand vizier. 'How naive, how hopelessly romantic.' He pointed to the gagged form of the Caliph Eternal. 'Meet the much-diluted, much-copied, twentieth-generation enculi of a very distant cousin who managed to wrest power centuries ago from an equally distant enculi of some inbred fool who was briefly ruthless enough to seize the throne. It was said that Ben Issman took five hundred wives. There's probably more of his blood in your veins, guardsman, than in this pathetic pair. There's certainly enough of some others . . .' He pointed at Farris Uddin. 'Does the last son of Barir know, officer of the Pasdaran? He's what, your great-great-great grandson?'

Farris Uddin said nothing as Omar stared at him in shock. *Is it true?* Was that the real reason why Farris Uddin had rescued the House of Barir's last half-blood bastard of a son from a bandit's blade?

'Special shackles for you, my aged Pasdaran friend. I have extracted most of your abilities from your blood code. You have been gifted with a shape-switcher's face and the ability to sweat acid and see in the dark. Enhanced strength, speed and senses. How old are you? The amount of trace drugs in your blood suggests you must have been taking pure lifelast for a very long time. You would have served my little enculi's flesh father for most of his reign. How fitting for you to be here at the founding of a new dynasty.'

At last, Farris Uddin spoke, jerking his head towards Salwa. 'An abomination as the power behind the throne? You are, I presume, the same as this thing?'

Salwa moved closer and punched him in the face. 'You should not listen in to other people's conversations.'

'Our present forms are a necessary deception,' shrugged the grand vizier. 'The empire is not yet ready for a female grand vizier. And my male form should not disgust you, for in a very practical sense, it was you and your kind that made me, my Pasdaran friend. You are as much my begetter as you are the boy's here.'

'What do you talk of?' spat Farris Uddin.

'Do you remember when the satrapy of Hakaqibla rebelled all those years ago? When the Pasdaran came and executed everyone in the sultan's family – all the males anyway. It's not an easy thing to be a twelve-year-old girl, raised in luxury as a princess, innocent and artless, knowing nothing of the world, and then to have all that ripped away from you in a single night of savagery.'

'You were there . . .'

'As were you, I expect. You have no care for what you and your people did to me, do you? What you did to all of us. After such a gentle upbringing to find myself being whipped as a slave, watching most of my sisters and cousins die as we were dragged half-drugged behind sandpedes across half the empire. But I was lucky, if you can call being kept alive after what I experienced lucky. I was the prettiest of the survivors – the slavers made sure I got just enough food and water not to stumble and perish in the desert. Eventually, when I went on the block in Bladetenbul, I was purchased at no small expense by a very old and powerful womb mage who stood senior in the order's ranks. I became his very special little slave, and somewhere in between abusing me, the sweaty old goat fell in love with what I still was in those days, as did his young fool of an apprentice. Between the two of them, I learnt every skill of the womb mage's craft, until the pair didn't even realize that their innovations were more my work than their own. I drove the old goat into a fit of jealousy by my dalliance with his apprentice, drove him into murderous fury, and made sure he pushed the young boy out of one of the towers of Mutantarjinn.

'It was then that I replaced the apprentice, in every sense of the word, having developed a changeling virus to assume his assistant's gender. How furious my owner was when he saw what his beautiful little slave had turned into. But he could say nothing without being executed by my side as the murderers we had become. And when the time was right, I slipped a draught into the old goat's wine that burst his heart like an overripe fruit, leaving me to claim his legacy.'

Omar stared appalled at Immed Zahharl. More of an abomination than anyone had suspected. How similar and yet how different they were. Both Omar and the grand vizier had once been slaves, both risen beyond their station. He freed – indirectly – by her machinations, and she clawing her way back to privilege, becoming a chimera through the darkest murder and treason. How many lives had ended in the fall of the House of Barir, the Sect of Ackron declared heretic to make room for her followers' rise in the Holy Cent; how many more would die in the war against the north? *My father, my people, my home.* She had slain Boulous, and worse yet, completely corrupted his beautiful Shadisa within and without. Filled the Sect of Razat with monstrosities made in her own image by sorcery – then filled them with the lust for power and the blood of men. How much better if that young princess had been left to her guileless pleasures in her distant province.

The grand vizier's eyes narrowed. 'I should plant you in the torture gardens, Farris Uddin, so I can thank you every morning for making me what I am today. Unfortunately, old man, you have too few years left for me to enjoy your company, so we shall have to put your body to a more practical use.'

The grand vizier was now near enough to Westwick's chair for her to spit at his feet as she cursed him for a traitor.

Immed Zahharl just seemed amused by the woman's little act of defiance. 'I would free you if I could and convert you into one of us. But you are as much a product of the Pasdaran as the old man here. How clever of the secret police to send agents across the border masquerading as escaped slaves. And every girl born of her mother's womb as much a slave to the Caliph Eternal as his troop of beyrogs. The changes in your body that imprint your loyalty to him run too deep and subtle for me to remove them without killing you. A pity. What an assassin's blade you would have made for me. But don't worry.' The grand vizier tapped the vials of blood that had been extracted from the prisoners. 'I have your design here. We can have a few more like you bred, I think, with the recipient of your devotion corrected to a more appropriate choice of candidate. The original, I fear, we must feed to the creatures in our stables. Some of them have quite a healthy appetite, you see.'

The grand vizier moved down the line to where Commodore Black was tied up. 'And here is a strange fellow to turn up as one of parliament's agents. The blood of kings runs through your veins, old man. I was led to believe that all of the Jackelian royalist rebels had perished with the fall of the u-boat fleet-in-exile at Porto Principe.'

'Not the ones who swam from the depth charges, lass,' said the commodore.

'Eminently sensible,' smiled the grand vizier. 'Half the people who serve my cause have switched sides. I rather count on it, or I would be ruling over a very depopulated empire. When the Kingdom of Jackals falls, I think I will crack open the cells of your people's royal breeding house and see if I can find someone malleable enough to become the puppet sultan for my new satrapy. A little continuity goes a long way in such matters. You shall act as my broker.'

'Parliament already has a blessed puppet queen locked up in the palace,' said the commodore. 'And I would sooner have her the prisoner of parliament's crew of dirty Jackelian shop-keepers than of some wicked Cassarabian caliph.'

The grand vizier's smile turned to ice on his thin lips. 'You'll change your mind in time, I believe.'

'No lass. I might feel sorry for you, but I won't be doing that. Because you're right about one thing, you're a creature of the Pasdaran alright. They created you in the cruelty of the life of a girl born to the empire and the crucible of slavery, they made you just as surely as a womb mage creates a drak. They didn't need a scalpel and blood splicer to do it. Just whips and murder and a slave collar.'

'They made me strong!' the grand vizier hissed.

'No, lass. They made you hard, and broke you into so many pieces you'll never be able to tell the difference. As one noble-born to another, strength has no purpose unless it's used to help the weak. Not this, not what you're about here.'

'We shall see what the true currency of strength is, you old fool. When there are crowds of Jackelians kneeling on the streets of Middlesteel as my armies march in procession down your lanes. We shall see which of us is right, then. I will give the empire a victory no man has ever been capable of achieving, and how they will love me for it.' The chief minister finished behind Omar's chair. 'And here we have the last son of Barir, the smallest and least significant of my loose ends. Of no account at all. I am told you were a slave on a desalination line, guardsman. How cruel for fate to push you so far beyond your limits. I clawed myself up through society one death at a time to get back to where I belonged. Perhaps you should have crawled back down to your natural station?'

'I'll crawl over glass to see you die,' spat Omar. He struggled madly against his bonds but they were too tight. Too tight to let him slip them for a second and break the neck of the beast who had turned Shadisa into a twisted shadow of the spiteful politician. *All this death, fate, all this suffering. Why have you put me here in front of this monster if not to kill it?*

'Just a proud, vain little peacock, that's all,' said the grand vizier, wagging a knowing finger towards Salwa. 'I told you, even in one who used to be a slave, his male pride would prove too strong for him to defect to our cause.' The grand vizier moved back to the start of the line of prisoners. 'So, the guardsmen among you came looking for the Caliph Eternal, and here he is for you now, conveniently trussed up. While my two curious Jackelian friends came visiting to see how it is I now have celgas enough to float an armada capable of outgunning the Royal Aerostatical Navy. That too, I have to show you!'

The grand vizier went to a control panel in front of the mirrored wall, and as his fingers ran over it, the surface of the wall became transparent, revealing a spacious cavern on the other side. Pointing to a series of large glass tanks on the ground of the cavern carpeted with decomposed vegetation and filled with a green mist. Within them, herds of white, bone-like spheres, each with six human-shaped arms, progressed slowly across the tanks as though they were drugged cattle. They walked on their hands whilst scraping up vegetation into a round mouth where a double set of teeth was slowly, constantly chewing.

'The creatures you see down there are called *skoils*. They have a voracious appetite for rotting foliage and the green gas you see is their sole output. Lighter than air, and you simpletons could barely understand the labours I went through to make it non-flammable.'

'Save your womb mage's tricks for someone who will appreciate them,' said Farris Uddin.

'Oh, but you should appreciate them,' insisted the grand vizier, pointing to another series of tanks facing those that housed the strange, sorcery-born creatures. 'It's not easy to produce a skoil, only someone as brilliant as I could find a way around the hurdles that have defeated every womb mage labouring on the problem for half a millennia.'

Omar stared down to where the grand vizier was indicating. He had seen such tanks before, being dragged through the womb mages' chambers beneath the caliph's palace. The yellow nutrient fog inside almost concealed the poor slaves within, their bellies unnaturally distended to allow them to give birth to the products of the sorcerers' art.

'Of course,' said the grand vizier. 'The previous attempts to manufacture our airship gas were made by mere men, and my solution would not have been one they could easily countenance.'

As the grand vizier stopped speaking, the yellow fog of nutrients cleared and Omar saw the faces of the slaves, straining and sweating under the unnatural load their wombs were carrying. Bearded and coarse, they were the faces of men!

Farris Uddin turned his head from the sight in disgust. 'Abomination, what have you done?'

'When Ben Issman wrote of the two souls held in a body's flesh, he was talking about something we womb mages refer to as a chromosome. And only the male chromosome can produce a skoil. Fortunately, the work I did on scouring away my gender can be modified for other uses . . . such as giving a male a fully functioning womb.'

'You are cursed under heaven!'

'Perhaps I am.' The grand vizier shrugged. 'Perhaps every one of us was. Not all of my sisters died on the long journey from the provinces to the heart of the empire. When I tried to locate my remaining two sisters, I found their death records here in the Citadel of Flowers – where they had spent their final years as producers. Do you know what they whisper to producers before their bellies are given a changeling virus to swell them to a useful size? *This is your duty to the Caliph Eternal, do your duty, woman.*' The grand vizier beckoned to Salwa who removed a large syringe from the chest and passed it to him. The chief minister leant close to Farris Uddin's head and whispered, 'This is your duty to the Caliph Eternal, do your duty. *Man.*'

He plunged the syringe into Farris Uddin's arm. 'Of course, it's not easy to give a man a producer's womb, even now. It takes many days for the changes to complete, and fifty per cent of those we attempt to alter reject the virus and die within the first few seconds.'

Farris Uddin was shaking in his chair, his face turning purple. The grand vizier kicked the chair over angrily, enraged that there would be no chance to inflict the ultimate indignity on the last of his surviving secret police enemies. 'Wasteful, I know. But there are always so many sons of the empire left.'

Omar looked on in horror as the chest of the man who had saved him from the sack of Haffa swelled up, choking Uddin, as the air could no longer enter his lungs. Omar's kin, the last of his family, by how many generations removed? Their eyes met briefly as he twisted on the floor, the features of his face distending in automatic reflex, as if all the faces he had worn across the ages were surfacing in turn during his death throes.

'Sorry – boy,' the man mouthed, and then with a series of gentle tremors, his eyes rolled to white and the long life of Farris Uddin finally came to an end.

Omar howled in rage, rocking his chair until the claw-guards weighed into him, giving him a taste of their rock-hard fists with their talons retracted.

'You really are the last son of Barir, now,' sighed the grand vizier, almost sounding disappointed by the lack of challenges left to face. 'And you shall honour your venerable ancestors by following in their footsteps.' He indicated to Salwa that another syringe should be made ready.'

'He is not one of them,' protested Salwa.

'Not raised as one, perhaps,' said the grand vizier. 'But he is a male and he wears a guardsman's uniform. He picked his side when you had him tied to a pair of draks.'

'I know Omar better than anyone – he is a joke, not a threat.'

'The woman called Shadisa knew him. Salwa of the Sect of Razat has chosen more aptly – or do you wish to reconsider your answer to me?' There was an edge of menace in the grand vizier's words, and suitably subdued, the new grand marshal of the guardsmen delved back into the womb mage's chest.

'Better,' said the grand vizier. 'One dose for the last son of Barir, one for the Caliph Eternal.'

Gagged and bound to the chair, the real caliph began to struggle madly, and with an imperious flick of his fingers, the grand vizier sent one of his claw-guards to beat the ruler to a quiet stillness with its fists. 'You have reached the end of your usefulness to me, Akil Jaber Issman. Let us see if it is to be death or a producer's tank for you.'

The false caliph moved to stand between the grand vizier and his twin, clearly troubled by the implications of what the grand vizier had just announced. 'We still need my flesh brother's blood, mother, we still need to milk him for the enzyme that controls the beyrogs and the other creatures of the Jahan.'

'Oh, my beautiful son,' said the grand vizier, hugging him close and speaking softly. 'We don't.' The grand vizier indicated the ranks of claw-guards. 'We have a new imperial bodyguard, more appropriately sized to travel on an airship's decks. And as for the Jahan, I believe the Citadel of Flowers will make a far more appropriate centre of power for the new, enlarged empire *I* shall create.'

'But you saved me from execution,' whined the enculi. 'You said I was the son you could never have, that your love for me was too strong to allow one of my flesh brothers to supplant me as the rightful Caliph Eternal.'

'My darling,' said the grand vizier, plunging a dagger deep into his pet's heart. 'You are quite correct, the one thing I can no longer have is a son.' The false caliph staggered back, looking in stupefaction at the blade buried in his chest, before collapsing slowly to the floor. 'By heaven's right, my future enculi shall be daughters.' The grand vizier knelt by the dying boy's side, taking his hand, kindly. 'Close your eyes, my son. You will be asleep soon. Sleep knowing your mother is claiming your throne. A calipha to rule the empire in the name of Ben Issman's blood line.'

As the dying boy's tremors ended, the grand vizier stood up and took one of the pair of syringes being proffered by Salwa. 'I suppose I shall have to have the beyrog barracks in the citadel flooded with poison gas, now that I can't control the stupid, lumbering things. Almost as stupid as my little enculi here. He always was the weakest of the last caliph's flesh children, whereas I have high hopes that you—' the grand vizier angled the needle towards the empire's real ruler, '—young ruler, will be able to survive the process of becoming a producer.' Walking up to the true caliph, the grand vizier plunged the syringe into his arm and stood back to watch his shaking palpitations. The grand vizier nodded in satisfaction as the fit passed after a couple of minutes. 'There, that is the vigour of youth for you. Now, Salwa, you shall prove your loyalty to me. Put the last son of Barir to the service of our sect as a producer, and let us see if his constitution proves as stout as the caliph's.'

'Pray,' said Salwa. 'Can you not do it? Or one of my claw-guards?'

'And would that be a true test?'

'Please,' Omar begged, as the new master of the guardsmen advanced on him, a strange, conflicted look in the creature's eyes. 'Shadisa, do not do this thing.'

'Shadisa shall not,' said the thing Omar had once loved as a woman. 'But I am Salwa.'

The needle plunged into Omar's arm, drawing blood as its terrible contents found their way into his body. His eyes went out of focus as his chest heaved, the skin around his arm burning, throbbing. The commodore was shouting something to Omar, but he couldn't hear the old man's words. *Please don't let me die here, fate. What would be the point of letting it end here for me? Who would you have to torment then?* The room seemed to judder with rough chemical violence, his body changing, twisting with the sickness of the sorcerer's foul art. Then, as quickly as it had taken Omar, perhaps a minute or two later – although if felt like mere seconds to him – the fit was lifted, his body left washed with cold sweat.

'Thank Lord Tridentscale's beard, lad,' said the commodore. 'You made it.'

'Welcome into our sect's service, last son of Barir,' smirked the grand vizier. 'We will require litters of ten skoils a time from you, a new brood every four months. Toss the boy in a cell with the Caliph Eternal and the two Jackelians. Make sure you remove the caliph and the boy when their bellies start showing.'

The claw-guards cut Omar's bonds and dragged him away. He shouted and struggled in panic as he caught a last glimpse of the long line of producers' tanks below, filled with slaves doing their hideous duty for the empire. Omar hardly needed the stomach cramps and fever to remind him of his fate. *I will be joining their ranks soon enough.*

CHAPTER FIFTEEN

Jack was helped to his feet by Lieutenant McGillivray, the young sailor's uniform covered in broken glass from the shattered compass next to the bridge's map table. *We've survived.*

'I don't think that manoeuvre has a name in the rulebook, laddie,' said McGillivray. 'But back in the uplands, we'd call that a Coldkirk kiss.'

Captain Jericho was still standing by the forward viewing port, as if he had remained vertical right through their violent ramming of the third Cassarabian vessel. 'Damn m'eyes, it seems that iron beats both carper and canvas after all. All stations report readiness and damage.'

Jack stumbled forward, half expecting to find the enemy airship wrapped around their nose cone, but it was drifting downwards, oily black clouds of smoke billowing out from what had been left of their engine room.

'She's breaking up, sir,' called the sailor on the rudder wheel. 'We've ripped her in half with our stern armour, right up to her lower lifting chamber. She's lost equilibrium.'

'They're heading for the ground, gentlemen. Down-gas to our optimum ceiling,' ordered Jericho. 'I want their main fleet to spy us running low and heavy on first sighting. Flash the guardsmen's flight leader when he's finished having his fun with those two dead pigeons we left for him. Get him to the boat bay, I need his flyers on m'wing.'

'Down-gas, aye,' confirmed the officer on the gas board.

They didn't have to wait long to make contact with the Cassarabian fleet sent to defend Mutantarjinn. A constellation of lanterns appeared drifting in the northern sky, running in close formation. The dark night suddenly felt a lot colder.

The guardsman's senior officer in the flight appeared a few minutes later on the bridge, ready to confer with the *Iron Partridge*'s captain.

'Good evening, colonel,' said Jericho. 'I am afraid the weight of numbers is not in our favour.'

'Luckily for you, captain, all our training is towards harrying such a fleet – although traditionally, the enemy's colours should be Jackelian. How do you propose to engage?'

'With the only advantage we have, sir,' said Jericho. 'The thick skin around our hull. I'll drive us into the centre of their disposition and trade blows at close quarters until we buckle. If you can take position on our wings and disperse before the first broadside to clog up as many of their engine cars as possible with your snarls, I believe we'll buy our people in Mutantarjinn the time they need.'

Jack rubbed his tired eyes. *The only advantage we have.*

'*I wish to hear music,*' Lemba of the Empty Thrusters, the spirit of the sky, had commanded in Jack's dream. '*Play, Play.*'

The words echoed around Jack's head until he found them coming out of his mouth unbidden, as if someone else was speaking. 'Captain, we have another advantage we've not brought to bear: the ship's automated systems.'

'You understand that the ship's automatics never passed our trials, Mister Keats?' said Jericho. 'Our sailors manning them is the only thing keeping this iron-plated bucket in the sky.'

'If I know only one thing, sir,' said Jack, 'it's transaction engines. The ship wasn't ready during the trials. She's evolved, sir. She's conscious now. I believe Mister Shaftcrank would bottle up the ship and send her back to King Steam to put her in a nursery body if he could.'

'When I issue an order, Mister Keats, I expect her to respond on m'command, not at her own whim. Running on full automation is too dangerous.'

The guardsman flight commander chortled.

'Do you find something amusing, colonel?'

'I find your Jackelian gradations of danger an interesting notion.' The guardsman gestured towards the sea of lights manoeuvring against the deep night. 'I know little of your technology, captain, but I understand the empire's feelings towards it. When we fight your people, it is never your discipline we fear, it is not your godless sailors, or the fact that you are a people so fierce and rebellious you imprison and mutilate your own king. It is this: every time you leave your rainy, frigid and sunless land, you come at us riding cold, soulless machines, not the warm flesh of a noble drak. It is that you trust all of this.' He pointed to the armada of lights coming towards them, larger now. 'There are some who call that progress, but if we begin to fight like you, how much longer will it be until we choke our cities with engine smogs, banish god from our hearts, let the Caliph Eternal be dictated to by bazaar hawkers, and become mere slaves to the cogs that are meant to turn in service for us?'

'Maybe we must both trust what we know, colonel,' said Jericho. 'Those aerial mines your airships carry have a main chute and a guide chute – could your draks get you close enough to slice the guide chords?'

'If the fleet release the mines, it would be simple work,' said the colonel.

'They'll use the mines,' said Jericho. 'Now we've downed their three pathfinder vessels, they'll want blood, eh? Everything they have, we shall see this night. A clear path, colonel, and as many of their engines snarled as you can attack, and may the gates of your paradise open for you.'

'We already fight in the heavens,' said the colonel, saluting, before turning to exit the bridge. 'The trick will be to stay here.'

The captain looked at Jack. 'The last time I bet against the house, Mister Keats, I ended up trading m'own for the accommodation of the debtors' prison.'

'Gambling is a sin, sir.' *But only if you lose.*

Jericho pointed to a line of out-of-action boards covered with dusty green canvas between the bridge's ballast board and altimeter station. 'That's what's meant to connect the bridge to your transaction-engine chamber aloft. Let's discover if building thinking machines into an airship was the worst or the best decision the admiralty ever made.'

Omar sat on one of the two bunks in the windowless cell, clutching at his gut as it churned in pain. 'In the end, I hardly knew Farris Uddin at all, and then he was snatched away from me – just as my father was taken.' *It seems I must lose everything. My father, my great-grandfather. Oh Shadisa, how great my destiny, to be punished so.*

'Farris Uddin was a rum old cove,' said the commodore, trying to make the boy feel better. 'And if he had as many years under his belt as I think he did during his long service, you probably have half-brothers and sisters scattered all over the empire.'

'Ah, the service of the empire,' sighed the caliph from the

other bunk. 'To tell you the truth, I sometimes wondered if I was its master or its slave. To be bought up in isolation, knowing only my tutors and their lessons, then at the age of eighteen to be told I was one of septuplets, six of whom had just been murdered. To be wheeled out and briefly introduced to my dying flesh father, whose sole legacy before he was snatched away to heaven was to inject me with a changeling virus that filled me with snatches of a string of lives I have never lived. We are not so different, you and I, guardsman. Families we never knew. Lives we did not choose, and now both to be brood mares for the ambitions of the grand vizier.'

'You must not say that, your majesty,' said Westwick. 'You were born to be the Caliph Eternal.'

'I was born to be nothing else, sweet lady,' said the deposed ruler. 'And now I walk with the echoes of my ancestors in my ears, hearing the voices of god in my head like some sun-maddened hermit stumbling through the dunes.' He reached out to touch Westwick's arm. 'So many memories within me. There are one thousand, seven hundred and fifty two discrete points of difference in your DNA that form the basis of your loyalty imprint to me. There is less in a beyrog, but they are simpler creatures – a lot of shark in their genetic composition.' Seeing that his words meant little to his fellow prisoners, the young ruler shrugged. 'Sorcerers' secrets. Ben Issman was the first womb mage, but then, it was he who discovered the ruins of the original Mutantarjinn back in another age.'

'Your sorcerers' secrets,' said Omar. 'Do they include whether this filthy magic they have inflicted on us can be undone?'

'The grand vizier's changeling virus must be recorded some-where in the citadel's library of spells,' said the caliph. 'With such knowledge we could restitch our base genome back to the normal order of things using another changeling virus.

But I do not believe the grand vizier intends to let me peruse his private library.'

'That will be a small matter to me, your majesty,' said Omar. 'I am the last son of your great and most loyal House of Barir. I have already achieved the impossible by rising from the rank of slave to serving as a guardsman. I am the apprenticed cadet of the great Farris Uddin, who taught me that no situation is without hope. We shall break out of here and make for the barracks where your bodyguard of beyrogs waits. With their strength we shall seize one of the producer's tanks and expose the nature of the abominations the grand vizier had built his airship fleet around. The Sect of Razat might wish to hide the truth, but there are at least enough womb mages from other sects inside the citadel who are not party to the grand vizier's twisted conspiracy that he must post warnings for them not to enter his flesh library.' Omar knelt before the young caliph. 'I am your guardsman, your majesty, and you are still the ruler of rulers.'

'Well then,' sighed the caliph. 'It seems we still have our old roles to play.' He looked towards First Lieutenant Westwick. 'You have the teachings of both the Pasdaran and the Jackelian secret police. Have you no craft that might free us from this cell, sweet lady?'

Indicating the commodore, the deadly woman scowled. 'We used specialist State Protection Board machinery to break the locks to reach you, your majesty, but my colleague here is reputed to have some small talent in that field.'

'Don't ask me that, lass,' said the commodore. 'Has poor old Blacky not done enough, already? Stuffed into an airship like the filling of some cheap sausage, shot and hacked at, dragged across the sands and led to some cursed pit in the ground filled with wicked sorcerers. Now you want to test my poor, tired genius against the most secure cell in this whole terrible citadel?'

'You know your duty.'

'It's a mortal hard thing to be lectured about it by a Pasdaran double agent, lass. You only came down here to see why your handlers in the Pasdaran had vanished on you; why the side you were really working for had gone quiet.'

'Our missions are both here, however they started,' said Westwick, 'yours and mine.'

'Ah, well, blessed duty will have to wait until I have been fed, lass. I can't work when I'm starving. They'll have to feed us, won't they, Maya? Two strapping young lads being made ready to give birth to their terrible monsters?'

'We need to get out now, old man,' said Omar. It was like coaxing a child. Is this how the old nomad Alim felt about him back at the water farm? 'Before the grand vizier gets around to poisoning the Caliph Eternal's beyrogs.'

'My genius needs a little mortal feeding first,' insisted the commodore.

And so, discovered Omar, it did, the four of them having to wait until four portions of lumpy gruel had been pushed through a slot in the armoured door. Omar felt so sick he could hardly look at the food, although the Caliph Eternal seemed able to eat the oatmeal and keep it down, while the commodore greedily finished his portion, then spooned all the others' remaining rations into his mouth.

'Ah now,' the commodore noted, smacking his lips, 'if only they had served us with a little wine along with their lumpy muck.'

'Womb mages forgo such stimulants,' said the Caliph Eternal. 'It is part of the order's code. You would be lucky to find a single bottle in the whole of Mutantarjinn.'

'That may be so,' whined the commodore, 'but I have heard that the sultan of Fahamutla produces the finest wines in the world, the grapes tickled into maturity by the sea breezes on

their slopes. A legend only among the vintners of my acquaintance, for none is allowed to be exported outside that province.
No bottle has ever made it as far as the Kingdom.'

The caliph finally lost his patience. 'For the love of the one
true god, if you get us out of here, I shall give you a whole
vineyard's worth from the sultan's private cellar.'

'Well, my need is now,' complained the commodore,
collecting the four small spoons from the empty bowls. 'I will
have to imagine your wine's fine taste on my dry lips as I
toil.' He began to rub the heads of the spoons, working as if
to polish them.

Omar looked on, puzzled, as the cutlery began to bend.
'What manner of fakery is this, Jared Black?'

'This is my sorcery, lad. The sorcery of locks. Hard learnt
from all the prisons and cells I've been thrown in over the
years. The kind of sorcery you must master when you don't
have a little box of tricks pushed on you by some too-clever
gang of enginemen in the pay of the State Protection Board.'

Omar watched in astonishment as the commodore fashioned
a set of tools out of their eating implements, and then began
to use one of them to prise open a panel in the cell wall,
humming with pleasure at what he found. 'Will you look at
this, now. Such fiendish cleverness. Triple encryption on a set
of three transaction-engine drums combined with three sets
of physical locks too. You not only need old Blacky here, you
need him to have the arms of an octopus to take on this
challenge.'

'Can you get us out of here?' demanded Omar. *God, please,
make it so this old trickster is clever and not touched by the
sun.*

'The fellow that designed this was a cunning one, lad. The
kind of man who you'd frisk, lift five knives and a brace of
pistols off, and he'd just reach out for a copy of the *Middlesteel*

Illustrated News on your desk, roll it up, and kill you with that instead. Rare to find in the great game today. But is he sharper than old Blacky, that's the question? Which of us is the better man?'

They were about to find out, watching the old man cursing and wheedling as he sweated over the exposed mechanism inside at times demanding complete silence from the other three prisoners, at times begging them to join him in humming obscure Jackelian ale-house songs. The commodore seemed to be possessed of a manic energy as he worked, shouting at the delicate machinery as if it could be made to leap to his command through the sorcery of his will alone, wheedling the locks, promising them riches and then threatening them with his makeshift tools.

There were times when Omar wondered if the shock of seeing their cruel fate mapped out for them had driven the old u-boat man insane. How had the infidel's secret police ever trusted such a man with the fate of their nation? If half the things the cur of a grand vizier had said about him were true, his service could hardly be relied upon.

'The fate of the empire,' whispered the Caliph Eternal. 'And it hinges on a set of broken cutlery.'

'No, your majesty,' said the commodore, as the bolts rattled open along all four sides of the vault-like door. 'It hinges on the nimble fingers and quicker mind of the last great player of the great game.'

Captain Jericho stood in the centre of the bridge where everyone could see him and lifted the speaking trumpet from the central station that would transmit his words throughout the airship. 'When we joined the RAN we took an oath to parliament's name, but those of you who have studied the words in detail will know that we did not give it to parliament, they only took it as agents: our word was given to the people of the Kingdom of Jackals. To protect them – to guard our wives, our daughters and sons, our parents and our sisters and brothers. It's what those who took the oath before us in the fleet have been doing for over six hundred years. That oath is without limit. No distance can diminish it; no number of enemy vessels can undermine it. I know of no god strong enough to smite the love I feel for our people; I know of no foreign emperor deserving enough to make Jackelians chattel, and I know of no better crew I would serve alongside here, today. There is a reason why the figurehead on our vessel clutches two bolts of lightning in her talons: those who would make slaves of Jackelians must first face the storm. What will they face?'

'Jack Cloudie!' roared the sailors on the bridge; echoes of the crew's roar carrying from every part of the airship.

'What will they face?' Jericho asked again.

'Jack Cloudie!'

'Give them the storm, gentlemen,' said Jericho. 'To your stations and to your duty.'

The captain turned to Jack and indicated the old cardsharp's station on the bridge. 'See those covers off, Mister Keats – reset the vessel to full automation and if you are wrong, may our next life along the Circle's turn prove kinder to us both.'

A sailor passed his cutlass to Jack and he sliced away the cords fixing the canvas to the metal board, every eye on the bridge hot upon the back of his neck as it slid away to reveal a long panel studded with dials and switches, a punch-card injector dead centre. Jack extended a small round seat on a metal arm from below the panel and pushed up the switches that would ease the ship out of her long sleep, the thinking machines in the transaction-engine chamber beginning to take control of wide swathes of the *Iron Partridge*'s systems.

'Sir,' called a sailor with his eye to a telescope at the front of the control car. 'Enemy vessels closing on us fast. They're breaking into two squadrons. Half their fleet appear to be staying at our altitude, the other half of their disposition are climbing.'

'Should we climb too, sir?' the man on the elevator wheel asked nervously.

'A partridge must stay close to the ground,' barked Jericho. 'And an iron one has a particular reason to stay low, d'you see. Close with them and hold our altitude steady. Make to cut their lower squadron straight down the centre.'

Pulling a speaking trumpet on a chord out of the panel, Jack managed to get in contact with Coss up in the transaction-engine room. 'The captain is with us; I'm pushing all systems to automatic. What's the situation up there?'

'We're feeding the boilers with everything we've got,' the steamman's voice came back faintly over the whine of noise at the other end. 'You're going to need to keep your cardsharping to your desk on the bridge, I don't have time to help you. The calculation drums are turning so fast inside the chamber, they're smoking oil faster than I can lube the machinery. We're burning the drums out up here.'

Overheating with less than half the ship's systems activated? What had Jack been thinking of, believing that he could run the vessel as her mad, dead designer had intended? *Setting our iron genie free of her bonds.*

'We're about to receive the lower squadron's broadside,' announced Lieutenant McGillivray behind Jack. 'And the second squadron will open their bomb bays above us, if we last long enough for them to overfly us.'

'We'll survive that long, Mister McGillivray,' said Jericho. 'Their broadside will be incendiary shells, designed for a normal airship. Even carper will burn if it's made hot enough

343

– but we're going to find out what this knightly mailshirt we're wearing is good for, eh. Bosun, what's our windage?'

'Southerly, sir,' called the bosun. 'We're tacking against it, they're riding it down onto us.'

'That fleet's admiral knows his trade, then,' said Jericho. 'Wind right behind them. In about a minute, the lower squadron's propellers are going to throw their rotors into full reverse and brake their formation, just as they release those aerial mines of theirs. The other squadron will rise above their mines and let the wind carry their full ordnance onto us – I believe they're counting on opening their bomb bays above a floating wreck. Mister Keats, how are you doing there?'

'Still restarting the ship's automation, captain,' called Jack.

'Helm, when they release their mines, throw our engine cars into reverse, make it look as if we're trying to avoid the mine field at first, but then I want you to plot a course directly through their ordnance.'

'Sir?' queried the ship's master pilot.

'Their mines are attracted to RAN canvas, man, not metal plate, d'you see? The lower squadron will pull back to avoid the killing zone. Their mines are going to become a buffer zone that will shield us from being raked at close quarters.'

'And the 'stats that are climbing to overfly us?'

'So much the better, we need to be exactly where they seem to want us, master pilot,' boomed Jericho. 'Put us right under the shadow of their bomb bays.'

'Squadron on our altitude is braking, sir,' barked the watch. 'Just as you said. Multiple launches from their bomb bays. Seventy, eighty, no, upwards of a hundred aerial mines in the air and running.'

Jack glanced up, the dark chutes of a host of mines blowing towards them, a swarm of charges spinning underneath shadows of billowing fabric. Jack had to fight to keep his eyes on the console in front of him rather than watching the moon-silhouetted cloud of death sweeping through the night towards the *Iron Partridge.*

The airship wasn't responding fast enough, Jack realized. The entire voyage he had spent trying to keep this beast of a craft slumbering and now he was trying to rouse her. His hands slippery with sweat, he cleared the dust off the dial indicating the transaction-engine chamber's processing cycles, its dial hand twitching in the blue zone. They were still running too cold.

Have I murdered everyone on the ship? Seconds away from hitting the enemy and the *Iron Partridge* was stuck in a fatal no-man's land somewhere between full automation and complete manual flight.

Jack picked up the speaking tube to the transaction-engine chamber. 'I can't lift all the seals on the automation, Coss. They're fighting my overrides. I'm not going to have enough time to do this . . .'

'You're acting as though your job is still to keep the ship locked down,' the steamman's voice sounded back. 'Kiss my condensers, but you have all the help you need, Jack softbody. You have the airship herself!'

The airship. Yes, Jack had the airship. His hands danced over the punch-card writer, composing a last desperate sequence of commands that was intended to let the *Iron Partridge* perform surgery on herself, allow the iron genie to crack her own bottle.

There was a second where Jack had fed the punch card into the injection mechanism before the hiss of the card being sucked out of his fingers merged with the decompression of the bridge as a mine detonated volcanically against their hull. Something happened, written in fire and debris and confusion. His consciousness blacked out for a second. The detonation sent him sprawling into his equipment and down, hard, to the deck.

Jack's head throbbed in agony as he pulled himself to his feet. The impact of the blast had turned the *Iron Partridge* into the wind, and smoke was billowing past the control car's cracked canopy, the chutes of the enemy's aerial mines visible through knives of broken glass, mines floating all around them like night-borne seeds blown off a meadow.

Jericho lay sprawled across the deck, part of the canopy embedded in his chest. The captain was just conscious enough to recognize Jack stumbling over to kneel down by his side.

'Is the helm – able to answer our control, Mister Keats?'

Jack repeated the skipper's faint query towards a group of sailors pulling the two dead pilots off their stations, then nodded in confirmation at the captain as the crew wrestled the *Iron Partridge* back onto her course.

Captain Jericho tried to turn his head as a clacking sound passed through the vessel, low at first like crickets chirruping in grassland, then louder and louder. Piston arms extending, pneumatic systems connecting, plates opening, steam-tensioned clockwork powering up, spars locking into place. A thousand hungry, chattering systems drawing mechanical breath for the first time, manual overrides themselves being overridden. A minute before, the *Iron Partridge* had been a dead thing, imperfectly flown by a full-sized crew of hundreds of sailors. *Now we've been demoted to mere components within the machine.*

'I believe you were – successful – Mister Keats,' coughed Jericho, blood spilling from his mouth across his high collar. He gestured for Lieutenant McGillivray to come over. 'Under – full – automation the master cardsharp has – equal rank to the first lieutenant. Given – First Lieutenant Westwick is not on board – you now have seniority on the bridge, Mister Keats.'

'Sir!' McGillivray protested.

'It's the – admiralty ordinances – Mister McGillivray,' Jericho smiled weakly. 'You – know – how highly – I respect the navy's confounded ordinances.'

'Of all your commands, captain, this is the bloody daftest,' said McGillivray. 'With respect, sir, of course.'

'When did – I ever – receive – that from any upland – officer?' asked Jericho. 'The – ship – is yours – Mister Keats. I would ask you – one favour.'

Jack had to stop himself from choking on his reply. 'Sir?'

'Not the navy's – graveyard for – me. I still maintain a family – plot. My wife and son are buried there. Plant – m'bones – down there next – to theirs.'

'I shall, sir.'

Jericho's final sigh joined the whistling of the wind through the bridge's broken canopy, merging and melding with it, until only the wind was left. Trying not to shake, from the cold and the shock of his captain's death, Jack got to his feet, every eye on the bridge gazing uncertainly at him.

Lieutenant McGillivray removed Jericho's jacket and slowly covered his corpse, making a makeshift blanket of the uniform. 'Difficult boots to fill, these. What are you orders, master cardsharp?'

'Is that it?' interrupted the bosun, pointing a finger at Jack. 'The skipper's gone and we're meant to salute the boy just because he knows how to cut a punch card for that white elephant on the upper deck?'

'Shut your trap, now, bosun,' barked Lieutenant McGillivray, 'and belay that bilge. I won't tolerate bellyaching on the bridge.'

'I'm just saying what's on everybody else's mind,' spat the bosun. 'He's a bloody pressed hand, one step ahead of the gallows. Our cabin boy's been in the service longer than this one – some twistery of the regulations, and the ordinances reckon he should be put in charge? Then damn the ordinances, I say!'

There were murmurs of agreement from around the bridge. *Just saying what was on everybody else's mind.* Jack's included. *What would Captain Jericho have done, what would the skipper have said, to reassert control here?*

The bosun looked as if he was about to launch into another tirade, but suddenly he was sent flying, collapsing against the altimeter station as a smoke-blackened figure weighed into him with ham-sized fists, beating him into unconsciousness. It was Pasco!

'Off him, man,' shouted Lieutenant McGillivray running over to pull the hulking engineer off the bosun. 'You're doing murder to him.'

Pasco angrily shoved the lieutenant back, his face as red as one of their airship's blazing engine cars. 'Aren't we all dead anyway? How many enemy airships are out there . . . one hundred, two? The only question is, are we dead as navy, as cloudies, or are we dead as stinking mutineers?' He pointed across to Jericho's body. 'The old man says that the master cardsharp is the ship's ranker when she's running on full automation, that's good enough for me.'

Jack looked back to the entrance to the bridge. Three of Pasco's men were standing there, two of them carrying the badly burnt body of a young rating. *He'll follow me, but I had better be damn sure where I want to lead him.*

'The engine room, Mister Pasco,' said Jack. 'What is our butcher's bill?'

'Thirty-two dead,' said Pasco. 'We've lost the port-forward engine car to their mines, blown clear off. Now, tell me that doesn't matter and that you have a bloody plan, sir?'

'Every life matters,' said Jack, looking at Jericho's arm

protruding from under the captain's jacket. 'We stand for them, we stand for them all. As for the *Iron Partridge*'s plan of engagement, we're exactly where we want to be.' Jack raised his voice so everyone on the bridge could hear, and even managed to keep it from trembling. 'We do what Jericho would have done. We press the attack, regardless.'

'Well, at least you've got the old man's daftness down pat, laddie,' muttered Lieutenant McGillivray, but softly enough so that only Jack heard it. *Yes, let's hope I've guessed right about his intentions.*

Somewhere in the distance Jack could sense the tide of triumph from the steamman's spirit of the sky, Lemba of the Empty Thrusters, as the Loa observed the changes happening across the airship. *I'm doing this for us, not for you. For the crew, for the memory of Jericho, for the Kingdom.* He hadn't even noticed he was no longer doing it for himself.

From the outside of the hull there was a fluttering wave of iron plates rising on tiny metal arms, the bridge shifting as the airship rolled slightly, the flight surface of the *Iron Partridge* becoming a dynamic thing, as manoeuvrable as the feathers on a hawk. Sprays of ballast water and vented gas exhaled from ducts below the plates, the airship's lungs breathing her first real breath. In the gun deck, sighting mechanisms pushed out from under the cannons' barrels, tiny windage rotors outside their rubber hoods dropping down to gauge the air currents. The occupants of the h-dome and crow's-nest dome scrambled out of the way as clusters of telescope arrays fell out of the ceiling and rose out of the floor, filling the space the sailors had been occupying only seconds before. The crew inside dropped their telescopes in consternation while something deep inside the turning calculation drums of the ship's transaction engines marked and noted the constellations outside against her charts, and then the vessel drew a small crosshair across every moving, turning lamp on every Cassarabian airship in the night sky.

On the bridge, the strangeness of the moment following Jericho's death was replaced with a wave of confusion as the boards and stations reconfigured themselves, sailors scrambling back as a new chair surrounded by an arc of dials and switches rose on a dais in the centre of the bridge. It was as if some throne from legend had appeared in their midst, beckoning the chosen one to anoint himself as war leader on its steps.

Jack took the seat – settling down into its hard, iron curves – how fitting that its support was never intended to be comfortable. On the controls in front of him there was a detachable speaking tube next to a rotating drum bearing copperscripted names – Bomb Bay, Observation Car, Sick Bay, Wardroom, Lower Lifting Chamber – and Jack rotated it around until it read Transaction-Engine Chamber, picking up the pipe to speak. 'Mister Shaftcrank, how stands our transaction engines?'

The steamman's voice warbled out of a voicebox set in the side of the chair. 'Jack, is that you? Thank the Loas. All our calculation drums are turning smoothly. Processing capacity is at seventy per cent on full automation ship-wide. We have one outstanding query process in queue.'

'Which system, Mister Shaftcrank?'

'The ship,' said the steamman. 'The whole ship. Query reads, "My orders?"'

'Your input, Mister Shaftcrank. Card in, *engage the enemy*. All the ship's spare processes to be dedicated to gunnery and navigation.'

'Engaging, aye.'

'Helm is becoming sluggish, sir,' reported the master pilot. 'It's as if our rudder is no longer responding.'

Jack settled into the chair. 'Do you ride, pilot?'

'Sir?'

'Horses, sir? To hounds? Originally I was a farming man, by trade. The knack of guiding a horse is to point her in the right direction, apply a touch of pressure on the reins, and then just let your beast do all your work for you. Don't fight the reins, master pilot. Just point her and let her lead you. That goes for everyone here. If your station is doing your work for you, allow your board its head.'

There were disconcerted murmurs from the crew, levers sliding around their stations and control dials flicking to peculiar positions. *It's as if the ghosts of the navy's legions of dead have returned to possess their vessel.* But this was the way that the airship had always been intended to fly. Jack knew transaction engines; he knew them as well as he knew anything. He had to be right about this, didn't he? The cleverest man in the Kingdom was said to have designed this bizarre oddity of a vessel. *And I'm gambling that the unfinished work he left behind as his legacy might just keep us alive.*

Then the enemy fleet was overflying the *Iron Partridge*, bomb bays opening to finish off the Jackelian airship for good.

Only minutes old, Jack Keats's new command was as good as murdered in the air. His very first command. His very last?

CHAPTER SIXTEEN

'Heaven's teeth, can't you do this any quicker?' asked the marine officer from the Imperial Aerial Squadron, his hand sweating on the pommel of his holstered pistol.

'Quicker, perhaps, with your silence,' snapped the bombardier squatting by the ventilation shaft to the barracks. He opened the last of the line of fin-bombs connected together by a knot of rubber pipes. 'Gas bombs are meant to be triggered by impact with the ground. They were never designed to have their mixing chambers detonated on a slow release.'

The marine officer glanced nervously across the tower concourse towards the large sealed doors of the barracks, and, seeing their anxiety, the womb mage from the Sect of Razat supervising the cull attempted to reassure the two airship sailors. 'You have all the time you need. The beyrogs have been ordered to stay inside their barracks.'

'That would be the same disloyal regiment of beyrogs with a serious fault in their breeding pattern?'

'They will stay confined inside, and the womb mage responsible has already been punished,' said the sorcerer. 'The Sect of Razat doesn't accept such errors in our followers' work.'

Kneeling by the shells, the sailor continued to work. 'Nearly there. I just have to disable the safeties on the gravity switch.'

'Last thing we need,' said the marine officer. 'God-cursed rogue drak riders outside dropping grenades on our heads, and now we could have one of our own regiments of beyrogs rampaging through the citadel. I sometime wonder who our enemy is.'

'That would be me,' said a female voice. As the marine officer turned, he was smashed back into the row of gas shells, his nose bone fatally struck back into his brain by the flat of First Lieutenant Westwick's hand.

Omar kicked the bombardier in the face, hard enough to spin him back unconscious just as Westwick grabbed the fleeing womb mage and broke his – or in reality, more likely, *her* – neck.

Commodore Black peered over the unconscious sailor's work and quickly slid some of the disassembled components on the floor back into the exposed shell's works before ripping out the rubber pipes connecting it to the ventilation shaft. The commodore lifted the pistol and holster from the marine, checking the body's leather ammunition pouch for the number of charges inside. Omar took the other sailor's gun and passed the cutlass-style sword to Westwick.

'Enough wicked dirt gas here to choke half of the sewer rats back in Middlesteel,' said the commodore.

'Larger prey than rats, my strange Jackelian angel,' said the Caliph Eternal. 'Let us see how disloyal my defective regiment of beyrogs truly is . . .'

Whatever genetic sorcery the caliphs had relied on across the ages to control their beyrogs, the potency of that power could not be denied. As soon as the young ruler entered the barracks complex, the monstrously large ranks of biologick soldiers came flooding towards him as though they were a pack of hunting hounds at feeding time and he the kennel keeper. Exhibiting much the same strange fascination as the caliph's murdered flesh brother had shown – not quite daring to touch his person, as if he were surrounded by an invisible wall – the beyrogs demonstrated their devotion by falling to one knee, excitedly shaking their scimitars and crossbows in recognition of the ruler of rulers. The power to command them quite literally running through the Caliph Eternal's blood.

'They're a grand old size,' noted the commodore, trying not to be jostled out of the way as the eager beyrogs crowded around to confirm their fealty in front of their master. 'They put me in mind of a bludger of my acquaintance who used to guard the door on a Spumehead harbour drinking house. Small Eli was his name, a brawler who could chew iron nails and spit them through a u-boat's hull when he was in a mood.'

'The beyrogs will follow the Caliph Eternal,' said Westwick. 'And that is enough.'

'Let us hope so, sweet lady,' said the caliph. 'I fear they are all we can count on inside the citadel.' He raised his arms in the air and the beyrogs ceased their excited shoving. 'Hear me, my guardians. I have uncovered treachery and treason of the vilest sort here within the citadel. The grand vizier is plotting to murder me and claim the empire's throne for himself.'

There was a wave of unease and agitated growls through the towering ranks and Omar realized that while the beyrogs could understand the Caliph Eternal's words well enough, they had no voices of their own to articulate their outrage at the reports of the chief minister's sedition.

'They cannot speak,' said Omar.

'The pattern of their minds is too far removed from the race of man's for them to attempt speech, guardsman,' whispered the Caliph Eternal. 'But they can reply well enough in war sign using the fingers of their hands.' The caliph raised his voice. 'Where are my captains?'

A grizzled pair of beyrogs emerged from the ranks, one sporting an eye-patch, the other with ugly scars running down his face.

Reaching out, the caliph grasped their arms in greeting. 'Still alive, then? Good. I must ask you to serve one last time, and not against any common guild assassins or palace conspirators. Apart from my three friends here, you should trust no one.'

One of the old beyrog officers twisted his fingers around in a dance that seemed too intricate for his oversized hands as he growled softly. Omar's war sign was not advanced, but he caught the gist of what the beast had said.

We trust our blades to your service. Only our steel should be trusted.

Nodding in sombre agreement, the caliph faced Westwick. 'You remember the way to the producers' chambers where the skoils are being bred, sweet lady?'

'I can retrace the journey,' said Westwick.

'There are two routes through the citadel to reach the chambers we saw,' explained the caliph. 'Once we leave the barracks with the beyrogs, the grand vizier will realize that we are moving to expose him and the Sect of Razat's deceit. He will come at us with every one of his new guardsmen beasts and all the soldiers and marines whose loyalty he thinks he has purchased.'

'You have a scheme, then, your majesty,' said the commodore. 'I can see it by the twinkle in your noble eyes – just as I can sense in my waters that it means a right bad end for brave old Blacky.'

'You and the First Lieutenant shall take a quarter of the

beyrogs and strike out first, retracing your route from the cells. Myself and my most loyal guardsman here will follow the alternative route with the main force and secure the evidence of the grand vizier's corruption from the citadel below.'

'I knew it,' said the commodore. 'Leading a diversion again. Made into a mortal sacrificial goat tethered to a stake in the hope of drawing out some sand lions to gnaw on my bones.'

'Anyone who can break out of the most secure cell in Mutantarjinn is not fated to die here,' said Omar. 'Old man, the hundred faces of the one true god are surely smiling down upon you.'

'If they are, lad, then they're laughing at my blessed misfortunes. Glad to squeeze some more amusement out of my unlucky stumbles through the world.'

'We will lead the diversionary force,' assured Westwick, without a trace of doubt or emotion in her voice. 'Success here is all that matters.'

'Not all that matters,' said the caliph, thoughtfully. 'But all that matters today, perhaps.' He turned to the beyrog officer sporting an eye-patch. 'A quarter of your brothers to follow these two, captain, and keep them as safe as the fates allow. Fight your way towards the chamber of producers on the citadel's lowest level; keep them busy long enough for us to secure proof of the grand vizier's vile sorceries.'

The officer pounded a fist against his gold breastplate in salute and the two Jackelians made to leave, a company of beyrogs falling into line behind them, drawing their helmets, weapons and supplies from racks on the side of the barracks, armour and weapons rattling as the creatures shook the floor with their massive boots.

Omar watched the two foreigners leave. *There goes a brave man.* 'He complains like a slave, but he fights like a guardsman.'

'No higher praise,' said the Caliph Eternal, with what might have been a touch of irony in his voice. 'I may be the most recent of the ruler of rulers, but there's one constant in my chain of inherited memories. They all serve, those who do not oppose. Come, guardsman, let us ensure that our Jackelian friends' sacrifice is not made in vain.'

'Are you sure you are not related to Little Eli?' the commodore asked the massive beyrog officer leading the company of flesh-twisted soldiers. 'You've much of the same taciturn nature and a cold eye towards an old u-boat man down on his luck.'

Westwick translated the flicker of oversized fingers as the officer replied in sign language. 'He says you talk too much.'

'But I'm the only one doing the talking here, lass,' said the commodore, indicating their surroundings. 'If you discount the shouts of those unlucky womb mages that tried to stop us entering this dark place.'

The two Jackelians and the beyrog company were traversing an ossuary – a gloomy hall filled with the dusty bones of hundreds of generations of the womb mages' creations, strung together with thin copper wire and marking the incremental evolution of the order's most successful accomplishments. Draks that had started out as barrel-ribbed, short-necked things with almost wholly human skulls, before being bred towards their present, elongated arrow-like forms. Beyrogs that had begun as hump-backed giants, some with four arms, before growing slightly smaller and less crudely formed over the centuries. Less primitive. More deadly. It was a terrible, eerie thing to see the skeletons' living descendants filing silently past the exhibits, fully flesh-laden and wielding mammoth weapons designed to strike fear in the hearts of any who saw them.

All the womb mage novices inside the hall had fled

screaming when the first of their number fell backwards into one of the skeletons, his chest broken by a beyrog crossbow bolt.

Only our steel should be trusted.

Commodore Black just counted his blessings that the beyrogs' orders were explicit about trying to keep him and Maya alive. Along the sloping wall of the hall, long, thin windows looked out onto Mutantarjinn, and the commodore caught the distant thump of a grenade and a brief glint of light blossoming from the explosion.

'The guardsmen are still out there, Maya. Harassing the city. Ah, what I'd give for one of those ugly flying man-lizards to land on the roof outside and whisk us to safety right now.'

'The drak riders will fight to the end,' said Westwick.

'What about you, lass? Does that stand for you too?'

'There's only one way you're getting out of here,' said Westwick, in answer.

'Now, I did rather figure that,' said the commodore, his eyes narrowing slyly.

Looking up as snarls sounded from the beyrogs surrounding them, Commodore Black spotted a group of the grand vizier's claw-guards fanning out across the end of the hall, Imperial Aerial Squadron marines too, the men trading shouted instructions between each other as they sprinted to take up position.

'Well then,' said the old u-boat man as he drew his heavy Cassarabian pistol. 'Can there be a more suitable place than this to leave my weary old bones?'

When the Caliph Eternal had talked of an alternative route to reach the grand vizier's twisted creations in the chambers below, Omar hadn't realized it would entail a gusty detour down the outside of the Citadel of Flowers' central tower.

While the maintenance stairwell corkscrewing around the tower was wide enough to accommodate their beyrog battalion marching three abreast, the stairs were completely unprotected by railings or a balustrade. It took every iota of Omar's drak training to keep his sense of vertigo under control while descending. To keep himself from ducking as lightning forked over the giant spinning blades scraping their wind-driven passage around the chasm's tallest tower. *This will not be my death, falling off a tower before I have a chance to remove the grand vizier's head from his sorcery-twisted body. It is too ridiculous to contemplate.*

At times it was hard for Omar to differentiate between the steady crack of the thunder and the relentless rumble of the beyrogs descending behind him. They were marching under the weight of yellow cuirass-style breastplates with gilded copper rivets, golden helmets mounted with red plume-like brushes on top, and a full canvas backpack loaded with canteens, rations, crossbow bolt quivers and scimitar sharpening stones. As much as their finery was designed to reflect their master's wealth and power, putting beyrogs inside the showy dress uniforms was like trying to disguise the feral nature of a sand lion with a gem-studded collar. It only served to underline that these vast creatures really required nothing more than a length of sharp, shining steel with which to hammer their enemies.

The Caliph Eternal hadn't ordered the beyrogs to change into their full field uniforms and he seemed almost blithely unaware of their presence as he walked down the lightning wreathed spire. Perhaps, Omar mused, it was as the caliph had confided during their captivity in the cells: his mind was full of past lives, all of the empire's petty jealousies and ambitions repeating before him like a shadow play. But whether it was by accident of nature, blood, or the final changes the previous caliph had worked upon his replacement's young body, Akil Jaber Issman had turned out nothing like the nervous, needy puppet whose life the grand vizier had preserved to install on the throne. *I suppose that the empire should at least be grateful for that.*

For Omar, there was nothing else left to him now but to follow this deposed ruler according to his guardsman's oath, and take one final chance to smash the schemes of the wicked Immed Zahharl. Everyone else had gone to their inescapable end – his father, Farris Uddin, Boulous, the drak riders he had trained and fought alongside, even the two Jackelian spies and their sailors on their outlandish ironclad airship. There was just Omar left with the Caliph Eternal and he had never felt so tired or alone.

By his side, the caliph slipped on one of the stairway's wet treads and Omar reached out to steady the ruler by his arm. 'Are you alright, your majesty?' Omar instinctively touched his own gut, noting the strange feeling of emptiness there. The changes being worked by the grand vizier's sorcery had quietened for the last hour, but how much longer before he swelled up like a whale and could only survive inside the choking nutrient mist of a producer's tank? *Oh Shadisa, why did you do this to me? Did you hate me so much back in Haffa?*

'It is not the grand vizier's foul virus that is making me sick,' said the caliph, as if reading Omar's mind – or at least his body language. 'I am starving. Apart from that gruel in the cells, I haven't had a meal for months that wasn't fed to me through a tube stuck into my veins. Heaven's silver gates, what I wouldn't give for a roasted side of gravy-soaked lamb from the palace kitchens.'

Their scar-faced beyrog officer commented with a flicker of his fingers.

The Caliph Eternal shook his head. 'No, I don't need my

sedan chair. This is not the Jahan, and I have been isolated enough from the empire, from the world. If it had been otherwise, the grand vizier would not so easily have been able to exchange my flesh brother and I as if we were both dolls from the same toy chest.'

'The distance of command,' said Omar. 'That is what Master Uddin called it.'

'It was an early lesson from my tutors, too. Detachment from those you must ask to die for you. I always used to wonder whose benefit that was for. My soldiers, or mine? When you detach yourself too much from life, the world and reality, I believe you start walking the path towards insanity.' The ruler threw his hands towards the storm, as if he could command the very heavens around the Forbidden City. 'I like the rain on my bare face. Have you got anything to say about it, all you caliphs who have passed before me? No whispers of advice for me? No pearls of wisdom to cast down before my sopping-wet toes?'

Protecting him from the wild discharges of energy in the sky, the beyrog formation gently eased the Caliph Eternal away from the open edge of the twisting staircase. 'My voices seem quiet today,' said the caliph. 'Perhaps they have been embarrassed to silence by failing to spot the perverted nature of Immed Zahharl's plot against me before it was too late. It was you and my two Jackelian angels that came to save me, guardsman, not the wisdom of the ages. When the time comes, I vow that I will see to it you do not suffer the producer's fate the grand vizier has set for you.'

'They all serve, those who do not oppose,' said Omar.

The caliph shook his head. 'Your faithfulness is much more than that, guardsman. Unlike that of my beyrogs, it is not instinctive. All that you have achieved, you have achieved for yourself.'

'The famous Barir luck,' whispered Omar. *To have lost everything. To be left nothing by fate except revenge.*

He was about to find out how far it could be stretched before it snapped. As they rounded the bend on the tower's stairs, Omar discovered himself facing rank after rank of the grand vizier's claw-guards on the steps below, their talons already outstretched and glinting in the evil electric light of the chasm. And in the middle of the first line was Salwa, resplendent in the full regalia of the grand marshal of the imperial guardsmen; the faint, hidden pulse of Shadisa concealed somewhere far deep within the rain-slicked uniform.

No, this is what I have been left.

Howling like a banshee, the claw-guard crashed back through the skeleton of a sandpede, hundreds of leg bones sent scattering through the air and spinning across the polished floor of the ossuary. Lowering his pistol's smoking barrel, the commodore broke the gun and cleared its spent charge, feeding in a fresh shell while Westwick emptied her own pistol into one of the charging monsters. The noise of her shot was lost against the splintering volley of the grand vizier's forces and the air-splitting thud of the beyrogs' crossbows replying in kind.

'There's too many of the wicked things, Maya,' coughed the commodore, snapping his pistol shut and pulling back its clockwork firing mechanism.

They were coming like a black flood through the exhibits, a vast, relentless tide of fury breaking against the beyrogs' cuirasses and swords. While the claw-guards loped forward en masse, snaking past the displays of the ossuary, the Imperial Aerial Squadron marines had taken snipers' positions at the rear of the hall, maintaining a constant rain of fire in their direction. Balls whizzed through the air, buzzing with the evil song of angry hornets.

'That is rather the point,' said Westwick. 'A diversion must divert.' She rubbed tiredly at her eyelids, just underneath where her forehead had been splashed by a claw-guard's blood. 'Damn my itching eyes; is the blood of these creatures poisoned?'

'No, lass. It's only sleep you need. Sleep and a good hearty meal with a fine bottle or two of wine to wash it down.' Commodore Black glanced around. The beyrogs had formed a semicircle-shaped double line halfway down the hall, the front row beating back the wave attacks of their more diminutive cousins with their blades. Behind them stood a second rank of crossbow-wielding beyrogs, pouring independent fire into the charges coming at them and exchanging bolts for bullets with the marine snipers at the rear.

It was proving a mortal effective defensive formation, but there wasn't enough cover in the hall as exhibits were smashed into clouds of bony shards, while the grand vizier seemed to have an entire citadel full of these new claw-guard regiments to throw against them. A diversion must divert.

Another wave of the stone-faced claw-guards came leaping and howling like wolves against the front line of beyrogs, the imperial bodyguard unit's scimitars swinging and cutting in response, claw-guards screaming as they died, beyrogs stumbling back where the beasts broke through the tight line and swarmed over the giant defenders.

This was no battle for men, no battle for old Blacky. Not with both armies supplied by the empire's dark womb mages. Attacking and defending without any sign of fear or care for their own skins. They were living machines driven only by raw animal instincts and the cruel whims of their masters. This wasn't a battlefield, it was a vast gladiatorial pit, starving lions and wolves thrown against each other for someone else's advancement.

A ball buzzed past the commodore's ear. Tracing the shot back to the short-stocked airship carbine pulled tight against a marine's shoulder, the commodore sighted his pistol and was rewarded with the sight of the man slamming back through a discharge of gun smoke as his pistol bucked once.

Still the relentless claw-guards crashed against the beyrogs' lines, the defenders' crossbow-fire finally faltering and slowing. Commodore Black noted the empty quiver swinging from the nearest beyrog's back. They were running out of ammunition.

'Fall back,' shouted the commodore. 'Move back out of the hall.'

'Those are not their orders,' said Westwick, translating for the massive one-eyed officer.

'Their orders were to keep them busy, not to die here like blessed fools,' said the commodore. 'The passages behind us are narrow. You can funnel their assault down tight and hold them with your front rank's bulk. You want to sell your mortal lives, then sell them dearer than this.'

'There!' shouted Westwick, interrupting the argument. She'd thrown a hand towards a figure at the far end of the hall. It was Immed Zahharl, the grand vizier waving a sword and urging the claw-guards forward to overwhelm the beyrogs.

'I can say goodbye to my blessed chance to act as broker for the next king of Jackals,' said the commodore.

'I'm out of charges,' said Westwick.

The commodore picked out the very last crystal shell from his cartridge pack and kissed it before tossing to the first lieutenant.

Westwick broke her pistol, pushed the charge into its breach and cocked her gun, sighting it along her forearm. She squeezed the trigger and a marine running past the grand vizier collapsed and went sprawling as the ball took him in the skull.

'Luck of the bloody devil,' she cursed.

The grand vizier looked across the marine's corpse and spotted the two Jackelians behind the beyrog ranks, then yelled in red-faced rage, shoving his monsters forward with the flat of his blade.

'And you've lost your chance to join the Sect of Razat,' said the commodore.

'For the Caliph Eternal,' yelled Westwick. 'For the honour of the Caliph Eternal, fall back and hold them in the citadel's passages.'

With the logic of the move undisputed by the officer this time, two of the beyrogs sounded the retreat using circular trumpets coiled around their cuirasses. Giving ground, the caliph's monstrous bodyguard marched back in lockstep even as the grand vizier's claw-guards intensified their assault. Wave after wave of the beasts harried the retreating line, leaving corpses spilled from both sides, many fastened around each other in death. With no more bolts left to fire, most of the beyrogs had thrown aside their crossbows and drawn their scimitars, the hall echoing to the clash of claws against tempered steel, the snarls and growls of an animal pit fight filling the chamber.

His empty pistol discarded, the commodore held his position in the retreating line alongside Westwick, his sword hacking and thrusting as the number of claw-guards pushing them back swelled, both Jackelians made mere components in the living war machines savaging each other. Every metre they lost littered with dead. Every minute they gained for the main attack purchased with their blood and bodies; every second closer to their ranks being thinned to a complete rout.

No place for a man – no place for Jared Black's unlucky bones.

*   *   *

'Go back, Omar,' called Salwa from the line of claw-guards blocking his passage down the tower steps. 'You do not have to die here tonight for the sake of someone else's palace intrigue.'

'It is not a palace intrigue I die for,' said Omar. 'It is the Caliph Eternal and my guardsman's oath. I already gave you my answer back on the walls of the palace fortress.'

'You thought you were giving your answer to Salwa,' called the new grand marshal of the guardsmen. 'Not to Shadisa.'

'No! I was right. Salwa did kill Shadisa, for I see nothing of her in *you*,' shouted Omar.

'Then you have been blinded by your stupid male pride,' retorted Salwa, 'for we are exactly the same. You never knew me at all, did you? Only the idea of a golden-haired girl you filled with all your hopes back in Haffa.'

And how I wish to the hundred faces of god that idea was still alive, somewhere.

'Order your soldiers aside,' demanded the caliph, stepping forward. 'You have fallen under the glamour of the grand vizier, I can see that. Stand down your force here and I will see that you are pardoned for your treason. There are womb mages inside the city who can undo the evil changes that have been worked upon you.'

'The changes that really count, little enculi,' spat Salwa, 'aren't the ones your sorcerers can undo at your whim. You and your ossified regime have held back progress for so long that you have forgotten how to bend with the winds of change. And if you can't bend, you must be made to snap.'

Omar rested his hand on the pommel of his sheathed sword. 'I only hear the propaganda of the Sect of Razat. None of your own words.'

Salwa slipped the scimitar out of his belt and raised it ready to commence the attack as the leather-uniformed ranks of his claw-guards jostled each other, preparing to spring up the stairs and begin the slaughter. 'Then you may hear mine now.'

There was a splintering sound behind Omar as the snarling beyrogs' massive crossbows were cranked back and projectiles pushed into position, ready to release the first of their heavy three-fletched bolts.

The caliph spoke softly to Omar. 'Let the beyrogs go in first. I heard your voice when you spoke of this Shadisa back in our cell; I would not order you to do this, guardsman.'

'You do not have to, your majesty,' said Omar, drawing his scimitar. 'This is my fate and this is my choice.'

The caliph smiled sadly. 'So be it, then. They are coming up the stairs while we are going down, with only enough space for one of us to pass. That's a story as old as time. Let us settle it now . . .'

There was a moment's silence, the claw-guards' quivering talons left shaking in the air, the wordless growling beyrogs holding their oversized scimitars out high as though they were totems to the storm shifting above them. Both sides' roars rose up almost simultaneously and the two ranks surged towards each other, Omar and Salwa's swords clashing in the centre of the mêlée as they ran to do murder. *It begins.*

Biologicks from both sides crashed into their enemies in multiple waves of animal frenzy, the claw-guards' charge fleet and furious, the beyrogs meeting them with the weight of moving mountains, beating aside sabre-fingered strikes with four-foot tall scimitars as bestial yells were hurled between the hacking, thrusting, howling forces. Dead soldiers spilled over the sides of the twisting staircase, living ones too, still locked in fierce combat. Lightning flashes illuminated the hellish scene while the heavens split and roared, two armies from a nightmare spiralling towards each other far above the black spires of the Forbidden City.

Lost in the sodden stench of the animal rage all around him, the world reduced down to his own private combat, Omar struggled against Salwa, his fingers locked around the wrist of his opponent's sword arm, as Salwa's were locked around his, the two of them desperately shifting and struggling for advantage.

'Is this,' Salwa panted through gritted teeth, 'what you want?'

'No,' said Omar, his arm burning as held back the blade inching towards his nose. 'But it is what we have.'

Salwa grinned through a snarl. 'Yes.' Their swords danced, and Omar turned one of Salwa's thrusts a little too clumsily, the point cutting his left cheek and drawing a bitingly painful thin rivulet of blood there.

'A duelling scar for you,' said Salwa. 'But there'll be none left among your old guardsmen friends to appreciate it.'

Try for my heart next time. You've already filleted it.

They both fell back as a beyrog collapsed into their space, three claw-guards slashing at the giant's yellow breastplate, taking out slices of metal armour with each swing. Free of Salwa's grasp, Omar warily circled the new commander of the guardsman, both their scimitars held high in the classic duellist's pose.

'I am stronger than you, Omar. Faster.'

'The grand vizier's sorcerers refashioned your muscles well,' spat Omar, not taking his eyes off the gently swaying blade. 'And your soul too. It used to be as clear as a lake. Now it is a dirty puddle.'

'The Sect of Razat freed me!'

'I felt your soul!' shouted Omar, turning aside Salwa's blade as it came out in an exploratory tap. 'You don't even know what they've done to you.'

Again Salwa's steel sprang out, far faster and more decisive this time. 'I could say the same about you, Omar. Spouting dull platitudes about the honour of the Caliph Eternal. Is this what the guardsmen have done to *you*? Made you care about a dying age? Made you pick the wrong side of history when all you used to care about was a life of ease and your belly?'

Omar feinted right and cut left, but Salwa was too quick, blocking his thrust. 'The guardsmen are right.'

'This makes right,' yelled Salwa, pushing forward with a quick sequence of thrusts so rapid that Omar had to give ground up the steps as he parried. 'Victory and nothing else. You've picked a bad time to learn to care about something at last, Omar Barir.'

Omar nearly stumbled back over one of the dead claw-guards. 'I used to care about you.'

'Another lost cause. What a pity you didn't join us when I offered you the chance. The future could have been ours.'

No future I want.

'I am going to gut your sect's future,' snarled Omar. 'And when I'm done with them, I'm going to hunt down Immed Zahharl and feed him my sword inch by inch for what he's done to you and everyone I ever cared about.'

'Through me first,' said Salwa, meeting Omar's blade with a chime of metal. 'I'm the future! These beautiful claw-guards are our new guardsmen. More loyal and reliable than you and your men ever were.'

Omar fell back again. Perhaps this twisted shadow of the woman he had loved was correct. *We're too alike, too evenly matched.* Salwa met every blow Omar gave out, turned every thrust, reversed every parry. Salwa was even wearing the same uniform as the claw-guards; monsters following their new grand marshal, in crude, bestial mockery of the brave men that Omar had served alongside. Omar's jacket was soaked with rain, sweat and the blood of the dying biologicks still impaling and battering each other around him. His muscles and tendons seemed made of living fire as he tried to summon up enough strength to beat his way through Salwa's guard. *Is this the fight you wanted, fate? Is this what you have spared me for? I must kill the sole piece of Shadisa that hasn't already been murdered by the grand vizier.*

A beyrog struggling with a pair of the claw-guards came smashing down the steps, and both Omar and Salwa leapt desperately over the slashing, rolling landslide of bodies, but Omar was a second too slow, his boot catching on a trailing crossbow strap. Unbalanced, he landed a single boot on the stair's blood-slicked surface and went falling down the treads. Omar saw Salwa following his tumbling passage like a mountain gazelle, leaping through the carnage of combat around the tower stairs. Omar landed hard by the edge, his momentum broken by the corpse of one of the claw-guards, the body nearly shifting over the stair's boundary with the sky and sending Omar plunging into the chasm's abyss. His scimitar had spun away in the fall and Omar desperately frisked the beast's corpse for a pistol, a knife, anything, but of course, its weapons were its claws.

Your sword is not the weapon. You are the weapon. The cadet master's words echoed in his mind. True for the grand vizier's bestial new army, at least.

The point of Salwa's sword turned him around, digging into his spine. 'I warned you. My body is faster than yours. Stronger.'

Omar looked up into eyes he did not know. 'Womb mages' tricks.'

'Call it progress,' said Salwa, raising the scimitar and striking down to bury it into Omar's chest.

Your sword is not the weapon. You are the weapon.

Omar seized the claw-guard corpse's cloak and whipped it

out, rolling and kicking as he wrapped it around Salwa's leg. The new commander of the guardsmen was sent sprawling forward, meeting Omar's sweeping leg and sent stumbling over the edge of the stairs with a surprised bellow. Omar looked down. Salwa was hanging just two feet below the ledge, body thrashing in the wind, one hand grasped around the rod of a rain-slicked lightning conductor.

Omar threw down the cloak, turning it into a makeshift line. 'Take it!'

Salwa's spare hand flailed up – trying to reach the cape, or perhaps the safety of the lightning conductor. 'What for?'

'For me.'

Salwa's hand flailed up again, catching the lightning conductor, desperately holding on against the fierce gusts with both hands. There was a flicker of a smile around Salwa's lips. 'What will you give me if I win?'

'A kiss.'

Salwa looked up, the rain cascading down the grand marshal's face. 'I've been a slave before, Omar, I didn't much like it.'

Omar dropped the cloak as far as his aching arm could stretch. 'Please, reach out.'

'*Freedom*!' Salwa called up, the fingers of both hands opening, letting gravity catch hold. Omar watched the body turning and shrinking in the wind, swallowed by the darkness and the storm until there was nothing left but the chasm below and the raging battle behind. He let the useless cloak drop after the vanished body.

The press of the skirmish had shifted further down the tower's stairs now, leaving dead beyrogs and claw-guards strewn in its wake. *So many times I lost her. So many times. All she wanted was to be free, and now she is. Free of every-thing. What have I made myself into? A slave pretending to be a soldier, the last son of a dead house. A uniform filled with muscle and blood, a uniform disguising a killer, a uniform holding onto nothing but duty and sharpened steel. Which of us is the larger monster now, Shadisa, you or Omar Barir, truly the greatest of all the guardsmen?* Falling to his knees, Omar turned his bleeding face to the sky and let the rain roll down his features, clearing away the blood from his cheeks. The storm ripped against him and he tipped his face back to howl at the heavens and rail at the fates. 'What more do you want from me? Why am I still alive? Is my blood so noble you will not shed it? Am I so celebrated you cannot crush me or cast me off this bloody tower?' *Do I have to avenge everyone in Haffa?*

He lay there weeping. It could have been for minutes, it could have been for days, until appearing through the litter of the carnage, the Caliph Eternal walked towards Omar. The guardsman's lost scimitar lay balanced in his untroubled hands.

The Caliph Eternal offered the blade. He didn't seem to notice Omar's tears in the rain. 'This is yours, guardsman.'

Omar rose shakily to his feet, grasping the pommel and cleaning its curved edge uncertainly against his trouser leg. As he stood, the shaking lessened, falling away until he was as still as the dark stones of the city towers below. Slowly then, his bearing grew straighter, his shadow longer across the stairs, darker across the dead. What was filling him? *Destiny or inevitability?* Then he looked at the weapon as if seeing it for the first time. 'Your majesty, you are mistaken. It is yours.'

CHAPTER SEVENTEEN

There were shouts verging on panic from the spotters on the bridge as the enemy fleet moved into position above them, bomb bays open and ready to fire.

Only seconds after Jack gave the order to engage the enemy, the spotters' calls tailed off as the forward starboard engine car fell silent, matching the port side with its damaged rotors.

She's compensating, the ship is offsetting the damage to port.

'That's the style,' Pasco said in bewilderment to the airship. 'Run us clear, old girl. Turn us back on bloody course.'

The *Iron Partridge* lifted upward, listing slightly, the manoeuvre accompanied by a strange clacking like a table of rapidly shifting dominoes being played. It was their armoured plates outside, rippling as they performed micro adjustments to the airship's pitch and yaw. The metallic chattering was suddenly drowned out by an explosion, a hollow thump followed by an echoing infill of air as the first of the frill of mortar tubes along their spine spat out fire.

Then came the enraged roar of a leviathan, the line of mortars punching out a rippling salvo of projectiles right along the airship's length. Each burning hot shell was visible from the bridge as an arc of red light, as though the *Iron Partridge* was a deep-water squid with multiple tentacles reaching out in the dark to seize every fish that surrounded it. A burning flower erupted at the end of each arc, quickly followed by crimson veins spreading across the envelopes of the Cassarabian airships, more detonations, as the enemy vessels shuddered and were torn apart.

'Enemy bomb bays struck above,' shouted the master pilot from the front of the bridge. 'We're putting our mortar shells right inside their magazines. There are mines and fin-bombs detonating all across the squadron's loading frames!'

Jericho's plan of action echoed in Jack's head. '*We need to be exactly where they seem to want us, bosun. Put us right under the shadow of their bomb bays.*'

Jericho had trusted Jack to do his work, just as he had trusted the ship to be about her business. The ultimate bet in the deadliest game, made with the only stakes the skipper had left to play . . . *our lives.*

'Yaw warning,' called a sailor from their inclinometer. 'Brace for port roll.'

Jack grabbed the sides of his command chair as the *Iron Partridge* rolled twenty degrees to port, the bombardment from the gun deck outside a deafening roar with the forward viewing canopy blown out. She had never been built to elevate her guns, but the ship was sighting them on the roll anyway.

'Yaw warning, brace for starboard roll,' warned the sailor again.

Thunder lifted out from their other side, enemy hulls lighting up in the night. Draks could briefly be glimpsed diving out of the way as the engine cars being targeted were blown free from their moorings, falling towards the ground with their rotors still turning.

Hissing a rain of ballast water from her sides, the *Iron Partridge* drifted upwards, rising like a wraith through the shoal of burning vessels. There was a different cadence to her manoeuvres now, the creaking carper decks almost silent as the airship picked a passage through the burning wreckage, ominously slow and deliberate.

They hovered on the crosswinds of flaming wreckage like a bird of prey, the telescope arrays in the crow's nest and h-dome extending to their maximum magnification in the search for any resistance. Jack imagined the enemy airship damage tables being consulted on the calculation drums above, poor old Coss dancing around the transaction engines, cursing and working as the junior ratings they had pressed into service on the boilers shovelled in enough coal to meet the steam-driven thinking machines' new voracity.

'Station gunner,' called Jack. 'Magazine capacity?'

'Magazine capacity, aye. Stores seventy per cent depleted on our cannons, and over eighty per cent empty on the mortar loading chamber,' the sailor on the gunnery board called across to Jack, not bothering to conceal his concern at how fast they were rattling through the contents of the ship's magazine. 'Although all our fin-bombs are still accounted for, master cardsharp. Quarter gunners are reporting that our thirty-two pounders are running hot.'

'Swab them out between the volleys,' barked Jack. 'I don't care if the gunners have to drop their britches and water them with last night's rum ration. Cool them off.'

Then the reverberation sounded again. Their ship not, it appeared, satisfied yet. Echoing in the thin night air, the *Iron Partridge*'s guns roared back into life, a ship-shaking snarl that became a constant thunder, one cannon after another, in perfect, timed synchronization, with just enough time for the first gun to be automatically reloaded on its shock-absorbing turntable mere seconds after the last cannon in the line had thundered to silence. The quaking under their boots grew stronger as the mortars added their voice to the massive barrage, Jack's teeth literally shaking in his mouth as the bridge – opened to the air with her smashed canopy – trembled at the violence being worked in the heavens outside.

It was only as they rose above the burning enemy fleet that the extent of the devastation and how targeted their action had been became evident to Jack and the bridge crew. Every enemy vessel had its engine cars picked off, their bomb bays erupting volcano fire along their keel decks, and where the Jackelian airship's recent broadsides had found their mark, the enemies' upper lifting chambers were blown open, spilling rising gas bags into the night air in waves.

Sailors were leaping out of ripped envelopes on emergency chutes from a few of the vessels, their pattern obviously copied from Royal Aerostatical Navy standard – and their crew just as badly trained in their use. Only meant as a last resort, only intended to exit a burning airship with no hope of landing, the triangles of fabric were caught in the burning crosswinds and sent spiralling downward like burning moths, the ones that survived picked off by the guardsmen on their wheeling draks.

I would almost feel sorry for them, if they hadn't done the same thing to the Fleet of the South.

Then, as if the entire wrecked fleet was merely an aerial display mounted only for the bridge crew's benefit, the great mass of burning airships began to lose equilibrium at the same time, their sole remaining lifting chambers unable to support the loss of ballonets topside. The enemy fleet's nose cones dipped, almost in salute, and began to sink groundward, trailing ugly coils of black smoke in their wake. Jack might have been mistaken, but he swore he glimpsed the shape of

Lemba of the Empty Thrusters forming in the smoke for a moment. Then the Loa was gone and cold starlight filled the night sky.

Jack turned in the hard-backed command chair, gazing out at the devastation, trying not to be startled by what had been worked upon the enemy fleet, by what had happened to him. He had forgotten himself. It was as if he had become Captain Jericho during the battle, worn the position of captain as though it was an officer's cloak, one possessed by the soul of its last owner. Was this what command was like? Death seen from someone else's eyes; the deaths he had ordered.

They had *won*.

Lieutenant McGillivray broke the stunned silence that had descended over the bridge crew as an evil whistling split the air outside. 'And what in the name of the Circle is that unholy caterwauling?'

'That, Mister McGillivray,' said Jack, leaning back into the hard confines of the iron chair, 'is the air of a rather imperfect rendition of *Lion of Jackals* cooling the tubes of our mortars. I understand that some call it progress.'

Holding back the claw-guards was like breaking the tidal rush of a river, the narrow passage they were retreating down restricting the enemy ranks to four or five snarling, slavering monsters, the head of a column hundreds deep, surging and jostling at the swinging scimitars of the surviving beyrogs. All of the stench and the shouts and the screams of the conflict funnelled down to a few feet of lashing blades, the commodore's arm aching from picking off the beasts that came leaping over the shoulders of the beyrogs. Flogging and slicing until his old shoulders were numb from the effort of it, his sword arm heavy with pain. *I might as well be an oarsman condemned to the seat of a wicked slave galley.*

Every minute or so they would lose another exhausted beyrog to the avalanche of claw-guards pressing in against their ranks, a giant soldier toppling over with his bright uniform torn to shreds and his cuirass opened up by the constant rain of talon strikes. By the commodore's side, Westwick looked every bit as exhausted as the commodore felt, her coffee-coloured skin slicked with sweat and her blade arm still and raised for the next attack, no more of the flourishes and fancy spins that he'd noticed she favoured when they had started fighting. Biding her time and preserving her energy for the next claw-guard to break through the retreating unit's lines. Only the one-eyed giant acting as the company's captain appeared to be undiminished by the constant, harrowing withdrawal. He kept his blade spinning around like a small windmill, decapitating his miniature cousins as they came leaping forward, seizing others mid-air, throttling them and contemptuously tossing their limp bodies against the walls.

For all of their animal snarls, the beyrogs' stone-skinned faces lent them a strangely stoical, immobile cast as they fought. Whereas soldiers from the race of man would have exhibited confusion, fear and anger in this relentless close-quarter's combat, the only sign of emotions from the beyrogs came from their eyes, their most human feature. Fighting alongside them was like fighting alongside the trolls from some polar barbarian's fireside legend. But even giants from legend could die when the odds were this appallingly stacked against their favour.

Who will remember me if I fall here? Who would remember poor old Blacky? His friends back home, perhaps. The friends with whom he shared his residence, Tock House? Poor old Jared Black, off on one of his mysterious little jaunts, and he simply never came back from his last journey. Lost like one of those mortal fool explorers in the jungles of the east. Not much time to grieve for him, not when he was lost to the storm that would emerge from the empire's borders, sweeping the entire Kingdom before it. Everything he had lived and fought for all of his life. The forested roads of their green and pleasant land echoing to the jingle of the campaign kit of creatures such as these claw-guards, the last few red-coated regiments of the Middlesteel Rifles broken by the grand vizier's forces.

Feeling a slight airflow on his neck, the commodore risked a glance behind him. Sweet Circle, they were running out of the passageway, the corridor opening out to their rear. He remembered where they were now, from their journey down from the barracks. The beyrogs were falling back towards the central chamber of the Citadel of Flowers, where the multiple wings of the evil construction joined in an inner concourse that had been speared through the core by a calliope of lifting rooms, dozens of the pipe-like conveyances linked by gantries and walkways. While the commodore's beyrog escort had been ignored well enough on the way down by the hundreds of womb mages and their servants in the order moving through the chamber – just another military unit marching through the citadel – something told him the citadel's denizens would find it harder to ignore a pitched battle being fought between two breeds of their own sorcery-created monstrosities. Damn his unlucky stars. A dim cavernous hall with minimal cover. Their depleted force would be overwhelmed within a minute of leaving the tight confines of the passage.

Westwick had spotted the danger as well. 'Hold your ground! Hold them here!'

'We can't do it, Maya,' said the commodore, dodging back as talons lashed through the beyrogs' ranks, trying to reach him. 'There isn't enough fight left in the few bodies we have remaining.'

'If they get behind us . . .'

'We have to cut and run, lass,' said the commodore. 'That's the only option we have other than planting our corpses here.'

'The Caliph Eternal's protectors will not turn tail and flee.'

Commodore Black hardly counted his tired old bones among that list, but perhaps the first lieutenant – along with all of the Pasdaran's other agents – did.

'I'll give them their mortal lead, then. A clean pair of heels – a strategy that's been used by many a great general.'

'You try to run and I'll bloody kill you myself. Hold them back!' shouted Westwick, hacking out at the legion of beasts.

But she might as well have been yelling at the tides of the sea for all of the effect that her orders had. Another beyrog slipped on the bloody floor, weighed down by a pack of roaring, slashing claw-guards, the gap left in the line allowing the grand vizier's pets to burst through. Westwick rolled across the floor, sweeping the feet out from under the attackers, the beyrog captain and Commodore Black hewing into the claw-guards before they could regain their balance.

The beyrog formation closed ranks, thinner then ever, trampling back across the fresh corpses, driven into retreat by the sheer weight and ferocity of the numbers coming towards them.

Even by the fierce standards of battle in Cassarabia, where the losers were so often given the sword, this battle was as bad and bloody as any that had ever been fought inside the empire. No quarter given, expected or asked for. *Has Mutantarjinn ever seen anything like it before?* The terrible city was no stranger to misery. The generations of slaves whose lives had leeched away here as they gave birth to the dark creations of womb-mage sorcery. Its dark towers squatting in a chasm cut out of a hellish plain and beaten by the devil's own storms. And now the empire's sorcerous armies were pitted against each other in a civil war that looked as if it would sweep across the face of the civilized world.

Inch by inch the beyrogs surrendered the passage to the foe, leaving the claw-guards' bodies piled up in front of their ranks, the corpses pushed aside and clambered over by fresh soldiers howling their anger towards the caliph's private body-guard. Edging closer to the citadel's cavernous central hall, until the cold currents of the open space were running like ice along the back of the commodore's neck.

Commodore Black stumbled back. They had long since lost their two buglers to the sabre-like claws of the grand vizier's pets, but the beyrogs didn't need the orders of a trumpet to form the only disposition that could preserve their lives for a few seconds more. They fell back towards the hall's centre, automatically making a square; their scimitars dripping gore and their cuirasses dented by rifle fire and talon strikes and streaked with blood. Hundreds of womb mages and their staff scattered across the ground level of the hall, clamouring as the tide of bloody violence spilled out into the open, while servants shouted on the walkways above and pointed down in disbelief. Pouring out of the passage as though they were a nest of angered ants, the claw-guards surged into the open, loping and circling the few beyrogs left alive, waiting until they had overwhelming numbers to rout the ruler's bodyguard in a single charge. Imperial Aerial Squadron marines and armed sailors were assembling at the edges of the chamber, pushing shells into their rifles' breeches. The commodore kicked an empty crossbow quiver in frustration. *We have nothing with which to match their guns.*

Then there was a strange sound that Commodore Black had never heard before, rising from the throats of the beyrogs. A wolf-like keening. Their death dirge, or – no it was directed at the figure emerging from the passage surrounded by claw-guards. *Immed Zahharl.* The grand vizier victoriously emerging like an emperor come to give the sign of life or death to gladiators lying in the sand. It was a song of pure loathing directed at the man who had dared to overthrow their beloved ruler of rulers and crown himself emperor over their master's corpse.

'Do you expect us to surrender?' Westwick shouted from the middle of the square.

The grand vizier shook his head slowly, smiling all the while. 'Knowing that this is the very last trouble I shall receive from a member of the secret police? Please, don't deny me that.' He pointed his sword at the huddled formation of survivors from the caliph's bodyguard. 'Make ready—'

He was interrupted by a shout from the gantry above. 'Not the last trouble, surely?'

Commodore Black gawked up at the sight of hundreds of beyrogs with their crossbows pointed down into the hall, the caliph standing with the young guardsman Omar Barir in front of a number of glass tanks being manoeuvred out of the lifting rooms at the chamber's centre.

'I am sure the Pasdaran are still interested in treason and,' the caliph flung a hand back towards the tanks, 'the perverted sorceries of the grand vizier.'

There were gasps of outrage from the womb mages scattered across the massive chamber as they gazed at the faces of the slowly squirming men in the tanks, prisoners' sweating bearded cheeks glowing in the nutrient mist; twisted, pregnant bellies laid out like hills of flesh before them.

'Hear me. Hear your Caliph Eternal. This is the progress which the Sect of Razat brings you!' shouted the young ruler, his voice carrying far across the quieted hall. 'The progress of slaves and criminals who were born women and who have perverted their bodies towards the male form through the use of an illegal changeling virus. Criminals who have dared to use a variation of that foul virus to turn men into producers to breed unlicensed monstrosities.' His arm swept across the chamber. 'They have done this so that you, all of you, will take their places in the tanks of the producers!'

'He lies!' yelled Immed Zahharl. 'This is not the Caliph Eternal, only a twisted product of the womb mages' arts created by rebels and traitors. Believe not a thing that this weak-minded dog says.'

Omar Barir moved forward to the edge of the rail, flinging his hand back towards the tanks. 'Believe in the evidence in front of your eyes. And believe in the loyalty of the Caliph Eternal's bodyguard. You all know that his beyrogs follow only the true emperor's word, and they follow this man, as do his imperial guardsmen and every drak rider soaring in the sky above this city.'

'As do the Pasdaran,' called Westwick, pointing her sword at the grand vizier as if her blade might leap out and skewer the chief minister.

'I am the future,' railed the grand vizier. 'I have given the empire a new golden age.' He pointed at the Imperial Aerial Squadron sailors and marines, a tone of pleading intruding into the ice of his voice. 'I have given you heaven's command. I have given you victories and plunder. I have given you a new beginning. This, this is only the start of what we shall achieve together.'

High above, the beyrogs laid into one of the producer's tanks with the butts of their huge crossbows, shattering the crystal walls and rolling its twisted, bloated occupant to the edge of the gantry.

'Take a good look,' yelled Omar. 'This is *her* new beginning.'

There was a series of enraged shouts from the airship sailors at the end of the chamber, officers desperately trying to keep their men in formation, followed by a series of yells as the officers collapsed to the ground to the echo of rifle shots, their mutinous troops surging forward. Lost in the roar were the frightened yelps from sorcerers wearing the symbols of the Sect of Razat, dozens of them fleeing from a mob made up of howling womb mages and their servants.

'I gave you the future!' yelled Immed Zahharl, backing away as the provoked Cassarabians surged towards him, his retinue of beasts standing by his side, cutting the air nervously with their sabre hands.

'The gratitude of kings,' whispered Commodore Black, looking up at the caliph. 'I told you it was a mortal poor thing, Maya.' *It's a hard thing I do for the Kingdom today; as wicked hard as any, to save it by putting down a slave uprising down here. Maybe that's why no Jackelian believes in hell . . . because when you find yourself in it, you can only pick the lesser of two demons.*

'He still has his regiment of monsters,' said Westwick, pushing her way through the defensive square of beyrogs as the claw-guards fell back around the grand vizier.

The chamber erupted into violence as the Imperial Aerial Squadron marines opened up on the grand vizier's claw-guards with their carbines, adding their balls and gun smoke to the rain of crossbow bolts suddenly being loosed by the beyrogs from above. Immed Zahharl and his bodyguard retreated out of the concourse under the fierce hail.

Omar Barir was sliding down the rails of the stairs towards their position and the caliph leant over the gantry to call down. 'Take the grand vizier alive if you can, guardsman. He has many secrets to tell us before he can be allowed to pass.'

A ball from a marine's gun buzzed between the commodore and Westwick, bouncing off the cuirass of one of their beyrogs.

'I'll keep the boy safe,' said the commodore. 'You make sure his majesty up there lives long enough to declare peace with Jackals.'

'And the grand vizier,' said Westwick, in a flat tone of voice that Commodore Black wasn't sure was a statement or a question.

'Best efforts, lass.' He patted his sword.

'The abomination will be heading for the citadel's airship harbour,' said Westwick. 'It's what I would do. Rendezvous with the fleet and then bomb the city into rubble. Leave no survivors alive to tell of what happened here.'

'There's a pity,' said the commodore. 'Given that surviving is what I do so blessed well.'

He ran after the young guardsman, the beyrog captain and his giant soldiers following and cutting a path through the ranks of claw-guards trying to stop them. *All down to me, again, curse my unlucky stars.* In the heart of enemy territory, two nations to save, and only the sword of an unlucky old fool to rely on.

CHAPTER EIGHTEEN

Omar was running through the Citadel of Flowers' oppressive halls and passages, a dozen beyrogs and the commodore fast on his heels, as the Caliph Eternal's voice finished echoing out of the voicebox in the wall. His order to hunt down the grand vizier and the Sect of Razat was fading from the corridor, but the promise of a caliph's fortune if the chief minister was handed over in chains had clearly had its effect on the commodore, the old u-boat man's eyes twinkling with new-found zeal for their task.

Omar suddenly drew to a halt.

'What is it lad?' the commodore wheezed, catching up with him. 'A stitch in that sorcery-poisoned gut of yours?'

'The grand vizier didn't come this way,' said Omar.

'This is the way to the blessed airship harbour,' said the commodore. 'Where that rascal's private packet is tied up snug alongside all the other pocket airships.'

'He's not running for the harbour,' said Omar, extending his senses through the citadel to confirm his suspicions. 'I can feel the venom of his soul, and he's not passed this way.' He pointed to the floor. 'That way. He's going lower into the citadel, to the east wing – I'd swear it on the gates of heaven.'

'Those gates won't be opening for the grand vizier any time soon,' said the commodore, scratching his beard as he recovered his breath. 'The gates of your hell, now, that's another matter. So, what's he up to?'

'Immed Zahharl must have realized we'd look to seize him at the harbour,' said Omar. *Always one step ahead of me, but not this time. I can smell your stinking soul, grand vizier. Soaked as it is with the blood of Shadisa and everyone else who's died to keep you in power.*

'The cunning devil won't be ducking into the city's streets on foot,' said the commodore. 'He might be able to get away with one of the slavers' caravans, but by the time he reaches the next town his mortal ugly mug will be plastered across the garrison's walls. His scalp carrying a sum of gold so large that he'd have every wicked bounty hunter in the empire turning over barrels trying to cut his throat. He needs to act fast if he's to stay in power and he knows it.'

Omar looked at the one-eyed beyrog officer waiting in front of his troops. 'What's in the east wing of the citadel, captain? What do they have down there that we won't find in the rest of the fortress?'

Commodore Black looked towards the young guardsman for a translation of the beyrog officer's rapid flicker of sign language.

'It's the great stables,' said Omar. 'Where the womb mages' new stock is bedded down before being sent across the empire.'

'Well, he's not heading down there to help the stable hands clean out their stalls, lad,' said the commodore.

'No,' sighed Omar.

What sly mischief would the murderous traitor who had

corrupted Shadisa be working against them among the womb mages' creations?

They ran, Omar driven by the frantic dread that the grand vizier would have vanished by the time they reached the stables. Vanished like a mist of pure evil, one of the life-leeching djinn of legend, reforming elsewhere to continue his perverted schemes. *Something undead and unkillable. But I'll try to kill him, fate, by the hundred faces of heaven, I'll try. And you will let me. You owe that much to me for Shadisa's death.*

By the time they gained the arch to the vast series of chambers that composed the great stables, Omar found they weren't the only ones attempting to hunt down the grand vizier's cabal. A company of Immed Zahharl's surviving claw-guards was locked in unequal combat with the stable staff – pitchforks and baling hooks no match for the monsters' sword-length talons. The beasts were assisted by a mob of robed figures – keepers and holy servants from the Sect of Razat – along with a scrum of highly placed womb mages. So, the grand vizier's inner circle had heard the Caliph Eternal's commands and were trying to flee the sinking ship alongside their master.

Omar's force raced into the carnage, the beyrogs battering aside Immed Zahharl's twisted creations, the sounds of scimitars connecting with leather armour stifled by the racket from hundreds of sandpedes in one of the side-stalls rearing up and clawing in panic at the iron bars with their segmented legs.

But where is the grand vizier? The dregs of the regime were here, trying to save their skins, but where was the dog himself? Omar could almost taste Immed Zahharl's rage, his hatred for the guardsman who had come so close to overthrowing his rule for good. He was still inside the great stable, his soul pulsing with venomous loathing for Omar.

Omar smashed aside a claw-guard, the beyrogs behind him covering his back as he sprinted down the central passage – fifty foot wide with two levels of cavernous stalls on either side, filled with creatures driven into a frenzy by the unexpected violence that had spilled into the normally quiet stables.

'Immed Zahharl!' yelled Omar. 'Come out. The smallest and least significant of your loose ends has come for you. Show me of how little account you find me now.'

'Watch out lad!' The commodore's shouted warning almost came too late.

Catching the movement above him, Omar desperately rolled forward, tonnes of moving metal almost slicing him in half as a vast gate composed of thousands of bars dropped down from the ceiling, locking into place in a concrete groove in the floor. As he came to his feet, Omar found himself the only one from the caliph's force on his side of the great stables – all of the beyrogs and the commodore still locked in battle against the grand vizier's cabal and their claw-guards on the other side.

Commodore Black had a stable keeper pushed up against the gate on the opposite side. 'Open the blessed doors.'

'I cannot,' yelled the man, looking in terror at the sabre hovering inches from his chest. He jerked a hand at a corpse on the floor wearing stable livery. 'Only the stable master has the codes to unlock the stampede wall.'

Commodore Black banged the bars in frustration. 'I'll force the lock. Crack it and get the beyrogs across to you. Stay there, lad.'

'He's here,' said Omar, feeling the intense ball of burning hate throbbing behind him. 'Old man, if I don't make it . . .'

'Don't say that, lad. Saying it can make it come true. You're a guardsman, the blessed blade of the Caliph Eternal himself. You remember that.'

'Yes,' said Omar. *That is all I have left.* His house, Shadisa, Boulous, Farris Uddin, his family, all swallowed up by the ambitions of a single hellion in human form. *But I'm still a guardsman.* 'Your friend, Jared Black, the Pasdaran woman. You know she's going to kill you here.'

The commodore winked at him through the bars. 'Aye, you might be right, but you worry about yourself, not me. There's many a slip, lad, between cup and lip.'

Omar turned down the stable's central passage, walking forward and ignoring the clash of swords and screams from the gate behind him. 'You've left your people to die, Immed Zahharl.'

'But the empire teems with so many people.' There he was, the grand vizier emerging on one of the stone walkways built into the wall, standing in front of stalls on the second level. 'And the future is always purchased by sacrifice.'

So it seems, but until now, never yours.

Omar pointed his scimitar up towards the grand vizier's heart. 'The future is one body short.'

'I do so hate wasting a good breeder,' the grand vizier called down. 'How does your stomach feel, last son of Barir? The first wave of agony should have passed by now. The second wave will begin to burn inside you some time tomorrow morning. In a couple of days you will need a company of beyrogs to carry you to your new duty. How fine it would have been, to see you and the boy king in labour, your faces turning purple as you squeezed out another litter of claw-guards to fight for me. Why must you always disrupt my pleasures?'

Is that the secret the Caliph Eternal talked of keeping the grand vizier alive for? Does he believe that without the creator of the changeling virus, the other womb mages will have no chance of curing us?

'Your little enculi wants me alive,' laughed the grand vizier. 'But do you think the empire's soldiers and sailors will still follow their precious Caliph Eternal so readily after his belly has bloated large enough to give birth to a sandpede? What about you? Does the last son of Barir wish me alive, or as a corpse?'

Omar wrestled with the conflicting feelings inside him. What did he want, what did he *need*?

'If I live, you are both dead,' jeered the grand vizier. 'If I die, you are both cursed. That is my revenge, guardsman, and it is purer than every last gold coin the caliph has placed on my head as a bounty.'

'A guardsman is the Caliph Eternal's right arm,' said Omar, climbing a wall rail to reach the stable's second tier. 'Bound to obey his oath.'

Still retreating, the grand vizier laughed at Omar. 'Come, little peacock, show me the strength of your oath.'

'Here's my vow. I'm a freed slave with the stench of the sack of Haffa still reeking in my nostrils,' yelled Omar, pulling himself up onto the second level of stalls. 'I was raised by water farmers and a tribesman of the Mutrah, a wild reformed bandit who was little better than a savage. I'm not going to take you alive, by the blood of my house and my family and Shadisa, I'm going to slice you into pieces.'

Immed Zahharl had stopped by the stall at the end of the row, stooping to unlock its gate with a key stolen from the stable master's corpse. 'That, at last, is the truth of it. And I am the last princess of the noblest house of Hakaqibla. You were given your pathetically limited existence only to serve me.' The grand vizier stepped back into the open stall and disappeared.

Omar caught a familiar smell from inside the stall. *Draks!* The grand vizier had been heading down to the stables to saddle a drak and try to fly out to the fleet on one of his enemy's own steeds. Omar entered the antechamber to the drak eyrie, a tack room racked with saddle storage, hay, bedding, forks and rakes, the draks held back by a second gate inside. The grand vizier had already reached a control panel on the far wall, and a hangar door in the outside wall was drawing back, revealing the towers of Mutantarjinn beyond, the storm still whipping through the chasm.

Unhooking a drak saddle from the wall, the grand vizier dropped it on the floor and drew his scimitar. 'Leave me to escape and I'll cure your infected belly, lowly slave. You do realize I'm the only womb mage alive with the skills to save you.'

Omar shook his head and pointed to the draks shifting about in the eyrie chamber behind them. 'I would give birth to every drak inside there just for the chance to carve you into pieces.'

Immed Zahharl kicked the saddle aside. Angrily raising the scimitar high in a guard position, the grand vizier drew out a long dagger from behind his back, turning it between his fingers in an intricate, hypnotizing motion. 'At least your stupidity has the benefit of consistency. Come, lowly slave, come and show me what you have been taught. My line's blood is destined to be mirrored down the ages – while yours shall be spilled here.'

Ignoring mocking jibes that were only intended to drive him in anger onto the pair of blades, Omar circled the grand vizier slowly, marking the expert way he turned the weapons. Someone had trained him to fight. Someone every bit the equal of the old cadet master back in the palace fortress. But then, given the grand vizier's wealth, he would have paid for the very best tutors from the finest duelling halls inside the empire.

There was a clash of steel as their blades lashed out at the same time, the grand vizier's feet moving and twisting in the steps of a sinister dance. Their swords clashed again, Omar side-stepping the dagger in the politician's other hand, kicking out with his boot towards Immed Zahharl's knee and nearly losing his balance as the grand vizier darted out of the way with balletic grace.

'Brutal and direct,' sneered Immed Zahharl. 'Every bit the guardsman and every bit the slave.'

There is nothing fancy about gutting a traitorous dog. Omar bit his lip and feinted left while changing his thrust at the last second and cutting right. The grand vizier swayed back, but a moment too slow, the tip of Omar's scimitar nicking his cheek and drawing blood. Immed Zahharl wiped it off with the back of his dagger hand and Omar hissed in frustration as he saw the line of his cut fading from the grand vizier's face as if it was being erased by an invisible pencil.

'I didn't just reverse my gender,' said the grand vizier. 'I remade myself into a weapon, a razor with which to flay the skin from my enemies.' He cut out viciously and Omar retreated a couple of steps under the force of the blows. The grand vizier hawked a gob of spit at Omar and the edge of the guardsman's sword began to burn and blister where the spittle had struck above the hilt. *Acid, he can spit acid.* 'I am an instrument of heaven, little slave. Divine justice given human form.'

'Tell that lie to the widows of Haffa.'

'Your father was nothing more than a corpulent vulture,' laughed the grand vizier. 'Complacently subsisting on the inventions of his ancestors. His coward's fear of a new age doomed your house and all its allies. I was only the cliff edge he and the fading glories of your failing sect chose to jump off. Truly, it was he who killed your people, not I.'

Omar grunted as they threw themselves at each other, blades crashing, thrusting and probing in a fierce exchange. The grand vizier was as thin as a whip, but Omar could see that his sorceries had done something to his muscles. They moved in strange, alien ways that gave him the purchase and raw strength of someone four or five times his size – as if his skin had been filled by a host of eels squirming and wiggling.

Another fierce clash, and the scimitar in Immed Zahharl's hand seemed to speed into a blur, breaking through Omar's parries as easily as a knot being severed. Omar yelled as the sabre sliced through his sword arm's biceps, its sudden bite burning, his arm plunged into fire. He dropped his scimitar into his left hand, his right arm hanging useless by his side.

'See how quick my new body is,' cooed the grand vizier. 'A little push from my mind, and you are moving so slowly to my eyes that you might as well be wading through a sand drift. Did your guardsmen tutors take pity on you, little slave, and teach you how to fight left-handed?'

Omar lunged out and the grand vizier easily turned his blade. 'I didn't think so. Tell me how exquisite my new body is, slave. Tell me how you want it, how you need it.'

Omar yelled in desperation, ignoring the burning pain and swinging out with the scimitar in his left hand, but the grand vizier darted aside, plunging the dagger deep into Omar's left shoulder. The young guardsman fell to the floor as the scimitar was kicked out of his hand to the crack of two or three of his fingers breaking.

'Heaven chose to make me this way,' the grand vizier whispered in Omar's ear, before stepping back and booting him in the gut. 'I am beautiful.'

Omar was left doubled up, coughing on the floor, blood spluttering out of his mouth and onto the stall's concrete and sawdust. 'A terrible beauty,' gagged Omar. 'So fast.'

'Yes,' agreed the pacing grand vizier, the scimitar rotating in his hand, measuring the length of the killing stroke. *The executioner's stroke that will sever my head from my body.*

'There's one thing I have,' Omar moaned in pain, pulling the grand vizier's dagger out of his shoulder with his numb, crippled fingers, as blood gushed out of the wound.

'Ah,' smiled Immed Zahharl. 'The great knife fighter from Haffa.'

Omar rolled forward in agony, pitching the blade at the grand vizier, the lazy rotations of the dagger missing the devil's side by at least a couple of feet.

'Perhaps you are more of a pistol master?' laughed the grand vizier.

'The one thing I had wasn't your knife,' said Omar, pulling himself to his feet. 'It's six months of foul-tasting, foul-smelling guards' rations inside my body.'

Omar let the keening howls behind the grand vizier distract the man, just long enough for him to pitch forward in a charge and carry both their bodies tumbling through the opening gate and into the drak eyrie. Perhaps the grand vizier's quick eyes even had time to notice Omar's stolen dagger still quivering in the lever of the stable release handle. Yes, after six months of cadet rations Omar smelled like something a drak might actually acknowledge as its rightful master. Even an unbroken, raw fledgling drak – even an eyrie full of the wild, untamed beasts.

A long sinuous neck lashed out, sweeping Omar's feet from underneath him, before a pair of more mature draks snapped out angrily at the young upstart beast that was daring to challenge a guardsman. Grunting in pain and allowing the more developed pair to protect him, Omar limped to the side of the tall eyrie.

In the centre of the chamber, Immed Zahharl was on his

feet, curving his sword threateningly in front of the dozens of draks now circling him. Such a fine, exquisite body. But to a drak, it smelled nothing like a guardsman should. Some of the draks were so young that their scales hadn't turned green yet, but even a fledgling drak weighed as much as a rhino.

'My womb mages created you,' shouted the grand vizier. 'I created you.'

Hissing and darting their heads forward, the draks began to test the grand vizier's defences. His scimitar leapt out and the snarling draks' heads snapped back.

'They don't care,' Omar called. 'They're the past and the guardsmen's traditions, thousands of years of them, and our traditions have finally caught up with you.'

'You are cursed, slave,' shouted Immed Zahharl as a drak snapped the grand vizier's blade away from him. 'You will never be cured now. My death has cursed you!'

Omar shook his head. 'No, I'm a guardsman, not a slave. And I've cursed myself.' *My choice. For what I did to Shadisa. But you first, you mangy bastard!*

Immed Zahharl tried to run, striking out with his quick hands at the draks, but as fast as his sorcery-twisted body was, he could not evade an eyrie full of angry, snapping draks, their powerful, muscled tails beating out at him, claws flashing. More and more of the enraged creatures emerged from the side chambers and launched themselves down on him with the force of falling sabres.

Omar backed away towards the eyrie's gate, the pair of draks trailing him stopping only to gaze at the dozens of their cousins feasting on the unexpected treat that had been thrown into their midst. The nearest of the pair grunted and Omar gasped as he caught sight of the human eyes buried inside the lizard-like features of the drak's armoured skull. *His eyes.*

This was the drak he had sacrificed his flesh for back in the palace. Omar's bonded drak. It hissed knowingly at him, attracted by the invisible affinity between them. They were the same. It would ride for him like no other drak would, sensing his every whim, anticipating his every command in the air. Together, they would become the ultimate living weapon.

'Don't worry,' said Omar, pushing the eyrie gate's closure lever. 'You'll feel the storm on your wings soon enough.'

Behind him, Commodore Black came running down the gantry of the stable's upper level, a trail of biologicks in the stalls tracking his steps and hooting plaintively for a long overdue feed.

'Immed Zahharl?' asked the man.

Omar waved his crippled hand towards the eyrie.

Commodore Black grunted when he looked through at the sight on the other side of the gate. 'Then we've won, lad.'

Omar propped his bleeding body against the wall. Shadisa was lost to him. Farris Uddin, Boulous, half the guardsmen, his father and his home gone. His very body was cursed with the grand vizier's foul sorcery.

'No.'

'You're learning, Mister Barir,' said the commodore. 'This is what victory tastes of. Clear your throat and spit the blood out, because you're alive enough to sup on its ashes.'

From the other end of the stables came the victorious cheers of the stable hands and the animal-like bellows of the beyrogs. The last claw-guard had fallen, the corpses of the Sect of Razat's inner circle left sprawled across the floor.

Victory had come to the citadel, but it wasn't nearly enough to fill the hollow inside Omar's soul. He had learnt the last lesson of being a guardsman, the one every soldier had to learn for himself.

CHAPTER NINETEEN

Omar winced as the gaggle of the citadel's surgeons and womb mages poked and prodded at his body, the spray on his shoulder leaving the skin inflamed. But as the commodore had pointed out before he left the surgery, better safe than sorry; the painful poison-cleansing sorceries of the womb mages weighed up against the chance that the dead grand vizier's blades had been dipped in something corrosive and lethal to the flesh.

Lying in the shadow of machines the size of the desalination tanks on his water farm, Omar raised his voice above the womb mages chanting the results of his blood-code tests, loud enough for the Caliph Eternal to hear him over the racket.

'They should be taking care of you first, your majesty. We—'

The Caliph Eternal rested a hand on the slab where Omar was laid out. *A prize steak at a bazaar for senior members of the order of womb mages to tenderize.* 'I have just been seen by the order.'

'They have already purged you of the grand vizier's poison? So soon—'

The Caliph Eternal shook his head and smiled. He sounded distracted, as if he was talking about some event in the distant past that had affected one of his ancestors. 'It seems that my blood contained dormant defences. When the first fever touched me, those defences emerged and turned into predator cells that burnt all traces of the changeling virus from my flesh.'

Omar's eyes widened at the news – his elation that the ruler was safe followed by a more selfish notion. *If only a humble guardsman is left infected, how hard will the senior womb mages work at developing a way of halting my transformation into a human breeding machine?*

Squeezing Omar's unwounded shoulder, the caliph indicated the womb mages clustered around them. 'I am protected by the one true god, guardsman, and my protection will be extended to you. You have my word. There are no resources in this city that will not be spent on curing you.'

The bowing of one of the obsequious cluster of womb mages interrupted the ruler's reassurances.

'Speak,' commanded the Caliph Eternal.

'The guardsman is clear of the changeling virus, your majesty. He is not infected.'

'But I had the fever,' said Omar. 'My stomach was in agony.'

Even the caliph's normally ethereal manner seemed thrown by the news. 'This guardsman's pedigree includes partial inheritance from a Pasdaran officer, but his immune system would not—'

'I have not adequately explained myself to your majesty,' pleaded the womb mage. 'Unlike your own noble body, the guardsman's contains no traces of the changeling virus. The resequencing vector was blank and the carrier he was injected with was empty. Any discomfort he felt was purely as a result of the carrier itself, EE4208.'

'A modified variant of *E.coli*,' said the caliph, nodding in understanding. 'You do not need my protection, guardsman, the hundred faces of heaven were already smiling down upon you.'

Omar felt only confusion at the sorceries being discussed. 'I was injected, I was sick . . .'

'Injected with one of two syringes, both prepared by Salwa. One syringe with the changeling virus, the other with a blank carrier virus that would only make its recipient ill enough to mimic the effects of the real thing.'

Omar remembered the sequence of events, Farris Uddin lying dead on the floor, Salwa holding two syringes, the Caliph Eternal struggling bound to his chair as the grand vizier poisoned him before ordering Salwa to do the same to Omar.

'But Salwa couldn't be sure which of us the grand vizier would choose to give the needle to first, you could have been injected with the blank virus instead of me.'

The Caliph Eternal smiled sadly. 'Do you think Immed Zahharl could ever pass up the opportunity to test Salwa's loyalty to the sect by demanding she infect you? Or that the grand vizier wouldn't reserve the pleasure of injecting me with a changeling virus that could easily have killed me in front of his eyes? Salwa knew the grand vizier would order her to inject you, that is why she passed the grand vizier the live virus and kept back the syringe with the blank virus in her own hands.'

Tears rolled down Omar's cheeks. It hadn't been Salwa who had plunged the needle into his neck, it had been Shadisa. What had she been planning on doing – faking his death and pulling him out of the producers' chambers, sending him out of Mutantarjinn with one of the slavers' caravans? Risking her life by defying the grand vizier. *By saving me*. If Immed Zahharl had caught a whiff of her betrayal, she would have been slaughtered by her own claw-guards a few minutes after the discovery.

'A miracle after all,' said the caliph. 'Saved by love. I have been witness to so many things over the ages, but that happens far less than it should.'

There was a tone of wonder in the ruler's voice, as if he had found a long-extinct breed of butterfly alighting on his wrist; but Omar barely heard the man's words.

Shadisa saved me. Omar hadn't failed to rescue Salwa from falling off the tower, he had failed to rescue Shadisa. His father's words whispered across the chamber.

'*We are what heaven wills us.*'

Commodore Black was swinging supply bales into the open gondola of the grand vizier's pocket airship when he caught the reflection of First Lieutenant Westwick advancing on him in the polished mahogany of the craft's prow.

'You've heard the news about the *Iron Partridge* then?' said the commodore. 'I was hoping to away and rendezvous with her without troubling you or any of the others here. Ingenious Jericho and his mad strategies. We made a grand choice in picking him, eh? Not that the list of candidates was that long to start with, and that's the truth of it.'

'No trouble,' said Westwick. 'In fact, we'd prefer it if you stayed.'

'She's a fine 'stat, isn't she, Maya?' said the commodore, patting the airship. 'All her instruments plated with gold rather than brass. Her blessed wheel a single piece of carved ivory instead of oak. Where do you wonder they found tusks large enough for that?'

'She's the Caliph Eternal's airship now,' said Westwick.

'They've very particular traditions when it comes to dividing out the plunder, do the locals,' said the commodore. 'And I was there at the grand vizier's end. So technically, I would say this fine little beauty belongs to me now.'

Westwick drew her sabre. 'We would really *much* rather that you stayed.'

'That would be the Pasdaran *we*, then,' sighed the commodore, drawing his sword in reply. 'Do you think the State Protection Board won't know about you, lass, if I don't report back? And the tale of how the empire was getting its airship gas is well and truly out of the bag now, too. No Cassarabian will stand for male producers being used as the price of your aerial navy.'

'All that you know,' said Westwick, 'and the secret of the enculi too.'

'Add one more secret then, lass – why the caliph's belly isn't swollen out as large as the canvas of my beautiful craft here.'

Westwick's eyes narrowed dangerously. 'And why would that be, old man?'

'The grand vizier's wicked sorcery changes the male to the female. How well do you think that such a virus would work on a lass to begin with?' He shrugged unconcernedly. 'The descendent of Ben Issman, or the descendent of Benitta Issman? Do you think the grand vizier discovered the sorcery of masking her true gender, or just *re*-discovered it from the ancient records in the city?'

Westwick raised her sword into a guard pose. 'You die for speaking blasphemy here.'

'The gratitude of kings, Maya,' said the commodore, saluting her with his blade. 'I was counting on it.'

Their steel clashed in the air between them, the commodore toppling over some of the supply sacks in front of Westwick. She spun out and struck, turning and dancing back.

'All very fancy, lass,' wheezed the commodore. 'That's what

you get when you learn from the State Protection Board's trainers. Assassins, not duellists. Too much ritual in it.'

He stamped forward, cutting low as she cartwheeled back, stepping into a quick flurry of counter strikes, every blow making the airship harbour ring with crashing steel.

'I've a third of your years,' hissed Westwick. 'I can keep this up for hours. How tired is your sword arm right now, how much does it ache from the battle?'

'You're a grand beauty, lass,' admitted the commodore. 'As beautiful as that wicked blade up your sleeve; the one you're hoping I haven't noticed.'

She sprung it and leapt across the bales of supplies, slashing out and missing the old u-boat man by inches. 'Let me sink this into your heart. It'll be quick and almost painless. That's a professional courtesy.'

Commodore Black groaned as she advanced on him a second time, close to exhaustion after the battle against the claw-guards. Their blades slashed back and forth in an intense, intricate and brutal exchange of fury that might have lasted minutes or hours.

As the first lieutenant backed him up against the airship hull, her arm struck out in a blur and the knife sank into the thigh of his left leg, only its hilt visible as he fell to one knee, yelling with the shock of the blow. *I forgot how much this wicked game bloody hurts.* He raised a hand out in supplication as she twisted around, kicking the sabre out of his fingers.

'One last secret to tell, lass.'

'Valuable enough for me to drag you to an interrogation cell rather than taking your head for a trophy?'

'More of an admission, Maya,' coughed the commodore.

There was a curious look on the first lieutenant's face as she drew her sword back ready for the killing strike. A look that turned to confusion as she began blinking peculiarly, her feet stumbling over one of the overturned supply bales as if she hadn't seen it lying there.

'It's not sleep those beautiful green eyes of yours need, Maya – it's a fresh shot of the womb mages' blessing against the dark curse of their Forbidden City. A dose that wasn't cut with so much water by me.'

She sliced out blindly, but the commodore had already rolled out of the way, removing the bloody knife from his leg and sending it spinning across the harbour. Screaming in frustration, the first lieutenant carved her blade through the air, missing the commodore and the landing rocket launcher he was pulling over the side of the airship by a couple of feet. It was Westwick's last cut before the commodore triggered the large metal tube he was hefting, the landing rocket impaling her leg and sending her flying back towards a rack of expansion-engine cylinders.

The commodore ignored her wailing oaths as he tossed the empty launcher aside and hauled himself into the pocket airship's gondola. 'Don't be too mad at me, lass. The secret police down here will need a new head to gather together all of your survivors. I'm sure the State Protection Board will prefer a known quantity like yourself in that office.'

Westwick swore and sent her sword spinning blade-first into the hull of the airship.

'Out by a foot or two,' said the commodore. 'You know, you were right all along, lass. I thought I was getting too mortal old for all of this. But I am still good for it.'

The commodore fired up the airship's twin expansion engines, a rotor on either side of the small packet spinning into life. Lighting up his mumbleweed pipe, he puffed contentedly as the richly appointed airship lifted away from the tower's harbour moorings.

EPILOGUE

'Now then, laddies,' said the gruff lieutenant on the desk at the front of the queue snaking across the airship field. 'Being two nice honest boys, I am sure you both have your state work records with you.'

Handing over the tattered punch cards, the eldest of the brothers shifted uncomfortably in his boots. 'I thought the navy took anybody on.'

'Did you now?' said the lieutenant, his voice half a growl as he fed the cards into a portable transaction engine and inspected the results rotating across the beads on his abacus-like screen. 'Well, you're not on the constabulary's wanted list, which's a start. But I see a lot of concerns' names on your cards. Aye, can't settle down to a trade, eh? What makes you think you can settle with the Royal Aerostatical Navy, I wonder? Good scores on your letters, but it's not clerks we need. Not now the Cassarabians have found a new way to produce those little arse-farting gas monsters of theirs without offending the great sky gods or whatever fancy they're worshipping this month. We need men-of-war; we need Jack Cloudies. You two lanky laddies think that's you?'

They nodded in a non-committal way.

The lieutenant stamped their punch cards with the official navy recruitment pattern, jerking a thumb towards the airship hangars where a short steamman appeared to be addressing the assembled crewmen. 'Over there to take the oath and look lively about it. Master Cardsharp Shaftcrank is officiating today and if you slouch like that in front of him, I can guarantee you laddies'll be stuck stoking in his transaction-engine chamber for the first six months of your service.' They went to walk over, but the lieutenant stuck an arm out first, blocking their passage. 'Being such fine readers, you two no doubt peruse a copy of the *Middlesteel Illustrated News* of a morning, maybe buy a penny-dreadful or two to read?'

Again the pair nodded in a non-committal way.

'Are the pensmen still writing about the youngest captain of the fleet's latest exploits; you know the one, boys, the hero of the Battle of the Mutantarjinn Flats?'

The oldest brother grunted in the affirmative.

'I thought they might be.' The lieutenant dropped his arm. 'On your way, Messrs Alan and Saul Keats. Welcome to the Royal Aerostatical Navy.' He glanced up at the next man in the queue, a grizzled old sailor with a wooden leg. 'Pete Guns. I had an inkling you might have been more than a wee bit deceased by now. Has the navy, by chance, stopped paying you your pension?'

'Not dead yet, Lieutenant McGillivray. Maybe another tour might do for me – if not, living on the admiralty's pauper generosity surely will.'

The lieutenant stuck his hand out for the sailor's work record, punching it through with the recruitment code. 'Aye well, nobody could tie a fuse quite as well as you, Mister Guns. Welcome back to the Royal Aerostatical Navy.'

* * *

Coppertracks curiously trundled to the front door of the tower-like mansion that was Tock House. One of the sage steamman's drones had reached the door before him in answer to the chimes of the bell pull, and Coppertracks hadn't recognized the image of the black-suited gentleman on the steps sent back by the drone, the man's stovepipe hat held ever so tight in his hand.

'Can I help you, dear mammal?' asked Coppertracks.

'This is the residence of Jared Black?'

Coppertracks hesitated before answering. This softbody looked like a parliament man. From the Customs and Revenue Department of the civil service, perhaps. They were always probing and poking into the poor old commodore's esoteric sources of wealth. Items such as the ridiculously expensive large ivory wheel that the steamman had helped transport to the auction rooms the summer before.

'That is correct,' said Coppertracks, a little loop of energy circulating through the crystal dome topping his head as he dismissed the opportunity to dissemble. 'Are you perhaps calling from the treasury?'

The dark-suited softbody inclined his head and then stepped aside, revealing a pile of wooden crates scattered along the lawn as if someone had tried to lay a path with them. He tapped the nearest box with a smart silver cane. 'Indeed not. Foreign and Colonial Office.'

Coppertracks thoughtfully scratched the side of his skull dome. 'This is most irregular.'

'On that, sir, I believe we can concur,' said the official, tipping his hat before replacing it on his head. 'For the commodore. Good day to you.'

'And these crates?' spluttered Coppertracks.

'What passes for diplomacy these days, courtesy of the Cassarabian embassy,' called the official, walking briskly back through the steamman's gardens.

Coppertracks' artificial servants had just levered the lid off the nearest of the crates when the commodore came to the door and, rushing down the steps, seized a bottle from the drone's metal fingers before it could attempt to brush off the wood shavings that had come out of the box.

'Jared,' said the steamman, 'could you kindly explain what this is?'

The commodore gleefully held the bottle of red wine up to the sun, running his hands lovingly over the elaborate alien script of the label. 'As rare a vintage as has ever graced a Jackelian's table. From the sultan of Fahamutla's private estate unless my poor blessed eyes are mistaken.'

'This is all wine!' The steamman's voicebox trembled somewhere between astonishment and annoyance. 'There must be the best portion of a vineyard's worth littering our lawn here.'

'What's the matter, old steamer, have you never seen the gratitude of kings before?'

When the rider came out of the sandstorm his eyes were red and his throat sore, despite the gauze filter mask that covered his face. The sandstorms were as bad this season as they had ever been, but even the drifting wall of dust could not disguise the works of construction being carried out in front of him. After the work was completed, the occupant would have a fine view of the beaches and harbour below the cliffs.

The rider's camel snorted uncertainly. It had caught the scent of something it did not like, but what? Most creatures with any sense would be sitting out this filthy hell-sent storm for the rest of the day in whatever shelter they could find or burrow into for themselves.

With the strength of the whipping winds, the rider almost missed the figure squatting on the ruins of a stone desalination pipe, a strong cape pulled tight around him, an ornate filter mast protecting his face from the fury of the gale.

The figure's voice carried across on the gusts. 'You are a long way from the sands of the Mutrah, nomad.'

That voice, there was something oddly familiar about it.

'Curiosity has carried me here on the storm,' shouted the rider. 'What else is there to do in such filthy weather?'

'Yes. What else?'

'Who rebuilds here?' demanded the rider. 'The ones who destroyed the town are no more, that much I know.'

'Those who have title to the land build here,' called the figure.

'And who has granted such title?'

'The Caliph Eternal.'

Snorting, the rider turned his camel towards the ruins of a line of water farms. 'We are a long way from the court. Who rebuilds here?'

'Filthy townsmen,' laughed the figure. 'Filthy civilized water farmers, Alim of the Mutrah.'

The rider's camel stumbled, snorting in alarm as it caught sight of the massive long neck of the creature half buried by sands in front of the ruins. A drak, one of the great flighted works of imperial sorcery; just the sight of it enough to chase away the shock the nomad felt at this strange devil appearing to conjure his name out of the very gale itself.

'There will be a large pipeline,' called the figure, rising and leaping onto the saddle behind the drak's neck. 'It will run water all the way from here to the capital. It would be a good thing for the bandits and vagabonds of the dunes to avoid while out raiding.'

'And why would that be?' challenged the nomad.

'Because it would sit badly with me, killing a dog who I still owed a fat purse full of tughra to. Rascals might say that

I killed him so I wouldn't have to repay the debt, and what would that do for a great man's reputation?'

Alim grunted as the drak powered into the air and disappeared into the twisting wall of dune dust, taking the visitor along with it. *So, it is you!* Alim started to shake, his grunt transforming into a monstrous shuddering laugh that bounced around the dunes like an artillery barrage. He reached out to scratch the back of the camel's head reassuringly, then turned it back into the face of the storm. 'Oh, that's a good one. Did you mark his sand mask? Jewels and filigree silver filters fit for a sultan. And on a bloody great drak too. Oh yes.'

Alim's laughter echoed around the roar of the storm, swirling with the wind, until the camel and its rider were swallowed by it.

And then only the desert was left.